DATE DUE

JAN 1 8 2008		
MAR 3 0 2008		

Gods and Pawns

The Anvil of the World
The Children of the Company
The Graveyard Game
In the Garden of Iden
The Life of the World to Come
The Machine's Child
Mendoza in Hollywood

Gods and Pawns

KAGE BAKER

TOR®

A TOM DOHERTY ASSOCIATES BOOK
NEW YORK

This is a work of fiction. All the characters and events portrayed
in these stories are either fictitious or are used fictitiously.

GODS AND PAWNS

The following stories have been previously published:

"The Catch," *Asimov's,* Oct.-Nov. 2004
"The Angel in the Darkness," Golden Gryphon Press, October 2003
"Standing in His Light," SciFi.com, July 2001
"A Night on the Barbary Coast," *The Silver Gryphon,* June 2003
"Welcome to Olympus, Mr. Hearst," *Asimov's,* Oct.-Nov. 2003

This book is printed on acid-free paper.

A Tor Book
Published by Tom Doherty Associates, LLC
175 Fifth Avenue
New York, NY 10010

www.tor.com

Tor® is a registered trademark of Tom Doherty Associates, LLC.

Library of Congress Cataloging-in-Publication Data

Baker, Kage.
    Gods and pawns / Kage Baker.—1st ed.
       p. cm.
    "A Tom Doherty Associates Book."
    ISBN-13: 978-0-765-31552-6
    ISBN-10: 0-765-31552-1
    1. Dr. Zeus Incorporated (Imaginary organization)—Fiction. 2. Immortalism—Fiction.
3. Time travel—Fiction. 4. Science fiction, American. I. Title.
    PS3552.A4313G63 2006
    813'.54—dc22

                                                              2006025841

First Edition: January 2007

Printed in the United States of America

0 9 8 7 6 5 4 3 2 1

This one's for David Hartwell, who underwrote
the second half of the long, long journey.

CONTENTS

Gods and Pawns

TO THE LAND BEYOND
THE SUNSET

Somewhere in South America, New World One, 1650 AD . . .

Well aware that it was probably the most pointless thing an immortal could do, Lewis sat slouched behind his desk with his chin on one fist, watching the clock.

He was stuck in a dull job working for an idiot, his love life was nonexistent, and he was bored.

As immortal servants of an all-powerful-cabal-of-scientists-and-investors-who-possess-the-secret-of-time-travel go, Lewis was an unimposing fellow: slightly built, with limp fair hair and eyes of twilight blue. He was handsome, in the earnest manner of a silent-film hero. When called upon to act he could be plucky, determined, and brave; but it had been half a millennium since he'd had to do anything but sit behind a desk and hand out brochures.

This might have suited timid and retiring mortals, but Lewis happened to be a cyborg programmed in library sciences. He was, in fact, a Literature Preservation Specialist. He had once wandered the British Isles with a harp, gathering hero stories from persons painted blue. Later still he had wandered France with a lute, troubadoring for all he was worth and slipping the odd illuminated copy of *le Romain de la Rose* into his parti-colored coat before making a quiet exit down the castle drainpipe.

Lewis had done his job cheerfully and well, so it had come to him as a complete surprise when, following a minor accident in the field, he had been abruptly transferred to the Company base at New World One and appointed Guest Services Director.

The clock struck three.

Sighing, Lewis got to his feet. Finding his hat, he stepped out into the lobby.

"Closing time, Salome," he said, and then realized he was speaking to thin air. Frowning, he went to the receptionist's desk. She had left a scrawled note: *Lewis—something came up. Be a dear and punch my time card? Thanks!*

Muttering to himself, Lewis punched her time card with quite unnecessary force, punched his own, and left the pyramid.

The tropical heat fell on him like a wet blanket. He gasped, wishing he had gills, and set off down the broad straight avenue between the pyramids. Beyond the Perimeter, animals screamed and fought in the jungle depths, but not here; a vast sleepy silence reigned, suffering only the trickle of fountains and the chatter of little parrots to disturb it.

And, now, the rhythmic pounding of bare feet. Lewis turned to look over his shoulder and groaned. Bearing down on him was a sedan chair borne by six immense Mayans in matching livery, splendidly kilted and adorned in jade and gold, with quetzal plumes nodding above their headdresses. He tried to wave them past, but they drew level with him and stopped.

"No, no, it's quite all right," he said. "Shoo."

"We respectfully implore the Son of Heaven to permit us to carry him to his destination," said the lead bearer, in well-bred tones that implied disapproval. Lewis looked up at him in despair. The bearers were mortal, descendants of intercepted child sacrifices, haughty beyond reason, and Lewis had had this same argument with their fathers and grandfathers to no avail. Still:

"I'd really rather walk. I need the exercise," he said. The lead bearer smiled indulgently.

"The Son of Heaven is pleased to be humorous. I respectfully point out that, being immortal, he cannot *require* exercise. Moreover, if he walks all the way to Administrative Residential Pyramid his divine garments will be soaked with sweat, and he will scarcely be in any fit state to attend the four o'clock cocktail reception mandated by the wise and just Father of Heaven," said the bearer, and knelt. So did the other bearers, in perfect unison, and Lewis found himself irresistibly (but *respectfully*) boosted into the sedan chair.

He gave up, taking off his hat and fanning himself as the chair rose smoothly and the bearers went bounding away down the avenue. From his seat he had a fine view of New World One, laid out with all the precision of a knot garden: red and white pyramids, manicured emerald lawns, lush flowerbeds, turquoise swimming pools. To an immortal who'd just come in from a field assignment working somewhere dirty and dangerous, it would have seemed a vision of hallucinatory beauty. Lewis had long since grown weary of its splendor.

"Administrative Residential," the lead bearer announced, as they pulled up in front of a particularly imposing pyramid.

"Thank you," said Lewis, and hopped out as they dipped for him. They went running on, having fixed on a drooping immortal trudging along some distance off, and Lewis went inside. It was cool and dim, save for a pink neon sign saying THE PALENQUE POODLE about twenty meters down the passage, by the elevator doors. He could hear the clink of glasses, the banal chatter with one voice braying above the rest. Lewis stood straight, threw back his shoulders, and marched into the bar.

Houbert, the Director General, was holding court under an immense potted philodendron, sprawled back at his ease on a divan with jaguar skin upholstery. He was large for an immortal, beefy in a way that did not suggest muscle, and thinly bearded.

"And he-ere's *Lewis*," he announced to the room, "punctual for our party! Really too good of you, sir. I suppose you made the extra effort for the special occasion?"

"What special occasion, Director General?" Lewis inquired, sweeping off his hat as he bowed.

"What a delightful hat! Makes you look like a little puritan. But, you haven't heard? Victor is leaving us!"

"Really?" Lewis turned and saw Personnel Coordinator Victor, surrounded by well-wishing immortals. *The lucky devil,* he thought.

"For Paris, the beast. But, what can one do? That's life with Dr. Zeus; the job's the job, we go where we're posted, and all that. Go over and say good-bye to him, do." Houbert waved a dismissive hand.

Lewis turned and had made it halfway across the room when a Mayan waiter loomed into his path, bearing a tray of violet martinis.

"Cocktail, Son of Heaven?" he said.

Lewis looked at the tray in horror. "Might I have a gin and tonic?"

The waiter shook his head, causing the plumes on his high headdress to shimmy gently. "The august Father of Heaven has ordained a special Beverage of Lamentation in honor of the departure of one of His divine Children from Paradise."

Lewis knew from tedious experience that there was no point in arguing, so he took a martini from the tray and forged on toward Victor. Victor, dressed in full cavalier rig, was smirking rather as he accepted congratulation from his fellow cyborgs. He spotted Lewis on the edge of the crowd and raised his violet martini in ironic salute.

"Lewis, old man! What shall you do without me to keep an eye on you, I'd like to know?"

"This'll be a duller place, by all the gods," said Lewis sincerely, shaking his hand. "*Paris!* Oh, how I envy you. I hear it's quite the city nowadays. I'd give anything to go back there."

"Well, don't despair; one never knows what the Company has in store for one," said Victor, with a significant lift of his eyebrow. He twirled his red mustaches. "I have a feeling no one will miss me here."

"Oh, no, that's nonsense." Lewis had a sip of his drink and shuddered. "Look at this turnout! We'll all miss your wit."

Victor regarded Lewis with the closest thing he could muster to affection. Lewis was possibly the only immortal at New World One not to have figured out that Victor was there in the capacity of Political Officer.

"No doubt," he said dryly. "All the same, half of 'em here are from Botany. They're hoping to assault Houbert *en masse* to get a definitive answer on the Pool and Gymnasium Exclusivity Question."

"Oh, my, is that still going on?" Lewis glanced over his shoulder at the head of the Botany Department, who was advancing on General Director Houbert with a glare of adamant. Botany Residential had had to share its recreational facilities with Support Tech Residential for the last four centuries, and furious interoffice transmissions had been flying back and forth like electronic wasps for decades now.

"Still unresolved, I fear," said Victor, swirling his martini. The candied violet sank to the bottom and lay there, rotating sluggishly. He regarded it in distaste a moment before adding, in a lower voice, "Mendoza's here, you know."

"She is?" Lewis turned his head sharply. Victor narrowed his eyes in amusement.

"Brought in as moral support for Botany Director Sulpicius. I can't imagine she gives a damn, though, can you? Why don't you trot off and relieve her ennui, like the good little knight-errant you are?"

"I rather think I will," said Lewis. He backed up to a potted palm, surreptitiously dumped the contents of his glass, and hurried off to the booth where the Botanist Mendoza sat alone.

He had known her since 1596. It had been the longest relationship he'd ever had with a woman he'd loved, possibly because she had never noticed that he loved her. He didn't mind. She liked him, at least, and the Botanist Mendoza liked hardly anybody. Somewhere in her past, a mortal lover had gotten himself burned at the stake, and it had left her with a fixed loathing of mortals and not much tolerance for immortals, either.

She raised a cold black stare to Lewis now, as he slid into the booth, but then she recognized him and smiled. Had he been a mortal man, his heart would have skipped a beat.

"Thank God," she said. "I was going mad with boredom. How are you, Lewis?"

"Just peachy-keen, now that I have the fragrance of violets on my breath," he replied. She snickered and drained the last of her martini.

"Ugh. They don't serve these every day, do they?" she asked.

"God Apollo, no. I gather Houbert invented them especially for the occasion," said Lewis. "Shame about Victor leaving, though, isn't it? I shall miss his sense of humor."

"Did he have one?" Mendoza looked genuinely surprised. "I always thought he was a pompous twit."

"Oh, no. You must never have seen his impression of—"

They were interrupted by a Mayan waiter sweeping in to pick up their empty glasses. He was in the act of setting down another pair of martinis when Mendoza said, "Not those damn things. Bring us a pair of gin and tonics, can't you?"

"But the divine Father of Heaven—" the waiter began.

"—can go and sit on his big jade throne," said Mendoza. "Do as you're told, mortal man."

The waiter left, looking miffed. Lewis wrung his hands in embarrassment. "Now, now, look at it from his point of view—he adores Houbert, and it can't be easy waiting on the lot of us, he must hate this as much as we do—"

"I suppose so," said Mendoza. "I just get so fed up. 'The Father of Heaven insists that all shall wear their hats backward today! The Father of Heaven ordains that all shall eat nothing but purple jelly beans today! The Father of Heaven commands that all shall do the Hokey Pokey!' And the mortals just bend over backward to obey."

"Cheer up; if Victor got a transfer out of here, perhaps we will, too," said Lewis.

"You'd really like to go back to Europe?"

"Lord, yes. How wonderful it would be to be able to do some *real* work for a change. Or at least, step outside the Perimeter walls!"

"I know how you feel," said Mendoza, patting his hand in sympathy. "Nothing matters but the work, as they say. There's this place in Bolivia—"

The waiter returned and sullenly slapped down in succession two cocktail napkins, two gin and tonics, and a pair of what resembled jade mahjongg tiles.

"Thank you. What're these?" Mendoza inquired.

"Raffle tokens," replied the waiter. "The incomparable Father of Heaven requests that His children retain them. There will be a drawing later."

"Oh, whoopee," said Mendoza glumly.

"You never know." Lewis toasted her with his drink. "It might be a box of fruit jellies. Perhaps even a set of shoe trees, this time. Cheers."

They clinked glasses and drank. "You were saying, about Bolivia?" said Lewis, when they had set their glasses down.

"Well, one of the field ops brought back something interesting from there," said Mendoza. Her voice dropped as though she were about to impart a secret. "You're aware I'm working with primitive cultivars of maize, right?"

"Of course," said Lewis, looking into her eyes. Like most immortals, her physical body had stopped aging at twenty or so; but Mendoza, more so than any other immortal Lewis had met, had an extraordinary quality of reflecting her moods in her appearance. Sad, she was pale and austere, a bitter old woman for all the smoothness of her skin. But if he could make her laugh—if he could delight her with a story, or with good news—then the color rose in her face and the years dropped away.

He watched the process now, and made himself pay attention to what she was telling him with such intensity.

"... bigger than the teosinte I've found anywhere else, but not only that—it was found in a deposit of *terra preta*."

"I'm sorry?"

"Also known as Amazonian Dark Earth," said Mendoza, in a seductive sort of voice. "Super-compost. Occurs near ancient settlement sites but not even the Indians know where it comes from. Reproduces itself, like sourdough yeast. Bury some in lousy rain forest soil and it'll convert it to arable land. One of those answer-to-world-hunger things about which mortals will never quite get a clue."

"Oh. But the Company will?"

"Probably. And probably find a way to market it to gardeners and make a profit, up there in the future. Anyway, I'd give a year's worth of damned pool privileges to be able to go down there and have a look at it."

"*But*, do we lowly Preservers ever get any budget for field excursions?" said Lewis, and she chorused with him: "Noooo!"

At that moment a particularly well-muscled Mayan stepped up to a gong and smote it with a tremendous mallet. The note reverberated in the room, rather painfully for the immortals with their augmented senses. All the petty chatter died at once and all heads turned to Director General Houbert, who had risen to his feet.

"And now, darlings, it's time for our weekly ration of delicious suspense," he announced. "Console yourselves through the endless nights with this thought: that though we, servants of an all-knowing godlike pseudo-entity, are cursed with foreknowledge of nearly all things that happen, *this* at least we cannot know. I refer, of course, to the matter of who shall win the fabulous door prize!"

"And what *is* the fabulous door prize, oh beloved Father of Heaven?" said his Mayan majordomo.

"Why don't you tell them, best of slaves?" said Houbert coyly.

"At once, Divine One!" The majordomo cleared his throat. "The lucky holder of this week's winning token will receive—a full week's liberty for two, complete with air transport to the holiday destination of his or her choice!"

There was a silence.

"Is it my imagination, or did the irony level just drop in here?" whispered Mendoza.

"We're all a bit stunned," Lewis whispered back. "Generally he awards things like potted orchids or spa coupons."

A Mayan waiter wheeled forth a dessert trolley on which sat a big glass bowl, filled with jade tokens.

"Victor, as our departing celebrity, perhaps you'll do us the honor of selecting our winner?"

"Certainly, sir." Victor stepped up to the bowl and delved in, stirring the tokens.

"Suspense suspense suspense suspense suspense suspense," chanted the Mayan waiters, until Victor drew out a single piece of jade. He held it up with a flourish, and then read aloud what was engraved thereon:

"Nine Flower Monkey Rain Cloud!"

A moment of hurried clicking, like a roomful of scorpions, as the immortals grabbed up their jade tiles and examined them. Lewis looked around, waiting for someone's exclamation of triumph.

"Hell," said Mendoza. "I've got Nine Flower Jaguar Stone Star." She looked across at Lewis. "Aren't you going to check yours?"

"Oh, I never win these things—great Caesar's ghost!" Lewis stared at his tile, unbelieving. "Nine Flower Monkey Rain Cloud! Oh! Oh, my gosh!"

"We have a winner!" shouted the majordomo, seizing Lewis's hand and holding it up.

"Olé!" cried Mendoza, applauding. "Lewis, you can go to Paris! Rome! London! Bravo!"

And his fellow immortals joined in the applause, and Director General Houbert himself condescended to come forward to shake his hand, but as the roaring wave of congratulation broke over him all Lewis saw was Mendoza's face, bright and happy for once, and for *him*.

He had to use every ounce of invention and tact.

"You see, the awkward thing is, it's specifically for *two*," Lewis explained.

"Myself and a guest. And, er, you know . . . I'm not a couple. Lucretia informed me it's not only over, it never even began . . ."

"She's an idiot, and you were too nice for her anyway," said Mendoza firmly.

"Funnily enough, that was what she said, too," said Lewis, grimacing at the memory. "So I thought, well, perhaps—after all, there we were, talking about that place in Bolivia you've always wanted to see, and then, bang, I won, and—perhaps it's destiny or something!"

Mendoza blinked. "You're going to use your week's liberty on a field expedition?"

"We could actually get some work done!" said Lewis. "You could, anyway. And it would do me no end of good to get in a little wilderness experience."

"Oh, Lewis, you can't! I mean, I can't—"

"Of course you can! It's my door prize, after all; I can invite whom I please," said Lewis. "And I've decided I really, truly want to explore Bolivia."

"You perfect gentle knight," said Mendoza, and threw her arms around him and kissed him.

He had imaginary heart palpitations for an hour afterward, and drew stares from the Mayan gardeners as he went skipping back to Administrative Residential Pyramid.

"You're lucky the rainy season hasn't started yet," Grover informed them, ordering their shuttle to begin its descent. He was a very old operative, distinctly Neanderthal of brow, so much so in fact that he could no longer go out among mortals without drawing undue attention to himself. His duties these days were limited to on-base jobs like piloting shuttles.

"I suppose all that turns to impassable mud?" said Lewis, peering down at the plain below them. It was dry and brown, distinguished only by the curious forested mounds that rose here and there from the general flatness.

"No; it turns into a lake," said Grover. "See all those hills? They're actually islands. You want my advice, you'll set up your camp on one."

"Are there mortals down there?" Mendoza scowled at the network of raised causeways between the islands. "Certainly looks like it. That land's been farmed."

"Not in recorded history," said Grover. "Thirty thousand square miles of isolation. You can play your music as loud as you like—nobody's going to slap your wrist over anachronisms out here!"

"Good," said Mendoza.

They landed and were left with four crates of gear, and the cheery promise that Grover would return for them in a week's time. Lewis watched the shuttle vanish away to the west. Lowering his head, he regarded the island-hill before them and felt the first slight qualm of concern, with a deeper uneasiness following.

"My gosh, that's dense undergrowth," he said. "I'm not sure we're really dressed for adventuring. We look like a Dresden shepherd and shepherdess."

"What?" said Mendoza. "My whole ensemble's khaki. We'll be fine!"

"I suppose so," said Lewis, reflecting that seventeenth-century costume in khaki was still seventeenth-century costume.

"Besides," said Mendoza, hoisting a crate on one shoulder, "I hate those damned Company-issue coveralls."

Halfway up the hill, however, she was using language that rather shocked Lewis, or at least it did after he did a quick idiom access of sixteenth-century Galician Spanish. He ducked as first one and then the other of her high-heeled shoes went flying down the trail.

An hour later, however, there was a neat camp on the plateau at the top of the hill, on one edge so as to take advantage of the view.

"All the comforts of home," said Mendoza happily, setting up a folding chair. "Did you bring the gin?"

"And a bottle of olives," Lewis replied, hunting for the cocktail shaker. He found it, activated the self-refrigeration unit, and set it aside to chill. "Shall I build a fire?"

"We've got something better," said Mendoza, reaching into the depths of a crate. She pulled out a cube of something resembling thick glass, about the size of a hatbox. Further search revealed a wrought-iron base for it; Mendoza set it out, placed the cube on top, and switched it on. "There we go!"

Lewis watched as the cube lit up and began to radiate heat, with stylized holographic flames dancing across its surface. "Oh, my! How did we mere Preservers rate that kind of field technology?"

"We didn't," said Mendoza smugly. "Pan Li in Accounting owed me a favor. Nice, huh?"

"Splendid," said Lewis, setting up his own chair.

"And, look at this perfect camping spot! Guava trees. Brazil nut trees. Peach-palms. Anyone would think it had been someone's little private orchard."

"Paradisial," Lewis agreed.

They relaxed, sipping cocktails as the gigantic tropical evening descended, and listened to the night coming to life. Drowsy parrots nestled together in the high branches; far off, some monkey set up a low monotonous hooting. The stars swarmed like white moths.

"Now, *this* is solitude," said Mendoza in satisfaction. "No fussy department heads. No tedious meetings. No mortals!"

Except for one, Lewis thought to himself. He gazed across at Mendoza and imagined once again the specter of the mortal man she had loved, looming beside her. He had long since learned that he'd never supplant Nicholas Harpole, though the man had been dead the best part of a century. Lewis cleared his throat and said: "Wonderful, isn't it? What shall we do tomorrow?"

"Go exploring!" said Mendoza. "Take the field credenza and go in search of specimens yet unclassified."

"Search for lost worlds and dinosaurs? Ancient civilizations? Forgotten colonists from lost Atlantis?" Lewis suggested.

They laughed companionably and clinked glasses.

Later, as she sat in the entrance to her tent, combing out her hair without the least self-consciousness, he watched her and thought: *This, at least, I have. And it's more than she'll grant to anyone else.*

A field bivvy is a compact and useful piece of gear, lightweight and eminently portable. Once zipped inside, however, Lewis found it rather cramped.

He lay flat on his back, staring up at the mesh screen scant inches from his nose. It was hot, but the profusion of little insects whining on the outside of the screen dissuaded him from unzipping the flap. He turned over, and the tarpaulin underneath crackled disagreeably. He attempted to punch some comfort into his flat camping pillow, and failed.

God Apollo, he thought irritably, *I used to tramp through half of Europe dossing down in ditches, and slept like a baby. Have I really grown so soft?*

Just as sleep began its hesitant approach, something out on the far plain shrieked. Lewis gave up and resigned himself to a night of insomnia.

For a long while he listened to Mendoza's distant breathing and heartbeat. The night sounds grew louder: tree frogs peeping by the millions, immense stealthy insects, moon-eyed things that haunted the upper branches . . .

He heard, quite distinctly, the crash of a metal door rolling open. A soft white light, only just brighter than moonlight, flooded the camp. Lewis opened his eyes and saw that a door had opened in the hillside. Little people were emerging.

"Hey," he said, and tried to sit up. To his horror, he found that he was unable to move. But they had heard him; they came quite purposefully and yanked up the bivvy stakes, and commenced dragging him, doubly shrouded, toward the door in the hill.

"NO!" he shouted, managing at last to thrash about, and sat up face-first into the mesh. Moonlight, shining into his face, dappled through the jungle canopy; silence. No door, no little people.

"Lewis, are you okay?" Mendoza's voice was cautious.

"Bad dream," he said.

"Oh. Sorry," she replied.

"Quite all right," he said, and lay down and stared up at the mesh, knowing he'd never close his eyes again.

But the next thing he saw was red radiance everywhere, and a concerted morning birdcall backed up by little monkeys screaming at the sun.

Lewis turned over, focused his eyes, and recoiled at the number and size of the insects perched all over the bivvy mesh. He heard Mendoza give a muffled shriek and begin flailing away, as bugs flew off in all directions from her bivvy.

"Horrible, aren't they?" he called.

"Ugh, ugh, *ugh.*" Mendoza unzipped her bivvy and scrambled out, and danced up and down. "Goddamned tropics! We should have brought one of those electronic bug killers."

"Watch out," said Lewis, beating upward to dislodge two tarantulas and a dragonfly with a twelve-inch wingspan. Mendoza retreated to one of the equipment crates. Lewis crawled forth into the morning and dutifully looked elsewhere as Mendoza got dressed.

"Oh! There are pineapple guavas growing over here," he announced. "Shall I pick some for our breakfast?"

"Go ahead," said Mendoza, sounding muffled. Lewis spent the next few minutes busily gathering fruit. Then a tarantula reached out of a clump of leaves and grabbed back a guava he had just picked, at which point Lewis discovered just how far he could jump from a standing start.

He came skittering back with his arms full of guavas, just in time to see Mendoza step forth from the crate dressed in hip waders, into the top of which she had tucked the hem of her gown. It looked more than odd. She met his stare and said proudly, "I don't care. I'm insect-proof!"

"You know, you've got a point," Lewis replied and, setting down the guavas, dove into a crate himself, to root through his gear for his own waders.

Fully armored against insect peril, they sat down and dined. The freshness of the morning was rapidly boiling away, as steam rose from the broad leaves all around them. Far to the horizon, where mountain peaks were visible, lay a low line of slaty cloud.

"Is it storming over there?" Mendoza remarked, frowning as she spooned up guava juice.

"I suppose so," said Lewis. He peered out at the distant clouds, bringing them into close focus. "Oh, dear, we may not have escaped the rainy season after all."

"We'll just take rain ponchos," said Mendoza, shrugging. "Never understood the way mortals get upset by a few drops of water. England, now—*that* was a rainy country. And wretchedly cold."

They finished breakfast in a leisurely fashion and loaded on their field credenza packs, after which they made their way down from their hill to the plain. Close to, it was possible to see that irregular bands of dark earth circled each of the islands on the wide land.

"Ah-ha!" said Mendoza, pointing. "Teosinte!"

"Where?" Lewis turned his head.

"There! Growing all over the *terra preta*. See?"

"That stuff that looks like giant crabgrass?"

"Well, yes, it does," said Mendoza impatiently. "But do you realize how significant its presence is here? Nobody thought teosinte was cultivated this far down the continent! The indigenes farmed manioc and amaranths instead."

"You don't say," Lewis replied, as his brain went into comfortable shutoff mode, its custom whenever Mendoza started in on the subject of botany.

For the next few hours he trotted after her through the shimmering heat as they explored farther afield, nodding and making polite exclamations, occasionally holding things when asked or standing beside plants she was imaging so as to provide a reference of scale. As he watched Mendoza working, his primary consciousness was focused in a pleasant fantasy.

The hip waders impaired his imaginings somewhat, but still there was something of human passion about her when she worked, not like the other immortals at all, with such an intensity she seemed ever so slightly dangerous.

And how could something lithe as a tigress have such apple-blossom skin? Her hair was coming undone as she worked, floating like flames around her face, and the long coiled braid drooping down . . . if he were to reach out and take hold of it, what would she . . .

". . . The odd thing is, it's immense but it doesn't seem to have been cultivated, ever," she was saying in a puzzled voice. "Just some gigantiform variant, but no disproportionate increase in the size or number of seed capsules."

"How curious," Lewis said, jerked from his reverie by something registering on his hazard sensors.

He turned his head. Far out upon the cracked and blazing plain, a mirage of silver water shimmered, rippled, advanced. Advanced? A sudden gust of hot wind buffeted his face.

"Er—" he said, just as Mendoza lifted her head and turned swiftly.

"What's that?" she demanded. "Oh, God my Savior!"

"I think it's—"

They winked out more or less simultaneously and wound up halfway up the side of the nearest island, perched on a tree branch. Watching in horrified fascination, they saw the shining flood roll onward, unhurried, unstoppable, surrounding their refuge and flowing on to the horizon.

"Damn," said Mendoza, staring. "Where'd all that water come from?" Lewis pointed to the sky, where the slate cloud front of morning was just blotting out the sun and taking on a nasty coppery tint.

"It must be from the storm in the mountains. Grover told us this turned into a lake," said Lewis.

"So he did. Well, it doesn't look all that deep," said Mendoza. "We can wade back to camp. We wore our waders, after all."

An anaconda, quite a large one, floated past their perch. They regarded it in thoughtful silence.

"Then again," said Mendoza, just as the sky opened with the force of a fire hose.

They clung to their branch as torrents of water beat down on them, gasping for air with their heads down. The rain shattered the silver mirror of the plain, turned it into a seething, leaping mass of brown water.

"I think we ought to wait it out," shouted Lewis. Mendoza nodded and pointed to a drier section of branch, one overhung with a canopy of broad leaves. They worked their way along until they reached its comparative shelter and huddled there, dripping. Below them, various Amazonian fauna displaced by the flood was hurrying up the hillside on four, six, or eight legs respectively, likewise seeking refuge.

"But . . . It never does this at New World One," said Mendoza, pushing back her wet hair.

"New World One has a force field projected over it," said Lewis. "Houbert only lets in enough to keep the lawns green."

"Ah," said Mendoza. "That would also explain why we aren't besieged by insects every night."

"Or snakes," said Lewis.

"That's right; snakes can climb, can't they?" said Mendoza.

They edged a little closer together on the branch.

"Well, we did hope we'd have an adventure," said Lewis. "And I suppose this beats sitting in on another departmental budget meeting."

Mendoza nodded doubtfully, watching the rain lash the surface of the water to muddy foam.

"I have to admit, this is as rainy as England," she said. "At least there weren't anacondas in Kent."

"Scarcely any snakes at all there, really," said Lewis.

"Except for Joseph," Mendoza added, narrowing her eyes. Lewis, well aware of her feelings for the immortal who had recruited her, made a non-committal noise. Seeking to turn the conversation elsewhere, he said brightly, "Think how wretched I'd be right now if I'd asked Lucretia along! She wasn't what you'd call a good sport."

"Mineralogist, isn't she?"

"Mm. Emphasis on jewels. Curates the Company's new world loot. All that plundered gold, jade, and whatnot."

"You never know; maybe she'd have found a few emeralds out here." Mendoza turned to look at him. "Wait a minute—there's a rumor that somebody over in Mineralogy is kinky for gemstones. Supposedly has a private trove she likes to scatter in the bedsheets when she's entertaining friends. Among other things. That wouldn't be Lucretia, would it?"

"It certainly wouldn't," said Lewis firmly, and untruthfully. Mendoza grinned.

"And you wouldn't tell me if it was, would you?"

"Of course I wouldn't."

"You really are the perfect gentleman, Lewis," said Mendoza fondly. "What a bunch of idiots your ex-lovers have all been. One of these days, the right one will come along. You'll see."

Lewis gave her a forlorn look, which she utterly missed.

The rain continued without cease or indeed any sign that it was ever going to grow less. More things were swept by: a jaguar, crouched on a floating tree trunk, its ears flattened down in disgust. Caymans, swimming in flotillas. A sloth, apparently drowned but possibly not.

And then, abruptly, the rain stopped.

"Oh, look, somebody turned off the taps," said Mendoza.

They sat there a few minutes, waiting expectantly for the water level to drop.

"I don't think it's going down anytime soon, somehow," said Lewis.

A few more minutes went by.

"Well, it's only—" Mendoza scanned. "Just over a meter deep. We could wade."

"We could," Lewis agreed. A raft of broken branches drifted past, crowded with unhappy-looking monkeys.

"Or we could wait a little longer," said Mendoza.

They did.

"Dry clothing," said Lewis at last. "Dry martinis. Comfortable chairs."

"Yeah," said Mendoza. The tree tilted outward, ever so slightly, but unmistakably.

"Oh, crumbs," said Lewis, as the tree tilted farther.

They jumped and landed some distance behind the tree, which keeled over gracefully and slid down the hillside in a runnel of flowing mud. It took a lot of the hilltop with it.

"I have this sudden compelling urge to return to our camp," said Mendoza. Lewis just nodded, speechless.

They picked their way down the sodden hillside and ventured out into the water, which was just precisely high enough to trickle in over the tops of their waders.

"Lewis, I am so sorry," Mendoza said as she slogged along. "You might have been sunning yourself in some Venetian palazzo or other right now."

"Oh, that's all right," said Lewis. "I don't mind."

Mendoza looked at him askance. "I'll bet you say that to all the other girls, too. Sweetheart, there's such a thing as being too much of a—" She broke off and turned, coming face-to-face with the cayman that had been advancing on them stealthily. It opened its jaws, but closed them on empty air as Mendoza dodged and brought her fists down on its flat head, with a *crack* that echoed across the water. It spasmed, rolled over and drifted away belly-up. "—nice guy," Mendoza finished.

"I suppose so," said Lewis. "All the same, this isn't so bad. We've made a few discoveries, haven't we? You've lots of samples of your, er, maize thing."

"Though not the cultivars I expected," said Mendoza, squelching on. "Odd, that. You can almost see what this place was like a thousand years ago—some vanished tribe of indigenes working out how to grow things here. No rice, or they'd have figured out rice paddies—no way to drain the marsh, the rainforest soil good for nothing, so they built these islands instead, out of *terra preta*. Each island a little orchard, and maybe some of them were used for amaranth or manioc crops . . ."

"I wonder what happened to them all? And where the *terra preta* came from?" said Lewis. "Surely the Company knows."

"If all-seeing Zeus knows, he isn't telling the likes of *us*," said Mendoza. "Bloody paranoid corporate conspira—oh, my God."

Before them rose an island. They could tell it was their island, beaten and lashed by the storm though it was, because the little clearing in which they had pitched their tents was clearly visible. It was visible because it was now halfway down the side of the hill. As they watched, it slid farther. The crates were still up on top, on the edge of what was now a precipice, but everything else had spilled down the slope and Lewis's folding chair was already bobbing away on the flood.

"NO!"

Another cascade of mud came down, and the clearing flopped over, burying most of what they'd brought with them.

Three hours and a lot of cursing later, they sat on the hilltop once more, amid what they had been able to find of their base camp.

"It could be worse," said Lewis. "We saved the cocktail shaker."

"Pity about our sleeping bags, though," said Mendoza bleakly, taking a sip of gin. "And Pan Li's flamecube. And my tent."

"You can have mine, of course," said Lewis.

"But what'll you sleep in?"

"I'm an old field campaigner," said Lewis, with a wave of his hand. "I used to lie up in the heather with nothing but my cloak, when I even had a cloak. This is nothing to Northern Europe! Why, I'll bet I can even get a fire going."

Mendoza gave him an incredulous look.

"With what? All the wood is wet."

"Only on the outside," said Lewis and, rising, he took a hatchet and strode off in search of a dead tree. It took him a while; most of the local dead wood had already rotted down to punky, bug-infested bits. Finally he was able to scramble up and hack a few dead branches down, and further hack them into shorter lengths, and at last he staggered back with his arms full.

"Et voilà!" he said, looking around for a place to start a fire. There were no rocks, there were no patches of bare dry earth. Finally he improvised a sort of basket of strips of packing steel.

"And now," Lewis said triumphantly, "the old field operative makes fire. What's that, you say? We have no flint? We have no matches? We have no magnesium shavings? But we do have *hyperspeed!*" He held up a pair of dry sticks and then his hands became a blur, and a moment later both sticks had burst into flame.

"Nice trick," Mendoza admitted. She watched as he coaxed the wood in the basket to catch. It smoked a great deal, but there was no denying it was on fire. She drew the rubber field poncho about her shoulders more tightly.

"So . . . when was your first mission?" she asked him.

"Anno Domini 142," said Lewis proudly, rummaging through the box of field rations they'd salvaged. He drew out two pouches of Proteus Hearty Treats, wiped off mud, activated their autoheat units, and passed one to Mendoza. "Ireland. Well, I had to spend a year in Britain first, to acclimatize myself to mortals."

"They did that to me, too," said Mendoza. "Spent a whole year in Spain. I hated it. Damned mortals! I'd done all my prep work programming myself for the New World, and I was desperate to get out here. Then, what does the Company go and do? It sends me to *England.*"

"I'd have been perfectly happy staying in Britain," said Lewis, taking a mouthful of Proteus Hearty Treats. He chewed, paused, and then said: "Is it me, or does this taste like a brownie steeped in beef gravy?"

Mendoza opened her pouch and ate some. "You're right." She looked into the pouch. "Not bad, though. So anyway—"

"So anyway it was Roman Britain by that time, and I was stationed at the Dr. Zeus HQ in Londinium. Oh, it was wonderful there! Heated rooms. Neighbors from all corners of the empire. Quite cosmopolitan, you know, you'd hardly think you were in a barbarian country at all. But then, of course, just as I'd got to taking clean clothes and indoor plumbing for granted—"

"Isn't that the way it always is?"

"—I was sent to Ireland. Which was quite a contrast."

"I'll bet it was. What the hell would a Literature Specialist have to do in Ireland, in that era?"

"Quite a bit, actually," said Lewis. "Learning tribal lays, and all that. So I just made the best of things. Learned to forage, make fire, get myself out of difficult situations. I did so well I was rewarded with a job in Greece for a few decades, but then—back to rainy old Eire. I got work as a druid."

"At least I was never sent anywhere that primitive," said Mendoza with a shudder. "How long were you in Ireland?"

"Until—" Lewis halted, frowned. "Until I . . . ow." He put his hands up to his head and squinted his eyes.

"What's wrong?"

"Old programming error. Something . . . I'm so sorry, my memory's never been right since. I had an accident. Spent ten years in a regeneration vat, would you believe it? And ages in reprogramming therapists' offices after that," he babbled. He had begun to sweat profusely.

"Did it happen in Ireland?" Mendoza was watching him closely, concern in her eyes.

"I don't know! I was in France afterward. Old World One, in the Cevennes. Lovely place. Have you ever been there?"

"No. Lewis, are you okay?"

"I'm fine, I'm just—there's just that little glitch. Something fairly traumatic happened, apparently." Lewis shook himself, trying to regain some composure. Mendoza reached over and took his hand in hers, which sent his composure flying again, but he smiled at her and hoped she wouldn't notice the way his heart was pounding.

"Happens to all of us," said Mendoza gently. "Damned tertiary-consciousness programming. The Company hides all sorts of little traumas down there, and they spring out and nail you at the worst times—usually just as you're about to do something Dr. Zeus doesn't want you to do. Like me with Nicholas."

"I'm so sorry," said Lewis, sitting very still so she wouldn't take her hand away.

"You should have seen the panic attack I had the first time some mortal suggested I might be a Jew," said Mendoza. "Complete hysterical collapse. Utterly humiliating. All pulled out of suppressed memories of being in the dungeons of the Inquisition. And the nightmares . . ."

"I have nightmares, too," said Lewis sadly.

"Like last night?"

"Yes. Usually . . . I'm lost somewhere, and there are these tremendous domed hills or, or mounds or something . . . and then I'm being pulled down a hole. Or a tunnel. It's hot and suffocating and I'm trapped . . . and I wake up yelling, which doesn't much impress—well, anyone who happens to hear me."

Mendoza gave him a thoughtful look.

"Well," she said finally, "maybe romance just doesn't work for immortals, eh, Lewis? It certainly didn't work for me. And maybe it's just as well. No passion, no pain. Good friendship's just as important, after all. Maybe even more so."

She withdrew her hand.

"To get back to the subject of roughing it—I've heard stories of some of these older field operatives who are really good at it. Don't take any gear with them at all. They've trained themselves to sleep upright, only it isn't sleep, it's a sort of altered consciousness—like their perception of time and the exterior world changes. They just sort of become one with the land-scape and blend in. Have you ever done that?"

Lewis shook his head. "Though I've known a few who did. People who have stayed out in the field too long. They're certainly the best at what they do, and some of them can do some remarkable things . . . one fellow I knew called it *stripping down to the machine.* Cutting away the inessentials. They're not bothered by rain or snow or heat."

"See, I think that would be marvelous. You'd be sort of this super Zen master ninja cyborg," said Mendoza. "You wouldn't need anything. What stories they must have to tell!"

"Except that they don't tell them," said Lewis.

"What?"

"They're not great talkers. I suppose that becomes inessential, too. They don't work well with other operatives, much, and they can't work around mortals at all."

"Oh." She lowered her gaze to the little fire. "Well, it's still an interesting idea."

They retired early, Mendoza crawling into the sole remaining bivvy and Lewis wrapping himself up in his poncho in one of the crates. He lay there a while, cold and uncomfortable, listening to distant thunder. Gradually the thunder moved closer, and the lightning became more frequent. He opened his eyes and looked up just as a blue-white flash revealed dozens of insects, including a tarantula, making their determined way over the edge of the crate, all of them looking for a warm place to spend the night.

"Yikes!" Lewis nearly levitated up and out of the crate, landing with a squelch in the long grass.

"What?" Mendoza leaned up on her elbows.

"Just, er, a few bugs," said Lewis, leaping to his feet and smacking at something crawling up his arm. "It's all right—"

"Look—" Mendoza unzipped the flap. "This is dumb. Crawl in here with me. There's room enough and we can lie back to back, okay? Chaste as anything."

"Okay," said Lewis, and scrambled into the bivvy. Mendoza zipped it shut again.

They slept, chaste as anything. The rain began to fall again. The night filled with the scent of green leaves.

Lewis opened his eyes. Sunlight, above his face, sparkling on water drops. Early early sunlight, just after a gentle misty dawn. He could glimpse blue sky through the canopy, and a flash of color as a macaw streaked by overhead. The storm had rolled through.

None of which made any impression on him, however, because he was lying on his back and Mendoza was resting her head on his chest, and had thrown one arm over him, and was holding him close.

He lay there, scarcely daring to breathe.

Lord God Apollo, this is Lewis. Remember me? I don't suppose you'd remember, actually, I'm not the sort of fellow people remember much, but anyway here I am, and I still pray to you occasionally even though I'm a cyborg now, and I was just wondering: I don't suppose you'd be willing to stop time, right this minute? Right here, in this moment, for the rest of Eternity?

She was warm. Her hair was fragrant with something. Roses? Her arm was bare. She was breathing quietly as a child.

He could almost—

"Mh . . . *Nicholas?*"

He felt her come awake, utterly relaxed one moment and utterly alert the next. He squeezed his eyes shut.

She started violently, and he heard her draw a sharp breath. A frozen moment of immobility; then, with great care, she drew away from Lewis and turned on her side, with her back to him.

She made no sound, but he felt the slight trembling as she wept.

Lewis waited an hour before stretching and yawning loudly.

"My gosh, the sun is shining!" he announced.

"And we made it through the night without being washed down the hill," said Mendoza in a bright voice. She turned to face him, red-eyed but calm and collected.

"What shall we do today?" said Lewis. "Other than pay a heck of a lot of attention to barometrical readings?"

"Hang things out to dry," she said, leaning up on one elbow to peer out through the mesh. "And I guess we really should see if we can dig out any more of the gear that got buried. Just so some Victorian explorer doesn't stumble on it and claim it's evidence for colonists from Atlantis."

A few strands of her hair were stuck to the side of her face. Lewis, unable to stop himself, reached out and smoothed them back. She pretended not to notice.

"Do you want to go any farther afield to look for your maize?"

"Teosinte. No . . . I think I've found pretty much everything there is to find, there," she said. "I'm starting to be more interested in the place itself."

Lewis nodded. "It must have been quite an engineering feat on somebody's part."

"There had to have been a huge resident population to build it all, and then to keep the land in production. I want to do some tests on the fruit trees here, to see if there's much genetic difference from the cultivars grown in other parts of Amazonia."

"Okay," said Lewis, unzipping the mesh and crawling out before the conversation could get more botanocentric. He dressed himself, performed such ablutions as were possible, and wandered off to see if he could find any more guavas for breakfast.

There was a bearing tree just at the edge of the slide precipice. He approached with caution, so busy scanning for unstable earth that he didn't notice the view until it was right before his eyes. When he did notice it, though, he stopped in his tracks, openmouthed.

The land had become a shallow sea, sky-reflecting as a mirror, brilliant blue. The high mounds rose from the water, an archipelago of green gardens, and on their lower slopes grew purple flowers. Macaws sailed out on brilliant wings, blue and gold, scarlet and green, between the islands. All of it in dreamlike silence, but for the rustling of their wings; not a bird or a monkey cried anywhere.

Mendoza came up behind him and gazed out.

"Beautiful," she said.

"Another Eden," said Lewis, but she shook her head.

"Mortals built this place," she said, and went to the guava tree and picked the fruit.

They put their waders and ponchos back on and made their slow way down the hill after breakfast, paralleling the smooth chocolate-colored track of the slide, digging into the mud at the bottom with camp shovels. They found Lewis's sleeping bag, very much the worse for wear, and a case of bottled water.

"And there was great rejoicing," said Mendoza, hoisting it on her shoulder. "Let me get this up the hill into the shade."

"I think I see the flamecube," said Lewis, poking with the handle of his shovel.

"Oh, good. That'd really give the Von Danikenists something to talk about, wouldn't it, if that got left behind?" She set the water down and came back to peer into the slush. Lewis raked with the upper edge of the shovel and levered up a corner of the cube. Before it sank into the muck once more, Mendoza was able to reach down and grab hold.

"Oh, no, you should have let me—"

"It's all right, just back up a little so I can—"

"Really, let me—"

So busy were they that neither one of them noticed the mortal's approach.

He was within arrowshot when they looked up and saw him at last, and then they stared in disbelief.

He was an ancient mortal, poling along toward them in a flat-bottomed skiff. His boat was elaborately carved to represent some kind of water bird. It moved without a sound across the glassy water, leaving no more wake than a dream. His own garments were elaborate, too, woven cotton in several colors and a headdress of bright macaw feathers, and little pendant ornaments of shell and hammered gold.

He brought his skiff up to the edge of the mound and stopped, leaning on the pole.

"Good morning," he said.

They did a fast linguistic access and realized that he was speaking in a Taino dialect, though his accent was strange and archaic.

"Good morning, sir," Lewis replied, in Taino.

"You wouldn't happen to be gods, would you?" inquired the old man.

"No, sir," said Lewis. "Only servants of a god."

"Ah," said the old man. "Well, that would explain the mud all over you. Tell me, children, is the lord Maketaurie Guyuaba anywhere about?"

"Er—no," said Lewis, doing a fast access on Taino mythology. *Maketaurie Guyuaba: lord of Coaybay (land of the dead) beyond the sunset.* Hastily he transmitted the reference to Mendoza.

"What a pity," said the old man, cocking an eye at the hilltop. "I had so hoped to speak to someone important. That would be his camp, up there, where his effulgence shone out the other evening?"

"No, sir, that's our camp," said Lewis. "The, er, effulgence was a sort of lamp, this one in fact," and Mendoza held it up, "but I'm afraid it washed down the hill in the storm, and we've just been digging it out."

"*Your* lamp?" The old man looked askance at them, mildly amused. "Yes, very likely indeed. You'd best get the mud cleaned off it, children, or your master will beat you. *I* know what servants will get up to, when the lord of the house is away. When may I find him at home?"

"I'm afraid he lives—er—that way," said Lewis, waving an arm, "Many moons—ah—quite a long distance off. He sent us here on a great bird to, er . . ."

Gather plants for him, transmitted Mendoza.

"Gather plants for him, and he's sending the bird back to collect us in a few days," Lewis finished.

"A great bird. I see," said the old man, in a tone of polite disdain. He coughed delicately and said: "The fact is, I had hoped to consult with him on a matter of some importance."

"We would be happy to deliver a message to him," said Lewis.

"I wonder if you might," said the old man. "Would you just let him know that a fellow deity wishes to discuss a matter of mutual advantage?"

Lewis and Mendoza exchanged glances.

Company business, transmitted Lewis. *We've encountered a member of a previously-unknown culture. We're supposed to investigate and report back to Dr. Zeus, so they can send an evaluation team.*

But we're not anthropologists! protested Mendoza.

We're Preservers, all the same. And, after all, how many people get a chance to discover a fabulous lost civilization?

Hmf. And if we don't investigate, we'll get nailed with a Section Sixteen, won't we? Damn. So much for a vacation away from mortals.

"Of course, sir," said Lewis to the mortal. "In the meanwhile, may we be of any assistance? Our master has given us some power to act for him."

"Has he?" The old mortal considered them, looked at the gear scattered about. "Perhaps."

"May we speak directly to the god?" Lewis inquired. The old man raised his eyebrows.

"Child, you *are* speaking to a god. I am Orocobix, Lord of Abundance."

Lewis gaped and then knelt, grabbing Mendoza's arm in his descent to compel her to kneel, too.

"Pardon our ignorance, Lord Orocobix," he said.

I'm kneeling to a mortal . . . Mendoza ground her teeth. The old mortal gaped, too, and then smiled. He drew himself upright, holding the pole like a scepter.

"Rise, children rise. You may be forgiven; you're dead, after all. However—" and he looked again at their gear "—you might want to present me with a suitable offering . . . ?"

Lewis glanced over his shoulder. With great presence of mind he ran and fetched the case of bottled water.

"Please accept this, great Orocobix! Pure water in conveniently reusable containers," he said.

"How nice," said Orocobix. "Perhaps the lamp as well."

But I borrowed it from Pan Li in Accounting!

Can't be helped. Technically it's Company property, you know.

"Certainly, great Orocobix," said Lewis, bowing. "Will you permit us to accompany you to your sacred place, bearing these gifts for you?"

"Yes," said the old mortal, "I think that would be best." He retreated to the stern of the skiff and sat down. Lewis loaded the water and the Flame-Cube into the bow, and handed Mendoza up onto one of the thwarts; when he stepped in himself, Orocobix handed him the pole.

"Due east," he instructed. He reached over and took the flamecube from Mendoza's hands, and, holding it up critically, brushed some of the mud off.

"How does it burn?" he inquired.

"I think it has to dry out first," said Lewis, pushing them off from the shallows. The skiff went gliding across the water. "I hope you'll pardon us, great Orocobix, but I'm certain our god will have a lot of questions to ask us about you. He was under the impression that this part of the world was deserted."

"Oh, no," said Orocobix, leaning back. "This has always been our country. We created all this kingdom." He waved an arm at the surrounding landscape. "Sadly, we have been without subjects for some time now. It is very inconvenient."

"I'm very sorry to hear that, sir."

Bloody mortal aristocrats, Mendoza transmitted, glowering.

Orocobix shrugged. "So it goes. Even gods may be obliged to endure difficulties. When did the august lord of the dead extend his dominion this far east, may I ask?"

"Actually, he hasn't," said Lewis, leaning into the pole to send their boat gliding forward. "We're just visiting."

"Of course."

"Though of course his kingdom is perfectly immense, you know," Lewis improvised. "What with mortals dying on a regular basis."

"How very interesting," said the old man, stroking his chin. "Has he many wives?"

"Well—not so many, no," said Lewis.

"Indeed," said Orocobix. He gave a slight smile and leaned back, clasping his hands in his lap. Seen close to, it was apparent that his garments were a little threadbare, and the feathers of his crown had a somewhat moth-eaten appearance.

Four miles more or less due east, they drew near to an island that was larger than any other they had yet seen. Its sides seemed to be terraced; some stonework was visible here and there. Mendoza stared hard at it.

Cultivation! she transmitted. *Lewis, somebody's farming those slopes. See the manioc? I don't notice any maize, though . . .*

"You are to be commended on the admirable silence of your sister," said Orocobix, a little uneasily. "Does your lord prefer his women without voices?"

"No," said Mendoza.

"She's just, ah—loath to chatter in the presence of gods," said Lewis hastily. That seemed to please Orocobix.

"Very wise policy," he said. "We have reached the sacred mountain, by the way. Put in there, at the boat dock."

Lewis poled them up to a fairly ramshackle little causeway built out over wooden pilings, and tied off the painter. Several boats had been moored there, but lay now just under the water in various stages of ancient decay. The old man did not trust his weight to the rotten planks of the dock. He hopped straight ashore. Lewis and Mendoza followed his example.

"Do bring the water gift as well, won't you? You may ascend to the Royal Palace," said Orocobix, waving a hand at the stone staircase that led up from the landing, a flight of a hundred moss-grown steps. As they gazed at it, a furious commotion broke out somewhere above.

"Merely the sacred birds," said Orocobix. "Pray do not mind them; they are kept penned up."

Animal domestication! Lewis transmitted, hefting the case of bottled water to his shoulder.

Whatever, Mendoza replied. She started up the long stair, peering at the terraces as she passed them. By contrast with the island on which they had camped, it was quite a tidy cultivation; manioc, sweet potatoes, small fruit and nut trees Lewis was unable to identify. Several plantings of what were apparently medicinal herbs, to judge from the fragrance. Some terraces seemed to be given over to fish ponds; there were also withy enclosures where geese came to the fence and put their heads over, honking dire threats.

It's a self-sustaining ecosystem! Lewis was terrifically excited.

Damned if you aren't right, Mendoza replied. She came to a dead halt on the stairs, staring. *What—?*

Lewis followed her gaze. *Those are cotton plants,* he informed her helpfully.

But they're the wrong kind! Mendoza stepped off the stairway and out onto the terrace, where she bent down to inspect what was growing there.

"My sister is impressed by your garden," said Lewis. Orocobix, who was following at a slow but steady pace, looked pleased.

"I take it your master has none such?"

"Well—no, not really."

"Ah," said Orocobix, with great satisfaction.

They ought to be growing Gossypium barbadense. *This is* Gossypium herbaceum. *It's African cotton, Lewis!*

Aha! Proof of Atlantis!

Oh, don't be a—

"We have other excellent plants here, also," remarked Orocobix, as he passed Mendoza. "Come along, child."

He led them up the last few steps. "The Royal Palace of the Guanikina," he said complacently.

They stared, and were stared back at.

The palace was a low sprawling building of thatched stone, with wings opening off a central courtyard, green with moss and overhung with forest canopy. In the courtyard sat two mortal women and a man. The man and woman appeared to be in early middle age, clad in the same sort of worn finery as the old man. The other woman was young, in her late teens or early twenties. She had been in the act of fanning herself and was looking rather disagreeable, though her expression changed to one of shock when Lewis and Mendoza stepped into the courtyard.

"My family, I bring you visitors," said Orocobix, looking smug.

"My lord," exclaimed the girl, and rising from her seat she threw herself at Lewis's feet.

"I'm sorry?" Lewis looked down at her.

Orocobix cleared his throat.

"My child, this is a mere servant of Maketaurie Guyuaba. A dead mortal."

"Oh!" Blushing furiously, the young lady scrambled to her feet. "How dare you, man of earth!"

"You should have known they were dead by the color of their skin," said the older lady to the younger, in tones of icy reproof. She turned a brilliant smile on Lewis. "How do you do, child? You may set your offering down. We scarcely expected a delegation from divine Maketaurie. Not in broad day-light, at least."

"*His* kingdom is apparently doing rather well," said Orocobix meaning-fully. "And he has few wives."

"Has he?" The older woman and the younger exchanged glances.

Lewis, they're all alone here! I can only pick up two other mortal signs. Who the hell are these people?

A royal family with no subjects?

"So, I suppose older deities, who are perhaps not such swift fellows as they once were but nevertheless have a certain amount of wisdom the young cannot possess, *do* have their uses," said Orocobix to the other man, with an air of triumph.

"You needn't preen yourself," said the other man. He was thickset, with something of the look of a dissipated politician. He turned dull eyes on Lewis and Mendoza. "There are only two of them."

"*But* they are authorized by their lord to negotiate on his behalf," said Orocobix. "And will return to him in a week's time. Therefore it behooves us to treat them as ambassadors, don't you think?"

"Of course it does," said the lady, taking the man by his arm in a rather firm clasp. "Welcome, proxies of great Maketaurie! I am Atabey, goddess of the earth, and this is Agueybana, god of the sun. Regard the goddess Ca-jaya. Is she not fair?"

"Most fair," said Lewis, bowing. In fact Cajaya was sallow, angular, and rather pigeon-breasted, but she simpered for him now and batted her goose-feather fan.

"You must excuse the sad state in which you find us," said Atabey. "No servants to wash your feet, no retainers to salute you! The truth is, our great family has suffered certain reverses."

"Very sorry to hear it, oh goddess," said Lewis.

"The end of the damned world, in fact," said Agueybana gloomily. "Ex-cept for us, of course. And your master, obviously." He gave Lewis and Mendoza a speculative look. "Tell me, has he any live servants at all?"

Careful, Mendoza transmitted.

"A certain number," said Lewis. "And great multitudes of our kind, of course."

"But surely it is not mannerly to interrogate our guests without refreshment!" cried Atabey. "Tanama! Tanama, attend at once!"

"Yes, mother," replied someone from the depths of the house, and a moment later a second girl came forth. She seemed no more than ten or eleven, small and thin, and wore a plain robe of brown cotton. She blinked in surprise to see visitors, but folded her hands and bowed low.

"Fetch chairs for our guests, child, and then bring wine. Bring it in the *good* service," ordered Atabey.

"At once, mother," said the little girl, and hurried away.

Within a few moments Lewis and Mendoza found themselves seated somewhat uncomfortably on cane chairs, watching as the little girl poured something fruity and fermented into cups of pure gold. She presented them with a brief dazzling smile.

"Here is your drink, dead people," she said. "It's made from guavas. Is that right? Can you drink the same as us? Because all the stories say—"

"Do not presume, Tanama!" said Atabey.

"It's quite all right," said Lewis, smiling as he raised the cup in salute. "We don't need much. Thank you."

What on earth is it? transmitted Mendoza, who was staring into her cup in a mixture of fascination and loathing.

It doesn't matter. Drink, Lewis replied, and sipped. Guava brew, fermented by human enzymes. Without shuddering, he set his cup aside and smiled at his hosts.

"Now, oh great ones, what message would you have me carry to my master?"

"First," said Agueybana, "extend our greetings to our most mighty fellow divinity—before whom the stars and planets prostrate themselves, before whom he who sends the rain gusts feels inadequate—and so forth and so on."

"And tell him we *do* apologize abjectly for not communicating with him earlier, but our situation here—" began Atabey.

"Don't tell him that! Gods never apologize to anyone!" said Agueybana indignantly.

"Perhaps you ought to say," said Orocobix, "that we, ancient and powerful as we are, have been so preoccupied with the administration of our own realm that it had not occurred to us to survey its outer regions in some time, and that therefore the discovery of great Maketaurie's proximity to our neighborhood comes as a pleasant surprise to us."

"And that we are happy to extend our hospitality to a pair of his servants," added Atabey.

"Whose undoubtedly unintentional trespass into our dominion we will generously forgive," said Orocobix, with a graceful inclination of his head in Lewis and Mendoza's direction. "That they may serve as couriers of our will. Which is, that we propose to our brother Maketaurie a dynastic union of great advantage to himself."

"We offer young Cajaya," said Agueybana, raising his voice, "of immaculate and perfect pedigree, in whose bloodline runs the wealth of the earth and golden immortality."

"I hear," said Lewis gravely. He remembered a timbered hall on a green hill, where he had watched a druid preside over the betrothal arrangements for a chieftain's bride in almost exactly the same terms. Not quite the same, though. *Golden immortality?*

"And in return for this magnificent gift," said Agueybana hurriedly, "we expect no less than the girl is worth."

This is like a Jane Austen novel, for God's sake, transmitted Mendoza.

I'm sure the Company can come up with a suitable trousseau, Lewis responded. Aloud he said: "I hear and will convey your message, great ones. I hope you'll permit a few discreet questions on my master's behalf?"

"Naturally," said Orocobix.

"Thank you, great one. Will it please you to relate the ancestry of lovely Cajaya?" inquired Lewis. "With, perhaps, a digression explaining how her glorious forebears came to rule this place?"

"Of course," said Orocobix, looking pleased. Agueybana exhaled loudly, folding his arms. Atabey and Cajaya rolled their eyes at each other. He ignored them and, clearing his throat, struck a majestic attitude.

"In the beginning of Time, great Orocobix floated in the void with his people," he announced. "He was the first great father. His children were Agueybana and Atabey, Kolibri and Tanama, Tonina and Cajaya. Many were the storm-spirits of the void he subdued. Yet in time his children wearied of the flesh of fish, and so great Orocobix thought it good to make a solid world.

"He drew up his celestial boat in this place, which was made up of void and firmament, and sent his servants out to live in it. They planted crops, but there was too much void still. The crops would not grow. Great Orocobix saw that he must make the world more solid, in order that his servants might not starve.

"Wherefore he created sacred Caonaki, who made the crops grow abundantly. And great Orocobix moreover created the solid mountains to rise above the void, where his people might live. There they prospered, and rejoiced, and praised great Orocobix for his wisdom and beneficence. As well they ought," concluded Orocobix.

Standard run-of-the-mill creation myth, transmitted Mendoza. *Void, firmament, mortals multiplying. Same old story.*

Not quite, Lewis replied. He bowed politely. "Indeed an impressive tale, great Orocobix."

"In time," Orocobix continued, "Great Orocobix wearied of the flesh he wore, and it pleased him to pass again into the shining void. When he wished to return, divine Atabey bore him new flesh. And so he came again to rule his children and his servants in wisdom. Thereafter, when any of the Children of Orocobix had worn out their flesh, they went away to the void, and shortly returned in new bodies. By this, you may see that divine Cajaya's ancestry is direct and is as pure as gold."

They're claiming to be their own ancestors. Mendoza looked coldly amused. *And what a shallow little gene pool it must be!*

You never know; maybe the Atlanteans could clone themselves. Lewis bowed and said aloud: "Pure as gold indeed, great Orocobix. I have no doubt my master will be delighted to marry fair Cajaya. Though it is my painful duty, as his servant, to make inquiry touching the apparent absence of your subjects . . . ?"

"Oh, they all got sick and died," said little Tanama. In the moment of mortified silence that followed, Cajaya looked away and fanned herself more rapidly. Atabey clenched her fists. Agueybana cleared his throat.

"They were disobedient," he said, "so great Orocobix smote them with pestilence. That's why we need new ones."

"It was a great while ago," said Orocobix, in a tone of sad wonderment. "I can't really remember it very clearly. In retrospect, it seems rather a foolish thing to have done; but apparently my wrath used to be formidable.

I incline to a somewhat more merciful temperament nowadays. Even we gods grow in wisdom."

"My master himself has often regretted the rashness of his youth," Lewis hastened to say.

"So you can appreciate our position," said Agueybana.

"We wouldn't require much," said Atabey. "I'm sure your master has plenty to spare—"

"But, of course, this is hardly the sort of petty accounting with which to annoy great Maketaurie," said Orocobix, with a severe look at his children. "Only slaves beg for favors, after all."

Cajaya's fanning reached a speed comparable to the beat of humming-bird wings. Agueybana flushed and stared at the ground. Atabey called sharply, "Tanama! Take yourself off to your duties, stupid child! Do you think anyone here wants to listen to your opinions?"

"At once, mother," said Tanama, and went back indoors. Mendoza turned to watch her go.

Interesting family dynamic. And . . . Lewis, there's another mortal in the house.

"Hem! Well," said Lewis, "quite right, great Orocobix. To continue, then: I take it that some members of your family are not presently here?"

"Tonina is refreshing himself in the void," said Orocobix. "We expect his return to the flesh presently. As for Kolibri . . . he is engaged in certain duties. You understand, of course, that there are matters beyond a servant's comprehension? Very good. Let it suffice that he also sends his most cordial greeting to our brother Maketaurie."

"Certainly, great Orocobix," said Lewis.

I think the one inside must be sick, Mendoza transmitted, *from what I can pick up of his life signs. And of course gods are never sick, so they're keeping it a secret, aren't they? Or perhaps he's just too inbred to be presentable.*

I suppose so. Lewis studied the royal family critically. There were a few signs of genetic trouble; Cajaya's high narrow chest, a trace of scoliosis in Agueybana. *Poor things. They must have been marooned here for generations. I wish I really were an emissary from another god; they could use some new blood.*

I somehow doubt the Company's going to patch up their little pantheon with a gift of chromosomes.

Lewis cleared his throat. "All this will I relate to my master, of course.

No doubt his munificence will be extraordinary. In the meanwhile, is there any service we may render you, divine ones?"

"Oh, of course not," said Orocobix airily. "Which is to say, other than one or two little things . . . I scarcely like to bring them up, they're hardly worth notice . . . but if you could see your way to, perhaps, putting a new roof on the palace? Now that the rains have begun, the leaks will be dreadfully inconvenient, you know."

"And the garden needs weeding," said Atabey.

Climbing the ladder with an armful of cut reed, Lewis reminded himself that he was *exploring a lost civilization*, after all. He peered down through the roof beams at the humble interior below—somebody's bedchamber, rough furniture many times repaired with jungle liana or braided cotton fiber.

"So great Orocobix floated in the void and ate a lot of fish," he speculated to himself. "And fought with storm-spirits. A seagoing culture, obviously, and they found themselves obliged to adapt to specialized agriculturalism.

"And if they came from some other place, let us say somewhere in the Caribbean, perhaps that was why they hadn't any interest in teosinte and grew manioc instead. But rain forest soil's dreadful to grow things in, so . . . Orocobix the First, clearly a clever chap, devised elevated fields of *terra preta*.

"The thing is, how? What, and from whence? Gosh, I wish I'd been programmed in anthropology . . ."

He worked on, lashing reeds in place with liana cord, wondering how Mendoza was faring down on the garden terrace. A voice floated up from some room in the house below him. A child? Yes, the little girl Tanama . . .

". . . they look very lively for dead people to *me*. And not at all like bats! Except for their clothes, which are sort of loose and shiny, like folded bat wings. The boy is pretty and nice, but the girl is angry. What do you suppose the dead have to be angry about? Anyway, isn't it exciting?"

A silence followed her remark. Or did it? Had there been a faint reply?

"You know what I think? I think the world is possibly a lot bigger than they always told us it was. And realer! Maketaurie is *real*. Coaybay beyond the sunset is a real place. I could tell Mother and Father were surprised by it all, they didn't know what to do. And you should have seen Cajaya being nice! It was just hysterical. She *smiled* and *smiled* and *smiled* until I thought her face would crack!

"Wouldn't it be lovely if she went away to Coaybay to be a queen? I wonder what would happen then? I suppose we'd have to get a new Cajaya from somewhere. But if I ask Grandfather—"

"What a splendid job you're doing, child," remarked Orocobix, wandering out to peer up at Lewis. "I shall certainly commend you to your master, when at last we meet. And such quickness! But then, the dead work swiftly, don't they?"

"Thank you, sir. We do our best," said Lewis, descending the ladder in some haste.

The little girl brought them their supper—a platter loaded with guavas—in the guest room they had been given, a dank chamber wherein painted murals were just visible on the crumbling plaster walls.

"You ought to like it in here, dear dead people," she said cheerily. "It's nice and dark. I'm afraid the beds aren't very good, but then you sleep hanging from the ceiling, don't you?"

"Sometimes," said Lewis. "I'm sure we'll be quite comfortable, thank you."

"What's it like in the land of the dead?"

"Er . . . well, it's . . . lovely, and everyone is happy," said Lewis.

"Is it dark there, on the other side of the sunset? Grandfather said he was going to go there and I just thought he meant he was going to die soon. I didn't think he meant it, you know, *literally,* or maybe he was going to take some Magic Medicine and dream he was going there, not really get in the boat and *go* there," Tanama chattered. "But he did! What a surprise!"

"Yes, wasn't it?" said Lewis, wishing Mendoza would take some part in the conversation. She merely sat on one of the low chairs with her arms crossed, clearly impatient for the little girl to leave. When Tanama left at last:

"Why is that child under the impression we're a pair of fruit bats?" she inquired.

"It's part of Taino mythology," said Lewis, sitting down. "The dead turn into bats, and go to live in the west, and eat a lot of guavas. At least, that's the story I'm getting from my folklore database. You don't have it?"

"I'm only a Botanist, remember?" Mendoza selected a guava and looked at it critically. "I wasn't programmed with that stuff. You're the Literature Specialist."

"It's a rather nice afterlife," said Lewis, a little wistfully. "No concept of eternal damnation or reward either, for that matter. Ever so much pleasanter than the Mesopotamian model. You just fly about in the night and have all the sweets you want. Not unlike Halloween."

"Not that *we'll* ever know," said Mendoza. "But I'll tell you something I did find out, Lewis. Ask me how my afternoon went!"

"How did your afternoon go, Mendoza?" Lewis said, drawing out his knife and slicing the top off a guava.

"It was an afternoon of discovery. I pulled a lot of weeds," she said. "And rebuilt a couple of dry-stone walls which had crumbled. Noted a lot of rare herb plantings; I'll tell you, Dr. Zeus's pharmaceuticals branch is going to be interested in those. Watched as little What's-her-name came and gathered watercress from one of the fish ponds, which are crawling with snails, to which the geese have no access. A textbook setup for parasites. Our hosts must have one helluva problem with liver flukes."

"Oh, dear. All that and inbreeding, too."

"Nasty, isn't it? But I digress! I worked my way around to the far side of the island, Lewis, following these cunning little Machu Picchu–style terraces, and guess what I found over there?" She withdrew her own dagger, sliced open a guava, and bit into it with gusto.

"The chariots of the gods?" said Lewis. "Prester John?"

"I'll tell you what I found," said Mendoza. Her eyes burned at him. "A structure of stone, like an enormous grain silo tipped on its side, or maybe a chute roofed over with slates. It runs from the back of the palace all the way down the hill to the lake below. And, all the way down that hill, the brush has been kept clear and the tree branches cut back, so that this immense stone tube gets full sunlight during the hottest part of the day. You know what else?"

"What?"

"It was *steaming*," said Mendoza, as though that were terrifically significant.

"So . . . it's a hot water conduit?" Lewis ventured.

"No," said Mendoza patiently. "It's a composter. The biggest composter in the world. I climbed up the hillside to see what went in at the top. Charcoal, broken pottery, fish bones, fruit and vegetable peels, and, yes, feces in astounding quantity. The smell would knock you down.

"Then I climbed down the hillside to see what comes out at the bottom, after what must be about two years of ripening in its slo-o-ow passage down the hill, pushed by all the muck thrown in above it. Guess what I found down there, oozing into the sunlight?"

"*Terra preta!*" cried Lewis.

"Bingo," said Mendoza calmly, reaching for another guava.

"It's just compost?" said Lewis. "How anticlimactic."

"No, no. It's made *with* compost; but there's some microbial content I can't identify. The stuff that makes it work like sourdough starter, I guess."

"A secret ingredient," said Lewis.

"That's right," said Mendoza. "A completely organic, self-renewing fertilizer so powerful it could convert the Sahara to prime farmland. And these mortals are the only ones left who know how to make it."

"Oh, dear," Lewis murmured. He looked at Mendoza with wide eyes. "You do realize, don't you, that once we make our report, the Company is going to do a lot more than send anthropologists to study these people? It'll do whatever it takes to get the secret out of them."

Mendoza shrugged. "Yes. Could it be much worse than leaving them up here to become a bunch of inbred idiots?"

"I suppose not," Lewis said. "Still . . . we discovered a lost world, perfectly intact, perfectly unchanged until we made contact with it. And now . . . it'll burst like a soap bubble."

Mendoza stared at the floor. "Funny how that happens, isn't it?" she said wearily. She took another bite of guava.

Lewis balanced precariously, straining to reach the roofbeam. He grabbed, made the cord fast, and dragged the next bundle of reed thatching into place. Pushing away to reach the ladder again, he looked down into yet another dark and empty room. The palace must have housed dozens of mortals at one time; but most of the rooms he had seen had clearly been unoccupied for years.

What had happened? Not famine, that much was certain. An epidemic of disease was much more likely. Not liver fluke. Probably something that killed swiftly . . . *An epic tragedy,* Lewis thought, *and the rest of the world never even noticed.*

"Good morning, Slave of Maketaurie," said someone at the base of the ladder. Lewis glanced down between the rungs and spotted Cajaya, peering up coyly. "Leave that work, for now. I've brought you a nice guava to eat."

"Many thanks, fair goddess," said Lewis, reflecting that he was going to be heartily sick of guavas soon. He descended the ladder and accepted the guava with a bow. Recalling his conversation with Mendoza, he scanned Cajaya for liver fluke. To his surprise, the girl was quite free of parasites.

Cajaya smiled widely at him—it really did look as though she found it painful—and waved her goose-wing fan.

"We've scarcely had any time to talk since you arrived here! And I was so hoping to pry a few details from you concerning dear Lord Maketaurie," she said.

"What do you wish to know, radiant Cajaya?" Lewis inquired.

"Well, silly, I want to know what he's like!" Cajaya demanded, blushing. "Tell me! Has he a man's form, like yours?"

"Why, yes, he does," said Lewis, wondering which lucky anthropologist was going to be assigned the role of Maketaurie by Dr. Zeus Incorporated.

"But he's taller than you are, I assume," said Cajaya, looking him up and down appraisingly. "And his skin's a better color, I hope,"

"I think so, goddess," improvised Lewis. "I, er, don't look at his divinity directly, you see. It's not proper etiquette for a servant."

"Oh! Well, that's understandable," said Cajaya. She gave him a sidelong look from behind her fan. "I wonder what you can tell me about his other wives? Does he give them many presents? Golden nose rings? Feather cloaks? Has each her own household, with a proper train of servants? They aren't all crowded together in one palace, are they?"

"I believe my master is very generous, goddess," said Lewis. He wondered what a Company Facilitator would say in his position. He decided an extravagant falsehood was likely. "And I believe each lady has quite a spacious suite to herself, but—"

"And are any of them as beautiful as I am?"

"Goddess, that is something on which a mere servant cannot possibly offer an opinion," said Lewis desperately. "I should be committing a grave breach of propriety, were I to do so."

"Of course," said Cajaya, touching his arm with her fan. "However . . . I shall give you an opportunity to do me a service, gentle dead man. You shall advise your master of my desires—indirectly, of course, dropping little details here and there in the most nonchalant fashion, about what you have observed. Let him know I expect a palace of my own, and servants, and heaps of gold—nose rings, ear plugs, necklaces, the whole lot. My favorite color is scarlet, although violet is acceptable."

"I will endeavor to let my master know these things, goddess," said Lewis.

"Discreetly, do you understand?"

"Without fail, goddess."

Cajaya turned and walked away a few paces; then turned back. She pulled a gold bead from the fringe of her gown and tossed it to him.

"I nearly forgot. For your trouble," she said.

Lewis was trudging back up the steps, dragging a sledge loaded with new-cut reeds, when he saw Atabey waiting on the near landing. He smiled and bowed, but his heart sank as he realized she was intent on speaking to him.

"Slave of Maketaurie, a moment of your time," she said.

"Of course, great goddess." Lewis pulled the sledge level and stopped. He drew off his hat and bowed. Atabey regarded his hair with displeasure. She reached out and touched it gingerly.

"Your hair is the color of dead grass. Appropriate for a dead person, I suppose, but—is your master's hair the same way?"

"I don't believe so, great goddess."

"What about his other traits? Is he—how shall I put this?—suitably virile?"

"I beg your pardon?"

Atabey pursed her lips. "Has he many sons by his other wives?"

"Oh. Indeed, great goddess, mighty Maketaurie has begotten abundant sons."

"Has he? Very good. And daughters?"

"Of course. He may rule the land of the dead, but is not *himself* dead, you see?"

"Oh, good! Yes, that's an important distinction. I wonder whether he would consider sending a few of his children by Cajaya back here, once she's settled in and bearing him sons on a regular basis?"

"Madam?" Lewis blinked at her.

"But, of course, *you* wouldn't know that," said Atabey, frowning and waving a dismissive hand. As though to herself, she muttered: "All the same . . . it never hurts to ask." She turned to Lewis again, and smiled graciously. "I merely inquire, you see, because we do need to keep our august and ancient family present in this plane of existence, and one does require a body of flesh in which to manifest, after all. And for that—" She gave a little embarrassed laugh. "One does need daughters, doesn't one?"

"I suppose so, great goddess," said Lewis, wishing hard that he were in a peaceful room somewhere far away, Londinium perhaps, with a martini at his elbow and a copy of the *Iliad* or perhaps the plays of Aristophanes . . .

"And, of course, there is the question of servants," Atabey went on. "Your master will certainly want to see that his in-laws are well attended. A mere hundred or so to see to our personal needs—really, we wouldn't require much. Oh, the difficulties and inconveniences we've had to face, the last few years!"

"I can imagine," said Lewis, doing his best to sound sympathetic.

"I don't think so," said Atabey severely, now clearly uncomfortable to have unburdened herself before a lesser creature. "It has been a great trial."

"Terribly sorry, great goddess." Lewis lowered his eyes.

"You may continue with your task," said Atabey, and stalked off. Lewis scanned her as she went; no sign of liver fluke at all, contrary to Mendoza's expectations.

I wonder who's eating all the watercress, then? he wondered. He sighed, gritted his teeth, and took another haul on the sledge.

Lewis had just thrown a bundle of reeds across his shoulder and was starting up the ladder when he spotted Agueybana approaching him. He stepped back down, dropped the bundle, and dusted his hands.

"Good afternoon, god Agueybana," he called, "Would you like a word with me in private?"

Agueybana winced and hurried nearer.

"Not so loudly, if you please," he said in an undertone. "Or we'll have them all about us, babbling away with their nonsense. Look here—we need to discuss a few practical matters."

"Such as, great god?" said Lewis innocently.

"Such as a bride price, for one thing," said Agueybana. "I'm sure your master is a practical fellow; he's sure to see what an advantage it'll be for him to take our Cajaya to wife. We are, after all, the most ancient of the divinities! To say nothing of the wealth of this land of ours."

"It is, indeed, a fruitful country," said Lewis.

"So it is," said Agueybana, with a sly look. "Let us just say that he who weds Cajaya shall never lack for guavas, eh? But, of course, he can't expect such advantages for nothing. We ought to be provided for *properly*."

"What did you have in mind, great one?" said Lewis.

"Mortal slaves," said Agueybana, without hesitation. "As well as building stone and artisans. A few thousand mortals to maintain the gardens, a retinue for the house. Preferably highborn—we couldn't be expected to put up with field slaves waiting at table."

"Ah," said Lewis, nodding noncommittally. He scanned the mortal for liver fluke infestation, continuing to murmur "Yes," and "I see," as Agueybana rambled on with demands.

No, the man was in perfect health, like the ladies . . . except . . . No! There was some trace of something after all . . . Lewis concentrated and focused his scan, going slightly crosseyed with effort, though Agueybana failed to notice.

". . . enough slaves to make the trip to the coast again, with sledges to bring back stones . . ."

Signs of an old infestation, long healed. At some point in the past Agueybana *had* suffered from liver fluke, but made a full recovery. And seemed, overall, quite robust now. Therefore . . . nobody was eating the cresses? Or the fish? Perhaps the pond was merely ornamental. But . . .

". . . glad you agree with me!" Agueybana was saying, and thumped him on the back with painful heartiness. "It's damned annoying to be the only level-headed person in the place, but there you are. Lord Maketaurie will sympathize, I'm sure. Tell me . . . has he an army?"

"I'm sorry?" Lewis came alert. "An army? Oh, no, great one. Why would the ruler of the afterlife need an army?"

"Hm. I hadn't thought of that," said Agueybana, pulling at his lip. "Pity. It might have come in useful. Oh, well. You present my terms, anyway, understand? And I'll see to it your master receives good report of you."

"You are too kind," said Lewis, genuflecting.

He was lying down on one of the two ancient cots when Mendoza entered their room, carrying another platter of guavas.

"I headed off our hostess," she said. "Told her the dead need a little peace and quiet now and then. My God, Lewis, you look exhausted."

"I've been lying like a Facilitator all day," said Lewis dully. "But I'm nearly done with the east wing of the palace."

"Bloody lazy mortal aristocrats," said Mendoza, setting down the platter. "I'm surprised they didn't make the child do it. They make her do everything else."

Lewis sat up and reached for a guava. "They don't have liver flukes, by the way. I scanned. No parasites at all."

"None?" Mendoza looked suspicious. "But that fish pond is crawling with the stuff. It's in the snails and the fish. It's encysted on the watercress. Lewis, we've got a tiny inbred colony of primates living together here on one hilltop. They ought to be loaded with fleas and lice and—just about every nasty parasite mortals can get."

"They're not, however," said Lewis, peeling the guava. "Odd, isn't it?"

"Distinctly odd. By the way . . . I don't suppose you'd do me a favor?"

"I'd be happy to. What is it?"

"Since you don't seem to mind talking to them . . . I wonder if you could sort of indirectly bring up the subject of plant composting in the garden, and ask them what their recipe is?"

"But I thought you discovered that," said Lewis, bewildered.

"No. I spent all day analyzing samples I took from the bottom of the chute—when I wasn't weeding their damn terrace paths and herb beds. Fish bones, broken pots, vegetable matter, mortal sewage. *And something else.* Some batch of microorganisms I could not, for the life of me, identify, *but* which is able to convert stinking muck into black gold."

"All right," said Lewis, mentally adding another to the long list of things for which the greatest delicacy and tact was needed. "Rely on me."

"Thanks," said Mendoza. She threw herself down on her bed, which promptly collapsed in a tangle of rotten wood and cord. With explosive profanity she rose and kicked it across the room, where it broke into bits with a sound like old bones shattering.

Lewis rose at once. "You can have mine."

"No! No, sweetheart. All I had to do for the wretched monkeys all day was weed their little plague-spot of a garden. They worked you a lot harder. You stay there," said Mendoza, controlling her temper with difficulty.

"Oh, I couldn't—" said Lewis dazedly, the word *sweetheart* pounding in his ears.

"No. Hell, you know what I'll do? I'll just see if I can't sleep standing up." Mendoza surveyed the room and found a patch of wall that was slightly less leprous with moss than the rest. She leaned against it, and balanced herself cautiously. "What's it called, *going into fugue*? If those old field ops can do it, I'll bet I can do it, too."

"It takes a little practice," said Lewis. "You have to sort of open your consciousness. The opposite of focusing, you see? Just . . . reach out into the Everything."

"So you've done this before?" Mendoza let her arms hang down, decided that was uncomfortable, and folded them instead.

"A little," Lewis admitted. "I had climbed a tree to get out of a flood. On the third day I was up there, I tried going into fugue, so I could get some rest."

"Did it work?"

"Yes . . . though I wouldn't call it a success. I found myself identifying entirely too closely with my tree. Next thing I knew, I was having a furious conversation with a family of gall-wasps. Had this overpowering urge to rub insect repellent on myself for months afterward."

"Ugh." Mendoza shuddered and closed her eyes.

Lewis peeled and ate another guava.

Mendoza opened her eyes.

"Wait a minute. These people survived an epidemic that wiped out the rest of their civilization. You don't suppose they've got some kind of genetic resistance to parasites in general? And, therefore, maybe, to certain diseases transmitted by the parasites?"

"Possibly," said Lewis, struck by the idea. He looked at her. "Interesting! But . . . you know, if you want to go into fugue, you need to stop thinking about anything specific."

"Oh. Right," said Mendoza, and closed her eyes again. "Well, good night, Lewis."

"Good night."

He ate one more guava, slowly, wondering why the mortals he'd scanned hadn't so much as a flea bite among them. What *if* they, alone of all their people, had some genetic characteristic that helped their ancestors survive an epidemic? He knew that Native Americans were dying, in the millions, of smallpox and other European diseases. They died, not because they were especially weak and susceptible, but because they were more genetically alike, one to another, than the mongrel Europeans.

So suppose, he thought to himself as he lay down, *this one family were just different enough to live through the plague? Some kind of favorable mutation. They might have decided they were gods. But then, with no one else with which to breed, they'd have fallen into the same trap of genetic homogeneity . . . ah, the ironies of history . . . shallow gene pool, just like the cheetahs . . .*

He thought over the absurd parade of requests he'd received from the mortals. The contrast between their royal expectations, and what was most likely to happen, was painful to contemplate.

If Dr. Zeus followed usual policy, every byte of data Lewis was absorbing would be wrung from him, and from Mendoza, too, as though they were a pair of sponges; then a team of anthropologists would be sent in, masquerading as Maketaurie and his entourage, no doubt.

These last survivors, with their culture, would be studied, collected, and packed off to some Company facility like so many rare butterflies. How would they adjust to life as mere Company dependents?

Too sad to dwell upon . . .

Lewis turned and watched Mendoza, intending to offer her helpful advice should she be finding it difficult to go into fugue. To his amazement, she appeared to have succeeded on the first try. Stiffly upright there in the darkness, she had taken on the immobility of a dead branch or a pillar of stone; she seemed nearly transparent, a shade among shadows. Her features were drawn, almost deathly, and yet there was something ecstatic in her expression.

It frightened him, for no good reason he could name. Lewis felt an irrational urge to leap up, to put his arms around her and carry her away from that inhuman void into which she slipped with such terrifying ease.

Perhaps she's meeting him *there,* thought Lewis. *Perhaps the void is Nicholas Harpole.*

Guilt, and regret, and weariness so overcame him that he turned his face away. He tried to remember a place he'd been happy once, a wine shop in Piraeus with a view of the sea, and he'd sat there with a fresh copy of Menander's *Dis Exapaton* all one sunny afternoon, with never a care in the world . . .

Dawn came with a thousand birds crying, and Lewis opened his eyes to an empty room. He started up, panicked; but after a moment of scanning he picked up Mendoza's signal down on one of the terraces. She was pulling weeds again.

Are you all right? he transmitted.

Yes! Lewis, it worked. What a great way to rest! I can't think why we don't fugue out more often.

I believe it's frowned on if you're posted in an urban environment around mortals, said Lewis. *The argument is, you might as well slap a big sign saying* CYBORG *across your forehead.*

Mendoza responded with a cheerful obscenity. Lewis sighed, got to his feet, and wandered out into the palace courtyard.

Orocobix sat there, gazing out at the morning. On a block of stone at his feet, the flamecube flickered away; someone had scrupulously cleaned it and figured out how to switch it on. It diffused a pleasant heat against the early morning chill. Little Tanama was just offering her grandfather a cup of something steaming. He accepted it, smiling, and bowed a greeting to Lewis.

"Good morning, child. I must say, the palace roof has never been so well repaired."

"Thank you," said Lewis, accepting a cup from Tanama. He sipped it: a bitter herbal tea. He had no idea what its botanic origin was; he detected caffeine, as well as chemical compounds intended to regulate metabolism and keep the prostate an acceptable size. Useful, for an elderly mortal male.

"Are you going to be working on the other side of the house today?" Tanama asked him. "I need to know so—" Orocobix held up his hand in a warning gesture, and she blushed and fell silent. Gathering up the tray with its pot and cups, she hurried indoors.

"Great Orocobix," said Lewis, setting aside his cup. "I must be frank with you. It is likely that my master will prefer to take you, and your family, to his own kingdom, rather than leave you here."

"I am aware of that, child," said Orocobix placidly. "The Lord of Coaybay takes all into his realm. It is his nature."

"Yes, but your family seems to believe that life will go on, unchanged," said Lewis. "That will not be the case at all."

Orocobix nodded.

"They are greedy and impatient," he said. "And not, I think, very great observers of the world. A great tree shoots up from the earth, it bears fruit, the fruit ripens and rots and falls; the tree sees many seasons come and go, watches many harvests drop from its branches. Yet in some hour the tree itself will die at the heart, and rot and fall, too.

"We were the tree, you see; our people came and went, and finally went away forever, but we Guanikina remained on awhile. And my children have proceeded on the assumption that we would always remain. But I knew our heart had rotted out.

"When I saw this light, shining out after the sunset, I thought perhaps that Maketaurie was advancing his borders. That was why I went in search of him. What would you have done, child, in my place? Wait to grow weaker, and fewer, as the years go by, dwindling to nothing at last? Or go to him voluntarily while we still had some shred of our former dignity? I have made the best bargain I can. It is, I think, better than we might have expected."

Lewis bowed his head. "You are a wise god, Great Orocobix."

"And, in any case, it's not as though we haven't done this before," added Orocobix.

"What?"

"When we came from the land beyond the sunrise," said Orocobix.

"What's the land beyond the sunrise?" Lewis asked, feeling all his senses come alert. Somewhere, some time, a Company official in a dark room would be listening very closely to this.

"The place we lived before we sailed in the void," said Orocobix. "Many, many lives ago. Guanike. I don't recall it personally anymore, you understand; one head can only hold so many memories."

"That's so true," said Lewis, with a surreal sense of mirth. *Unless you get called in for an upgrade.* He edged closer. "What can you tell me, great Orocobix, of what you know? Is it a real place?"

"It was," said Orocobix. "Sadly, it sank into the void, and we were obliged to leave. We traveled westward, and found a little country, with mortals to be our servants there. In time we left that land, too—I don't know why, anymore—and found this place, which was much more suitable because it was simply immense, you know. And now, we travel on again. I think it's all for the best."

Mendoza! Mendoza, you won't believe what I just heard!

What? From her tone she was doing something boring in a methodical manner.

These people have an Atlantis story! They came from some place in the east that sank into the sea!

Lewis, that's dumb. Atlantis never really existed. The Company would know if it had.

What if it was Thera? What if it was in the Black Sea or the Mediterranean?

Lewis, they are Indians. Run a DNA sample, for heaven's sake.

Lewis cleared his throat. "Tell me, great Orocobix: did you bring anything with you from lost Guanike?"

"Nothing very much," said Orocobix. "Not a lot of room in an open boat, after all. There's a little box in my chambers. A few old ornaments."

"I would very much like to look upon them, Great Orocobix."

"One of these days," Orocobix replied, with a yawn. "I'll ask the child to find them for me."

Lewis bowed. He scanned the old man; but was able to determine only that he was in good health for his age. And . . . had evidently once, long since, suffered hepatic insult consistent with parasitic infestation, and recovered completely.

Lewis staggered up the ladder with a bundle of reeds in his arms and a positive frieze of ancient Atlantean figures processing through his head.

Lost Guanike! Where could it have been? Having reached the top of the wall, he peered down into the chamber within, where the ancient plaster crumbled from the walls. Any traces of a painted mural there? Any suspiciously amphoralike jars?

No.

But, not far distant, mortal voices raised . . . Lewis tilted his head, listening.

"I can't move him again! That's twice in one week, and he gets so tired!" It was Tanama, sounding angry, even tearful.

"Then I'll help you move him." That was Agueybana, sounding peremptory. "We can't leave him in here; do you want the dead man looking in at him as he mends the damned roof? If we lose our secret, we'll bargain from a weaker position."

"But . . . if Cajaya marries his master, won't he find out anyway?"

"Not likely," said Agueybana. "He's a *servant,* after all! Do you suppose Maketaurie involves such creatures in his private affairs?"

Lewis, I'm going back to the camp. Mendoza's transmission so took Lewis by surprise that he nearly fell backward off the ladder.

What?

I've taken the old man's boat. I won't be gone long; but I've got to have a credenza to analyze this stuff.

What stuff?

The terra preta!

Oh. Right. Perhaps we could do a quick DNA analysis as well?

So you can find out whether your Indians are actually from Santorini? Mendoza sounded as though she were grinning. *Oh, why not?*

But what am I going to tell them if they notice the boat's gone?

Oh, I asked the old man. Startled the daylights out of him when I spoke, but he was polite as anything. See you soon . . .

From the ladder he spotted her returning, later in the day, poling along with a credenza strapped to her back; she put in at the landing and started up the steps with a purposeful stride.

Lewis went wearily through the purple twilight, as a fine drizzle fell. New World One had begun to gleam in his thoughts with a luster it hadn't possessed in ages; how could he ever have been bored with flush toilets, hot showers or crisp white bed linen?

Mendoza was already in their room when he walked in, sitting on the edge of his bed with the credenza on her knees, staring into its screen.

"Hello," she said in an absentminded way. "I got us a few things while I was over there."

"Zeusola bars!" Lewis cried in delight, and seized up one and tore off its wrapper. "Oh, gods . . . Caramel Oat Nut, mmm mmm . . ."

"A change of clothing, too," Mendoza added. Lewis looked around for his bag and didn't see it. She waved a hand at the bundle on the head of the bed.

"You brought me underwear?" he said, disconcerted. ". . . Thank you."

"You're a very neat packer," she said. "It was easy to find. Say, did you happen to ask anybody about the compost formula?

"Oh! No. I'm sorry. But I did learn something—"

At that moment they felt the little girl's approach.

Oh joy, Mendoza transmitted grumpily. *More guavas.* She slid the credenza out of sight.

"Good evening, dead people," said Tanama. "Look! I brought you some lovely fruit! You're lucky, we had a really good year for guavas. Grandfather says fruit's always in season in the Land of the Dead. Is that true?"

"Why, yes, it is," said Mendoza, startling Lewis. "We get good watercress, especially. Though of course we don't grow things the way you do, here, on these hills. Very nice compost you use. How is it made?"

"Oh, it's just—" The little girl clapped her hand over her mouth. "It's—just some stuff. That's, um, lying around."

"I notice it's a much darker color than the earth of the plain," said Mendoza, with an interrogative stare like a hot poker.

This is not the way to ask, Lewis transmitted. Mendoza gave him an impatient look, but subsided as he said: "In the Land Beyond the Sunset, you see, we have no such earth. It's, er, pink."

"Pink?" Tanama looked enchanted. "Like Cajaya's dress? Really?"

"Yes, and all the trees grow on flat ground," said Lewis. "In straight lines."

"How strange! That must make them hard to water, when the rains stop," said Tanama.

"Oh, our master is clever. He has spirits that fly about with jugs of water tending to them," said Lewis. "They're called, er, *amphorae*. Have you ever heard of such things?"

"No," said Tanama. "We use gourds for that. Oh, dear, one of the beds broke. Shall I go get you another one?"

"Most kind! But I wouldn't hear of you fetching such a heavy piece of furniture, little goddess. If you'll show me where another bed is, I'll bring it back myself," said Lewis, as smoothly as he was able. Tanama, however, bit her lip and backed off a pace.

"I'm not supposed to—that is, Father says—"

"It's all right," said Mendoza quickly. "I'll just sleep hanging from the ceiling again. Don't trouble yourself."

"Thank you!" said Tanama, and ran from the room.

Lewis and Mendoza exchanged glances.

"I had been about to tell you," said Lewis, "that the royal family seems to be keeping a secret."

"I'd guessed as much." Mendoza turned her head and eyed the doorway. "Something other than the obvious secret ingredient in *terra preta*?"

"I'm afraid so," said Lewis. He told her what he'd overheard, and she frowned.

"Why would a drooling inbred idiot be considered a bargaining chip?" she said.

"Perhaps a negative one? In any case, I'm afraid we don't have much choice," said Lewis. "Company procedure, and all that."

Mendoza sighed. "Pass me a guava. It's going to be a long night."

They sat up in silence as the night darkened. The soft mist became driving rain, thundering down on the broad leaves of the tree canopy above the house; soon there was a counterpoint of *plinks* and *plonks* from pots hastily placed in rooms Lewis's thatching had not yet reached.

Breathing deeply, Lewis attuned himself to the night. Under the drum and spatter of the rain, the fearful song of a million tree frogs chanting their lust. He made out the slower rhythms: mortal heartbeats, mortal breathing, a drowsy conversation, the popping of embers in a low fire. The creak of a bed frame: someone was tossing impatiently.

There were the scents, too: the smoking fire fragrant as incense, the sweetness of overripe fruit, the bitterness of mold. Over all, the immense raw wet black smell of the night outside; under all, a faint mortal reek.

The mortals grew still. The conversation drifted into snores. The impatient sleeper lay quiet, finally at peace.

Lewis waited until he thought he could hear centipedes rustling through the garden mold. He opened his eyes and looked at Mendoza. Her eyes were wide and vacant, dreaming awake. Gently he took her hand. She turned her face to him blindly; gradually she pulled her consciousness to the here and now, and met his eyes. He smiled and rose to his feet, taking her with him.

They walked out into the dark house.

A black corridor stretched before them, and only faintly glowing mushrooms along the baseboards gave any light; but they needed none. Silent they proceeded over the damp flagstones, through the vacant wing of the palace where they had been housed. Empty rooms opened black mouths, all along the wall to their right; now and again an arcade opened to the left, where rain gurgled in all the cistern runnels of the courtyard.

The mortal scent became stronger, the walls dryer and in a little better repair. It was now possible to see where painted frescoes had been, peeling and flaking away. No dainty ships or wasp-waisted ladies; only clubbed geometric figures, with here and there a dead-eyed face protruding its tongue through gapped teeth, and things that might have been intended to represent flowers or stars.

And now, a surreal flickering on the wall, making the murals seem to writhe and grimace. Mendoza halted. Lewis raised a hand to point at the line of doorways ahead, where rush lights smoked and threw fitful illumination.

They can't harm us, he told her.

I have nightmares, too. Mendoza stood rigid. *Sometimes I dream I'm awake, and standing in the house where my mortal family lived. They're lying there together in our bed, my mother and my father, and my little brothers and sisters. They're all asleep; only I am awake and alone, in the night. I can't wake them to keep me company, no matter how I try. And then I remember that they've all been dust this many a year, and I can never, never rest.*

Lewis put his arms around her. She clung to him. He held her until she stopped trembling. Without a word, then, he led her on along the corridor.

They looked in through the first doorway. Orocobix, Lord of Abundance, lay on his plain bed. He was gaunt and ancient, composed as though he had been laid out on a bier. His clothing was neatly folded on a chest. Under the bed frame was a clay chamberpot.

Lewis scanned the room. Unable to take her eyes from the old mortal, Mendoza fumbled in the credenza case she had brought and took out a glass vial, tipped with a needle point. She passed it to Lewis, who stepped forward soundlessly and bent over Orocobix where he slept, placing a hand on his brow. Orocobix sighed; he passed into deeper sleep. Lewis jabbed his upper arm once with the cell collector; the vial filled with a pinkish mist, and its needle point retracted inward. He passed the vial to Mendoza, who capped it and put it away.

In the next room was a wide bed, where Agueybana and Atabey curled together snoring. Their room was cluttered with what must have been the best surviving furniture from the palace; the atmosphere, even in that roaring wet night, was thick and airless. Mendoza withdrew two more vials from the case; Lewis stepped very carefully as he took cells from the mortals. Agueybana grunted and shifted, but did not wake; Atabey slept on.

The room beyond was Cajaya's. It was strewn with clothing and discarded ornaments. On a small table sat several jars of scent and powders, most of them with their lids ajar, diffusing a sickly sweetness. Some attempt had been made at daubing flowers on the walls here; Lewis examined them hopefully, but they bore no resemblance to the graceful lilies of Thera. The room's mistress sprawled under furs, and her snore was high-pitched. She never so much as stirred when the needle nipped her arm.

One more room, Mendoza noted, as they returned to the corridor. Lewis nodded. Prepared as they were for another shabby bedchamber, they stepped through the doorway and halted in astonishment.

This room had been maintained above all others. The plaster seemed to have been renewed regularly, and it was painted, polychrome in barbaric splendor, red and yellow and black. Fernlike trees grew on black cone mountains, bowed with black fruit under winking stars. Birdlike things stalked and gestured. Abstract patterns shimmered by the fluttering light of the lamp. From an incense brazier a solid blue fume arose, smoke straight and thick as an arm, vanishing in a cloud of shadows near the ceiling.

The incense did nothing to dispel the sickroom atmosphere. For it was a sickroom: upon a bed grand as an altar lay a young man in an agony of illness, feverish and shaking, emaciated. His body shone like gold in the lamplight. For one moment Lewis thought, *Good gods! It's El Dorado himself!*

He stepped close to see, and realized that the illusion came from the film of sweat over the boy's skin, which was yellow as a harvest moonrise.

But his bed had been decked with ornaments of shell and beaten gold, with bright-dyed cotton ribbon, with macaw feathers, and the massy crown upon his brow was gold, too. A jaguar pelt was spread on the floor beside the bed, where little Tanama was curled up like a devoted puppy. Something gleamed beside her. On closer inspection, it proved to be a great vessel of hammered gold. It stank like a latrine.

Mendoza gasped for breath. *He's got the worst case of liver fluke I've ever seen.*

Lewis scanned him and winced. Chronic hepatic fascitis, all right; it was a wonder the boy was still alive. *He must have been infested for years.*

His bones are poking through his skin. Mendoza dug in the case and thrust two more vials at Lewis. *Hurry! I can't bear it in here.*

She stepped to the side and looked away as Lewis bent over the bed. The young man opened wide dark eyes, but did not see him, or thought he was only one more in a lifetime of fever dreams. Lewis touched his brow gently, sent him into deep sleep, and looked for a likely place to take a sample; there was very little spare flesh.

Getting a sample from Tanama went much more easily. Lewis stepped away, turning to hand the vials off to Mendoza. She was staring fixedly at the back wall of the room, where the mural pattern swirled around a hole that opened into utter darkness.

Do you realize what that is? she transmitted.

A ventilation shaft?

No! Triangulate its position. The composting chute is right below this room.

It's a . . . sewer drain?

Mendoza pointed at the big vessel. *They gave him a solid gold bedpan. That, and a golden crown. What compensation! The little girl waits on him, and dumps everything in here.*

How happy they'll be to encounter Company plumbing. Lewis backed away from the smell, which intensified as a gust of wind backed and sent appalling vapor up the shaft.

Let's get out of here!

They fled back through the nightmare corridors.

So . . . the family has some genetic resistance to liver fluke, Lewis theorized. *Except for one or two members in a generation.*

Dr. Zeus will be interested in whatever gives them immunity, Mendoza replied. *Possibly even more than in the source of* terra preta. *Oh, God, how I want a hot shower in a clean room.*

They ducked back into their chamber. It seemed almost fresh and wholesome to them now, and they sucked in great breaths of dank air.

You'll take the bed tonight. Lewis led her to it with a firm grip. Mendoza did not resist, but sank down on it.

I think I've had a bit more mortal company than I can stand . . . She lay back and curled on her side. *You're very kind, Lewis . . .*

The rain intensified, roared down in torrents, and thunder cracked sullen and slow. Lewis leaned against the wall, avoiding a leak that streamed in, and watched as Mendoza slept.

When he opened his eyes, after a long night of being hyperaware of the bacterial life of the wall, he saw Mendoza awake. She was sitting up with the credenza on her lap, studying its screen while she munched a Zeusola bar. The rain had stopped.

"Morning, Lewis," she said. "I have a surprise for you."

"Good morning." Lewis stretched painfully and looked around for the cache of bars. He had torn one open and was wolfing it down before the import of her words sank in on him. "Mmf?"

"I've been running analysis on the samples from the males," said Mendoza, rubbing her eyes. "I'm running the boy now. Guess what? The old man and his son aren't entirely Indians. Had a lot of odd genetic markers. Closest match I could find was the aboriginals of the Canary Islands."

Lewis did a fast access. "What, the Guanches?" He slapped his forehead. "Of course! And they call themselves the Guanikina!"

"Do they? And the Canary Islands have a lot of volcanic activity. Villages wiped out by eruptions, survivors paddling off to other islands in the chain to start new villages. My guess is, at some point in the past somebody paddled due west and wound up in the Caribbean," said Mendoza. She shrugged. "It isn't exactly Atlantis, but . . ."

"But it's fascinating!" Lewis rubbed his hands. "What a story, what a journey it must have been! And then . . . they must have conquered a Taino tribe somehow or other, and . . . and interbred, but not much. And later emigrated here to the mainland, where they founded this astonishing agricultural civilization! What else have you been able to find out?"

"Not a lot," Mendoza admitted. "I'm a botanist, remember? If they were maize cultivars instead of mortals, I could really do some analysis. That'll have to wait for the anthropologists. At least now I know where the African cotton came from."

"Of course," said Lewis automatically, but his mind was racing with speculation. "Maybe this would explain how the royal family survived whatever it was that killed off all their subjects! They were *from the Old World!* They had a greater genetic variation, therefore greater resistance to disease—"

"Maybe," said Mendoza. "Access the data. Old World natives have better immunoresponse to disease; New World natives have better immunoresponse to parasites."

"Which would explain why that poor boy is so ill with liver fluke!"

"But why's the rest of the family perfectly healthy, then?"

"Oh." Lewis frowned. "Favorable mutation? Or some miracle herb in their garden?"

"I think we'd better leave this for the Company to figure out," said Mendoza.

She was silent a moment, and then added: "By the way . . . sorry about last night. I behaved like an idiot."

"Not at all! Perfectly understandable, under the circumstances."

"I have issues with mortals," said Mendoza stiffly. It was the most outrageous piece of understatement Lewis had heard in a while, but he merely nodded and reached for another Zeusola bar. The credenza beeped. She peered down at the screen. Her eyes widened.

"Well, this is interesting," she said. "The boy's different. Significantly . . ."

"Isn't he related to the others?" Lewis leaned past her to look, but made out only dense columns of code.

"Oh, no question, but look . . ." Mendoza ordered up other columns of code and juxtaposed them with the other results.

"It's probably whatever genetic variation that makes him susceptible to the liver fluke, when the others aren't," said Lewis.

"Maybe," said Mendoza, sounding unconvinced. She looked at the screen suspiciously. "I think I need to do a blood analysis, too."

They left the credenza running tests on the samples, and slogged away to their respective tasks.

The island rose above a lake of white mist now; the vapor flowed like a white river, trailing through the treetops, veiling the lower terraces. Lewis went splashing across the courtyard and found the bundles of reed he had cut yesterday, undisturbed by the storm. Hoisting one to his back, he went up the ladder with it and set to work.

As he labored, Lewis let his awareness expand a little. He felt the little household coming to life in their corner of the vast ruinous palace. Creaking, grumbling, coughing, the padding of bare feet. Cajaya's high thin voice raised in query. There was the raking back of coals, the snap of kindling catching fire. Tanama's cheery voice beginning its chatter, like a bird greeting the day. Splashing from a cistern. The smell of amaranth porridge cooking.

He watched when they came wandering out into the courtyard, one by one, avoiding the pools of rainwater. Cajaya folded a blanket on which to sit, complaining about the wet stone. Orocobix wandered out to the edge of the courtyard and seemed to pray a while, gazing out into the mist. Agueybana and Atabey were bickering, with no particular heat, about whether or not he ought to go hunting.

Tanama came out, carrying bowls of pure gold and a cooking pot that steamed. Orocobix came back and sat down; the child dished up a serving for each of them, and then retreated back into the palace.

"She's left lumps in it again," Cajaya said. "*I* never used to leave lumps in it."

"You certainly did," said Agueybana.

"Don't eat them, if you don't like it," said Atabey. "Just think! Soon you'll have servants cooking for you. Servants! And a divine husband. So you've nothing to complain about."

"I suppose not," said Cajaya. "If that dead man is any kind of an ambassador."

"He's doing a nice job on the roof," Orocobix remarked, glancing up at Lewis. He caught Lewis's eye and nodded graciously.

"They really do seem to work astonishingly well," said Agueybana. "Think what it'll be like to have a few thousand of *those* laboring for us, eh? We'll do nothing all day but sit about at our ease!"

"How lovely!" said Cajaya, fanning herself.

"How like ancient times!" said Atabey, with a sigh. Orocobix looked into his empty bowl and said nothing.

And there they sat, in expectant pettiness, as they must have sat every day of their lives. They looked out on their empty kingdom. Lewis shook his head sadly.

Did all mortal adventure end like this? Once, there had been journeys into the unknown, and struggles against great odds, and grandeur.

Around noon, Mendoza transmitted: *Lewis, I'm back in the room. Thought I'd see how the analysis is going. You want another Zeusola bar?*

I'd love one, thanks.

There was no reply. He worked on placidly, and had only paused to remove his hat and wipe sweat from his face when there came a wave of astonishment through the ether, without coherent words. Lewis cocked his head, turning, triangulating. Where was she? Still in the room?

Mendoza, what's going on?

The emotion subsided a little. When he heard her again, he had the impression she was overwhelmed with disgust.

I have the blood analysis results.

Well?

That boy has more than liver fluke, Lewis. He must be dying of septicemia.

What? Lewis called up his memory of the ghastly room, the stick-thin figure on the bed. *But . . . no. We'd have picked it up in our scans, if that were the case. Why do you think—*

His blood's rotten with bacteria.

What kind of bacteria?

There was a long pause. The next burst of emotion nearly knocked him off the roof.

When he had regained his grip on the ladder, Lewis heard Mendoza laughing.

Well, we've just solved another mystery. I now know the secret ingredient in terra preta.

Lewis thought rapidly. *The mystery microbes? They're from* him?

That's right. Remember the drain in his room, that empties straight into the compost chute?

No! You don't mean . . . There's some sort of bacteria that makes mortals deathly ill, but when passed into the soil—no, wait—

Wait, that doesn't add up—

Maybe whatever it is that makes him particularly susceptible to the liver fluke—

But that doesn't make sense—because when you compare his DNA to the others . . . Her thought trailed into a sense of bewilderment, frustration.

You've solved the mystery of Super-Compost, anyhow. You'll get a Commendation, do you realize that?

If I do, you'll deserve it. You'll get a week in Monte Carlo yet, Lewis.

He wondered if he dared to reply: "Would you come with me?"

But before he could screw up his courage, she was brisk again: *I'm setting up to run tests on the samples from the females, now. See you in a minute.*

And in precisely sixty seconds she walked up to the base of his ladder, tossing him a Zeusola bar.

"Bon appétit! I'm off to weed the garden again. I really ought to get some samples of the infested watercress, too, don't you think?"

"Probably," Lewis agreed. He watched her walk away, down the hillside into the weeds.

He paused long enough for his snack, then went back to work. The mist was burning away; macaws called and sailed across the blue on wings like fragments of shattered rainbow. The mortals drowsed in their courtyard, save for Agueybana, who finally decided to go hunting. He took his bow and arrows and went down to the boat landing. A little while later Lewis saw him, far off, poling out to a distant island.

Only one boat left, Lewis thought to himself. *Household furniture falling apart. They must have forgotten how to make things for themselves, if they ever knew. Poor creatures. It's just as well . . .*

He heard the commotion before the scream came; incandescent wrath scorching through the ether, hissed interrogation, the child's stammering

replies. Then the scream followed, but by that time he was already down
from his ladder and running.

They were on the terrace with the fish ponds. Tanama was clutching a
golden basket half full of watercress, but the cress was spilling out because
Mendoza had caught her by one wrist. The child was sobbing.

"I *have* to!" she protested. "It's his sacred food!"

"Mendoza!" Lewis grabbed her arm. "You're hurting her!"

"They're infecting that boy *on purpose*," said Mendoza. She was shaking
with anger. "They know exactly what they're doing. And they could cure
him if they wanted to! Look!" She let go Tanama's wrist, but pointed an ac-
cusatory finger at the plantings on either side of the walkway.

"*Baccharis Trimera*," she said, spitting out the botanical name like a
curse. "*Pemus Boldus. Boerhavia Caribaea.* All of them specifics for liver
trouble, all of them vermifuges. But what are they giving him? This stuff!"
She seized up a frond of watercress and held it out to Lewis.

Dazed, Lewis took the cress. Yes; the leaves were full of cysts that would
develop into liver fluke, if ingested. More significant just now, however,
was the fact that Orocobix was coming down the steps, followed by Atabey
and Cajaya.

"What did you do, you little fool?" Cajaya shouted.

Tanama threw herself down before Orocobix, hiding her face.

"I didn't," she wept. "The dead lady—she saw—"

Orocobix lifted her gently to her feet, and she clung to him. He looked at
Lewis.

"Oh, dear," he said.

"I'm afraid you have not told us everything," said Lewis, with all possible diplomacy.

"And why should we?" cried Atabey. "You're nothing but a servant—"
Orocobix lifted his hand and she fell silent.

"It's the *terra preta*, isn't it?" Mendoza demanded, speaking in Cinema
Standard. "The microbe's only produced by infecting someone with liver
fluke! They're *sacrificing* him, and by inches—for goddamned *compost*—"

"Mendoza, wait," said Lewis. Orocobix was watching their faces closely.

"I trust you'll pardon us our omission," he said. "It's a state secret, you
see. But I suppose you must be told . . ."

"We have become aware of another member of your family. The dead notice these things," Lewis improvised. "Why is the young man so ill?"

"He was Kolibri, but became Caonaki," said Orocobix. "The King, whose honor it is to suffer for the good of all mankind. The very sweat of his agony makes the earth bear in abundance. Without him, I could never have made these islands. We should have starved on a barren and watery plain long since."

Savages—mortal savages—barbaric devils— Mendoza was not trusting herself to speak aloud anymore, for which Lewis was grateful. He cleared his throat.

"He seems very young," he observed.

"He never lives very long," said Orocobix regretfully. "But he always comes to us again, for he loves us. He understands his duty. And now, you understand the advantage we are offering your master, do you not? For it is likely Cajaya will bear his next body. The land of the dead will become a garden of all loveliness."

It's a favorable recessive! Mendoza shouted silently, thinking even through the red fog of her anger. *He's not less able to resist the parasites— he'd have died by now. He fights them off! That's why the damn mortals keep re- infecting him! And his body fights them off by producing the bacteria—*

Which also produce the terra preta. Lewis almost heard the *click* as the puzzle pieces snapped into place. He stared at Orocobix. He must have been tested in childhood—so must Agueybana—and found wanting. Their bodies did not generate the magic microbes. They'd been cured and al- lowed to live normal lives. The women were never tested, but carried the recessive.

For a moment Lewis saw so clearly the immensity of what had been here, once: the great agricultural empire expanding, the black islands rising from the plain of thin poor soil, the unfruitful rain forest conquered and made to bear. The royal family, presiding over the people they had subju- gated with promise of eternal plenty. Their thousands of subjects lived in peace in hilltop gardens, never knowing hunger, with death merely the promise of a more carefree life.

But, at the heart of this earthly paradise . . . always somewhere a young man suffering in darkness, voiding gold from his bowels and bladder.

The royal family had understood exactly the genetic reasons for their wealth, and the mechanism of infestation.

Here on this island they had issued commands, received tribute, and calculated their bloodlines to a nicety. Here they had huddled together, immune, when the unknown epidemic came, and their subjects died to the last man, woman and child. The stench of the far gardens must have risen up to heaven. Here they had dwindled over the decades, as the extended family died back. Here they had married cousins and finally brothers and sisters, and in a few more years would have come to nothing anyway.

And no poet to sing their story! Lewis cried from his heart.

The bastards, Mendoza transmitted bitterly. *The mortal bastards. Send them a miracle and they'll never fail to nail it to a cross.*

All this in a split second, and Orocobix was still looking at Lewis, hoping his proposition had found favor. Lewis drew breath and bowed, knowing what he must say.

"I think my master will be pleased, Great Orocobix," he said, blandly.

They left the next morning, before the mists had cleared.

Orocobix accompanied them, though he sat as a passenger while Lewis poled the boat across the green water on the journey out. He looked up at their island as it loomed out of the fog, and shook his head at the raw scar of the slide, which had grown bigger.

"They're all going like that now," he said. "No one to tend them, you know. I suppose, given enough time, they'll all melt down onto the plain. It's just as well we won't be here to see."

Mendoza stepped from the boat without a word to him, shouldering the case that held her credenza. Lewis turned and helped him to his feet, passing the pole over before he stepped ashore.

"Many thanks for your splendid hospitality, Great Orocobix," he said. "I can assure you, my master will respond promptly to your offer."

"She was a prettier girl, when she was younger," said Orocobix. "I think it likely she'll improve with a little plumpness, as she matures; they tend to be a good deal less flighty after the children start coming."

"No doubt," said Lewis. The old man fumbled for something inside his robe.

"By the way," he said, "I meant to send you with something . . . ah! Here it is. Present this to Lord Maketaurie, with my compliments. We honor him with the most ancient heirloom of our house, as an earnest of our sincerity."

He handed Lewis a small bundle. Lewis accepted it with a bow, sticking it in an inner pocket.

"Good day to you, then, children," said Orocobix. "Pray excuse me; so much to do, you know . . ."

"Farewell, great god," said Lewis. He watched as the old man dipped the pole and sent the boat around, light as a leaf on the water; it went gliding away, and vanished into the mist.

Lewis started up the hill after Mendoza, who had paused halfway up to retrieve a few buried items washed out by the storms. He was rehearsing a speech, and it began: *Look here, I was wondering . . . we get on pretty well, don't you think? I have nightmares, and a little glitch or two, and you have nightmares, too, and bad memories, but—we could sort of form a mutual support alliance. I know I'll never replace your Englishman, but—*

"Oh, look," Mendoza said glumly, and held up a martini glass. "Ancient visitors from space left us a ritual object. Do you suppose they preferred shaken, or stirred?"

Lewis took the glass and tilted it so the mud trickled out. "Looks like they drank espresso."

"Ugh," said Mendoza. "Do you realize, this whole time we've been living on a mountain of—"

"Don't think about it," said Lewis. "Just don't. Think about anything else. Fairies dancing in the moonlight. The meaning of *Rosebud*. The far-off tinkle of little golden temple bells."

"Or, for example, my disciplinary hearing," said Mendoza.

"What disciplinary hearing?"

"The one I'll get when the anthropologists discover what I did. I sneaked into the damn Room of Sacrifice again last night. Gave that boy a dose of medication to kill liver flukes," said Mendoza, starting up the hill again. Lewis stared after her a moment, then ran to catch up.

"Bravo," he said. "Bravo! But it won't make any difference, I'm afraid. He'll only be reinfected."

"No, he won't." Mendoza reached the top and swung around to face Lewis. "Because after I dosed the kid, I went out to the fish ponds. Yanked out every last little bit of watercress. *And* smashed every damn snail I could find."

Her eyes were sullen, her mouth was hard, and Lewis thought he had never loved her more than in that moment.

"I had to, Lewis. That temple room was the most obscene thing I'd seen since . . . since England." England, where a young man had gone willingly to the stake because he believed it was his duty.

"I know," said Lewis gently, seeing the tall specter loom beside her, and knowing it would never go away. Nicholas Harpole's shadow rose with her in the morning, walked with her in all her ways, and lay down beside her at night.

"It still won't make any difference," she went on. "You can bet Dr. Zeus will infect him again, once the Company gets its hands on him. They'll want to experiment on him, won't they?"

"It won't be that bad," Lewis said. "The Company isn't inhumane. They'll cure him again once they get their answer, and then—well, the Guanikina will learn they're not gods, and will that really be such a bad thing? Better than living in ever-increasing squalor and—and—"

"And incest," said Mendoza. "You're right, of course."

"And who cares what the anthropologists think anyway? We've still made an amazing discovery. How often do lowly field operatives discover something about which All-Seeing Zeus didn't already know?" said Lewis, more cheerfully.

"That's true." Mendoza brightened up a little.

They waded into the remains of their camp, which was already disappearing under creepers, and began to throw what they'd salvaged into the packing crates.

"By the way," said Mendoza, "what was that, that the old man gave you?"

"A relic of ancient Atlantis, ha ha," said Lewis. He reached under his poncho and pulled out the bundle. Carefully, he unwrapped rags of colored cotton.

"Oh," he said. Mendoza came and peered at the little lidded basket, woven of pink and yellow straw.

"Talk about cheesy souvenirs," she said. She lifted off the lid. "Something in there? Those look like somebody's keys."

Lewis reached in and pulled out a bunch of metal tags, all fastened together on a loop of braided cord. They were rectangular, apparently made of polished steel, and engraved on one side. He separated one out from the rest and held it up to examine it. His eyes widened.

"What?" Mendoza craned her neck to look.

"*Numerus XXXV. Pertinens ad Stationem XVII Experimentalem Hesperidum,*" Lewis read aloud. He tilted the tag so she could see the stylized thunderbolt logo underneath the inscription.

"Hesperides Experimental Station?" Mendoza stared at the tag. "Wasn't that the old Company base out in mid-Atlantic they had to close when . . ." She trailed off and was silent for about thirty seconds before turning away and doubling up with laughter. Lewis joined her, laughing so hard he had to lean against a tree. At last he stood, threw his hat in the air and whooped in despair:

"So much for discovering something unknown to Dr. Zeus! Ladies and gentlemen, please take your places for the Causality Quadrille!"

THE CATCH

The barn stands high in the middle of backcountry nowhere, shimmering in summer heat. It's an old barn, empty a long time, and its broad planks are silvered. Nothing much around it but yellow hills and red rock.

Long ago, somebody painted it with a mural. Still visible along its broad wall are the blobs representing massed crowds, the green diamond of a baseball park, and the figure in a slide, seeming to swim along the green field, glove extended. His cartoon eyes are wide and happy. The ball, radiating black lines of force, is sailing into his glove. Above him is painted the legend:

WHAT A CATCH! And, in smaller letters below it:

1951, The Golden Year!

The old highway snakes just below the barn, where once the mural must have edified a long cavalcade of DeSotos, Packards, and Oldsmobiles. But the old road is white and empty now, with thistles pushing through its cracks. The new highway runs straight across the plain below.

Down on the new highway, eighteen-wheeler rigs hurtle through, roaring like locomotives, and they are the only things to disturb the vast silence. The circling hawk makes no sound. The cottonwood trees by the edge of the dry stream are silent too, not a rustle or a creak along the whole row; but they do cast a thin gray shade, and the men waiting in the Volkswagen Bug are grateful for that.

They might be two cops on stakeout. They aren't. Not exactly.

"Are you going to tell me why we're sitting here, now?" asks the younger man, finishing his candy bar.

His name is Clete. The older man's name is Porfirio.

The older man shifts in his seat and looks askance at his partner. He doesn't approve of getting stoned on the job. But he shrugs, checks his weapon, settles into the most comfortable position he can find.

He points through the dusty windshield at the barn. "See up there? June 30, 1958, family of five killed. '46 Plymouth Club Coupe. Driver lost control of the car and went off the edge of the road. Car rolled seventy meters down that hill and hit the rocks, right there. Gas tank blew. Mr. and Mrs. William T. Ross of Visalia, California, identified from dental records. Kids didn't have any dental records. No relatives to identify bodies.

"Articles in the local and Visalia papers, grave with the whole family's names and dates on one marker in a cemetery in Visalia. Some blackening on the rocks up there. That's all there is to show it ever happened."

"Okay," say the younger man, nodding thoughtfully. "No witnesses, right?"

"That's right."

"The accident happened on a lonely road, and state troopers or whoever found the wreck after the fact?"

"Yeah."

"And the bodies were so badly burned they all went in one grave?" Clete looks pleased with himself. "So . . . forensic medicine being what it was in 1958, maybe there weren't five bodies in the car after all? Maybe one of the kids was thrown clear on the way down the hill? And if there was *somebody* in the future going through historical records, looking for incidents where children vanished without a trace, this might draw their attention, right?"

"It might," agrees Porfirio.

"So the Company sent an operative to see if any survivors could be salvaged," says Clete. "Okay, that's standard Company procedure. The Company took one of the kids alive, and he became an operative. So why are we here?"

Porfirio sighs, watching the barn.

"Because the kid didn't become an operative," he says. "He became a problem."

1958. Bobby Ross, all-American boy, was ten years old, and he loved baseball and cowboy movies and riding his bicycle. All-American boys get bored on long trips. Bobby got bored. He was leaning out the window of his parents' car when he saw the baseball mural on the side of the barn.

"Hey, look!" he yelled, and leaned *way* out the window to see better. He slipped.

"Jesus Christ!" screamed his mom, and lunging into the back she tried to grab the seat of his pants. She collided with his dad's arm. His dad cursed; the car swerved. Bobby felt himself gripped, briefly, and then all his mom had was one of his sneakers, and then the sneaker came off his foot. Bobby flew from the car just as it went over the edge of the road.

He remembered afterward standing there, clutching his broken arm, staring down the hill at the fire, and the pavement was hot as fire, too, on his sneakerless foot. His mind seemed to be stuck in a little circular track. He was really hurt bad, so what he had to do now was run to his mom and dad, who would yell at him and drive him to Dr. Werts, and he'd have to sit in the cool green waiting room that smelled scarily of rubbing alcohol and look at dumb *Humpty Dumpty Magazine* until the doctor made everything all right again.

But that wasn't going to happen now, because . . .

But he was really hurt bad, so he needed to run to his mom and dad—

But he couldn't do that ever again, because—

But he was really hurt bad—

His mind just went round and round like that, until the spacemen came for him.

They wore silver suits, and they said, "Greetings, Earth boy; we have come to rescue you and take you to Mars," but they looked just like ordinary people and in fact gave Bobby the impression they were embarrassed. Their spaceship was real enough, though. They carried Bobby into it on a stretcher and took off, and a space doctor fixed his broken arm, and he was given space soda pop to drink, and he never even noticed that the silver ship had risen clear of the hillside, one step ahead of the state troopers, until he looked out and saw the curve of the Earth. He'd been lifted from history, as neatly as a fly ball smacking into an outfielder's mitt.

The spacemen didn't take Bobby Ross to Mars, though. It turned out to be some place in Australia. But it might just as well have been Mars.

Because, instead of starting fifth grade, and then going on to high school, and getting interested in girls, and winning a baseball scholarship, and being drafted, and blown to pieces in Viet Nam—Bobby Ross became an immortal.

"Well, that happened to all of us," says Clete, shifting restively. "One way or another. Except I've never heard of the Company recruiting a kid as old as ten."

"That's right." Keeping his eyes on the barn, Porfirio reaches into the backseat and gropes in a cooler half full of rapidly melting ice. He finds and draws out a bottle of soda. "So what does that tell you?"

Clete considers the problem. "Well, everybody knows you can't work the immortality process on somebody that old. You hear rumors, you know, like when the Company was starting out, that there were problems with some of the first test cases—" He stops himself and turns to stare at Porfirio. Porfirio meets his gaze but says nothing, twisting the top off his soda bottle.

"*This* guy was one of the test cases!" Clete exclaims. "And the Company didn't have the immortality process completely figured out yet, so they made a mistake?"

Several mistakes had been made with Bobby Ross.

The first, of course, was that he was indeed too old to be made immortal. If two-year-old Patty or even five-year-old Jimmy had survived the crash, the process might have been worked successfully on them. Seat belts not having been invented in 1946, however, the Company had only Bobby with whom to work.

The second mistake had been in sending "spacemen" to collect Bobby. Bobby, as it happened, didn't like science fiction. He liked cowboys and baseball, but rocket ships left him cold. Movie posters and magazine covers featuring bug-eyed monsters scared him. If the operatives who had rescued him had come galloping over the hill on horseback, and had called him "Pardner" instead of "Earth boy," he'd undoubtedly have been as enchanted as they meant him to be and he would have bought into the rest of the experience with a receptive mind. As it was, by the time he was offloaded into a laboratory in a hot red rocky landscape, he was far enough out of shock to have begun to be angry, and his anger focused on the bogusness of the spacemen.

The third mistake had been in the Company's choice of a mentor for Bobby.

Because the Company hadn't been in business very long—at least, as far as its stockholders knew—a lot of important things about the education of young immortals had yet to be discovered, such as: no mortal can train an immortal. Only another immortal understands the discipline needed, the pitfalls to be avoided when getting a child accustomed to the idea of eternal life.

But when Bobby was being made immortal, there weren't any other immortals yet—not successful ones, anyway—so the Company might be excused that error, at least. And if Professor Bill Riverdale was the last person who should have been in charge of Bobby, worse errors are made all the time. Especially by persons responsible for the welfare of young children.

After all, Professor Riverdale was a good, kind man. It was true that he was romantically obsessed with the idyll of all-American freckle-faced boyhood to an unhealthy degree, but he was so far in denial about it that he would never have done anything in the least improper.

All he wanted to do, when he sat down at Bobby's bedside, was help Bobby get over the tragedy. So he started with pleasant conversation. He told Bobby all about the wonderful scientists in the far future who had discovered the secret of time travel, and how they were now working to find a way to make people live forever.

And Bobby, lucky boy, had been selected to help them. Instead of going to an orphanage, Bobby would be transformed into, well, nearly into a superhero! It was almost as though Bobby would never have to grow up. It was every boy's dream! He'd have super-strength and super-intelligence and never have to wash behind his ears, if he didn't feel like it! And, because he'd live forever, one day he really would get to go to the planet Mars.

If the immortality experiment worked. But Professor Riverdale—or Professor Bill, as he encouraged Bobby to call him—was sure the experiment would work this time, because such a lot had been learned from the last time it had been attempted.

Professor Bill moved quickly on to speak with enthusiasm of how wonderful the future was, and how happy Bobby would be when he got there. Why, it was a wonderful place, according to what he'd heard! People lived on the moon and on Mars, too, and the problems of poverty and disease and war had been licked, by gosh, and there were *no Communists!* And boys could ride their bicycles down the tree-lined streets of that perfect world, and float down summer rivers on rafts, and camp out in the woods, and dream of going to the stars . . .

Observing, however, that Bobby lay there silent and withdrawn, Professor Bill cut his rhapsody short. He concluded that Bobby needed psychiatric therapy to get over the guilt he felt at having caused the deaths of his parents and siblings.

And this was a profound mistake, because Bobby Ross—being a normal ten-year-old all-American boy—had no more conscience than Pinocchio before the Cricket showed up, and it had never occurred to him that he had been responsible for the accident. Once Professor Bill pointed it out, however, he burst into furious tears.

So poor old Professor Bill had a lot to do to help Bobby through his pain, both the grief of his loss and the physical pain of his transformation into an immortal, of which there turned out to be a lot more than anybody had thought there would be, regardless of how much had been learned from the last attempt.

He studied Bobby's case, paying particular attention to the details of his recruitment. He looked carefully at the footage taken by the operatives who had collected Bobby, and the mural on the barn caught his attention. Tears came to his eyes when he realized that the sight of the ballplayer must have been Bobby's last happy memory, the final golden moment of his innocence.

"What'd he do?" asks Clete, taking his turn at rummaging in the ice chest. "Wait, I'll bet I know. He used the image of the mural in the kid's therapy, right? Something to focus on when the pain got too bad? Pretending he was going to a happy place in his head, as an escape valve."

"Yeah. That was what he did."

"There's only root beer left. You want one?"

"No, thanks."

"Well, so why was this such a bad idea? I remember having to do mental exercises like that, myself, at the Base school. You probably did, too."

"It was a bad idea because the professor didn't know what the hell he was doing," says Porfirio. The distant barn is wavering in the heat, but he never takes his eyes off it.

Bobby's other doctors didn't know what the hell they were doing, either. They'd figured out how to augment Bobby's intelligence pretty well, and they already knew how to give him unbreakable bones. They did a great job of convincing his body it would never die, and taught it how to ward off viruses and bacteria.

But they didn't know yet that even a healthy ten-year-old's DNA has already begun to deteriorate, that it's already too subject to replication errors for the immortality process to be successful. And Bobby Ross, being an all-American kid, had gotten all those freckles from playing unshielded in ultraviolet light. He'd gulped down soda pop full of chemicals and inhaled smoke from his dad's Lucky Strikes and hunted for tadpoles in the creek that flowed past the paper mill.

And then the doctors introduced millions of nanobots into Bobby's system, and the nanobots' job was to keep him perfect. But the doctors didn't know yet that the nanobots had to be programmed with an example to copy. So the nanobots latched onto the first DNA helix they encountered, and made it their pattern for everything Bobby ought to be. Unfortunately, it was a damaged DNA helix, but the nanobots didn't know that.

Bobby Ross grew up at the secret laboratory, and as he grew it became painfully obvious that there were still a few bugs to be worked out of the immortality process. There were lumps, there were bumps, there were skin cancers and deformities. His production of Pineal Tribrantine Three was sporadic. Sometimes, after months of misery, his body's chemistry would right itself. The joint pain would ease, the glands would work properly again.

Or not.

Professor Bill was so, so sorry, because he adored Bobby. He'd sit with Bobby when the pain was bad, and talk soothingly to send Bobby back to that dear good year, 1951—and what a golden age 1951 seemed by this time, because it was now 1964, and Bobby had become Robert, and the world seemed to be lurching into madness. Professor Bill himself wished he could escape back into 1951. But he sent Robert there often, into that beautiful summer afternoon when Hank Bauer had flung his length across the green diamond—and the ball had smacked into his leather glove—and the crowds went wild!

Though only in Robert's head, of course, because all this was being done with hypnosis.

Nobody ever formally announced that Robert Ross had failed the immortality process, because it was by no means certain he wasn't immortal. But it had become plain he would never be the flawless superagent the Company had been solving for, so less and less of the laboratory budget was allotted to Robert's upkeep.

What did the Company do with unsuccessful experiments? Who knows what might have happened to Robert, if Professor Bill hadn't taken the lad under his wing?

He brought Robert to live with him in his own quarters on the Base, and continued his education himself. This proved that Professor Bill really was a good man and had no ulterior interest in Robert whatsoever; for Bobby, the slender kid with skin like a sun-speckled apricot, was long gone. Robert by this time was a wizened, stooping, scarred thing with hair in unlikely places.

Professor Bill tried to make it up to Robert by giving him a rich interior life. He went rafting with Robert on the great river of numbers, under the cold and sparkling stars of theory. He tossed him physics problems compact and weighty as a baseball, and beamed with pride when Robert smacked them out of the park of human understanding. It made him feel young again, himself.

He taught the boy all he knew, and when he found that Robert shone at Temporal Physics with unsuspected brilliance, he told his superiors. This pleased the Company managers. It meant that Robert could be made to earn back the money he had cost the Company after all. So he became an employee, and was even paid a modest stipend to exercise his genius by fiddling around with temporal equations on the Company's behalf.

"And the only problem was, he was a psycho?" guesses Clete. "He went berserk, blew away poor old Professor Riverdale and ran off into the sunset?"

"He was emotionally unstable," Porfirio admits. "Nobody was surprised by that, after what he'd been through. But he didn't kill Professor Riverdale. He did run away, though. Walked, actually. He walked through a solid wall, in front of the professor and about fifteen other people in the audience. He'd been giving them a lecture in advanced temporal paradox theory. Just smiled at them suddenly, put down his chalk, and stepped right through the blackboard. He wasn't on the other side when they ran into the next room to see."

"Damn," says Clete, impressed. "*We* can't do that."

"We sure can't," says Porfirio. He stiffens, suddenly, seeing something move on the wall of the barn. It's only the shadow of the circling hawk, though, and he relaxes.

Clete's eyes have widened, and he looks worried.

"You just threw me a grenade," he says. *Catching a grenade* is security slang for being made privy to secrets so classified one's own safety is compromised.

"You needed to know," says Porfirio.

The search for Robert Ross had gone on for years, in the laborious switchback system of time within which the Company operated. The mortals running the 1964 operation had hunted him with predictable lack of success. After the ripples from that particular causal wave had subsided, the mortal masters up in the twenty-fourth century set their immortal agents on the problem.

The ones who were security technicals, that is. The rank-and-file Preservers and Facilitators weren't supposed to know that there had ever been mistakes like Robert Ross. This made searching for him that much harder, but secrecy has its price.

It was assumed that Robert, being a genius in Temporal Physics, had somehow managed to escape into time. Limitless as time was, Robert might still be found within it. The operatives in charge of the case reasoned that a needle dropped into a haystack must gravitate toward any magnets concealed in the straw. Were there any magnets that might attract Robert Ross?

"Baseball!" croaked Professor Riverdale, when Security Executive Tvashtar had gone to the nursing home to interview him. "Bobby just loved baseball. You mark my words, he'll be at some baseball game somewhere. If he's in remission, he'll even be on some little town team."

With trembling hands he drew a baseball from the pocket of his dressing gown and held it up, cupping it in both hands as though he presented Tvashtar with a crystal wherein the future was revealed.

"He and I used to play catch with this. You might say it's the egg out of which all our hopes and dreams hatch. Peanuts and Crackerjack! The crack of the bat! The boys of summer. Bobby was the boy of summer. Sweet Bobby . . . He'd have given anything to have played the game . . . It's a symbol, young man, of everything that's fine and good and American."

Tvashtar nodded courteously, wondering why mortals in this era assumed the Company was run by Americans, and why they took it for granted that a stick-and-ball game had deep mystical significance. But he thanked Professor Riverdale, and left the 1970s gratefully. Then he organized a sweep through time, centering on baseball.

"And it didn't pan out," says Clete. "Obviously."

"It didn't pan out," Porfirio agrees. "The biggest search operation the Company ever staged, up to that point. You know how much work was involved?"

It had been a lot of work. The operatives had to check out every obscure minor-league player who ever lived, to say nothing of investigating every batboy and ballpark janitor and even bums who slept under the bleachers, from 1845 to 1965. Nor was it safe to assume Robert might not be lurking beyond the fruited plains and amber waves of grain; there were Mexican,

Cuban and Japanese leagues to be investigated. Porfirio, based at that time in California, had spent the Great Depression sweeping up peanut shells from Stockton to San Diego, but neither he nor anyone else ever caught a glimpse of Robert Ross.

It was reluctantly concluded that Professor Riverdale hadn't had a clue about what was going on in Robert's head. But, since Robert had never shown up again anywhere, the investigation was quietly dropped.

Robert Ross might never have existed, or indeed died with his mortal family. The only traces left of him were in the refinements made to the immortality process after his disappearance, and in the new rules made concerning recruitment of young operatives.

The Company never acknowledged that it had made any defectives.

"Just like that, they dropped the investigation?" Clete demands. "When this guy knew how to go places without getting into a time transcendence chamber? Apparently?"

"What do you think?" says Porfirio.

Clete mutters something mildly profane and reaches down into the paper bag between his feet. He pulls out a can of potato chips and pops the lid. He eats fifteen chips in rapid succession, gulps root beer, and then says: "Well, obviously they *didn't* drop the investigation, because here we are. Or something happened to make them open it again. They got a new lead?"

Porfirio nods.

1951. Porfirio was on standby in Los Angeles. Saturday morning in a quiet neighborhood, each little house on its square of lawn, rows of them along tree-lined streets. In most houses, kids were sprawled on the floor reading comic books or listening to Uncle Whoa-Bill on the radio, as long low morning sunlight slanted in through screen doors. In one or two houses, though, kids sat staring at a cabinet in which was displayed a small glowing image brought by orthicon tube; for the future, or a piece of it anyway, had arrived.

Porfirio was in the breakfast room, with a cup of coffee and the sports sections from the *Times,* the *Herald Express,* the *Examiner,* and the *Citizen*

News, and he was scanning for a certain profile, a certain configuration of features. He was doing this purely out of habit, because he'd been off the case for years; but, being immortal, he had a lot of time on his hands. Besides, he had all the instincts of a good cop.

But he had other instincts, too, even more deeply ingrained than hunting, and so he noticed the clamor from the living room, though it wasn't very loud. He looked up, scowling, as three-year-old Isabel rushed into the room in her nightgown.

"What is it, *mi hija?*"

She pointed into the living room. "Maria's bad! The scary man is on the TV," she said tearfully. He opened his arms and she ran to him.

"Maria, are you scaring your sister?" he called.

"She's just being a dope," an impatient little voice responded.

He carried Isabel into the living room, and she gave a scream and turned her face over his shoulder so she wouldn't see the television screen. Six-year-old Maria, on the other hand, stared at it as though hypnotized. Before her on the coffee table, two little bowls of Cheerios sat untasted, rapidly going soggy in their milk.

Porfirio frowned down at his great-great-great-great-(and several more greats) grand-niece. "Don't call your sister a dope. What's going on? It sounded like a rat fight in here."

"She's scared of the Amazing No Man, so she wanted me to turn him off, but he's *not* scary," said Maria. "And I want to see him."

"You were supposed to be watching *Cartoon Circus,*" said Porfirio, glancing at the screen.

"Uh-huh, but Mr. Ringmaster has people on sometimes, too," Maria replied. "See?"

Porfirio looked again. Then he sat down beside Maria on the couch and stared very hard at the screen. On his arm, Isabel kicked and made tiny complaining noises over his shoulder until he absently fished a stick of gum from his shirt pocket and offered it to her.

"Who is this guy?" he asked Maria.

"The Amazing No Man," she explained. "Isn't he *strange?*"

"Yeah," he said, watching. "Eat your cereal, honey."

And he sat there beside her as she ate, though when she dripped milk

from her spoon all over her nightgown because she wasn't paying attention as she ate, he didn't notice, because he wasn't paying attention either.
It was hard to look away from the TV.

A wizened little person wandered to and fro before the camera, singing
nonsense in an eerily high-pitched voice. Every so often he would stop, as
though he had just remembered something, and grope inside his baggy
clothing. He would then produce something improbable from an inner
pocket: a string of sausages. A bunch of bananas. A bottle of milk. An immense cello and bow. A kite, complete with string and tail.

He greeted each item with widely pantomimed surprise, and a cry of
"Woooowwwwww!" He pretended he was offering the sausages to an invisible dog, and made them disappear from his hand as though it were really
eating them. He played a few notes on the cello. He made the kite hover in
midair beside him, and did a little soft-shoe dance, and the kite bobbed
along with him as though it were alive. His wordless music never stopped,
never developed into a melody; just modulated to the occasional *Wowww*
as he pretended to make another discovery.

More and more stuff came out of the depths of his coat, to join a growing heap on the floor: sixteen bunches of bananas. A dressmaker's dummy.
A live sheep on a leash. An old-fashioned Victrola, complete with horn. A
stuffed penguin. A bouquet of flowers. A suit of armor. At last, the pile was
taller than the man himself. He turned, looked full into the camera with a
weird smile, and winked.

Behind Porfirio's eyes, a red light flashed. A readout overlaid his vision
momentarily, giving measurements, points of similarity and statistical per-
centages of matchup. Then it receded, but Porfirio had already figured out
the truth.

The man proceeded to stuff each item back into his coat, one after another.

"See? Where does he make them all go?" asked Maria, in a shaky voice.
"They can't all fit in there!"

"It's just stage magicians' tricks, *mi hija*," said Porfirio. He observed that
her knuckles were white, her eyes wide. "I think this is maybe too scary for
you. Let's turn it off, okay?"

"I'm not scared! He's just . . . funny," she said.

"Well, your little sister is scared," Porfirio told her, and rose and changed the channel, just as Hector wandered from the bedroom in his pajamas, blinking like an owl.

"Papi, Uncle Frio won't let me watch Amazing No Man!" Maria complained.

"What, the scary clown?" Hector rolled his eyes. "Honey, you know that guy gives you nightmares."

"I have to go out," said Porfirio, handing Isabel over to her father.

"You were living with mortals? Who were these people?" asks Clete.

"I had a brother, when I was mortal," says Porfirio. "I check up on his descendants now and then. Which has nothing to do with this case, okay? But that's where I was when I spotted Robert Ross. All the time we'd been looking for a baseball player, he'd been working as the Amazing Gnomon."

"And a gnomon is the piece on a sundial that throws the shadow," says Clete promptly. He grins. "Sundials. Time. Temporal physics. They just can't resist leaving clues, can they?"

Porfirio shakes his head. Clete finishes the potato chips, tilting the can to get the last bits.

"So when the guy was programmed with a Happy Place, it wasn't baseball he fixated on," he speculates. "It was 1951. 'The Golden Year.' He had a compulsion to be there in 1951, maybe?"

Porfirio says nothing.

"So, how did it go down?" says Clete, looking expectant.

It hadn't gone down, at least not then.

Porfirio had called for backup, because it would have been fatally stupid to have done otherwise, and by the time he presented his LAPD badge at the studio door, the Amazing Gnomon had long since finished his part of the broadcast and gone home.

The station manager at KTLA couldn't tell him much. The Amazing Gnomon had his checks sent to a post office box. He didn't have an agent. Nobody knew where he lived. He just showed up on time every third Saturday and hit his mark, and he worked on a closed set, but that wasn't unusual with stage magicians.

"Besides," said the mortal with a shudder, "he never launders that costume. He gets under those lights and believe me, brother, we're glad to clear the set. The cameraman has to put VapoRub up his nose before he can stand to be near the guy. Hell of an act, though, isn't it?"

The scent trail had been encouraging, even if it had only led to a locker in a downtown bus station. The locker, when opened, proved to contain the Amazing Gnomon's stage costume: a threadbare old overcoat, a pair of checked trousers, and clown shoes. They were painfully foul, but contained no hidden pockets or double linings where anything might be concealed, nor any clue to their owner's whereabouts.

By this time, however, the Company had marshaled all available security techs on the West Coast, so it wasn't long before they tracked down Robert Ross.

Then all they had to do was figure out what the hell to do next.

Clete's worried look has returned.

"Holy shit, I never thought about that. How do you arrest one of *us*?" he asks.

Porfirio snarls in disgust. His anger is not with Clete, but with the executive who saddled him with Clete.

"Are you ready to catch another grenade, kid?" he inquires, and without waiting for Clete's answer he extends his arm forward, stiffly, with the palm up. He has to lean back in his seat to avoid hitting the Volkswagen's windshield. He drops his hand sharply backward, like Spider-man shooting web fluid, and Clete just glimpses the bright point of a weapon emerging from Porfirio's sleeve. Pop, like a cobra's fang, it hits the windshield and retracts again, out of sight. It leaves a bead of something pale pink on the glass.

"Too cool," says Clete, though he is uneasily aware that he has no weapon like that. He clears his throat, wondering how he can ask what the pink stuff is without sounding frightened. He has always been told operatives are immune to any poison.

"It's not poison," says Porfirio, reading his mind. "It's derived from Theobromos. If I stick you in the leg with this, you'll sleep like a baby for twelve hours. That's all."

"Oh. Okay," says Clete, and it very much isn't okay, because a part of the foundation of his world has just crumbled.

"You can put it in another operative's drink, or you can inject it with an arm-mounted rig like this one," Porfirio explains patiently. "You can't shoot it in a dart, because any one of us could grab the dart out of the air, right? You have to close with whoever it is you're supposed to take down, go hand to hand.

"But first, you have to get the other guy in a trap."

Robert Ross had been in a trap. He seemed to have chosen it.

He turned out to be living in Hollywood, in an old residency hotel below Franklin. The building was squarely massive, stone, and sat like a megalith under the hill. Robert had a basement apartment with one tiny window on street level, at the back. He might have seen daylight for an hour at high summer down in there, but he'd have to stand on a stool to do it. And wash the window first.

The sub-executive in charge of the operation had looked at the reconnaissance reports and shaken his head. If an operative wanted a safe place to hide, he'd choose a flimsy frame building, preferably surrounding himself with mortals. There were a hundred cheap boardinghouses in Los Angeles that would have protected Robert Ross. The last place any sane immortal would try to conceal himself would be a basement dug into granite with exactly one door, where he might be penned in by other immortals and unable to break out through a wall.

The sub-executive decided that Robert *wanted* to be brought in.

It seemed to make a certain sense. Living in a place like that, advertising his presence on television; Robert must be secretly longing for some kindly mentor to find him and tell him it was time to come home. Alternatively, he might be daring the Company problem solvers to catch him. Either way, he wasn't playing with a full deck.

So the sub-executive made the decision to send in a psychologist. A *mortal* psychologist. Not a security tech with experience in apprehending immortal fugitives, though several ringed the building and one—Porfirio, in fact—was stationed outside the single tiny window that opened below the sidewalk on Franklin Avenue.

Porfirio had leaned against the wall, pretending to smoke and watch the traffic zooming by. He could hear Robert Ross breathing in the room below. He could hear his heartbeat. He heard the polite double knock on the door, and the slight intake of breath; he heard the gentle voice saying, "Bobby, may I come in?"

"It's not locked" was the reply, and Porfirio started. The voice belonged to a ten-year-old boy.

He heard the click and creak as the door opened, and the sound of two heartbeats within the room, and the psychologist saying: "We had quite a time finding you, Bobby. May I sit down?"

"Sure," said the child's voice.

"Thank you, Bobby," said the other, and Porfirio heard the scrape of a chair. "Oh, dear, are you all right? You're bleeding through your bandage."

"I'm all right. That's just where I had the tumor removed. It grows back a lot. I go up to the twenty-first century for laser surgery. Little clinics in out-of-the-way places, you know? I go there all the time, but you never notice."

"You've been very clever at hiding from us, Bobby. We'd never have found you if you hadn't been on television. We've been searching for you for years."

"In your spaceships?" said the child's voice, with adult contempt.

"In our time machines," said the psychologist. "Professor Riverdale was sure you'd run away to become a baseball player."

"I can't ever be a baseball player," replied Robert Ross coldly. "I can't run fast enough. One of my legs grew shorter than the other. Professor Bill never noticed that, though, did he?"

"I'm so sorry, Bobby."

"Good old Professor Bill, huh? I tried being a cowboy, and a soldier, and a fireman, and a bunch of other stuff. Now I'm a clown. But I can't ever be a baseball player. No home runs for Bobby."

Out of the corner of his eye, Porfirio saw someone laboring up the hill toward him from Highland Avenue. He turned his head and saw the cop.

The too-patient adult voice continued: "Bobby, there are a lot of other things you can be in the future."

"I hate the future."

Porfirio watched the cop's progress as the psychologist hesitated, then pushed on: "Do you like being a clown, Bobby?"

"I guess so," said Robert. "At least people *see* me when they look at me now. The man outside the window saw me, too."

There was a pause. The cop was red-faced from the heat and his climb, but he was grinning at Porfirio.

"Well, Bobby, that's one of our security men, out there to keep you safe."

"I know perfectly well why he's there," Robert said. "He doesn't scare me. I want him to hear what I have to say, so he can tell Professor Bill and the rest of them."

"What do you want to tell us, Bobby?" said the psychologist, a little shakily.

There was a creak, as though someone had leaned forward in a chair.

"You know why you haven't caught me? Because I figured out how to go to 1951 all by myself. And I've been living in it, over and over and over. The Company doesn't think that's possible, because of the variable permeability of temporal fabric, but it is. The trick is to go to a different *place* every *time*. There's just one catch."

The cop paused to wipe sweat off his brow, but he kept his eyes on Porfirio.

"What's the catch, Bobby?"

"Do you know what happens when you send something back to the same year often enough?" Robert sounded amused. "Like, about a hundred million times?"

"No, Bobby, I don't know."

"I know. I experimented. I tried it the first time with a wheel off a toy car. I sent it to 1912, over and over, until—do you know where Tunguska is?"

"What are you trying to tell me, Bobby?" The psychologist was losing his professional voice.

"Then," said Robert, "I increased the mass of the object. I sent a baseball back. Way back. Do you know what really killed off the dinosaurs?"

"Hey there, zoot suit," said the cop, when he was close enough. "You wouldn't be loitering, would you?"

". . . You can wear a hole in the fabric of space and time," Robert was saying. "And it just might destroy everything in the whole world. You included. And if you were pretty sick of being alive, but you couldn't die, that might seem like a great idea. Don't you think?"

There was the sound of a chair being pushed back.

Porfirio grimaced and reached into his jacket for his badge, but the cop pinned Porfirio's hand to his chest with the tip of his nightstick.

"Bobby, we can help you!" cried the psychologist.

"I'm not little Bobby anymore, you asshole," said the child's voice, rising. "I'm a million, million years old."

Porfirio looked the cop in the eye.

"Vice squad," he said. The cop sagged. Porfirio produced his badge.

"But I got a tip from one of the residents here—" said the cop.

"*Woooowwwww,*" said the weird little singsong voice, and there was a brief scream.

"What happened?" demands Clete. He has gone very pale.

"We never found out," says Porfirio. "By the time I got the patrolman to leave and ran around to the front of the building, the other techs had already gone in and secured the room. The only problem was, there was nothing to secure. The room was empty. No sign of Ross, or the mortal either. No furniture, even, except a couple of wooden chairs. He hadn't been living there. He'd just used the place to lure us in."

"Did anybody ever find the mortal?"

"Yeah, as a matter of fact," Porfirio replies. "Fifty years later. In London."

"He'd gone forward in time?" Clete exclaims. "But that's supposed to be impossible. Isn't it?"

Porfirio sighs.

"So they say, kid. Anyway, he hadn't gone forward in time. Remember, about ten years ago, when archaeologists were excavating that medieval hospital over there? They found hundreds of skeletons in its cemetery. Layers and layers of the dead. And—though this didn't make it into the news, not even into the *Fortean Times*—one of the skeletons was wearing a Timex."

Clete giggles shrilly.

"Was it still ticking?" he asks. "What the hell are you telling me? There's this crazy immortal guy on the loose, and he's able to time-travel just using his brain, and he wants to destroy the whole world and he's figured out how, *and we're just sitting here?*"

"You have a better idea?" says Porfirio. "Please tell me if you do, okay?"

Clete controls himself with effort.

"All right, what did the Company do?" he asks. "There's a plan, isn't there, for taking him out? There must be, or we wouldn't be here now."

Porfirio nods.

"But what are we doing here *now*?" says Clete. "Shouldn't we be in 1951, where he's hiding? Wait, no, we probably shouldn't, because that'd place even more strain on the fabric of time and space. Or whatever."

"It would," Porfirio agrees.

"So . . . here we are at the place where Bobby Ross was recruited. The Company must expect he's going to come back here. Because this is where he caused the accident. Because the criminal always returns to the scene of the crime, right?" Clete babbles.

"Maybe," says Porfirio. "The Company already knows he leaves 1951 sometimes, for medical treatment."

"And sooner or later he'll be driven to come *here*," says Clete, and now he too is staring fixedly at the barn. "And—and today is June 30, 2008. The car crash happened fifty years ago today. That's why we're here."

"He might come," says Porfirio. "So we just wait—" He stiffens, stares hard, and Clete stares hard, too, and sees the little limping figure walking up the old road, just visible through the high weeds.

"Goddamn," says Clete, and is out of the car in a blur, ejecting candy bar wrappers and potato chip cans as he goes, and Porfirio curses and tells him to wait, but it's too late; Clete has crossed the highway in a bound and is running across the valley, as fast as only an immortal can go. Porfirio races after him, up that bare yellow hill with its red rocks that still bear faint carbon traces of horror, and he clears the edge of the road in time to hear Clete bellow: "Security! Freeze!"

"Don't—" says Porfirio, just as Clete launches himself forward to tackle Robert Ross.

Robert is smiling, lifting his arms as though in a gesture of surrender. Despite the heat, he is wearing a long overcoat. Its lining is torn, just under his arm, and where the sweat-stained rayon satin hangs down Porfirio glimpses fathomless black night, white stars.

"*Lalala la la.* Woooowww," says Robert Ross, just as Clete hits him. Clete shrieks and then is gone, sucked into the void of stars.

Porfirio stands very still. Robert winks at him.

"What a catch!" he says, in ten-year-old Bobby's voice.

It's hot up there, on the old white road, under the blue summer sky. Porfirio feels sweat prickling between his shoulder blades.

"Hey, Mr. Policeman," says Robert, "I remember you. Did you tell the Company what you heard? Have they been thinking about what I'm going to do? Have they been scared, all these years?"

"Sure they have, Mr. Ross," says Porfirio, flexing his hands.

Robert frowns. "Come on, *Mr. Ross* was my father. I'm Bobby."

"Oh, I get it. That would be the Mr. Ross who died right down there?" Porfirio points. "In the crash? Because his kid was so stupid he didn't know better than to lean out the window of a moving car?"

An expression of amazement crosses the wrinkled, dirty little face, to be replaced with white-hot rage.

"Faggot! Don't you call me stupid!" screams Robert. "I'm brilliant! I can make the whole world come to an end if I want to!"

"You made it come to an end for your family, anyway," says Porfirio.

"No, I didn't," says Robert, clenching his fists. "Professor Bill explained about that. It just happened. Accidents happen all the time. I was innocent."

"Yeah, but Professor Bill lied to you, didn't he?" says Porfirio. "Like, about how wonderful it would be to live forever?"

His voice is calm, almost bored. Robert says nothing. He looks at Porfirio with tears in his eyes, but there is hate there, too.

"Hey, Bobby," says Porfirio, moving a step closer. "Did it ever once occur to you to come back here and prevent the accident? I mean, it's impossible, sure, but didn't you even think of giving it a try? Messing with causality? It might have been easy, for a superpowered genius kid like you. But you didn't, did you? I can see it in your eyes."

Robert glances uncertainly down the hill, where in some dimension a 1946 Plymouth is still blackening, windows shattering, popping, and the dry summer grass is vanishing around it as the fire spreads outward like a black pool.

"What do you think, Bobby? Maybe pushed the grandfather paradox, huh? Gone back to see if you couldn't bend the rules, burn down this barn before the mural was painted? Or even broken Hank Bauer's arm, so the Yankees didn't win the World Series in 1951? I can think of a couple of dozen different things I'd have tried, Bobby, if I'd had superpowers like you.

"But you never even tried. Why was that, Bobby?"

"*La la la,*" murmurs Robert, opening his arms again and stepping toward Porfirio. Porfirio doesn't move. He looks Robert in the face and says: "You're stupid. Unfinished. You never grew up, Bobby."

"Professor Bill said never growing up was a good thing," says Robert.

"Professor Bill said that because he never grew up, either," says Porfirio. "You weren't real to him, Bobby. He never saw *you* when he looked at you."

"No, he never did," says Robert, in a thick voice because he is crying. "He just saw what he wanted me to be. Freckle-faced kid!" He points bitterly at the brown discoloration that covers half his cheek. "Look at me now!"

"Yeah, and you'll never be a baseball player. And you're still so mad about that, all you can think of to do is to pay the Company back," says Porfirio, taking a step toward him.

"That's right!" sobs Robert.

"With the whole eternal world to explore, and a million other ways to be happy—still, all you want is to pay them back," says Porfirio, watching him carefully.

"Yeah!" cries Robert, panting. He wipes his nose on his dirty sleeve. He looks up again, sharply. "I mean—I mean—"

"See? Stupid. And you're not a good boy, Bobby," says Porfirio gently. "You're a goddamn monster. You're trying to blow up a whole world full of innocent people. You know what should happen, now? Your dad ought to come walking up that hill, madder than hell, and punish you."

Robert looks down the hillside.

"But he can't, ever again," he says. He sounds tired.

Porfirio has already moved, and before the last weary syllable is out of his mouth Robert feels the scorpion-sting in his arm.

He whirls around, but Porfirio has already retreated, withdrawn up the hillside. He stands before the mural, and the painted outfielder smiles over his shoulder. Robert clutches his arm, beginning to cry afresh.

"No fair," he protests. But he knows it's more than fair. It is even a relief.

He falls to his knees, whimpering at the heat of the old road's surface. He crawls to the side and collapses in the yellow summer grass.

"Will I have to go to the future now?" Robert asks piteously.

"No, son. No future," Porfirio replies.

Robert nods and closes his eyes. He could sink through the rotating earth if he tried, escape once again into 1951; instead he floats away from time itself, into the back of his father's hand.

Porfirio walks down the hill toward him. As he does so, an all-terrain vehicle comes barreling up the old road, mowing down thistles in its path.

It shudders to a halt and Clete leaps out, leaving the door open in his headlong rush up the hill. He is not wearing the same suit he wore when last seen by Porfirio.

"You stinking son of a bitch *defective*," he roars, and aims a kick at Robert's head. Porfirio grabs his arm.

"Take it easy," he says.

"He sent me back six hundred thousand years! Do you know how long I had to wait before the Company even opened a damn transport depot?" says Clete, and looking at his smooth ageless face Porfirio can see that ages have passed over it. Clete now has permanently furious eyes. Their glare bores into Porfirio like acid. *No convenience stores in 598,000 BC, huh?* Porfirio thinks to himself.

"You knew he was going to do this to me, didn't you?" demands Clete.

"No," says Porfirio. "All I was told was, there'd be complications to the arrest. And you should have known better than to rush the guy."

"You got that right," says Clete, shrugging off his hand. "So why don't you do the honors?"

He goes stalking back to his transport, and hauls a body bag from the back seat. Porfirio sighs. He reaches into his coat and withdraws what looks like a screwdriver handle. When he thumbs a button on its side, however, a half-circle of blue light forms at one end. He tests it with a random slice through a thistle, which falls over at once. He leans down and scans Robert Ross carefully, because he wants to be certain he is unconscious.

"I'm sorry," he murmurs.

Working with the swiftness of long practice, he does his job. Clete returns, body bag under his arm, watching with grim satisfaction. Hank Bauer is still smiling down from the mural.

When the disassembly is finished, Porfirio loads the body bag into the car and climbs in beside it. Clete gets behind the wheel and backs carefully down the road. Bobby Ross may not be able to die, but he is finally on his way to eternal rest.

The Volkswagen sits there rusting for a month before it is stolen.

The blood remains on the old road for four months, before autumn rains wash it away, but they do wash it away. By the next summer the yellow grass is high, and the road is white as innocence once more.

THE ANGEL IN THE
DARKNESS

August 6, 1991.

Maria Aguilar slammed the door of her apartment, dropped her keys and purse on the coffee table, threw her head back, and screamed in perfect silence. She had not had a good day at work.

She seldom had good days at work, lately; she was an underpaid insurance underwriter in a firm that had just been sold to new owners, and the future was dubious. Today, with rumors of relocation and layoffs, it was especially dubious. The weather was stickily hot, the air acrid with smog. She was forty-six, single, overweight, and drove an eight-year-old Buick Century.

And the red light on the answering machine was blinking at her.

She stepped out of one of her high heels and threw it at the wall, not quite close enough to hit the phone table.

"What the hell is it *now,* Tina?" she muttered, as she undressed. "Philip's daddy didn't show up to drive you to the clinic for his shots? Philip's cutting another tooth and you can't get him to stop crying? Philip ran out of Similac and you need somebody to drive you to the market? Or maybe you just can't get the cork out of your goddam bottle of Pink Chablis?"

Stalking back through the living room in her bathrobe, Maria glared at the answering machine. "You can damn well wait," she told it, and leaned sideways into her tiny kitchen. Rummaging in the freezer, she withdrew a pint of Ben and Jerry's Cherry Garcia. She pulled a spoon from the drainer, shoved a pile of unfolded laundry to one end of the couch, and settled down to work her way through some consolation.

Halfway through the pint, however, she sighed, set it aside, and pressed the PLAY MESSAGES button. She braced herself for Tina's voice weepy and alcoholic, or, worse, with the abnormally bright and chirpy tone that meant something had gone really wrong. Instead, she heard a total stranger.

"Uh . . . Ms. Aguilera, this is Marcy Jackson of Senior Outreach. Mrs. Avila at the Evergreen Care Home gave me your number and suggested we might discuss the best possible outlook for your father, uh, what we can do to make him more, uh, to improve the quality of his care. There are some other facilities I can recommend—"

Maria said a four-letter-word. Five minutes later, having pulled on sweats and sneakers, she was back in the Buick Century fighting traffic, on her way to the Evergreen Care Home.

Mrs. Avila was younger than Maria, but she always spoke as though she were a kindergarten teacher gently rebuking a five-year-old.

"It's specifically stated in the terms of admission," she said. "*No* open flames in any room at any time. He's had two warnings now. Today was his third infraction."

"Why the hell didn't you tell me he had a lighted candle in his room?" Maria cried.

Mrs. Avila pursed her lips. "We had assumed you'd noticed. When you visited your father."

"But—" Maria fell silent, realizing she had seen the candle after all. As long as she could remember, there had been a votive candle flickering in its little ruby-glass cup in front of the wooden figure of the Virgin of Guadalupe, familiar to the point of invisibility. For most of Maria's life, the Virgin had stood on the mantelpiece of the house on Fountain Avenue. Recently, she had relocated to a shelf above Hector's television set in the Evergreen Care Home.

She was still there, smiling through five generations of candle-soot, when Maria stepped into her father's room; but there was no light in the glass cup now.

Hector, seated on the edge of his narrow bed, blinked at her and smiled wide.

"Hey, shweetie," he exclaimed, rising painfully to his feet. "It's sho good to see you!"

He struggled forward and she came quickly to take his hands, seat him again. His hands were soft now, felt fragile as chicken feathers. "Papi, we have to talk. Do you understand they want you to move out of here?" said Maria.

He smiled, nodding, looking into her eyes; then the meaning of her words got through and he scowled, looked away.

"I'm moving back to my daughter's plashe," he said.

"No, no, Papi, listen—why are you talking like that? Did you break your upper plate again?"

"No, no. I—wait! Yesh I did." He fished in his mouth, produced it for her inspection. Maria stared at it bleakly. She dug in her purse and found the Papi kit: disposable plastic gloves, antibacterial ointment, Band-Aids, denture adhesive, tube of Superglue. She pulled on a pair of gloves.

"Christ Jesus, Papi. Give it here."

He looked on mildly as she dried the pieces with a paper napkin and fitted them together.

"Did you know, my wife used to be in the movies?" he said.

"I know, Papi. Three Republic Studios serials, one monster flick, and a TV commercial for bananas. I'm your daughter Maria, remember?"

"Oh. When's Tina bringing the little man?" he asked, smiling again.

"Pretty soon, Papi. He's teething right now, and he's a handful. Here we go; you have to make this last, Papi, *please*, okay? I still haven't got your paperwork straightened out at the dental clinic. The only time I can do it is during the day when I'm at work, and there's only so long I can wait on hold on a personal call. You see?"

"Uh-huh."

"Have they said what your white blood cell count was, from last Tuesday?"

"No. Nobody tells me anything."

"Damn. And where have you been getting votive candles for Our Lady?"

"Corner store."

"You mean somebody went down there and got them for you?" Maria looked up sharply.

"No. I take my walk."

"Oh, my God." Maria closed her eyes, imagining her father toddling through traffic like Mr. Magoo. "Nobody told me they were letting you out for walks. Papi, you can't do that! You get lost. Remember?"

He just shrugged, smiling in a vague kind of way.

"Look, Papi—Papi, are you listening to me? You aren't supposed to have candles in your room. They're this close to throwing you out of here, Papi, you hear me? I got them to give you one more chance. But you have to promise me you're not going to break the rules again. No more candles, okay? You could burn the place down."

When that sank in on Hector he looked askance, elaborately scornful.

"Why, they're crazy. I never burned our house down," he stated. "Fifty years Our Lady has her candle, on Fountain. S'not dangerous."

"It's the law nowadays, Papi," Maria said. She had a flash of inspiration. "Listen, you know what they're doing now, in churches? They've got little electric votive lights in front of the statues. You drop in a dime, you push the button, a light comes on in the cup." Gingerly she set his upper plate on the top of the bureau, wedging it between Hector's Bible and water glass, and peeled off the disposable gloves. Grabbing up her purse, she searched through it.

"Here! I'll show you what we're going to do." She pulled out her keys and unclipped the mini Maglite flashlight she kept there for emergency occasions. "See this teeny flashlight? Cute, huh? Red, just like a rose. Look, Papi, we're going to dedicate this flashlight to the Blessed Mother, okay? Here!" Maria turned on the mini Mag and stuck it in the candle cup, then hastily tilted it outward so the Blessed Mother didn't look quite so much as though she were telling a scary story at a slumber party.

"Ta-da! And, uh, look, see the little spot of light it throws up in the corner? Think of that as, like, a little window into Heaven. That's where your guardian angel is watching over you, all right?"

Hector eyed it doubtfully.

"You're wasting the battery."

"It's not wasting!" Maria threw her hands up in the air. "It's burning in honor of our Lord and Savior Jesus Christ, okay? Papi, I'll go to Bargain Mart and buy you a whole case of triple-A batteries, I swear. It'll be just like candles, only safer. And then you can go on living here."

Hector's mouth trembled.

"I want to go home," he said.

"Oh, Papi, don't start that again," Maria begged. "These are nice people. They drive you to your doctor appointments. They make sure you take all your medications, don't they? And you know I can't do that unless I quit my job. And I can't afford to quit my job. I used up my personal leave when you had pneumonia as it is. Please. This is how it has to be."

But his attention had wandered away, and he gazed up at the light on the ceiling now.

"My guardian angel," he mused. "Your Uncle Porfirio came to see me, you know?"

She nearly screamed out *Uncle Porfirio has been dead for thirty-five god-damned years, Papi!* Containing her fury, she merely said: "Gosh. Did you have a nice visit?"

Hector just nodded, smiling now, tranquil and enigmatic as Buddha.

She got him to promise he'd be good, to promise he'd leave his upper plate out until tomorrow morning when the glue would be set, promised in turn she'd be back the next evening with more batteries, and kissed him good-bye. His kiss was wet and soft. Maria fled from his room down the pastel hallway, hating herself for her anger.

At the elevator, a man waited. He merely turned and smiled at Maria, as she drew near; but something about his smile chilled her.

She smiled back, though, and studied him out of the corner of one eye. What was it? She knew, if she looked long enough, she'd figure out what was setting off subliminal alarm bells in her mind.

Maria had been sensitive, all her life, to physical differences in others. Her acuteness of observation had often embarrassed her parents, when she had been too little to know better than to blurt out *Mama, that lady has a wig on her head!* or *Papi, why is that man dressed up like a lady?* It had enraged her sister, when Maria had been able to spot dilated pupils or smell the chemical sweat that betrayed drug use in Isabel's boyfriends. Isabel had remarked often, acidly, that Maria would make a great vampire hunter.

What was it about this man, now? Glass eye? Prosthetic limb? A trace of ketones on the breath? He wore a white coat, though somehow he didn't look like a doctor. He was young, too, perhaps in his mid-twenties. And the smile was still on his face even though he was no longer meeting her eyes, a self-assured smirk that reminded her of, of, of . . . the Cat in the Hat.

The elevator arrived, the doors slid open. Maria stepped in and turned, but the man remained where he stood. He lifted his eyes to her look of inquiry.

"No thanks, Maria, I'm going up," he said.

"How'd you—" she said, before the doors closed and the elevator dropped with her.

"Well, that was creepy," she remarked aloud.

Two ambulances had pulled up outside the lobby, sirens wailing, lights flashing. She barely noticed them, striding back to her car. Somebody was always dying at the Evergreen Care Home.

She drove too fast heading back into LA, through a lurid purple evening shot with red sunlight. Would there be a thunderstorm tonight? An earthquake? The freeway rose and fell like a serpent, offering her chaotic glimpses of the tumbled city as she sped along. Aztec pyramids, palm trees, Babylonian ziggurats, graffiti cryptic as hieroglyphs along the dry river channels. The air was muggy with wet heat, trembling. Something was out of balance somehow, something portended doom; but that was normal for Los Angeles.

Still, the feeling nagged at her enough to make her pull off the freeway and stop in at the house on Fountain, to check on Tina and the baby.

Everything looked normal enough there, if sad: old bungalow set back from the street in its unkempt garden, half hidden by banana trees, rubber trees, hibiscus bushes. Even the FOR SALE BY OWNER sign was beginning to be engulfed by creepers. Again, the reproachful little voice in her memory told her *Papi used to keep all this so nice . . .*

"Everything changes," she replied stolidly, and made her way up the front walk to the door.

Tina, to her pleasant surprise, was being Good Tina. She was sober, cheerful, and the house was clean. Philip was rolling about in his walker, chewing on a toaster waffle.

"Baby, look! It's Auntie!" cried Tina, and Philip grinned and bounced in his walker. He waddled it laboriously across the floor, right up to Maria's feet, and stared up into her face. Her heart broke with love and she leaned down to scoop him up, kiss his fat little chin and cheeks. He gurgled, waving his waffle.

"How's everything been today?" Maria inquired. Tina, washing her hands in the kitchen, shouted:

"Really fine, Auntie! I cleaned that little storage room behind the garage. Hauled out tons of old junk Grandpa had hoarded in there. Most of it had been rained on and was just a mess, so I trashbagged it, but there was this one box I thought you'd want to see—" She emerged from the kitchen drying her hands on a dishtowel, and tossed it aside as she stooped to lift a cardboard carton from the floor.

"It's mostly old photo albums," she added.

"That's the only box that wasn't ruined?" said Maria, with a sinking feeling. "Honey, some of that stuff was Mama's, from the house back in Durango—"

"It was covered in black mold," Tina told her firmly. "And we have to learn to let go of the past, like my therapist says. Look, I thought we could sit down and look at the pictures together. You should see Grandma's old movie stuff! It'll cheer you up. Want a glass of wine?"

So she had alcohol in the house again. "Okay," said Maria heavily, and sank down on the couch with the baby.

But Tina brought out only the one glass, and though Maria disliked Pink Chablis intensely she drank it, grateful that Tina wasn't joining her.

They went through the first album, as Philip babbled and reduced his waffle to eggy bits. This album contained a few black and white glossies, glamorous Lupe Montalban's publicity shots, including one hilarious shot from a monster B-movie where she was standing at the mouth of a cave, screaming in terror at a robot who looked like a trash can. The rest were family snapshots from the fifties, tiny black-and-white images with white scalloped borders.

"December 25, 1951. See how new the house looked?" said Tina, smiling and pointing. Maria sighed. Everything looked new, and full of light: what a tidy lawn, *dichondra* for God's sake, who had dichondra lawns anymore? And the front porch empty and clean, the hibiscus bushes clipped to neat boxes, the front walk straight and clear. Who were the two little girls on Christmas-morning-new tricycles? Why, the pretty one would grow up to be the famous Isabel Aguilar O'Hara, gracing the cover of *Vanity Fair* only last year! And the older one? Oh, that was her sister. Maria somebody.

"That was Grandpa, can you believe it?" Tina shook her head at the handsome young man crouched on the walk behind the little girls. "And Grandma. This was before she got sick?"

"Years before." Maria peered at the figure half-shadowed on the porch, smiling from a swing chair. "She didn't get the cancer until I was a sophomore. You look a lot like her."

"Why'd she give up acting?"

"It was just what women did back then, once they married and settled down," said Maria. *And her career was over, thanks to Uncle Porfirio,* she added silently.

"And here you are at your First Communion," said Tina, "And that's my mom, and there's Grandpa and Grandma with the priest, right? And that's you on a streetcar with Grandpa somewhere."

"It's not a streetcar. That was Angel's Flight. It was a funicular railroad with two little cars, one block long. It's gone now; used to be downtown. That's your mom and your grandmother behind us."

"And this is all of you in Chinatown, I guess, huh?" Tina angled the book in the light. "Or is that Olvera Street? The thing I began to wonder about, looking through these, was: who took the pictures? Most of the time it's Grandma, Grandpa, you and my mom in one shot."

"Uncle Porfirio had a camera. He was sort of Papi's cousin," said Maria, setting Philip back in his walker. She thought of Hector, staring up dreamy-eyed at the spot of light on his ceiling, and grimaced.

"What's the matter?" said Tina, watching her.

"Nothing."

"Was he the one who was a policeman?"

"LAPD," Maria affirmed, getting up and going to the kitchen to pour out her wine. "Plainclothes detective. He got killed when I was eleven. That's why there aren't that many pictures later on."

"How come there's no pictures of him?"

"There's one," said Maria, returning. She sat down and paged through the book, past the Christmases, past the trips to Disneyland, past the loving color portraits of the brand-new two-tone 1956 Chevy Bel-Air (pink and black!).

"Here," she said at last, setting her finger on a shot taken in this very room. A black-and-white picture of Isabel, seated on this very couch, proudly holding up for the camera the cardboard model she'd made for school: Mission San Fernando, with kidney bean tiles glued on its roof.

"That's just my mom," said Tina. She leaned closer. "Oh!"

The big mirror had still hung over the fireplace back then. Its surface reflected a glimpse of the breakfast nook, otherwise out of sight through the doorway. A man in a suit could just be seen there, seated at the table, head bowed over a newspaper.

"He looks . . . mean," said Tina at last.

"He was mean," said Maria. "He was a real hardass, and he had a face like Satan. But he was a good man."

And nothing had ever been the same, after he had been killed.

Tina, watching her face, said a little sharply: "Look, this wasn't supposed to get you depressed."

You're telling ME not to get depressed? thought Maria. Aloud she said, "I'm sorry. Rough day at work."

"Don't let it get to you. Things are going to get better now! As soon as we sell this place, there'll be plenty of money," Tina advised. "We'll pay off Grandpa's medical bills. I've even been thinking about buying an RV to live in, you know? Philip and me can go see the world! Maybe move out of California, to some place less expensive, huh? And you could come with us. Leave that crappy job. You could get an RV of your own, maybe."

Great, thought Maria, *And so, from being property owners, we'll become people who live in trailer parks.* "I thought you were going to go back to school and get your degree," she said.

"Well, of course I'm going to do that," said Tina quickly. "A-and get a job, too, of course. I'm already looking. I've got a friend helping me with a résumé."

Her hands began to tremble, imperceptibly to anyone but Maria. She closed the album, got to her feet, and headed for the kitchen.

"I could really do with a glass of wine, after all that dust," she called in a bright voice. "You want more?"

Maria drove through the hot night with her windows rolled up, because she had to scream. She screamed obscenities. She drew out one particular four-letter word over three whole blocks, and only stopped because there was a police car in the lane next to hers at the intersection. Uncle Porfirio had been a plainclothes cop.

Uncle Porfirio, with his holster and badge. Uncle Porfirio with his flat headstone at San Fernando Cemetery.

Nothing had ever been the same, after he'd been killed.

Her father had been an amiable young used-car salesman, an orphan as far as he'd known. Hector's life was fun, and he had a fast car, and he'd never saved a dime, but he owed nobody anything. Then Pearl Harbor had happened, and he'd enlisted. In some distant tropical hell, every man in his unit had fallen to Japanese machine-guns, and he'd fallen, too; but an unknown Good Samaritan carried him out, and he woke up in a field hospital.

One of the medics there had the same last name as Hector. They compared notes and discovered they were second cousins. Uncle Porfirio became his buddy, the older brother Hector had never had. They went back to Los Angeles together, after the war was over.

Uncle Porfirio made Hector get a better-paying job, and save his money. He introduced Hector to pretty Lupe Montalban, who was in the movies. When the studio gangster who had been dating Lupe objected, Uncle Porfirio had had a quiet word with him. Uncle Porfirio was best man at Hector and Lupe's wedding, and cosigned on the loan to buy the house. Uncle Porfirio became godfather to their two baby girls. Uncle Porfirio rented a room from them, in the attic loft above the porch.

Uncle Porfirio ran their lives.

Nobody had seemed to mind that, though, except little Maria.

Forty-six-year-old Maria watched the light change, realized her heart was pounding dangerously, and pulled off Franklin down a residential street so she could calm down. Groping in her purse for the medication, she muttered, "Goddam know-it-all control freak, that's what you were."

"*You* promised!" eight-year-old Maria had yelled, "*You said I could have a real bike if I got straight As, and I did!*"

"*Sweetie, I know we promised,*" Hector had said. "But—"

"But Uncle Porfirio reminded us about that freeway ramp they're building," Lupe had said firmly. "There's already too much traffic on Fountain, and it's only going to get worse. We don't want you getting killed."

Uncle Porfirio hadn't said anything, just folded his arms and looked opaque.

So Maria had never gotten a real bike; and if there had in fact been three fatal accidents on their block in the next three years—one of them Bobby Schraeder from next door, smacked off his Schwinn and into the next world by a delivery truck—it wasn't much consolation.

And if Uncle Porfirio had taken them to Catalina Island on holidays, and had bought little Isabel her first set of paints, and had known an infallible way to make the Good Humor man stop exactly in front of their house on every one of the long summer evenings of childhood—still, he was *never ever wrong*, in any argument.

The last straw, the ultimate injustice, was when he had refused to let Maria go to Camp Stella Mare.

"Are you nuts?" eleven-year-old-Maria had yelled. *"I worked my fingers to the bone to go on this trip! I sold thirty subscriptions to* The Tidings!"

"I know," Uncle Porfirio had replied. *"I bought twenty of them, remember?"*

"Sweetie, it's a long way up into the mountains, and the roads aren't good," said Hector apologetically. *"And it's a rickety old bus. Uncle Porfirio was talking to the mechanic across the street from the convent, and he says the undercarriage is all rusted out. We just don't feel it's safe."*

To which Maria had responded with the worst word she dared to say, and ran sobbing into the backyard.

She had been sitting on the roof of the garage, staring out at the cars zooming past on the freeway, when Uncle Porfirio came out to find her.

"Get down off there, *mi hija*, it's dangerous," he said quietly. "You want to break your neck?"

"I don't care," she snapped. "I hate you."

He sighed and walked close, vanishing from her sight under the edge of the roof, and a moment later vaulted up beside her. He had always been able to move faster than a cat. She tensed, expecting him to pull her down, but he seated himself instead.

"You hate me, so you don't care if you break your neck. That makes a lot of sense, doesn't it?" he said. "Come on, *mi hija*, you're smarter than that. You're the smart one in the family."

"A lot of good it does me," she said.

"Well, somebody has to be the smart one. Somebody has to look out for the others, and stop them from doing dumb things that'll get them killed."

"But that's always you," she replied. "You always know better than anybody else."

"But I won't always be here," he said. "And the family's going to need somebody strong and smart, right? And it's going to be you, I can tell that already."

"Huh," she said, not mollified. He was silent a moment, and then he said:

"You remember that man you told me about, the one who was hanging around the fence talking to Isabel?"

"The creepy man who said he was friends with Mickey Mouse?"

"That one. It was a good thing you spotted him, baby; he was a really bad guy. Lieutenant Colton and I took him downtown. He's back in jail now, where he belongs."

"Really?" Maria turned to look at him, wide-eyed.

"Yeah. But Isabel will be mad that the nice man isn't there to give her candy bars anymore. You think she'd say you were unfair to tell?"

"Oh, my gosh," said Maria, appalled. Uncle Porfirio turned to her, holding her gaze with his cold dark stare.

"You see?" he said. "And you think it's unfair that you don't get to go to camp. But I see danger you don't notice. When you're a grown lady, you'll have eyes as sharp as mine. It's a dangerous world, *mi hija*."

"I don't want it to be," she'd cried, furious because she knew he was right again. She'd scrambled down and run into the house, but the truth of what he'd said lay on her heart like an iron bar.

A week later he'd been murdered, killed while on an undercover operation. His body had been found sprawled on the concrete of the Los Angeles riverbed, so badly beaten the face was unrecognizable, but his gun and his badge were still with him. Maria had thought: *See, he made somebody else as mad as he made me*, and was instantly horrified at herself.

And the week after that the Camp Stella Mare bus lost its brakes coming down a steep mountain road, and eleven little girls and two nuns had gone straight to heaven. Maria felt worse then.

And four years later Lupe had been diagnosed with cancer, and had endured years of interminable indignities in treatment, with Hector scrambling through layoffs and pay cuts in the meanwhile as he tried to care for her. Maria had given up her plans for college and stayed home to help out. Her mother had died anyway, not soon enough for anyone. Maria stopped going to Church, and nobody noticed.

And Isabel had grown up, begun dating boys, gotten in trouble, presented her parents with Tina, and run off to join an artist's commune in San Francisco. Isabel never felt guilty about anything. She had sent postcards to Tina from San Francisco, Maui, New York, Paris, Katmandu, and finally Taos. Tina had, understandably, felt this was insufficient attention from her mother, and had gotten her revenge by becoming a severely depressive unemployed single parent.

And the untended garden had gone wild, full of black wet leaves. The house had shrunk, year by year more shabby. The cars roared by ever louder on the freeway. Gunfire began to punctuate the night. The Communist Invasion/Apocalypse/ Nuclear War never happened, but everything else did.

And at forty-six, in her rusty Buick Century on a darkened street, Maria Aguilar felt the future close on her like steel pincers. It's a dangerous world, *mi hija*.

"Damn you for having the last word," she whispered. A man strolled past her car.

"Hi, Maria," he said, and kept walking. She sat up and stared after him. A white coat: was he the man who'd been waiting at the elevator in the Evergreen Care Home? Narrowing her eyes, she started the car and drove away, checking the mirror frequently to see whether she was being followed.

"This really frosts the cake, huh?" she muttered aloud. "A goddamn stalker."

But nobody seemed to be lying in wait at her apartment. She locked herself in, went straight to the Tupperware bin in which she kept her handgun, removed it and loaded a clip. Then she made the rounds of all her windows, checking for signs of breaking and entry. Satisfied that all was as it should be, she noticed that the light on the answering machine was blinking again.

"Maria, this is Rob O'Hara. Apparently there's been some snafu with your father's nursing home? You need to get it straightened out. Some woman called here because she couldn't get in touch with you, and now Isabel is very upset. She can't paint when she's upset. You know that."

Maria made certain the safety catch was in place before putting the pistol to her head and miming blowing her brains out.

"So please get it taken care of, whatever it is, and if you need money or anything, maybe we can help. By the way, there's a wonderful review of Isabel's latest exhibit in *The New Yorker*. Calls her our generation's Georgia O'Keeffe. Isn't that exciting? I thought you'd—"

Mercifully, the machine cut him off.

There was another ambulance in front of the Evergreen Care Home when Maria arrived the following evening. She merely glanced at the corpse being wheeled out, shifted her grip on the case of triple-A batteries and shouldered her way into the lobby. To her surprise, Hector was there, staring out though the glass.

"Whoa, Papi, where are you going?"

"They got Steinberg," he said somberly.

"I'm sorry, Papi. Come on back upstairs. Was that a friend of yours?"

He didn't say anything on the ride up in the elevator. Maria hefted the batteries, trying to draw his attention to them. "Look! Lots of lights for the Virgin. She can a have a fresh one every day."

He just nodded, shuffling along beside her as they went down the hall to his room. There she opened the case and showed him how to put a new battery into the mini Mag. He didn't speak, and as Maria looked closely to see whether he was paying attention, she realized he wasn't wearing his upper plate. Her gaze went at once to the top of the dresser, where she'd left it between his Bible and his water glass. They were still there, but the upper plate wasn't.

"Papi, what did you do with your plate?" she demanded. .

He just shrugged.

"Papi, did it break again?"

He peered up at the dresser. "One of those damn Jap nurses must have stole it," he muttered.

"Papi, that's an awful, awful word, okay? It's not right to call Japanese people that anymore. And anyway, most of the housekeepers here are Filipinas, and *anyway* why the hell would somebody steal your busted upper plate?"

He sat silent, offended. She groaned and got down on her hands and knees to peer under the dresser, under his chair, under his bed. She moved the dresser a few inches out from the wall and peered down its back. Not a trace of pink and ivory plastic to be seen.

"Punks steal from me all the time," Hector said. "Took my crossword book, too."

"I'll have to talk to Mrs. Avila about it," said Maria, climbing to her feet with effort. "The nutritionist, too. You have to be able to eat, Papi."

"Get your uncle on the case, huh?" said Hector, who had wandered to the window and was looking out.

"Papi—" Maria bit back her retort, took a deep breath. She went to the window and kissed his cheek. "I have to go, Papi. I'll see you tomorrow."

He began to cry, holding her hands.

"I love you, honey . . ."

"I love you, too, Papi. Look, tomorrow I'll bring you some takeout. We'll have a picnic in here, okay?"

"Okay . . ."

She had worked herself into the necessary righteous wrath by the time she got to Mrs. Avila's office, but Mrs. Avila was on the phone, with her door closed, and in the time it took before Maria saw her hanging up the emotional momentum had fallen off. She rapped on the window politely. Mrs. Avila put her head in her hands, leaning her elbows on her desk, and didn't seem to hear.

"Mrs. Avila?" Maria opened the door halfway. "Um—my father had his upper plate out, and it seems to have disappeared from his room. I was wondering if you—"

"I beg your pardon?" Mrs. Avila looked up at her with such a strange expression that Maria took a step backward.

"Is something wrong?"

Mrs. Avila blinked rapidly. "We just lost a long-term resident. We were all very fond of Mr. Steinberg. I'm sorry, you had a complaint?"

"Just that—ah—my father seems to have misplaced his upper plate. Is there any chance I can talk to the nutritionist about getting him on the soft diet, until I can get him new teeth?"

"I'll make a note of it," said Mrs. Avila, twisting her hands together. "Unfortunately, Mrs. Ng went home ill today, but I'll see that she calls you to discuss this at the earliest opportunity."

"Okay, thank you," said Maria, and exited hastily.

She dreamed that night that a tightrope had been stretched from the roof of the Evergreen Care Home to the roof of another tall building across the gulf of the freeway. Hector and the other residents were lined up patiently on the roof, waiting their turns. Each ancient had been issued a brightly-colored parasol. The ones who had ventured out on the tightrope already were falling, gently as autumn leaves, down toward the roaring river of traffic, and the traffic was all hearses and ambulances.

She was trying, desperately, to get into the elevator to get up to the roof, to pull Hector back; but the Cat in the Hat kept hitting buttons that sent the elevator to the basement instead, smiling at her, insufferably pleased with his cleverness. Finally she leaped into the elevator anyway, trying to work it from the inside, but it dropped with her. The door opened on the basement, and there by the laundry chute stood Uncle Porfirio, gun in hand. Natty three-piece suit, Aztec cheekbones, mandarin beard and mustache. He looked at her without expression. His eyes were black as night.

It took Maria three trips to three separate drive-through restaurants and a visit to a drugstore to get what she wanted, so it was a little past her customary time the next evening when she pulled up in front of the Evergreen Care Home. The sky had flamed up orange and pink, and birds were crying from the tops of the trees. Trudging up to the lobby with an assortment of greasy paper bags, she glanced down curiously at the police tape festooned across the walkway.

"Did something happen here today?" she inquired of one of the housekeepers, as they ascended in the elevator.

"One of the residents reported somebody jumping off the roof," the housekeeper replied.

Maria shuddered, remembering her dream. "You mean there was a suicide?"

The housekeeper shrugged. "We called the cops, but they couldn't find anything in the bushes."

The door opened on Hector's floor and Maria hurried to him, fearful of finding his room empty, the window open on a void of glaring air. But no: he was seated placidly in his chair, listening to one of his tapes of Big Band music.

"Hey, you figured out how to work the tape player!" Maria greeted him, leaning down for a kiss. "Good for you."

"He fixed it for me," said Hector, jerking his thumb at the boombox. "Just push the red button, he said."

"What?" Maria peered at it. Someone had affixed a bright red adhesive dot to the PLAY button on the tape machine. "Oh. That's clever. Who's *he*, Papi?"

Hector's smile went away, came back, and he looked sidelong at her.

"Social worker," he said. He looked with interest at the greasy bags. "We gonna eat?"

Pushing the mystery to the back of her mind, Maria opened the bags and set up the little feast: mashed potatoes and gravy from KFC, hot dogs from the Hot Dog Show, a chocolate malt from Foster's Freeze. She cut the hot dogs into manageable pieces, stuck a plastic spoon in the potatoes, and presented it to Hector on a TV tray.

"Mm, good! See, it's all stuff you can manage with your plate out. Just in case they screw up downstairs and serve you the wrong meal. And I got this, too—" Maria pulled two cans from her purse. "It's like a vitamin shake. If you get hungry between meals, you just open one. I'll put them up here by the Blessed Mother so you don't forget, okay?"

"Mmhm," Hector replied, through a mouthful of hot dog.

She brought out her own hot dogs and soda, and they dined together companionably.

"I saw your mother today," said Hector.

Maria halted, soda halfway to her mouth. "Papi . . . Mama's in Heaven, remember?"

"I *know* that," he replied, indignant. "It was on TV."

"Oh! You mean, one of her movies? Omigod, which one?"

"The one with the spaceships." Hector strained for his malt, unable to reach it. She got up and handed it to him.

"*Aztec Robots from Mars*? No kidding! Maybe they'll finally put that out on tape, huh? Then I'll buy you a VCR, so you can see her whenever you want."

But Hector was blinking back tears.

"I miss your mother . . ."

"Oh, Papi, don't cry," said Maria hurriedly, kissing his cheek. "One of these days Mama's going to come for you in a pink Cadillac, okay? And you'll live happily ever after, up with the angels. You just have to hang on until then."

As she was wadding up paper bags for the trash basket afterward, Maria noticed the gauze pad taped to his inner arm.

"What happened to your arm, Papi?"

"Lab work," Hector replied.

"What kind of lab work? What for?"

"Don't know," said Hector, waving a hand. "Doctor came and did it."

"They're supposed to tell me if you need to go to the clinic. Did you have to be taken to the clinic?" Maria narrowed her eyes.

"Nope," said Hector. "Doctor made a house call."

"House call?" Maria was baffled. "And what's this I hear about somebody jumping off the roof?"

"There was a big fight up there," said Hector, nodding.

"A fight?"

"Yeah." Hector's smile vanished again. He looked uneasy. "I mean, I don't know."

She tried to see Mrs. Avila to ask her about what kind of lab work Hector had required, but the office door was closed and the blinds were drawn. Fuming, Maria drove home, deciding to call on her lunch hour tomorrow.

When she walked through the door of her apartment, the first thing she noticed was that Hector's upper plate was sitting beside her answering machine.

The second thing she noticed was the slip of paper under the plate.

Standing perfectly motionless, she thought: *Wow, it really does feel like ice water along your spine.* She looked right, at the closet door; she looked left, at the door to her bedroom. Ahead of her was the kitchen doorway. Her gun was in the bedroom.

Quietly as she could, she withdrew a can of Mace from her purse and advanced. No masked killer burst from closet, bedroom, or kitchen, and so she was able to get to the phone table. She read the note under the plate, being careful not to touch anything, and called the police. Then she withdrew to her bedroom and sat, shaking.

The note read simply: WE CAN TOUCH YOU.

————

The cops were interested in her love life to an excessive degree.

"You're sure this wouldn't be an ex-boyfriend?" the younger one wanted to know.

"Yes, I'm sure," Maria snapped, because it was the third time she had been asked that question.

"No ex-husbands?" asked the older one.

"None."

"Well, why would anybody leave a note like this?" The younger cop hefted the plastic bag and peered through it at the note, stashed in there with the plate for fingerprinting.

"Because somebody's a total psycho and has decided to terrorize a complete stranger?" said Maria. "That happens, doesn't it?"

"So, you've got, like, no—uh—nephews or brothers who might be in gangs?" the older cop inquired.

"No brothers. One grand-nephew, ten months old. Gosh, maybe he's in a gang," said Maria. "I should have thought of that before, huh?"

"Anybody in your family ever assaulted?"

"My father, two years ago, when he lived with me," Maria admitted. "He's nearly eighty. He used to open the door to anybody, during the day when I was at work. I came home and found he'd been beaten up and robbed. He's in a care facility now."

"Anybody in your family ever murdered?"

"Only my uncle who was a cop," Maria replied. "Shot five times and beaten to death. He worked Vice Squad. You can look him up: Lieutenant Porfirio Aguilar, 1956."

There was a silence, and a perceptible change in the temperature of the room. The older cop cleared his throat.

"Well. You should probably get your locks changed. And, uh, go and stay with somebody until you get that taken care of, okay? And you can call me if anything else happens." He took a card from his wallet and gave it to her. "Do you have anyplace else to stay?"

The house was dark, though it was only eight-thirty. Maria climbed the porch steps with her overnight bag, heart hammering. On the porch, closed in by ivy and hibiscus, it was nearly pitch-black.

"Tina?" she called, pounding on the door. No answer.

She found her old key and opened the door; reached in to the right and flipped the switch that turned on the porch light, and instantly stood in a pool of yellow illumination from the cobwebbed glass globe above her head. The door was open about six inches, and through its gap she could make out toys scattered on the carpet, surreal, fearful-looking in the gloom. She groped farther inward, trying to find the interior light switch, and heard something dragging itself toward the door.

"Jesus," she murmured. She froze there with her arm halfway into the room, as the rattling came nearer; then mastered herself and pushed the door open.

The light from the porch fell on Philip's little upturned face. He rolled himself to the door in his walker and peered up at her.

"Honey bunny, what's going on?" she said, trying to keep the fear out of her voice. She picked him up—he was soaking wet, stinky, how long since he'd been changed?—and turned on the overhead light, bracing herself for what she'd see.

Not so horrible as it might have been. *Sufficient unto the day are the horrors thereof,* she thought numbly.

Tina on the couch, passed out. Two empty wine bottles, an empty glass, an ashtray, a plastic Baggie with a little pot in it, a box of kitchen matches and a book of rolling papers. Philip's toys all over the floor, along with what looked like the contents of the kitchen trash basket.

"Jesus," Maria repeated. Leaving Tina where she lay, she took the pot and flushed it down the toilet. Then she went through the house with Philip, turning on lights in every room. He watched her in solemn silence.

She gave Philip a bath, fed him, put him into jammies and fixed him a bottle; then retreated with him to Hector's armchair, and sang quietly to him. It took a while to get him to sleep. He kept sitting up to stare across at his mother, black eyes wide and worried.

"Mommy's just depressed again, sweetheart," Maria said quietly. "I wonder what did it this time?"

He nestled back down, took his bottle, and fell asleep at last.

Maria looked across the room and time and saw herself on that couch at twenty-three, with a bottle of gin and a bottle of Seven-Up and a big glass of ice, getting drunk fast, furious with the world, as Hector sat in the other room staring at Lupe's empty bed. And little Tina had sat next to her and watched, with black eyes wide and worried.

I could tell her I'm this close to calling Child Protective Services; but she'd only try to commit suicide again. I could actually call Child Protective Services; they'd take Philip away to foster care, where somebody would molest him, and then she really would check out. I could call Philip's daddy and tell him to take custody; I'm sure his wife would love being presented with Philip, especially when she's just had her own baby. I could call Isabel . . . and she'd move to New Zealand.

"What am I going to do, *mi hijo*?" she wondered. "Please, God, somebody, tell me."

She was late for work the next morning. Tina had been weepy, apologetic, resentful, and finally indignant when she discovered that her stash had been disposed of. Maria had countered by telling her about the stalker. While this had been enough of a shock to abruptly change Bad Tina to Good Tina, it had also terrified her, and Maria had to spend a half-hour calming her down.

There was no point in explaining any of this to Yvette, the new departmental supervisor. Yvette lived in a world where such things didn't happen. Maria simply apologized for oversleeping and offered to work through her lunch hour.

On her afternoon break, however, she called Mrs. Avila's office.

She got a recorded message informing her that the switchboard was temporarily unavailable due to the high volume of incoming calls, and she could leave a message after the tone. Wondering grumpily how that many people could be calling the Evergreen residents, most of whom never heard from their kids except at holidays, she left a message for Mrs. Avila.

Two hours later, as she was on the phone explaining rate increases to a client, Yvette appeared at the doorway to her cubicle. She bore a message scrawled on a yellow legal pad: EMERGENCY CALL IN MY OFFICE.

Maria knocked over a chair in her haste to get to Yvette's desk, relaxing only momentarily when she heard Mrs. Avila's voice on the line, rather than the police.

"Ms. Aguilar? I'm afraid I have some bad news." Mrs. Avila's voice was trembling. "We've had to admit your father to County General."

It never rains but it pours, Maria thought. "Has he had a stroke?"

"No," said Mrs. Avila, and it sounded as though she was drawing a deep breath. "He has—ah—a virus."

"What? He was fine yesterday!"

"This is—" Mrs. Avila's voice broke. "This is some new thing. We've had several cases. He's in the ICU, and I don't know if you'll be able to get in to see him—"

By the time Maria had explained to Yvette, fought traffic all the way downtown to County General, found a parking space and bullied her way upstairs, Hector was dead.

"What do you mean, I can't see him?" she asked the floor nurse, but the presence of men in hazmat suits going in and out of the Intensive Care Unit answered her question. She fought her way to the window and stared through. All she could see was a confused tentage of plastic, tubes, pipes, one skinny little mottled arm hanging down. Hector looked like an abandoned construction site.

The doctor, whose name she didn't catch, explained that Hector had died from a rapidly-progressing pneumonic infection, just as all the others had, but because he had fought it off longer, there was some hope that—

"Longer?" Maria said. "What do you mean, *all the others*? How long were you treating him for this? He had no immune system, you know that?"

"He was brought in this morning," said the doctor.

"But—he said a doctor came and did some kind of lab work on him yesterday. There was a bandage on his arm," Maria protested. "He said the doctor made a house call."

The doctor looked at her in silence a moment.

"Really," he said. "That's interesting."

Maria was numb, going back down in the elevator, wandering past the gurneys full of moaning people parked in the hallways, threading her way between the cars in the parking lot. It wasn't until she got to the Buick and opened her purse for her keys that she saw the Papi kit, and the reality sank in: *My father is dead.*

And for about thirty seconds she felt the sense of release, of relief, that she had expected to feel. Then the mental image of the old man, the shrunken, childish, infinitely vulnerable thing he had become, vanished away forever. All she could remember was her father the way he had been in her childhood, young Hector who had put on dance records and waltzed in the living room with his two little girls, one on either arm, as Lupe sang from the kitchen where she fixed breakfast . . .

The memory went through Maria like a knife. She leaned against the car and wept.

The next day it was in all the papers and even on the local news: how the Evergreen Care Home was being evacuated following the deaths of more than half of its residents and three members of its staff, of what was thought to be a new super-virus. Maria had to go to Kmart to buy clothes for Hector to be buried in, once his body was abruptly released, because she was unable to enter the Evergreen's building; it was full of more men in hazmat suits, carrying equipment in and out. Too surreal.

The funeral was surreal, too. Hector had been a member of the Knights of Columbus and they turned out for him in full regalia, a file of grandfathers in Captain Crunch hats. They were most of them too frail to be pallbearers—six sturdy ushers wheeled Hector's coffin down the aisle—but they drew their sabers and formed an arch for him. Philip stared, absolutely fascinated, turning now and then to his mother and great aunt to point at the feathered hats.

There were more old men at the cemetery, ancient rifle-bearing veterans, one of whom carried a cassette player identical to the one Hector had owned. He slipped in a cassette and set it down to salute as "Taps" played, tinny and faint. The veterans fired off a twenty-one-gun salute; Philip started in his mother's arms and lay his head on her shoulder, trembling until the noise had stopped. At the end they folded the coffin flag into a triangle, just as Maria remembered the Marines doing at JFK's funeral long ago. As a final touch, they zipped it into a tidy plastic case, presenting it to her solemnly. Before leaving they asked for a donation, and Maria fished in her purse for a five-dollar bill to give them.

The old veterans left in a Chevy van painted with the Veterans of Foreign Wars insignia. The Knights of Columbus departed in two minivans and a Mercury Grand Marquis. Were Hector and Lupe going, too, away in a pink Cadillac to live happily ever after in the Land of the Dead?

Maria and Tina were left staring at Hector's coffin, poised on its gantry between the mounds of earth neatly covered by green carpet. Lupe's grave was hidden by them, and so was Uncle Porfirio's, but when the earth had been shoveled back in its hole the cemetery custodian would hose away the mud. They would lie there all three together, tidy, filed away, their stories finished. End of an era.

As Tina was buckling Philip into his car seat, Maria noticed a man standing alone by a near grave, head bowed, hands folded. He wore sunglasses. Their black regard was turned on her, just for a moment. She stared hard at him; no, he wasn't the man with the Cat in the Hat smile. He lowered his head again, apparently deep in a prayer for his dead.

Maria shrugged and got into the Buick, wincing at the hot vinyl seat. She drove out carefully through the acres of manicured lawn, flat and bright in the sticky heat of the morning. Questing for the nearest freeway on-ramp, she passed Mission San Fernando. It sat like a postcard for Old California, orange groves, graceful adobe arches, painted wooden angels, pepper trees. The past stood guard on the past.

They drove home in a weary silence that was not broken until they walked into the living room, when Maria played the messages on the answering machine. There were two.

"Hi Maria, hi Tina, this is Rob O'Hara. I just thought I'd call and let you know again how sorry Isabel is that she can't make the funeral—"

Tina stormed out of the room with Philip, muttering, "Fucking selfish bitch!"

"—know how much her father would have wanted her to do well, and the New York exhibit is turning out to be a terrific success. I'm sure he's looking down from Heaven, very proud of all of you . . ."

Rob's message ended abruptly, cut off in mid-sentence, and Maria smiled involuntarily. She expected him to resume in the second recording. Instead, there was a moment of silence but for background noise, and a hesitant throat-clearing. Maria tensed.

"Maria, Isabel, this is Frank Colton. Will you give me a call? I'm still at the same number in Seal Beach. I have some information for you."

Frowning, Maria sorted through the junk on the phone table for the

family address book. She flipped through it. Who on earth was Frank
Colton? She found a listing for him, seeing with a pang that it was in her
mother's handwriting. As she dialed, she began to place the name: a
long-ago Saturday drive to the beach. She had been twelve. Hector
and . . . yes, his name had been Frank, had sat together on the sand and
talked about Uncle Porfirio. They had both gotten drunk, and Lupe had
had to drive home.

She remembered him as a young man, with freckles and a crew cut:
Uncle Porfirio's partner. He must be a retiree now. His voice had sounded
old, tired. Maria dialed the number, hoping he wouldn't be home. But:
"Colton," said the voice on the other end of the line.

"Mr. Colton? I'm Maria Aguilar. I'm sorry I didn't call you in time—"

"Oh! Hector's daughter. Right."

"You were the lieutenant who worked with my uncle, weren't you?"

"That's right." There was a long pause. "Look . . . I'm retired now, but I
still get news. Your uncle's case was never solved, you know, and when anything related turns up, they . . . I get told. I heard you had some trouble,
you thought, with a stalker?"

"Somebody *was* stalking me," Maria said. "My dad had some, uh, property stolen from his room. It tuned up in my apartment, with a threatening
note. The cops took it away to test for fingerprints."

"Yeah, honey, I know. That's what I was calling about." The voice on the
other end of the line sounded embarrassed. "Hector's teeth, of all things. I
guess we all get older, huh? Anyway . . . they're not going to tell you this,
but they didn't find anything. No usable prints."

"Usable?"

"Well, there was a partial. Hector'd mended his teeth with Superglue,
apparently, and that was where the print was. They ran it through, but—"

"No records on file?"

"None that made sense. Some kind of file error. The nearest match they
could get was a guy who died in 1937. No prints on the note at all. So, ah,
it doesn't look as though the investigation is going to go anywhere. I
thought you should know, though."

"Thanks," said Maria dully.

"Tell your dad I'm still working on the murder, will you?"

"What?" Maria cried.

"Tell Hector, I'd like to maybe come up there sometime, talk over the old days—"

"Mr. Colton—Mr. Colton, I'm sorry, I thought you'd heard. My father passed away last week. He was at the Evergreen Care Home. It's been in the news—"

"Oh, my God." For a moment the voice on the other end of the line sounded young again, in its shock. "He was *there?* Oh . . . oh, son of a bitch!"

"I'm so sorry, Mr. Colton—"

"Son of a *bitch*! Ambrose Muller!"

"Mr. Colton?"

"But that makes no . . ." Suddenly the life drained out of the voice, and it was an old man's once more. "Miss, I'm sorry, please excuse my language. I just—"

"Who's Ambrose Muller?"

There was a long pause on the other end of the line. Maria could even hear distant surf, the cry of a seagull.

"He was the guy who committed suicide in 1937," said the voice. Frank Colton's breathing was labored now. It sounded as though he took a sip of water. "The one whose partial they thought they found on your dad's teeth. He, uh, was a doctor who worked in an old folks' home. Arrested on suspicion of poisoning his patients. Never stood trial; he committed suicide in his cell, like Hermann Goering. It just startled me, you know, the coincidence. This Evergreen Care Home thing."

"Right," said Maria, feeling slightly stunned.

"Listen, I'm so sorry about Hector. So sorry. I . . . will you call me if anybody bothers you again? Promise?"

"Okay," said Maria, wondering if he was about to cry.

"God and His angels protect you, sweetheart," said Frank Colton, and he did begin to cry, and hung up abruptly.

She went back to work the next day, having used up her Compassionate Leave time. Just after morning break all the employees were called into a meeting, where the sword fell: the new owners were relocating the company to South Carolina. Severance pay and unemployment benefits, or relocation incentives to work for one third her present salary a continent's width away from her family . . .

Maria walked back to her desk, almost tranquil, observing the black tidal wave of anger rising but not feeling it yet. Her supervisor stepped in front of her, and she blinked at Yvette in mild surprise.

"Maria, I'm so sorry this had to come at this particular time, for you," she said. "If you need to take the rest of the day off, ah . . ."

The black wave broke.

"Oh, so now I'm a human being and not just a machine part?" Maria said. "Don't you pretend they care anything about us! I've been here seventeen years and I was good at my job, and that counts for nothing? Jesus, there weren't even computers when I started working here. And now I'm forty-six, and where the hell am I going to find another job?"

"I'm sorry," said Yvette, and burst into tears. "They don't care. They have to look at the big picture. I feel just awful, but what can I do? It's not personal, Maria."

"You bet it's not. Clerical workers don't matter a damn to anybody. But if the new owners think they can find Hispanics who'll work for nothing in South Carolina, good luck to them," Maria snapped. She stormed out to the Buick, where her rage abruptly guttered to ashes in her shame at having played the race card. She drove away. The morning sunlight looked strange, unreal.

There were black plastic trash bags lined up on the curb in front of the house, when she drove up; Tina had been cleaning again, scouring away the pointless past. She met Maria at the door with a preoccupied frown.

"Auntie? What are you doing home?"

"I was laid off," said Maria, and watched the effect.

"But you've been there for seventeen years!" Tina shrieked.

"Bummer, huh?" said Maria, and walked past her and sat down on the couch. Philip came rolling up at once, reaching for her. She lifted him out, held him close.

"Those *bastards!*" Tina slammed the door. "Well—well, look, it's going to be okay. They never appreciated you there anyhow. You'll get another job right away, I know you will." She peered closely at Maria. "You're white as a sheet. You want a drink?"

"No, thank you," said Maria with great care, feeling the black wave begin to crest again. "Remember all those little talks we've had, about how alcohol doesn't help us in a crisis?"

Tina glared at her. Then she looked down, unclenching her fists.

"Somebody from Evergreen called. It's okay to go get Grandpa's things, now."

The tide went out abruptly, leaving a surreal landscape full of melted clocks. Maria stood up, dazed. "Well, let's go, then. We can get some lunch at a drive-through, eh? My treat. You can even have a Happy Meal."

"Thanks a lot," Tina muttered, but went to the hall closet for Philip's car seat.

Hector's boom box, his tapes, his statue of the Virgin of Guadalupe went in a big raffia purse that had belonged to Lupe. His clothes went into a black trash bag. Tina hefted it down to the car while Maria did a last check of the room. She pulled the bed, already stripped of its linen, away from the wall to be certain nothing had dropped down the side; there was only a book of crossword puzzles there, the last one she'd brought Hector, the one he had insisted had been stolen. Sighing, she picked it up. She opened the drawer in the bedside table to see if anything had been left there.

Yes, something white. An envelope. She picked it up. Something was written on the outside, in a familiar hand.

REALLY, MARIA, ISN'T IT BETTER THIS WAY?

She stared at it a long moment.

"All right, you bastard," she murmured. "You're dead, you know that? If I ever get my hands on you, you're dead as nails."

She slipped the envelope into her pocket as Tina returned with Philip.

In the car, Maria said: "Let's go to the library."

She left Tina and Philip in the Children's Room and made her way to the reference desk, where she explained what she needed. The slim young man on duty was friendly and helpful, and Maria retired at last to a microfilm viewer with file spools for all the major Los Angeles papers for the year 1937.

What a lost world, she thought. William Randolph Hearst sounded off on matters of national policy; real estate was painfully cheap, making her wish she had a time machine so she could buy a three-bedroom house for eleven thousand dollars. Charlie McCarthy and Edgar Bergen were hot. The advertisements were charming, quaint. The classified ads were so absorbing that she lingered over them, and so took a while to find her quarry.

But there it was at last in the *Los Angeles Times* on October 14, 1937, the headline story: DOCTOR INDICTED ON MURDER CHARGES. Ambrose Muller. Brilliant young physician. Resident at the Avondale Home, a hospital for the elderly. Staff shocked. Relatives demanding answers. "ANGEL OF DEATH" MULLER? Names of the pitiful deceased, their ages, the suspicious circumstances surrounding their departure into the next world. And here was the picture, Dr. Ambrose Muller in handcuffs between two big cops, the three of them caught by a barrage of flashbulbs exploding.

Maria stared at his face. The picture was dreadful, grainy, must have been poor even by the standards of 1937. She studied it a long moment. Finally she got up and went back to the reference desk. She asked for, and got, *LIFE* magazine for the year 1937 on microfilm. It was a local scandal, not a national one, but even so she found an article in the issue for the first week of November. There was the same picture of young Dr. Muller and the cops, beautifully sharp and clear now. He was smiling into the bright lights, smiling as though at his own cleverness.

She had seen him before, of course.

Great, she thought, *ghosts and vampires. My life has just become an episode of* Kolchak.

There was a quote from a noted psychologist on the subject of megalomania and delusions of grandeur. There was a photograph of one of the pieces of evidence that would have been produced at the trial, had Dr. Muller not committed suicide: a prescription for a diabetic patient, ordering a drug no sane physician would have given to anyone with that condition. With a feeling of resignation, Maria took out the envelope she had found in her father's room and studied it.

"Yep," she said. Same handwriting. *But families look alike*, she told herself. *Ambrose Muller died in 1937, right? So maybe this is his grandson, or something. Maybe he inherited his grandfather's M.O. as well as his face. And handwriting? Riiight. Stranger things have happened . . . but not people rising from the dead.*

There was something in the envelope, something she hadn't noticed in her anger. She opened it cautiously. It was a photograph, so old it had gone to sepia. Taken outdoors, it showed three young men, possibly *vaqueros* from their dress, standing together by an adobe building. One held the reins of a horse, quite a fine horse, obviously showing him off. In the background a fourth man had just walked into frame, blurred, frozen as he turned a startled face to the camera.

What was this supposed to prove? Maria wondered, turning it over in her hands. She didn't recognize the landscape. The men might have been Mexicans, or Indians; no other clue.

She stuck the picture back in the envelope. She rummaged in her purse for dimes, fed the microfilm machine's copier, and made three copies of the picture of Dr. Muller. Having returned the microfilm spools to the young man at the desk, she hurried out to the Children's section.

Tina was sitting at one of the little tables with Philip on her lap, reading to him in a whisper from *Madeline.* Her high breathless voice sounded like a child's voice. Maria vividly remembered holding Tina on her lap, pointing out Madeline at the end of the line of little orphaned girls . . .

But that had been in the old library, the one with its quaint tiled mural of Our Lady Queen of the Angels that little Tina had insisted was a dolly. It was gone now, torched by an arsonist in the late seventies.

Half my world is dead, Maria realized. *Why shouldn't there be ghosts and vampires?*

"Come on, *mi hija,*" she said, jerking her thumb at the door.

In the car, Tina remarked: "You haven't called me *'mi hija'* in a long time."

"I'm getting old," Maria replied.

"So . . . are you going to move out of your apartment now?"

"I guess so," said Maria, feeling the last of her short-lived independence slip away.

"It makes sense," said Tina. "You'll save money if you live with Philip and me. You don't want to stay there alone anyway, right? Not with the stalker, or whoever he was, bothering you. This way, we can be there for each other."

You mean I can be there for you, Maria thought, downshifting. It made sense; for what else was she going to do with her life, now? Take up crafts? Run away to Tahiti and get a gorgeous young husband? Wait: maybe she'd become a fearless vampire hunter.

Tina patted her on the shoulder.

"Let's stop by your apartment," she said. "You can't go on living out of your overnight bag. We'll pick up some of your things."

They entered Maria's apartment cautiously, but no one was lying in wait for them.

"Philip says, 'You better watch yourself, creepy man!' " Tina said, mock-fierce as she brandished him. " 'You mess with my Auntie and I'll punch you in the nose,' he says. Don't worry, Auntie. You've got a little angel looking out for you!"

"It'll be all right," said Maria automatically, scanning the phone table. No notes from anyone. No blinks on her answering machine. She went first to the stacked plastic boxes; her gun was there in its Tupperware, apparently untouched. She resealed it and set it on the table.

Five assorted bags and boxes of clothes, toiletries, and music cassettes went down to the trunk of the Buick. There was still room for her blankets and pillows; Maria sent them with Tina and stayed behind long enough to pull one of the photocopies she had made from her purse. She set it on the phone table, fended off Philip's attempts to grab it, and wrote across Dr. Muller's smiling face: I CAN TOUCH YOU, TOO, SMART GUY.

"Come on, sweetie." She shifted Philip to her other arm, picked up the Tupperware, and left the apartment.

Back at the house on Fountain, Tina drew the statue of the Virgin from Lupe's bag and set it on the mantelpiece.

"She's home again," she said, looking wistful. "We need to light a candle in front of her now. Grandma brought her from Durango, didn't she?"

"That's right," said Maria, methodically unpacking the rest of the bag. Something slipped out of Hector's crossword book: his plastic magnifying card. She picked it up off the floor and stuck it in her pocket.

"She looks really old. How long has she been in the family?"

Maria shrugged. "I think she belonged to Abuela Maria; that was your great grandmother. The one who lived on the big ranch."

"So she's looked after us for generations," said Tina, smiling.

"I guess so." Maria felt a pang, realizing that she was the only one left who knew the family stories about Durango. Isabel might remember, but Isabel didn't care. Did Tina really care? Would she be able to remember, would Philip inherit any sense of who he was, where he came from?

Something tugged at her memory. After a moment she placed it, and scowled to herself. "Why don't you go feed the baby? I'll unload the car."

Sitting among the boxes in her old room, she opened her purse and drew out the envelope again, and shook the old photograph out on the bed. *The big ranch in Durango . . .*

Maria took the magnifying card from her pocket and examined the picture minutely, especially the faces of the men. Not one of them bore any resemblance to Ambrose Muller. The one holding the reins of the horse was almost certainly an Indian. High cheekbones on him, and on the mustached man walking into frame—

Maria stared at that one a long, long time. He looked familiar, but the blur of motion made it impossible to place him.

Okay, she thought, *these people must be related to us. So, whoever he is, whatever he is, he was trying to show me that he knows all about us. Trying to scare me? Get my attention? Well, the ball is in his court now.*

She put the photograph back in its envelope and set it aside. Opening the Tupperware container, she took out her gun and slid out the clip, and proceeded to clean it.

Next morning Maria half-expected to find another note tacked on the front door, but there was nothing out of the ordinary there. She dropped off Tina at the mental health clinic and drove on down McCadden, through the same dreamlike sunlight, to the unemployment office.

Philip stared up from his stroller through the forest of adult legs, and only got cranky after the first hour in line. She placated him with one of the plastic gloves from the Papi kit, inflating it and tying off the end to make a rooster balloon. He thought it was hilarious, and bellowed with laughter as he flailed it through the air.

Wheeling him back to the Buick, Maria spotted the envelope under her windshield wiper. Moving deliberately, she put Philip in his car seat, fastened him in, folded up the stroller, and put it away before she allowed herself to pick up the envelope.

On its outside was written: CLEVER GIRL!

It was heavy, felt as though it contained a lot of folded paper. She weighed it in her hand, looking around to see whether anyone was watching her. Not a soul in sight. At that hour of the morning on a weekday, the mean streets were as wide and sunlit and empty as a desert.

Maria stuck the envelope into her purse, unopened. She got into the car and drove off.

Tina was smiling as she waited outside the clinic, clutching a paper bag. Maria's gaze riveted on it as she pulled up. Were they wine bottles?

"Sorry I'm late. What have you got in the bag?"

"I walked down to the little Mexican market on the corner," Tina replied, getting in. A heavy cloud of rose perfume came with her. "I bought candles for the Virgin, see?" She held open the bag to reveal three big pink candles, in glass cups color-lithographed with the Virgin of Guadalupe. "Don't you love that smell? Hi, baby, Mommy's so glad to see you! Were you a good boy for Auntie?"

"He was fine," said Maria, as she pulled away from the curb. "How was therapy?"

"Therapy was wonderful. Marvelous. Fabulously fantastic," said Tina, in a tone of such dreamy ecstasy Maria glanced sidelong at her, suspicious.

"Really," she said.

"Uh-huh," Tina said. She was still smiling.

"Well, don't keep me waiting," said Maria. "What was so good about it? You made a breakthrough?"

"You could say that," said Tina. "You know how I've told you what an incredibly nice man my therapist is? He's sensitive and caring and . . . and it's as though he's known me my whole life. He's like my angel."

"Yeah?" Maria tensed, guessing what was coming.

"Well . . . today he said he might like to, you know, go out with me. Socially."

Maria ground her teeth.

"*Mi hija*, doctors don't date their patients," she said.

"What do you know about it?" demanded Tina, coming down off her pink cloud a little.

"It's not something ethical doctors do. Especially not psych doctors with emotionally vulnerable patients," said Maria, trying very hard to keep the anger out of her voice.

"When two people fall in love, it doesn't matter who they are," said Tina. "You've never been in love, so you don't know, do you? He understands me, and I feel completely safe with him. I thought you'd be happy for me! Are you jealous, is that what it is?"

"No," said Maria, out of all the things she might have said.

"This could be the answer to *everything*," said Tina in a louder voice, leaning back in her seat. "We could get married. Philip would have a real daddy who's there all the time. And he's a doctor, you know? He lives in Bel-Air."

"Huh," said Maria. "And that would solve all your problems." Silently she screamed, *You wouldn't have to get a job, you wouldn't have to go back to school. You really think a doctor who lives in Bel-Air is going to ride to your rescue on a white horse.*

"Philip's happy for me, anyway," said Tina sullenly. "Aren't you? Wouldn't you like a new daddy?"

Maria waited until she was at home, alone in her old room, to open the envelope. It contained fifteen sheets of paper. She spread them out on her bed and studied them. They were not what she had expected, at all.

They seemed to be photocopies of scrapbook clippings, culled from newspapers and magazines, over a period of many years. Here and there they had been highlighted with a yellow marker, drawing her attention to certain points.

Maria read a story about a rare native species of bunch grass, long thought to be extinct, found again growing at a construction site out in Antelope Valley. The story next to it concerned another species once thought extinct, a kind of Asian deer, of which a small herd had just been discovered in a remote park in China.

Just below that story was an interview with a man in Sweden who had been cleaning out the attic of an old house and found a sixteenth-century quarto copy of a Shakespeare play. Next to it was a brief account of a cabinet in an old country house in England, opened by a new owner who discovered something locked away and forgotten: a concert piece by Handel, known to music scholars from contemporary references but formerly thought destroyed.

Wondering, Maria read on. All the articles had a common theme: the miraculous survival of lost things. Extinct species of plants and animals, works of art, manuscripts, early films. Somehow, in each case, they came to light once more, from whatever dusty shelf or hidden valley they had occupied all the while.

On the last page, someone had written:

WHAT IF SOMEONE HAD FIGURED OUT A WAY TO MAKE MONEY OUT OF THESE LITTLE SURPRISES?

HOW CAN YOU EVER BE SURE OF DEATH?

FOOD FOR THOUGHT, ISN'T IT?

"Okay," said Maria quietly. "You really are an obsessive psycho. What's next? UFOs?"

The doorbell rang.

"Can you get it?" Tina called from the kitchen. "I'm washing dishes."

Maria went out to the living room, noting that Tina had lit one of her pink candles and placed it before the Virgin of Guadalupe. The air was already warm with perfume. Going to the window, she peered through the blinds; a young man in a suit stood on the porch, looking at something he was holding in his hand.

She opened the door. The young man was a stranger to her. As he held up the leather case to display his badge, his coat opened and Maria saw the holster under his left arm.

"LAPD, ma'am. I'm Lieutenant John Koudelka. How are you today?"

"Fine," Maria replied, thinking that he sounded like a salesman.

"Would you be Maria Aguilar?"

"Yes."

"I take it you're no longer at the place over on Hobart. Would it be all right if I came in and asked you some questions about your father's death?"

"Sure," said Maria.

didn't he? What was that you stuck him with?" Maria swerved, accelerated as Emrys sprinted across the empty intersection.

"Tranquilizer. The only one that works on us, Theobromidan. But he didn't get much, and it wears off fast. I've got darts, though," said Porfirio, pulling his own gun from its holster. He slipped the safety off, sighted along the barrel. "If I can get him in the back with one of these—oh, shit."

Bounding ahead of them up Fountain, Emrys had leaped into the back of a pickup truck full of newspapers that waited at the stoplight. He turned, leering hugely in the Buick's headlights, brandishing Philip at them. Philip was screaming, tears coursing down his cheeks. Emrys hurled a bundle of newspapers at them, and had seized up another as the truck's driver—an elderly Asian man—jumped out in protest. Turning, Emrys swung the bundle with such force that the old man was knocked flying. He vaulted out of the back with Philip tucked under one arm, slid into the cab, and drove off.

"Come back here, you bastard!" Maria cried, flooring the accelerator pedal. Uncle Porfirio muttered an oath as they surged forward and followed the truck around a corner.

"*Mi hija*, watch it! You'll sideswipe somebody."

"I don't care," she said wildly. "Put your stupid dart gun away and use mine! Shoot out his tires!"

"Honey, at this speed, he could flip over—"

"Oh, NO, you SOB, don't do it! Oh, he's getting on the 101!"

"God damn," said Uncle Porfirio, sinking into his seat. "Follow him. How fast can you get this boat to go?"

"We're going to find out," said Maria, turning up the on-ramp so sharply that the Virgin of Guadalupe flew off her perch on the dashboard. Uncle Porfirio's hand shot out and he caught her in midair, stuck her in his coat pocket.

The freeway was nearly empty at this hour, a dark river winding through the heart of Hollywood, and black ivy climbed its banks and waved down from its overpasses. The taillights might have been red eyes in the jungle night. The air even now was hot, dead, heavy, smelling like warm milk. When Uncle Porfirio cranked down his window it pushed into the car with a roar, like a big animal.

The truck ahead of them slowed down, sped up, changed lanes recklessly. Maria followed, grim, steering with her left hand.

"I think he broke my arm," she said, almost as an aside. Uncle Porfirio turned his head and stared fixedly at her right arm a moment.

"No. But the muscles are torn and you've got a hell of a subdural hematoma. You'd better go to a doctor about that, *mi hija*."

"What, you've got x-ray eyes, too?" Maria laughed without humor, showing her teeth. "Hey, what happens if the cops get in on this chase? Does Doctor Angel of Mercy get hauled off to cyborg jail again? Or is there a cyborg looney bin? Or does he just get handed over to the Cyborg Police Department?"

Uncle Porfirio didn't say anything, watching the truck.

"You're with the Cyborg Police Department," Maria guessed.

"That's one way of putting it," said Uncle Porfirio. "He's exiting at Cahuenga. Change lanes!"

Maria cursed, steered the car across three lanes to make the off-ramp, and Uncle Porfirio had to haul on the wheel with her. They came off the ramp in time to see the lights of the truck speeding away over the hill, in the direction of Franklin.

"You miserable bastard," said Maria, gunning the engine and shooting up the hill like a rocket. As they crested the top and followed the long curve down, she added: "You don't save things, do you? Not like the other people who work for this Dr. Zeus Company."

"No," said Uncle Porfirio, so quietly she could barely hear him over the rush of air from the window. "I solve problems."

"And that's why he said he respected you? Christ Jesus, you're some kind of corporate hit man. Damn! He's going left on Franklin. Hope we make the turn!"

They careened around the corner on two wheels and zoomed up Franklin, climbing another hill, never managing to close the distance between the pickup and the Buick.

"It was the price I had to pay, *mi hija*," said Uncle Porfirio. "My special arrangement. I'm the only operative I know of with a mortal family. So the Company made an exception for me. Because of what I do for them."

"What about that studio executive Mama was dating when she met Papi?" asked Maria. "Was that a Company job, too?"

"That was different," said Uncle Porfirio, after a pause. "He was a mobster. He was bad for Lupe, and then he threatened Hector."

"Don't tell me any more," said Maria.

"Deal," he replied.

Down the hill and along the corridor of Franklin, and the night air was sweet again with jasmine and copa de oro from terrace gardens. Ahead of them the truck accelerated suddenly and was gone, vanishing left.

"That's Bronson," shouted Uncle Porfirio. "He's going up to Bronson Canyon. Make a left!"

Maria obeyed. Within a block they were going uphill through old Hollywood, residential streets laid out in the 1920s, green gardens clinging to the canyon walls. There were Spanish haciendas, there were English Tudor cottages, and French châteaux, and here and there an ersatz Neutra apartment building like a raw scar; but they went by in a blur, every one of them, and the cool night air streamed down the canyon like water.

"I know where he's going now," said Uncle Porfirio. There was a certain grim satisfaction in his voice.

"Where?" Maria leaned forward as she drove, concentrating, for the street had narrowed.

"Old Bronson Quarry." Uncle Porfirio checked his pistol.

"The place with the cave? Where they shot *Teenagers from Outer Space?*" Even in her terror and rage, Maria was incredulous. "And, like, I don't know how many *Star Trek* episodes?"

"Yeah. That's it," said Uncle Porfirio. "The great thing about it is that it's invisible. You go there, and you recognize it immediately because of *Outer Limits* or Ed Wood or whatever. And because it's familiar, your brain just turns off what's actually there and shows what you remember from TV instead. The Company uses places like that all the time. Concealed storage, transport stations . . . and places to rendezvous."

They had the truck in front of them once more, as the road climbed, as the houses became fewer and farther between. Two cylinders were making a big difference; the little truck did not like hills, and they were closer now, close enough to see Emrys's hunched shoulders as he drove. Far above them the Hollywood sign loomed, ghostly in the reflected light of the city.

Abruptly they were out of the residential area, as canyon walls loomed close on either side of the road, which seemed as though it was about to end in a narrow parking lot. But the truck sped straight through it and turned right, smashing open a barred gate, making another sharp right, and losing speed abruptly as it climbed.

"I hope this car has good suspension," said Uncle Porfirio, and a moment later Maria understood why; for now they were bouncing up an unpaved track. Bushes clawed at them to either side, boulders scraped the oil pan underneath. Even with the racket, they were now so close to the truck that Maria could hear Philip's screams coming from its cab.

"Oh," Maria wept, "*mi hijo*, please hold on. Please!"

"As soon as you get the chance," said Uncle Porfirio, "pull up on his right." He unbuckled his seat belt.

And then he was gone, having writhed out the passenger window like smoke, apparently onto the roof of the Buick, for Maria heard the sheet metal above her head flexing as he leaped. Then he was abruptly in the back of the pickup, and then he had punched in its rear window, and then he was gone. But the cab of the truck was full of a writhing darkness, and it veered suddenly to the right.

Maria sped up, pulled around the truck on the right as she had been told, and now she saw why; for on the right the embankment dropped away, and what a long way down it went, with the paved road far below! She wondered briefly how many filmed car chases had ended in a gangster's Packard or De Soto tumbling end over end down this drop, to finish in a nicely cinematic fireball: Crime Does Not Pay.

Her car was straddling the verge, the oil pan was grinding on gravel, now, but she cranked the wheel ferociously to the left and fendered the pickup, forcing it to stay on the road. Horrible, horrible noises were coming from the truck's cab. Suddenly an arm shot out the window, holding Philip by the scruff of his jammies like a little sack of mail.

Maria lunged, grabbed him with her good arm, stamped on the Buick's brakes, and prayed. She was able to drag Philip in over the window frame and clutch him to her chest, with an overpowering sense of relief. His arms went around her neck, his wet screams deafened her, and she cradled him and told him everything was all right, all right, all right. The Buick lurched to a stop on the edge of the trail.

The truck went rumbling on, purely on momentum, for it was no longer being driven or steered, and the trail was no longer climbing but opened instead into an immense amphitheater, towering rock walls all around three sides. Right where a stage ought to be was the cave Maria had seen in so many cheesy movies. The truck rattled toward it crazily, lighting its black mouth as the high-beams swept across. And . . . there was a figure standing in the cave, not thirty yards away.

Maria blinked through her tears, as she patted and crooned to Philip. For a moment her brain fought with her, telling her it had seen the Robot Monster, complete with gorilla suit and fishbowl helmet. Or had that been Tor Johnson in a torn shirt, with a glimpse of boom mike above his head? Or even the Aztec Robot from Mars? She remembered what Uncle Porfirio had told her about such places, as the figure walked forward from the pitch-black into starlight. Another slow circle of the truck, moving quite aimlessly now, lit the figure up white.

It was a starship captain in a federation uniform. *No!* It was a man in a business suit. Just a man.

Yet it wasn't just a man . . . was it?

The truck juddered to a halt at last. Something went flying out of the driver's side window. Had that been a gun? Maria looked around her on the seat and realized Uncle Porfirio had taken her gun. Which gun had just gone out the window?

"Philip, sweetie," she whispered huskily, "we have to get out of here."

She tried to set him on the seat beside her, but he clung and whimpered. She reached across the wheel with her left hand, found the gear shift, put the Buick in reverse. Turning to look over her shoulder as best she could with Philip there, she began to edge the car back down the trail.

She might have made it, if her front left tire hadn't been shot out.

The car jolted, sagged leftward; Philip screamed again, struggling. She turned and saw Emrys, who had emerged from the truck and was standing, braced with legs apart, clenching the gun with both hands. His Cat in the Hat smile was back, even creepier now because his face was scored with red lines. He looked as though he'd been in a fight with a much bigger cat; possibly a jaguar.

He raised the gun, pointing it high, at the stars; then brought it down, slowly, aiming at her face.

Then he lurched sideways, as Uncle Porfirio came from nowhere and leaped on him. The second shot went wide, spurted dust harmlessly ten feet from the car. The two men were a blur of motion and hideous noise on

the ground, in the white light and black shadow from the Buick's headlights, and dust rose in the beams like smoke.

The man in the space suit—*No!*—the man in the *Armani* suit was walking toward them. He was tall, dark-visaged, with autocratic good looks. He
might have been an Egyptian high priest, or a Roman senator, or an English headmaster. He wore the frown of a judge about to reprove an un-
wise counsel. When he spoke, clear across that amphitheater in the silence
of the night, Maria heard the measured tones of Patrick Stewart—*No!* But
something very like them.

"*If* you please, gentlemen," he said. "Stop that at once. Get to your feet."

The blur rolled apart. The two men struggled upright. Their clothes were
torn, they were gashed and bleeding. As Maria stared, the wounds began
to close. The bleeding stopped and their edges flowed together like melting wax.

Uncle Porfirio folded his arms, looking as much like a scornful Satan as
she could ever remember, even in his ruined suit. Emrys, by contrast,
smiled and bowed, rubbing his hands as though in gleeful anticipation.

"I brought him, Labienus," he said. "See? I knew you wanted him, and I
found a way to get him for you! Isn't this a coup? Isn't this a feather in my
cap? You can excuse a few little quirks of independence, can't you, for such
a prize?"

But the dignified man was shaking his head.

"Emrys," he said, "you really are a loose cannon."

Emrys lost his smile at once.

"Don't call me that," he said.

"Are you raising your voice to me?" inquired the dignified man. "I think
you'd better not do that."

"You ungrateful cretin!" Emry's voice became shrill. "Don't you know
who I am?"

"I know who you were, Emrys," said the dignified man. "Nowadays
you're simply a nuisance. On your knees!"

Maria jumped at the change in his voice on the last command. Emrys
folded at the knees as though pushed from behind. He looked up at the
man in astonishment, rage fading into fear. The man stepped closer, and
spoke quietly once more.

"You were warned repeatedly, Emrys, weren't you? We did give you

every chance, in view of your not inconsiderable talents. But you've become a liability to our organization, I'm afraid. This really has been the last
straw."

"But—you wanted him." Emrys, beginning to sob, waved a hand at
Uncle Porfirio. "And he was perfect. He has a weakness you can exploit!"

"I wanted *a* Security Technical," said the dignified man. "Not this one.
He has entirely the wrong psychological profile for our organization, however talented he may be. However vulnerable his personal arrangements
make him. And you were told that, weren't you? Yet you disregarded orders, Emrys.

"You took it on yourself to stage a bizarre and highly theatrical recruitment campaign. Were you aware that the police have tracked you down?
They're waiting at your office. They're waiting at your apartment. I myself
had the honor of a conversation with a plainclothes detective, not six hours
ago. I had to spin them quite a story."

"As though we care what the mortals think!" said Emrys.

"That is not the point," said the other. "You have drawn unnecessary attention to our organization, to say nothing of contravening some of the
most elementary laws concerning Company security in general. I am extremely disappointed."

How grave, how sorrowful was his voice.

"But I'm useful," Emrys wept. "I'm a genius. You need me."

The dignified man just shook his head.

"Genius? I've never seen such an amateurish job in my life. A Section
Seventeen violation, for heaven's sake!"

"What? No!" Emrys looked up, startled. The dignified man arched his
nostrils in disgust.

"Security Technical, kindly explain a Section Seventeen violation to the
prisoner."

"I know what—"

"It's 1991, asshole," said Uncle Porfirio. "You sent a mortal a digital image inkjet-printed on paper."

"But—within another few years—even months—"

"But not *now*," said the dignified man. "You are guilty of an *anachro-
nism*," and he spat the word out as though he hated the taste of it, "that any
neophyte would have been able to avoid. To say nothing of deliberately

revealing the Company's existence to a mortal. This business is finished. Bow to me, Defective."

Emrys began to cry, really bawl like a child, but he leaned forward. The dignified man reached into the inner breast pocket of his coat. What he brought forth was small, silvery, only glimpsed in his hand as he thumbed a button. He swung his hand over Emrys's neck.

There was a flash of blue and Emrys's head fell off, not with the expected sputter of wires and broken circuits but with a fountain of blood, and the headless trunk flopped forward. The dignified man stepped back to avoid being splashed. He tucked the unseen instrument back in his pocket.

Uncle Porfirio did not move.

"What happens now?" he asked.

"Ah," said the dignified man, smoothing his lapels. "Why, it's a stalemate, isn't it? Surely you see that. You know of the existence of our organization. We, on the other hand, know your little secret." He nodded toward Maria and Philip. Maria just stared back at him, mechanically rocking Philip, who had subsided into sniffles.

"I want my family left alone," said Uncle Porfirio. The man looked pained.

"Please," he said, with a dismissive gesture. "So long as they exist, we have a certain leverage with you. Isn't that so? And while I'd never be so foolish as to pressure you to help us, I do expect you to look the other way from now on. You may, in fact, be called upon to be absolutely blind on one or two occasions."

Uncle Porfirio said nothing for a long moment. Far off across the city, the first faint sirens of the morning started up. Somewhere, robbery or rape or murder was in progress. Somewhere, some bright new policeman with a bright new badge believed he could do something about it. Uncle Porfirio sighed.

"What about him?" He nodded at Emrys's body.

"Do as you please," said the dignified man. "Take his head, perhaps? Consider it an earnest of good faith on our part. And leave his body here a few hours, to let the coyotes eat their fill of him. That's what I'd do.

"I suspect you'll do the honorable thing and deliver his parts to the Company. Another defective rounded up and deactivated! Bravo, Security Technical Porfirio. One more success in your distinguished record of service to Dr. Zeus."

Smiling, he turned and walked away a few paces; then stopped and turned back.

"A word of advice," he said. "As part of our mutual avoidance policy. Get your family out of Los Angeles. We're going to be rather busy here, over the next few years."

He vanished into the shadows.

Uncle Porfirio walked back to the Buick.

"You have a spare in the trunk, right?" was all he said.

"Yeah," said Maria. "Who was that? The Lord of Evil?"

"Something pretty close," said Uncle Porfirio, reaching past her for the keys. "We're not going to talk about it anymore, okay?"

She got out of the car and stood under the pale stars with Philip, who had fallen asleep, while Uncle Porfirio changed the tire. As he was putting the flat tire and jack in the Buick's trunk, Uncle Porfirio asked: "What's in this plastic bag?"

"My box of laundry soap."

"I need to use the bag, *mi hija.*"

"But I hate getting detergent spilled all over the inside of the trunk."

"Better that than something else."

"Oh. Okay," she said, and watched numbly as Uncle Porfirio walked back toward the cave. A moment later he returned, carrying something in the green bag, and set it in the trunk beside the jack.

"So . . . I thought he was an immortal," said Maria.

"He is," said Porfirio, slamming the trunk. "Too bad for him. Get in the other side, *mi hija.* I'll drive back."

Maria sat beside him, watching as he backed the car down the trail, as he expertly pulled out on the paved road, drove away from the realm of flying saucers, giant mutant tarantulas, and creatures out of legend. And yet . . . here, at the wheel of her car, was an undying creature who had seen twelve generations pass into dust. She looked furtively at his Aztec profile.

She was silent until Franklin Avenue, when she said: "Please, tell me. Is there a God? Do we have souls? Is there any fucking point to this life?"

His voice was flat with exhaustion. "How would I know all that, *mi hija*?

I don't know. Nobody I've talked to in four hundred years has told me, either."

"Then what the hell do you know?"

He looked sidelong at Philip as he drove. Reaching out, he touched the child's sleeping face.

"That this is all we have, *mi hija*. And it doesn't last, so you have to take good care of it."

The Virgin of Guadalupe was still on duty, in her cloud of rose perfume. Tina still lay where she had fallen, in the silent house, but she was breathing. They lifted her onto the couch and covered her with a blanket. While Uncle Porfirio was cleaning up and changing into an old suit of Hector's, Tina became foggily conscious. Maria told her she'd been sleepwalking and fallen down the stairs. When Uncle Porfirio came back, he pretended to be an EMT, checking her vital signs and asking her questions about how she felt.

Maria left him sitting beside Tina, speaking to her in a low and soothing voice, while she went upstairs and bathed Philip. He woke crying, staring around; but, seeing no monsters, he calmed down and let her put him in fresh diapers and a sleeper. It took twice as long as usual with only one hand. When she carried him downstairs, in the pale light of dawn, Tina was sitting up, smiling if glassy-eyed.

"There's my little guy!" she said, reaching out for Philip. "Mommy fell down and went boom! Were you scared?"

Philip wriggled into her arms, beginning to cry again, and she hugged him. Looking over his shoulder at Maria, she added: "I don't think that new medication Dr. Miller prescribed was good for me, you know?" A shadow crossed her face. "I . . . don't think I want to go back to Dr. Miller. I had a really creepy dream about him."

"Okay," said Maria. Uncle Porfirio cleared his throat.

"Ms. Aguilar, I need to give you a list of symptoms you need to watch for."

"Sure." Maria picked up the TV remote, handed it to Tina, took the baby from her arms. "Why don't you find some cartoons to watch, okay, *mi hija*? I'll get breakfast for Philip."

They left her happily watching Bugs Bunny. In the kitchen, Maria made coffee while Uncle Porfirio looked into Philip's eyes, spoke to him to in a voice so quiet Maria could barely make out what he said. Philip was tranquil after that, feeding himself, eating Cream of Wheat with his right fist while carefully holding the spoon in his left. He watched, in mild interest, as Uncle Porfirio fashioned a sling for Maria's arm and made her take two aspirins.

"What happens now?" Maria inquired in a murmur.

"Now I steal your gun. And your car," said Uncle Porfirio. "Too much to clean up, *mi hija*, and you won't want it back when I finish what I have to do. It's insured, right?"

"I haven't paid the premiums in a month. I'm unemployed right now," said Maria, bemused. The night and all its horrible wonders had receded like tidewater, and the mundane rock of her old problems stood exposed again, quite unchanged.

"I'll send you money," Uncle Porfirio told her, as though reading her mind. "I have some saved. Buy another car. No SUVs, okay?"

"What's an SUV?"

"You'll find out. Get another Buick, maybe, or a Volvo. Put the house on the market with a Realtor. Take Tina and the baby and go, get the hell out of Los Angeles. Find a place in Taos, near Isabel. She needs to meet her grandson."

"Oh, she'll love that, being reminded she's a grandmother!" Maria grinned involuntarily. But he wasn't smiling.

"You're serious, aren't you? About what that guy told you. Labienus."

Uncle Porfirio flinched. "Don't even mention his name." He gulped his coffee and stood. "I made a deal with a devil, so I'm not about to waste any inside information I get from him."

"But . . . you're not really going to just look the other way, when he wants you to?"

Uncle Porfirio shrugged into his coat, not answering.

"But what you told me, about what those people do . . . doesn't that mean innocent people will die?"

"And other innocents will live," he said. "There's a price to pay for everything. But I made the deal, *mi hija*; not you. That weight, you don't have to bear."

He stepped to the back door and opened it.

"Keep the family together," he said, and slipped out, and was gone into the morning.

She never saw him again.

One month and an epic garage sale later, Maria stood on the front porch of the house on Fountain. Tina was buckling Philip into his car seat, in the new—well, 1986—Buick Skylark, which was crammed to the roof with all their remaining possessions. But it was solid, dependable, insured, had side mirrors and a good spare, and there were no severed heads in the trunk.

They were leaving late. The last-minute packing had taken longer than Maria had expected. All the same, she lingered on the porch, turning the key over in her hand. Closing her eyes, she took a deep breath. Acrid smell of dry rot, old plaster, dead leaves. The place of her childhood was long gone.

This place would be a parking lot, in another year. The Hollywood sign would look down on . . . what? Riots? Epidemics? Ruins? This cycle of time was ending, but what could she do about it? Run through the streets shouting a warning, like the man at the end of *Invasion of the Body Snatchers*? As though anyone listened to the Maria Aguilars of this world.

She walked down the front steps, scowling up at the hazy sky. Summer was gone, too; the late sunlight gave no warmth where it slanted, and the green leaves looked tired, frayed. Far off to the west, a few rifts of fog were drifting in from the distant sea. It would be a chilly night, and an early winter.

But the family would be somewhere else by then, safe in a new place. When the new cycle started, that had been paid for in blood, they would endure.

And she had to admit she felt less of a weight on her shoulders, now. Somebody else remembered her parents, so that Hector was more than a gravestone and Lupe more than a flickering black-and-white image in an old movie. Somebody else knew about Abuela Maria and the ranch in Durango. Somebody else was the guardian of their past, kept the family's story safe, a long and perfect and unbroken chronicle. It could never be forgotten, and maybe it would never end.

Doggedly she walked to the car, refusing to look back.

"Auntie!" Tina was leaning out the Buick's window, her face shining with awe. "Look at this. The Blessed Mother's in the car!"

"She's in the trunk," said Maria, going around to the driver's side. "I packed her in with the bath towels."

"No, I mean the one that got stolen with the old car!" cried Tina, pointing. Maria slid behind the wheel and halted, staring. There on the dashboard was the plastic Virgin of Guadalupe, robed in the starry heavens, crowned in the glory of the setting sun.

"If that isn't a miracle, I don't know what is," said Tina, wiping away a tear. "You see? Everything's going to be all right now. It's a sign that somebody's watching over us."

Maria nodded slowly.

"I guess so. Fasten your seat belt, *mi hija.*"

She closed the door, fastened her own seat belt, adjusted the mirrors. Pulling carefully out into traffic, she headed for the nearest freeway on ramp.

Unseen, five cars behind her in a Lincoln Continental, Porfirio followed.

STANDING IN HIS LIGHT

The country was so flat its inhabitants had four different words for *horizon*. Its sunlight was watery, full of tumbling clouds. Canals cut across a vast wet chaos of tidal mud, connecting tidy redbrick towns with straight streets, secure and well ordered behind walls. The houses were all alike behind their stepped façades, high windows set in pairs letting through pale light on rooms scrubbed and spotless. The people who lived in the rooms were industrious, pious, and preoccupied with money.

A fantasist might decide that they were therefore dull, smug, and inherently unromantic, the sort of people among whom the Hero might be born, but against whom he would certainly rebel, and from whom he would ultimately escape to follow his dreams.

Nothing could have been further from the truth. The people who lived in the houses above the placid mud flats had fought like demons against their oppressors, and were now in the midst of a philosophical and artistic flowering of such magnificence that their names would be written in gold in all the arts.

Still, they had to make a living. And making a living is a hard, dirty, and desperate business.

The Inn, 1659

The weaver's son and the draper's son sat at a small table. They had been passing back and forth a pipe of tobacco slightly adulterated with hemp, and, now it was smoked out, were attempting to keep the buzz going with two pots of beer. It wasn't proving successful. The weaver's son, thin and threadbare, was nervously eyeing his guest and trying to summon the courage to make a business proposition. The draper's son, reasonably well fed and dressed, seemed in a complacent mood.

"So you learned a thing or two about lenses in Amsterdam, eh?" said the weaver's son.

"I'd have gone blind if I hadn't," replied the draper's son, belching gently. "Counting threads on brocade? You can't do it without a magnifying glass."

"I had this idea," said the weaver's son. "Involving lenses, see. Have you looked at de Hooch's paintings lately? He's using a *camera obscura* for his interiors. They're the greatest thing—"

"You know my Latin's no good," said the draper's son. "What's a *camera obscura*, anyway?"

"All the words mean is *dark room*," explained the weaver's son. "It's a trick device, a box with two lenses and a focusing tube. The Italians invented it. Solves all problems of perspective drawing! You don't have to do any math, no calculations to get correct angles of view. It captures an image and throws a little picture of it on your canvas, and all you have to do is trace over it. It's like magic!"

"And you want me to loan you the money for one?" asked the draper's son, looking severe.

"No! I just thought, er, if you knew about lenses, you might want to help me make one," said the weaver's son, flushing. "And then I'd cut you in for a share of the paintings I sell afterward."

"But your stuff doesn't sell," said the draper's son.

"But it would sell, if I had a *camera obscura*! See, that's my problem, getting perspective right," argued the weaver's son. "That was the problem with my *Procuress*. I'm no good with math."

"That's certainly true."

"But the device would solve all that. I've got a whole new line of work planned: no more Bible scenes. I'm going to do ladies and soldiers in rooms, like de Hooch and Metsu are doing. The emblem stuff with hidden meanings, that people can puzzle over. That's what everyone wants, and it's selling like crazy now," said the weaver's son.

The draper's son sighed and drained his beer.

"Look, Jan," he said. "Your father died broke. He made good silk cloth, he ran a pretty decent inn; if he'd stayed out of the art business he'd have done all right for himself. Our fathers were friends, so I'm giving you advice for nothing: you won't make a living by painting. I know it's what you've always wanted to do, and I'm not saying you're not good—but the others are better, and there are a lot of them. And you're not very original, you know."

The weaver's son scowled. He was on the point of telling the draper's son to go to Hell when a shadow fell across their table.

"I'm very sorry to interrupt, *Mynheeren*," said the woman. They looked up at her. The weaver's son stared, struck by the image she presented, the way the light from the window fell on her white coif, glittered along the line of brass beads on her sleeve, the way the layered shadows modeled her serene face.

"What do you want?" asked the draper's son. She didn't look like a whore; she looked like any one of the thousand respectable young matrons who were even now peeling apples in a thousand kitchens. What, then, was she doing in the common room of a shabby inn on the market square?

"Well, I couldn't help but overhear that you two young gentlemen were talking about making a *camera obscura*. And, I said to myself, isn't that the strangest coincidence! Really, when a coincidence this remarkable occurs it's got to be the work of God or the holy angels, at least that was what my mother used to say, so then I said to myself, whether it's quite polite or not, I'll just have to go over there and introduce myself! Elisabeth Van Drouten, gentlemen, how do you do?"

And she drew up a three-legged stool, and sat, and thumped her covered basket down on the table. Looking from one to the other of the men, she whisked off the cover. There, nestled in a linen kerchief, were a handful of objects that shone like big water drops, crystal-clear, domed, gleaming.

"Lenses!" cried *Mevrouw* Van Drouten triumphantly. "What do you think of that?"

The two gentlemen blinked at them like owls, and the draper's son reached into the basket and held one up to the light.

"Nice lenses," he admitted. "Are you selling them?"

"Not exactly," said *Mevrouw* Van Drouten. "It's a long story. There's a friend of my family's in Amsterdam, actually that's where I'm from, you could probably tell from my accent, yes? Well, anyway, he grinds lenses, this friend of mine. And because he got in trouble with his family—and then later on the Jews kicked him out of their synagogue for something, I'm not sure what it was all about, but anyway, bang, there went poor Spinoza's inheritance. So we were trying to help him out by selling some of his lenses, you see?

"So last time I was here in Delft visiting my auntie, which was, let's see, I guess it was five years ago now, I brought some lenses to see if I could sell them, which I did when I was at my cousin's tavern to this nice man who was maybe a little drunk at the time, and I understood him to say he was a painter and wanted them for optical effects. Fabritius, that was his name!"

The two men grunted. In a gesture that had become involuntary for citizens of their town, they both turned to the northeast and raised their beers in salute. The woman watched them, her brows knitted.

"He died in the explosion," the weaver's son explained.

"Oh! Yes, the 'Delft Thunderclap,' we called it," said *Mevrouw* Van Drouten, nodding her head. "When your city powder magazine went *blooie*! Awful tragedy. And that's what my cousin said, when I went back to her tavern yesterday. That poor Fabritius had been so drunk that he left the packet of lenses on the table, and he never came back to get them because the explosion happened the next day. So she kept them until she saw me again. And I said, 'What am I supposed to do with them now? He paid for them, so I don't feel right keeping them,' and she said, 'Well, Elisabeth, why don't you find some other painters to give them to?' And I said, 'Where would I find some other painters?' and she said, 'Try that inn over in the market square,' so I came straight over, and here you are, fellow artists, I guess, eh? Maybe you knew Fabritius?"

"I did," said the weaver's son. "He was a genius."

"Well then! I'm sure he'd want you to have these, wouldn't he?"

The weaver's son reached into the basket and the lenses rattled, clicked softly as he drew one out. He peered at the tiny rainbowed point of light it threw. It magnified wildly the lines of his palm, the yellow hairs on the back of his hand. He held it up to the window and saw his thumbprint become a vast swirl etched in silver. The draper's son held his lens up beside it.

"Ooh!" *Mevrouw* Van Drouten clasped her hands in pleasure. "I wish I could capture this moment, somehow. Can't help thinking it's portentous, in a way I can't explain. Fabritius's ghost is probably smiling down from heaven at you two fine young fellows. Now you can build your *camera obscura*, eh? And maybe find one or two other uses for the lenses."

"Are you sure you want to give them away?" said the draper's son, a little vaguely because he was still entranced by the play of rainbows across crystal. The buzz from the hemp hadn't quite vanished.

"Quite sure," said *Mevrouw* Van Drouten cheerfully. She spilled the remaining lenses out on the table and stood, tucking her empty basket under her arm. "There. Much as I'd love to stay and chat, I've got a boat to catch. *Mynheer* Leeuwenhoek, *Mynheer* Vermeer, may God keep you both."

Then she was gone, as suddenly and inexplicably as she'd arrived. The weaver's son tore his gaze away from the liquid contours of the piled lenses and looked around. The light still streamed in, clear and soft, but the room was empty save for a drunk snoring on a bench in the corner.

In the twenty-fourth century, it was unanimously conceded by art authorities that Jan Vermeer was the greatest painter who had ever lived.

The other Dutch masters had long since been dismissed from popular taste. Rembrandt didn't suit because his work was too muddy, too dark, too full of soldiers, and too *big*, and who wanted to look at Bible pictures anyway in an enlightened age? To say nothing of the fact that his brushstrokes were sloppy. Franz Hals painted too many dirty-looking, grimacing people, and his brushstrokes were even sloppier. The whole range of still life paintings of food were out: too many animal or fish corpses, too many bottles of alcohol. Then, too, a preoccupation with food might lead the viewer to obesity, which was immoral, after all!

Had they known of their demotion, the old gentlemen of Amsterdam and Utrecht might not have felt too badly; for by the twenty-fourth century, the whole of Medieval art had been condemned for its religious content, as had the works of the masters of the Italian Renaissance. The French Impressionists were considered incoherent and sleazy, the Spanish morbid, the Germans *entartete*, and the Americans frivolous. Almost nothing from the twentieth or twenty-first centuries was acceptable. Primitive art was grudgingly accepted as politically correct, as long as it didn't deal in objectionable subjects like sex, religion, war, or animal abuse, but the sad fact was that it generally did, so there wasn't a lot of it on view.

But who could find fault with the paintings of Jan Vermeer?

It was true he'd done a couple of religious paintings in his youth, before his style had become established. The subject matter of his *Procuress* was forbidden, but it too was atypical of the larger body of his work. And his *Diana and her Companions* was enthusiastically accepted by the Ephesian Church as proof that Vermeer had been a secret initiate of the Goddess, and since the Ephesians were about the only faith left with political power or indeed much of a following, the painting was allowed to remain in catalogs.

There was, of course, the glaring problem of the *Servant Pouring Milk*. But, since Vermeer's original canvases hadn't been seen in years due to their advanced state of deterioration, it was no more than the work of a few keystrokes to delete the mousetrap from the painting's background and, more important, alter the stream of proscribed dairy product so it was no longer white, in order that the painting might henceforth be referred to as *Girl Pouring Water*. This would avoid any reference to the vicious exploitation of cows.

Those objections having been dealt with, Vermeer was universally loved.

He glorified science—look at his *Astronomer* and *Surveyor*! He was obviously in favor of feminism, or why would he have depicted so many quiet, dignified women engaged in reading and writing letters? There were, to be sure, a couple of paintings of women drinking with cavaliers, but everyone was decorously clad and upright, and anyway the titles had been changed to things like *Girl with Glass of Apple Juice* or *Couple Drinking Lemonade*. He valued humble domestic virtues, it was clear, but refrained from cluttering up his paintings with children, as his contemporary de Hoogh had done. All in all his morality, as perceived by his post-postmodern admirers, suited the twenty-fourth century perfectly.

They liked the fact that his paintings looked real, too. The near-photographic treatment of a subject was now considered the ultimate in good taste. An orange should look like an orange! The eventual backlash against Modern Art had been so extreme as to relegate Picasso and Pollock to museum basements. Maxfield Parrish and the brothers Hildebrandt might have been popular, had they not unfortunately specialized in fantasy (read *demonic*) themes, and David painted too many naked dead people. So, with the exception of a few landscape painters and the flower paintings of Delongpre, Vermeer was pretty much the undisputed ruler of popular art.

Having been dead nearly seven centuries, however, it is unlikely he cared.

The Room Upstairs, 1661

The *camera obscura* had worked, after a fashion. The image hadn't been especially bright, muzzily like a stained-glass window out of focus, but Jan had been able to sharpen it up by sealing all the gaps in the cabinet with pieces of black felt. All he had to do then was set up the picture: so he tried a variation on a popular piece by Maes, *The Lazy Maid.*

Catharina obligingly posed at the table, pretending to sleep. Above her, Jan hung the old painting of Cupid from the stock his father had been unable to sell. Beside her was the view through to the room where the dog posed with simpleton Willem, both of them apparently fascinated by circling flies. Jan had laid their one Turkey carpet on the table, and carefully set out the symbolic objects that would give the painting its disguised meaning, to be deciphered by the viewer: the jug and wineglass to imply drunkenness, the bowl of fruit to suggest the sin of Eve, the egg to symbolize lust.

"Why don't these things ever have anything good to say about ladies?" Catharina complained.

"Damned if I know," Jan told her, adjusting her right arm so she was resting her head on her hand. "But it's what the customers want. Hold it like that, see? That symbolizes sloth."

"Oh, yes, I know all about sloth," she retorted, without opening her eyes. "I'm a real woman of leisure, aren't I?"

"Mama, the baby's awake," little Maria informed them cautiously, edging into the room.

"See if you can rock her back to sleep, then."

"But she's really awake," Maria insisted, wringing her hands.

"Then give her a toy or something! Just don't let her cry."

"All right." Maria left the room. Catharina opened one eye and glared at Jan.

"If she starts crying, I'll run like a fountain, and that'll ruin this gown, and it's my best one! Unless you can get me a pair of sponges in a hurry," she said.

"I'll be as fast as I can." Jan retreated into the black cabinet with his palette.

Working quickly, despite the panicky realization that he'd installed the cabinet too far away from the light of the window, he roughed out everything he could see in a few wide swipes of the brush, applying the pale paint thinly. The main thing here was to get the perspective nailed down. Afterward there would be plenty of time to lavish on color and detail . . .

A thin wailing floated into the room. He saw the reflected image of Catharina sit upright, saw her eyes snap open, saw her clutch at her bodice.

"Jan, I've got to go," she said, and fled from the sight of the lens.

Six weeks later, he sat at the easel and contemplated his *Girl Asleep* sadly.

It hadn't worked. The perspective was correct, certainly, the *camera obscura* had done its job there; but left to himself he hadn't been able to nail down the direction from which the light ought to be coming. Was it strong sunset light coming through a nonexistent window? Firelight? Was it in front of the table or to one side? What was lighting the room beyond, where he'd finally settled for painting out Willem and the dog?

Growling to himself, he took a bit of lead-tin yellow on his brush and picked out a pattern of brass tackheads on the back of the chair. Halfway through the job he stopped and considered it. No, because if the light was falling *on* the table—

"Papa?" Maria came up to him.

"You're standing in my light, baby," he told her, gently nudging her to one side.

"I'm sorry, Papa. There's a lady to see you."

He came instantly alert, started to sweat. "Is it about a bill?"

"No, Papa, I asked." Maria raised her little pinched face to his. "Because then I would have said you were out. But she wants to buy something. That would be a good thing, wouldn't it? So I told her she could come up."

"But—" Jan looked up in panic as *Mevrouw* Van Drouten swept into the room, basket over her arm.

"Good day, *Mynheer*!" she cried gaily. "I see you remember me. So this is where you work, eh? And there's the *camera obscura*! Yes, that's a nice big one, but are you sure you don't want to move it closer to the windows?" She came straight to his shoulder and bent to look at the painting. "Yes, you definitely want to move it over. The light didn't work out at all in this one, did it? Nice painting, though."

"Thank you—but—" He rose clumsily, wiping his brush with a rag. "If you've come to buy, I'm afraid this one is already sold. I've got to deliver it to the baker. I have a lot of fine paintings by other artists, though, and they're for sale! Would you perhaps like to see—?"

"No, no." *Mevrouw* Van Drouten held up her hand. "I had a commission in mind, if you want to know."

"Certainly, *Mevrouw*," Jan exclaimed. "Can I offer you—" He halted, mortified to realize he was unable to offer her anything but bread and butter.

"That's all right," she told him. "I didn't come here to eat." She reached into her basket and brought out a small paper parcel. Turning with a smile, she offered it to Maria. "There you go: *spekulaas* with almonds! Baked this morning. You run along and share them with the little brothers and sisters, yes? Papa and I have to talk in quiet."

"Thank you," said Maria, wide-eyed. She exited and, with some effort as she clutched the parcel, pulled the door shut after her. If the big lady wanted privacy, Maria would make sure she had it, so long as she bought something. A painting sold meant Mama and Papa not shouting at each other, and no dirty looks from the grocer.

Mevrouw Van Drouten pulled up a chair. She paused a moment to smile at the little carved lion heads on its back rest. Seating herself, she crossed her arms and leaned forward.

"This commission of mine is a bit unusual, dear sir. My late husband was an alchemist—well, actually, he kept a lodging house, but alchemy was his hobby, you see? Always fussing with stinky stuff in a back room, blowing off his eyebrows with small explosions now and then, breaking pots and bottles every time. Geraert, I told him, you'll put an eye out one of these days! And of course he never made any gold. About all he ever came up with was a kind of invisible ink, except that it's no good as ink, because it's too thick. Well, he poisoned himself at last, wasn't trying to commit suicide so far as we could tell but he was still just as dead, there you are, and left me with nothing but the house and a book full of cryptic scribbling and that one formula for invisible ink, only it's more of an invisible paste, and what good's that to a spy, I said to myself?"

"I'm so sorry, *Mevrouw*," said Jan, feeling his head spin at her relentless flow of words.

"Oh, that's all right. I'm containing my grief. The thing is, I figured out a use for the invisible stuff." She leaned back and, from under the cloth, drew out another parcel. This one was a flat rectangle, about the size of a thin account book. It was tightly wrapped in black felt and fastened with string. Holding it up for Jan to see, she said: "This is a little canvas that's been coated in it."

She set it on the table and reached into the basket again, drawing out a small covered pot and a brush. "This is the reagent. If the ink was worth a damn as ink, this would make hidden messages appear when you brushed it on. I think we can do something better, though."

"What are you talking about?" Jan asked, wondering if she were a little crazy. "And what has this got to do with me?"

"You've got a *camera obscura*, that's what it's got to do with you, and you're a painter, besides. You've got flint but no steel. I've got steel but no flint. If the two of us got together over some tinder, though, I'll bet we could make a nice little fire," said *Mevrouw* Van Drouten. "I'll show you. You go stand in front of the cabinet and put your hand over the lens, eh? Nice and tight, so it's pitch-black inside."

Mystified, Jan obeyed nonetheless, cupping the palm of his hand over the focusing tube. *Mevrouw* Van Drouten moved rapidly to the cabinet, carrying what she'd brought, and stepped inside and closed the door.

"Oh, my, this is nice and dark! You did a good job. We'll need to seal it up a little more, that's all. Now, what I'm doing is unwrapping my little canvas . . ." He heard a rustling and thumping from inside the cabinet. "Here's where you put your pictures, obviously. Very good. Now, *Mynheer*, keep your hand on the tube but back away at arm's length, yes? And when I give the signal, drop your hand, but stand perfectly still there."

"What'll happen?"

"Well, eventually, guilders will rain out of the sky on us. No, that's just my little joke! Are you ready? Now!"

Jan dropped his hand. Nothing happened. He was relieved.

"Don't move," *Mevrouw* Van Drouten admonished him in a muffled voice. "Just stay like that. I'm counting to sixty. Wait."

When a minute had passed, she said: "Now, quickly, put your hand back."

He obeyed. He heard more bustling and thumping from within the cabinet, and a gentle splashing; then the room filled with an acrid smell that made his throat contract. He heard *Mevrouw* Van Drouten sneeze.

"Whew! Nasty stuff. We'll want to open the windows after this. Oh, but, yes! Here we go! Just a minute more. You should make a cap for the tube so you don't have to keep doing that with the hand, you know, maybe out of a sheet of lead? And lined with more of the black felt. Oh, hurray! Here, my friend, now you'll see I'm not at all mad."

Mevrouw Van Drouten emerged smiling from the cabinet in a blast of chemical fume, waving her little canvas. She thrust it at him. "Looky!"

It was a moment before Jan realized what he was seeing.

The canvas appeared to have been primed with a pale gray undercoat. On it, rendered in various grays ranging from silvery to charcoal, was the portrait of a man. He was staring out at the viewer with a doubtful expression. Behind his right shoulder was a wall, with a corner of a painting in its frame, the naked leg of Cupid just visible—

"Jesus God!" Jan shouted, having recognized himself at last.

"The stuff on the canvas reacts to light, you see?" chortled *Mevrouw* Van Drouten. "The way words drawn in lemon juice react to a flatiron! You just slap it on a canvas, expose it to light—*and the picture draws itself!*

"At least, it does as soon as you brush on a coat of reagent," she added, sneezing again.

Jan held the picture close, wrinkling his nose at the smell but unable to look away from it. Every detail, perfect and exact, as though—

"As though God Himself had painted it, yes?" said *Mevrouw* Van Drouten, watching his face. "We can make a lot of money out of this, my friend, wouldn't you say?"

"I haven't got a guilder to invest," said Jan reluctantly.

"Who needs to invest? We want to keep this a secret, yes? Or we'll have Saint Luke's Guild bringing a lawsuit against us on behalf of painters everywhere," said *Mevrouw* Van Drouten. Jan, pacing back and forth with the portrait, only half heard her.

"Not only the problems of perspective solved," he said, "but the lighting problems, too! God in Heaven, look at it! It's the perfect study for a portrait. You could take as long as you needed with this—wouldn't matter if your model had to get up to feed the baby, wouldn't matter if you lost the day-light! It's all laid out before you, permanent!" He turned to look at her in awe. She smiled at him and, from the seemingly bottomless basket, drew forth a bottle of wine.

"Shall we drink to our partnership?"

Over a convivial couple of glasses, they worked out the details of their arrangement. *Mevrouw* Van Drouten would mix the secret formula herself, and purchase and prepare the canvases. She would have them delivered, along with a supply of the reagent, to Jan, who would capture images on them and then complete the paintings. He would return the finished can-vases to her and receive half the proceeds when she found a buyer.

There were complications, of course. The images would only appear if the canvas received limited, focused exposure to light, which was why the *camera obscura* was necessary. Take a prepared canvas out of its wrapping in an open room and all it would show, when the reagent was brushed on, would be a uniform dark surface. The reagent was poisonous, the fumes mustn't be inhaled for long, so it was a good idea not to take more than one image a day, and best to leave a window open. The cabinet must be moved to the corner under the windows, to take the most advantage of daylight, but every crack and sliver of light visible inside must be covered over. Also, the images weren't truly permanent; left in the air they would fade to nothing, so it was vital that he begin painting over them as soon as he could after the images developed.

Because it was a secret formula, no one was to know about the use to which the *camera obscura* was being put. This meant that Jan must take no pupils, and entertain few guests. Poor as he was, this wasn't much of a problem.

And *Mevrouw* Van Drouten would decide what was painted.

"I know what the public likes," Jan protested.

"I'm sure you do, my friend. But I have a particular customer in mind, you see, and I know his tastes! A rich old doctor in Amsterdam, a collector in fact, but he's very particular about what he buys. No religious scenes, for example—he's a bit of an atheist," *Mevrouw* Van Drouten explained. "Likes pretty girls but in a nice way, you know what I mean? No boobs sticking out, no whores. Likes scholarly stuff. By the way, how's your friend Leeuwen-hoek? Seen him lately?"

"Not much," said Jan, feeling uncomfortable. "We move in different cir-cles nowadays. The friendship was more between our fathers, really. But he took a lot of those lenses you gave us. I think he's fooling around with lens-grinding himself, now, as a hobby."

"How nice," said Mevrouw Van Drouten.

"HEARST NEWS SERVICES UPDATE!" cried the bright electronic voice, as, in a million wells of dark air below holoprojectors, a million clouds of light formed and focused into the image of a reporter. She smiled and told the world: "Really important discovery! Look! Old paintings by Vermeer found!"

She vanished, and in her place appeared a five-second clip of footage showing first the entrance to a salt mine somewhere, then a bemused-looking miner poking his torch into what was evidently the newly made entrance to a previously hidden cave, and a closer shot of rows of flat stacked bundles.

The footage ended abruptly and the woman reappeared. "Some old salt mine in Europe! How'd they get there? Maybe it was Hitler! Who's Ver-meer? He painted this!"

Behind her appeared an enlargement of the *Girl Pouring Water*. In a mil-lion homes and public gathering places, viewers grunted in recognition.

"See? So this is really important. Lots of paintings found that *nobody knew about!*" The woman's eyes widened significantly. "Experts speak!"

Another clip of footage appeared, showing a man in a white lab coat saying: "They're real Vermeers, all right—"

The footage ended. The woman reappeared, crying: "Buried treasure for the art world!" Then she vanished, briefly replaced by the logo of Hearst News Services before it too vanished, leaving viewers blinking at the darkness.

This had been an extraordinarily long and in-depth piece of coverage; but, of course, it wasn't every day that lost masterpieces were found. This was big news. The art world of the twenty-fourth century, what there was of it, was all agog. Even the ordinary citizens were impressed. On the public transports, many a commuter turned hesitantly to his or her fellow passenger and ventured some remark like: "Isn't that something, about those lost paintings?"

And the fellow passenger, instead of shrinking away and ringing for a Public Health Monitor, would actually nod in agreement and might even venture to reply something like: "Really amazing!"

Even the transport's assigned Public Health Monitor, watching them narrowly, would silently agree: this was really amazing.

The world's moneyed elite had much more to say about it, of course, because they knew more big words.

"How much?" Catchpenny barked into his communicator.

"They'll be auctioned," replied Eeling. "But it'll run into the billions, I can tell you that right now. You've got until autumn to raise the money."

"*This* autumn? I thought there'd be lawsuits! Don't tell me the Bohemians have settled ownership that fast."

"Actually, they have. There was documentation with them. The whole collection was taken from some old family by Goering's art people. Just stolen; no money changed hands. There's a living descendant with proof. All the Bohemians are doing is fining her for back inheritance taxes."

"But what about verification? They might be more, what was the man's name? Van Meegerens? Forgeries."

"They're in the labs. Five have already been pronounced authentic. X-rays, all the chemical tests. The rest are expected to pass, too. Seventy canvases, Catchpenny!"

Catchpenny caught his breath. "There isn't that much money in the world." But he felt gleeful, lightheaded.

"I've already made your bid for the print rights. Sell your house."

"Yes!" Catchpenny ordered up a list of Realtors' commcodes and eye-circled three of them. "Find out who else is bidding, and make the usual arrangements."

"That will run into money, too," said Eeling cautiously, after a momentary pause during which she had ordered up a private list of commcodes for certain persons who did necessary, if unsavory, things at a price.

"Doesn't matter!"

"Agreed." Eeling signed out. The less discussion now, the better.

One week later, Hearst News Services featured a ten-second newsdab mentioning that exclusive print rights for the new Vermeers had gone to a prestigious gallery in London, but did not mention the name.

The Kitchen, 1665

"It's wonderful," said *Mevrouw* Van Drouten. "But I can only give you a hundred guilders for it."

"But it's worth more than that!" Catharina cried. "Look at all the detail!" She tilted *The Lens Grinder* forward. "You know how long it took to set up that scene? We had to borrow all the lens-grinding tools. My poor brother had to be dressed and made to sit still, which is miserably hard, let me tell you. And it's a big canvas!"

"My dear, I know. I think it's worth a couple of hundred at least, but what can I do?" *Mevrouw* Van Drouten opened her wide blue eyes in a frank stare. "It's not my money. The Doctor gives me a hundred and tells me to bring home a painting. It's not my fault he's a wretched old miser. At least he buys from you, eh? Cash instead of trade to the grocer."

Catharina, knowing she was defeated, pursed her lips and set *The Lens Grinder* on a piece of sacking, preparing to wrap it for transport. A dismal screaming erupted from the next room, and a tempest burst in at knee level: fat Beatrix running from little Jan, clutching a mug of soapy water that slopped as she fled.

"*I* want bubbles," little Jan was roaring. Now in close pursuit came Maria, burdened by the infant she lugged in its long gown, too late to prevent Jan from slipping in the spill and falling flat. His roaring went up in volume.

"Oh, look what you did—" she wailed, and her eyes widened in horror as she saw the adults. "Mama's *working*," she told the little ones, grabbing Jan by the back of his skirts with one fist and bending double as she strained to haul him backward out of the room. Catharina turned a basilisk stare on Beatrix, who gulped and exited swiftly. Maria paused in her dragging to smile frantically at Van Drouten.

"How nice to see you again, *Mevrouw*," she panted. "Wasn't that a nice picture Daddy did this time? I knew you'd like it, and we really need the money—"

"Jannekin, get up this instant," said Catharina, and the little boy left off yelling and scrambled out of the room on hands and knees.

"I must be going, please excuse me," said Maria in an attempt at adult gentility, and curtsied, nearly dropping the baby. "I'm sorry, Mama, but he wanted to drink the bubble stuff and—"

"Not now," said Catharina.

"Yes, Mama. God go with you, *Mevrouw* Van Drouten."

Mevrouw Van Drouten bit her lip.

"I'll tell you what," she said to Catharina. "I'll give you a hundred and fifty for it, if you'll throw in this little one for fifty." She held up a head-and-shoulders portrait of Maria. Catharina glanced at it.

"Done," she said at once. It had been nothing more than a test shot on a cloudy day, to see if there was enough light for a serious portrait. Maria had obligingly donned the yellow bodice and posed with a loaf of bread, offering it out to the viewer with an eager expression on her little pale face. There hadn't been enough light, so the shot hadn't really worked, but Jan had gone ahead and wasted paint and time on it anyway: ghost child smiling hopefully in a dark room. Catharina took the little canvas and tossed it down on the larger one, nesting it behind the wooden stretchers, and tied the sacking over them with string knotted tight.

"And here," Van Drouten said, remembering the paper parcel and drawing it forth from her basket. "Here's a dozen almond biscuits, enough for two each, eh? So they don't fight over them."

"You must have had children of your own," said Catharina.

"Hundreds," said Van Drouten absently. "I'd like to buy more of the pictures, you know. I love them. If the Doctor gave me a bigger budget, I'd take everything Jan cranked out."

"He's an old fool, your Doctor," Catharina said. *Mevrouw* Van Drouten shrugged.

"Maybe, but he knows what he likes, and he has money," she replied.

"And that's what counts," said Catharina, smiling as Van Drouten opened her purse.

In the studio upstairs, Jan paced and wondered if Catharina was presenting his complaints as he'd asked her to do.

For the first year or so, he'd enjoyed the work: the endless experiments with lighting, the race to capture the evanescent gray images in color by painting directly over them, the thrill of seeing perspective effortlessly perfect on canvas after canvas. Canvas after canvas after canvas . . .

But the novelty wore off, especially with the limit in his choice of sub-jects. All *Mevrouw* Van Drouten's client wanted to see was the same sub-ject, repeated in endless variation: a calm woman standing under a window, doing something industrious. Sometimes even that subject failed to please. The painting of Catharina's sister pouring milk in the kitchen, what had been wrong with that? But Van Drouten had shaken her head re-gretfully, said it was fine but declined to buy. Likewise the painting of Maria with the lute. And why did everything have to be in tones of ultra-marine blue and yellow?

Though Van Drouten had explained about that: it seemed her client, the mysterious Doctor, had a lot of his furniture upholstered in blue and yel-low, and so he wanted paintings hanging in his rooms to match. Jan hadn't mixed a good warm red in years now. It was all he could do to sneak a few terracotta jugs into a background.

He got occasional relief when the Doctor decided to order what *Mevrouw* Van Drouten referred to as a *scientific* picture, which involved a man under a window with the trappings of a particular field of study. Even though it meant coaxing Willem into costume and persuading him to sit still, and then rushing to catch the shot before he broke the tools in his hands, at least it was different. Even so, Jan could not for the life of him understand why *Mevrouw* Van Drouten had passed on the *Surveyor*, or the *Astronomer*. But she had; again, that regretful head shake, and the inexplicable remark that some paintings had to make it into the history books.

He bit his nails, now, looking at his half-finished work ranged around the room. There were the two studies of *Girl Wearing a Turban*, the lighting dummy he'd set up with Maria in costume and the real painting, for which he'd used pretty Isabella from next door. Catharina wearing the blue bodice and slicing bread: Catharina wearing the yellow bodice and picking out tunes on the virginal. Catharina waving angrily at a moth, in the tatty jacket with its once-elegant fur . . .

He heard the relentlessly pleasant voice flowing out into the street, bid-ding Catharina good day at last, and he stepped swiftly to the door of his studio. He listened for the slam of the front door before emerging onto the landing, and as Catharina mounted toward him he demanded: "Well? What did she say?"

Catharina looked him in the eye, and he looked away.

"You didn't tell her," he muttered.

"No, I didn't tell her! For the love of God, Jan, what am I supposed to do?" she cried. "Do you want to eat? Do you want your children to eat? It's the only money we've got coming in, and you want to lose even that much because you're *bored*? Lord Jesus!"

"It isn't that it's boring," he shouted back. "My art's been killed, do you understand at all? She gave me an eye that could see like God and then shut me up in a room where there was nothing, almost nothing to look at, so the gift is useless! It's wrecked my soul!"

"Then go dig ditches for a living," Catharina told him. "Better still, send me out to dig ditches, eh? With the girls? And you can paint whatever your heart desires, then. Get your womenfolk earning your bread and waiting on you hand and foot, just so long as your painting goes well. Who needs a rich patron? Not us."

She said it wearily, almost without bitterness nowadays, and turned away and went back down the stairs.

"It isn't art," he shouted after her.

"I know that," she replied. "But it's money."

He drew breath to shout a retort, and went into a coughing fit instead. That was another problem with the damned picture business; the fumes from the magic developing fluid were eating into his lungs. He retreated into his studio and collapsed into one of the lion-headed chairs, staring at the *camera obscura* with loathing.

But he could never really manage to loathe the canvases, dull as they were. Within the hour he was on his feet again, back at the easel, clouding the lead-tin yellow with white and making the fall of sunlight ever more softly luminous, ever more subtly the light of Eden before sin arose in the garden to ruin everything . . . and pale Maria, backlit by yesterday's sun, stood in yesterday's room and offered for inspection the white apple, her young face solemn. The long pared curl of peel at her foot suggested the Old Serpent, trampled and crushed at last perhaps, the secret allegory doubled upon itself, sin and redemption in one . . .

The sigh of the brush became the only sound, drowned out bells that marked the passing hours. He didn't need food. He didn't need drink. All he really needed was this room, wasn't that so?

And the light.

––––––––

"Calvin Sharpey for Hearst News Services!" cried that celebrity, striking a pose for the kameramen. He flashed the brightest of smiles, waved his microphone (it was a dummy, ceremonial and functionless as a scepter, studded with rhinestones; kameramen had been picking up both image and audio for generations now) at the woman beside him, and went on: "Look! Hearst 'sclusive interview! This is the lady who owns the old paintings! Auction today! Liz Van Drouten, what do you think?"

"Well, I hope that some of them will go to museums here in Euro—"

"Hearst News Services making a bid for holomuseum rights!" Calvin announced. "Hoping to bring the art of Jim Vermeer to you, the public!"

"Jan Vermeer," said the woman, quietly, but the kameramen Heard her.

"So! Wasn't it really amazing about your ancestors having all these in some castle or something? And nobody knew? It sure was different back then!"

"Yes, it was," Van Drouten agreed.

"Think maybe Jim was a friend of your family? Maybe hiding from Hitler?"

"No," Van Drouten explained, "You're getting your history mixed up, my dear. Jan Vermeer and Hitler lived two centuries apart."

"Wow! That is *so* much old stuff!" Calvin winked knowingly at the kameramen. He sang a snatch of that week's popular tune: "Can't get it into my *pooor little heaaad*! Pretty but dumb, folks, what can I tell you? Here's another look at the paintings on auction today!"

The kameramen relaxed, turning away as the prerecorded montage of paintings ran. Calvin Sharpey dropped his flashy smile and shouted for a glass of water, ignoring Van Drouten, who remained on her mark. She merely adjusted the drape of the gray gown that had been cut to make her look as dull as possible, a nonentity the audience would forget thirty seconds after her interview had ended, especially when contrasted with Calvin Sharpey's rhinestones.

Now the montage was ending, to judge from the way the kameramen stiffened and swung their blank avid faces back to center stage. Immediately *on* again, Calvin Sharpey grabbed the pasteboard sheet his PA handed him. He held it up—it was a color print of the *Girl with Pearl Earring*, with the face cut away to an oval hole—and thrust his face through, mugging as the kameramen focused on him again.

"Welcome baa—aack!" he said. "It's Calvin Sharpey! Weren't those paintings really something?"

In a high, dark, and distant room, someone stopped pacing and regarded the floating image of Calvin Sharpey's magnified smirk.

"Fire that dumb son of a bitch," said a cold soft voice.

"Right away, Mr. Hearst," said somebody else, running to a communications console, and, five minutes later on the other side of the globe, Van Drouten watched with interest as Calvin Sharpey was hustled off between two men in gray suits, protesting loudly, but the kameramen had done with him, and with her, too; they were turning away, closing like glassy-eyed wolves to See the media event of the year: the auction of the lost Vermeers.

Unnecessary now, Van Drouten faded into the sidelines, unnoticed behind the kameramen and the security forces. To be perfectly honest, she had no mystic powers of invisibility whatsoever: just fifteen centuries' worth of experience at letting mortals see only what she intended them to see. Liz Van Drouten had been an interesting role, but there wasn't much left of her. Two or three publicity shots, perhaps, before she could drop from sight, and a brief post-auction interview, when she would mention that she had decided to donate to charity whatever fabulous sum the auction had raised.

This was a lie, of course. All the proceeds were going straight into the coffers of her masters in the Company, and seven centuries of careful planning would pay off at last. But the words *charity* and *donation* tended to deflect an audience's interest.

Van Drouten sighed, looking out over the faces of the crowd that waited to bid. Some watched the podium with fixed stares, willing the clock to speed up; some whispered together behind their bidding fans, or peered around at the competition to assess them. To a man and woman, they might have stepped out of one of Daumier's engravings, might have been models for Rapacity personified, Desire, Obsession, whole-hearted Need. Van Drouten thought they were sad, and rather endearing. But then, she had always liked mortals and their passions.

There were so few passions left in this day and age.

So she savored the murmur that ran through the crowd, the audible pounding of seventy mortal hearts, the hissed or caught breath as the auctioneer stepped up to the podium at last. Intent as lovers, the kameramen dove close, Saw his rising hammer and Heard him as he drew breath and said: "Ladies and gentlemen! May I draw your attention to Item Number One?"

And it lit on the black screen behind him, the projected image of Vermeer's *Girl with Peeled Apple.* Van Drouten smiled involuntarily: there was young Maria again, greeting her across the dead centuries.

"Jan Vermeer's original oil on canvas, signed, circa 1668. Includes all rights of reproduction worldwide. Bidding starts at one million pounds, ladies and gentlemen, one million—"

Before he could even repeat the phrase, bidding fans had sprung up like flat flowers in a garden of greed.

The Path to the Tomb, 1673
"See?" *Mevrouw* Van Drouten was telling him gleefully, pointing to the easel. "You don't even have to think anymore. All you have to do is paint them in!"

He tried to reply but the words stuck in his dry mouth. He could only moan in horror at the line of little gray canvases stretching to the horizon, as many as the days of his life; and they were numbered. He couldn't breathe.

"See?" *Mevrouw* Van Drouten put a brush in his hand, a housepainter's brush of all things. "All the spaces marked with a One you paint in blue. All the spaces marked with a Two, you paint in yellow. What could be easier? And look, here, the paint is already mixed for you. But you have to crank them out quickly, or you'll lose the light!"

And with revulsion he felt himself drawn to the canvases, because she was right: he only had so much time before he lost the light. He slapped on the thin color over the meaningless black-and-white images, and *Mevrouw* Van Drouten watched, grinning, but looked constantly over at the clock, the enormous clock, saying: "Not much time. Not much time," but somehow he could never paint fast enough, and meanwhile the house was getting shabbier and more bare, the children thinner, his cough was getting worse, and Catharina was staring at him, crying, "Soup!"

". . . nice soup the lady next door sent, won't you even try?"

"I don't have time, I'll lose the light!" he told her, but she slipped the spoon into his mouth and he realized with a start that he was in bed. Catharina was leaning over him, looking sadly into his eyes. She gave him another spoonful of soup and felt his forehead, felt his stubbled cheeks. Her palm was cool.

"The fever broke, anyway. Did you think you were painting again?" she asked, and gave him another spoonful of soup before he could reply.

"Has she been here?" he demanded, wheezing.

"Who?"

"*Mevrouw* Van Drouten!"

"No, she hasn't. Don't worry, Jan. We can get by the next month or two, if we don't see her."

He lay still a moment, thinking that over, as she fed him soup. "You sold some of the stock," he guessed, noting the bare places on the walls. "You found another buyer!"

She smiled at him, and rubbed her eyes with her free hand. With the light full on her face, as it was, he was struck by how much silver was in her hair, and felt a pang at what she'd endured with him. And still another baby on the way, Jesus God . . . If only they hadn't loved each other.

"A gentleman came to see your stuff," Catharina told him, determinedly cheerful. "I explained we didn't have anything of yours for sale right now, you know, I played up how fast your stuff sells, and I think I've almost got him talked into commissioning something. And he did buy a couple of the old canvases. So, you see? You don't have to depend on the little witch paintings. You're good enough to paint your own work, too."

"As long as it sells."

"It'll sell, my heart."

He pushed himself up on the pillows, took the soup from her in his shaky hands, and tilted the bowl to drink. Handing it back to her, he gasped: "If I can talk him into an allegory—say a nice big canvas, maybe three or four figures on it, eh, that we can get a good price for? Maybe a heroic theme!—Lord God, if only I can stretch my muscles for a little with some reds and violets, won't that be something?"

"I had an idea about going to the priests, too," Catharina told him seriously. "They've got the money for paintings, and they know what's good."

"That's right, they do." He turned and considered his studio. "Can we afford a good sized canvas? Or even paper and charcoal. I'll get ideas, Catsi, I want to be able to block out a study."

"I'll see what I can do," she said, and bent to kiss him. "You sleep some more, now. Think about your allegory. We'll manage this somehow."

Jan lay still listening to her descend the stairs, and tried to close his eyes and sleep again; but the light in the room was too strong. He looked at the beautifully empty spots where the old paintings had been, and his eye filled them with new canvases. Should he rework *Diana and Her Nymphs?* With each figure in a different-colored gown, pink, green, purple! Or something else classical, one of the Muses maybe? Pull out all the stops, lots of little emblematic detail, a painting the viewer could mull over for hours! Or a religious one the priests would be sure to like, yes, say a risen Christ with a robe scarlet as the blood of martyrs . . .

He glanced over at the cabinet resentfully, the black void that had swallowed up so much of his strength, so much of his time. What a devil's bargain! And what a paradox, to spend his days in darkness to preserve the light.

When the idea hit him, it seemed to shake him physically, it was so powerful. He gaped at the blank wall, seeing the allegory there in all its detail. It wasn't *Diana and Her Nymphs* he'd rework, no. Another allegory entirely. It would be his revenge.

Sliding his skinny legs from under the blanket, he staggered upright and found a stick of charcoal. He lurched across the room and braced himself at the wall, blocking in the cartoon in a few quick swipes on the plaster, just far enough to see that his initial instinct for the composition had been correct. The charcoal dust was making him choke; but everything made him choke these days. Dropping the charcoal, he wiped his hands on his nightshirt and looked around for his breeches. This couldn't wait. He needed pen and ink.

Van Drouten walked through the echoing rooms of the old house in the Herengracht, which had been her home for nearly a thousand years. She had run the Company operation out of it, in one mortal disguise or other, since 1434, and every room was furnished with memories.

Here was the parlor where Spinoza had embraced her, before leaving for Rijnsburg; in this chamber, she still had the chair in which Rembrandt had sat when he'd come to supper. Upstairs was the bed in which Casanova, nasty fellow, had romped with her mortal maid. The kitchen had long since been modernized, but still around the baseboard ran the painted tiles at which Van Gogh had stared unseeing, gaunt young man with such good intentions, while he'd wolfed down the hot meal she'd offered him along with advice: that he might serve God best by painting His light.

And here was the broom closet hiding the so-narrow passage leading up to the attic rooms where she'd sheltered so many Jewish children from the Nazis, too many to count as they'd been smuggled through, but she could still summon each little frightened face before her mind's eye.

It was a quiet house, now, in this last age of the world, and her work was nearly over. There were only a handful of Company operatives left on duty in Amsterdam, where once they had come and gone like bees in a hive. Van Drouten sighed as she climbed the stair to her room. She had always liked a noisy house. She liked life. Some immortals grew weary and sick of humanity after a few millennia, but she never had.

Her private quarters, at least, were still comfortable and cluttered. She edged past centuries' worth of souvenirs on her way to the clothes closet, where she slipped out of her gray gown. This time she remembered to take off the little cloisonné pin before she hung it up, the emblem of a clock face without hands, and when she had slipped into denim coveralls she refastened it on the front pocket.

The pin was not a favorite piece of jewelry. Its supposed intent was to honor those who had the job of traveling through time, effectively defeating time's ravages; that was why the clock had no hands. Company policy, however, had recently tightened to require all operatives of her class to wear the badge at all times, to enable them to be readily identified by Company security techs on Company property.

Van Drouten avoided her own gaze in the mirror, steadfastly refusing to think as she made certain the pin was securely fastened and visible. There were just things you couldn't think about. Hadn't that always been so? The brevity of mortal life, for example. You had to keep yourself distracted from the sad things. You had to have an escape.

She glimpsed over her shoulder the painting in its alcove, and turned to regard it with a certain pleasurable nostalgia. It had cost her a lot, good hard cash out of her own household budget, because the Company had abandoned Vermeer once they'd got what they wanted; but she had never been sorry she'd spent the money. The picture gave her an escape, always. For a little while.

The Empty Room, 1675

Catharina, red-eyed with weeping and a little drunk, had looked up at her as she'd stepped into the chilly parlor.

"You're out of luck, my dear," she'd told Van Drouten. "No more paintings for your damned cheap doctor. Jan's dead."

"I heard," she said, as gently as she could. "I am so sorry. How are the children?"

"Scared. They're at Maria's."

"They'll be all right, I'm certain," said Van Drouten, wishing she could say more. Clearing her throat, she continued: "That was Leeuwenhoek I passed outside, wasn't it? The microscopist? Was he able to help you at all?"

"Oh, no." Catharina gave a sour laugh. "Respectable *Mynheer* Leeuwenhoek is going to be appointed executor of the estate, if you must know. He's only interested in seeing that all the debts get paid. So if you're looking for a bargain, you'd better hurry. They're coming in to do the inventory this afternoon. And you'd better pay cash!"

"I have cash," said Van Drouten, hefting the small chest she'd brought. Catharina looked at her sidelong.

"How much?"

"Seven hundred guilders."

Catharina put her hands to her face. "Jesus God," she said. "All right; come on upstairs with me now, quick! I'll show you something.

"Maybe you'll think it's funny," she continued, as they hurried together up the echoing stair. "It was his little joke, you see? Maybe you'll want it. Maybe you'll be angry. I don't give a damn either way anymore, to tell you the truth, but it'll be yours for seven hundred guilders. Here."

She pushed open a door and Van Drouten followed her into the studio. It had the reek of a sickroom and was bone-chilling cold, and canvases were stacked against the walls. The easel was bare; the paints were nowhere to be seen, and the sheets and blanket had already been stripped from the narrow cot. There was no sign of the *camera obscura*.

"Looking for the magic cabinet?" Catharina grunted, rummaging through the stacks. "You're too late for that; we sold it a year ago. Even a dying man has to eat, eh? Here. Look at this." She pulled out a painting, held it up with a defiant smile. "It's called *The Visit of the Holy Women to the Tomb of Christ.*"

Van Drouten caught her breath.

"Oh, it's wonderful! How clever!"

"But your pissy doctor won't want it, will he?" Catharina said fiercely. "Not enough blue and yellow!"

"This isn't for him," said Van Drouten. "This is for me. I liked Jan, Catharina. I liked you both."

"Then much good may this do you," Catharina replied, and tossed it at her. Van Drouten dropped the chest, putting up both hands to seize the painting. The chest burst open when it hit the floor, and guilders flooded out in a torrent of bright coin, ran and rolled into the four corners of the room.

Catharina, looking down at it, just laughed and shook her head.

In the street outside, late-night traffic roared and hissed along, and far up the pinpoint satellites orbited against the stars; but within the alcove Van Drouten regarded a spring morning in ancient Jerusalem, in a place of silver olive trees and white lilies, and green grass beaded with dew. Mortals, and God, could make such places; a cyborg couldn't. A cyborg could only preserve them. Van Drouten blinked back tears as she sank into the picture, escaped her immortal life and its immortal terrors for a moment . . .

There were the three women. Little Maria was at the left, peeping from the angle of the olive tree, her face bright with anticipation; Catharina was in the center of the canvas, her hands lifted in elaborate astonishment, her face haggard with bitter experience. There was the tomb of Christ, but it was not a stone rolled back that disclosed the interior. It was a cabinet door standing wide, hinges and all, with a lens-tube in its center.

And the third woman, Van Drouten herself, was highlighted against the sooty blackness of the tomb's walls. She smiled out at the viewer and offered forth in her hands the linen cloth on which the miracle was printed, in tones of gray and black: the trick, the joke, the alchemical cheat, the negative image of the man. It wasn't art; but there on the treated cloth his light had been captured for all time, a bargain at thirty pieces of good hard silver.

A NIGHT ON THE
BARBARY COAST

I'd been walking for five days, looking for Mendoza. The year was 1850.

Actually, *walking* doesn't really describe traveling through that damned vertical wilderness in which she lived. I'd crawled uphill on hands and knees, which is no fun when you're dressed as a Franciscan friar, with sandals and beads and the whole nine yards of brown burlap robe. I'd slid downhill, which is no fun either, especially when the robe rides up in back. I'd waded across freezing cold creeks and followed thready little trails through ferns, across forest floors in permanent darkness under towering redwoods. I'm talking *gloom*. One day the poets will fall in love with Big Sur, and after them the beats and hippies, but if vampires ever discover the place they'll go nuts over it.

Mendoza isn't a vampire, though she is an immortal being with a lot of problems, most of which she blames on me.

I'm an immortal being with a lot of problems, too. Like father, like daughter.

After most of a week, I finally came out on a patch of level ground about three thousand feet up. I was standing there looking *down* on clouds floating above the Pacific Ocean, and feeling kind of funny in the pit of my stomach as a result—and suddenly saw the Company-issue processing credenza on my left, nicely camouflaged. I'd found Mendoza's camp at last.

There was her bivvy tent, all right, and a table with a camp stove, and five pots with baby trees growing in them. Everything but the trees had a dusty, abandoned look.

Cripes, I thought to myself, how long since she's been here? I looked around uneasily, wondering if I ought to yoo-hoo or something, and that was when I noticed her signal coming from . . . *up?* I craned back my head.

An oak tree rose from the mountain face behind me, huge and branching wide, and high up there among the boughs Mendoza leaned. She gazed out at the sea; but with such a look of ecstatic vacancy in her eyes, I guessed she was seeing something a lot farther away than that earthly horizon.

I cleared my throat.

The vacant look went away fast, and there was something inhuman in the sharp way her head swung around.

"Hi, honey," I said. She looked down and her eyes focused on me. She has black eyes, like mine, only mine are jolly and twinkly and bright. Hers are like flint. Always been that way, even when she was a little girl.

"What the hell are you doing here, Joseph?" she said at last.

"I missed you, too, baby," I said. "Want to come down? We need to talk."

Muttering, she descended through the branches.

"Nice trees," I remarked. "Got any coffee?"

"I can make some," she said. I kept my mouth shut as she poked around in her half-empty rations locker, and I still kept it shut when she hauled out her bone-dry water jug and stared at it in a bewildered kind of way before remembering where the nearest stream was, and I didn't even remark on the fact that she had goddam *moss* in her hair, though what I wanted to yell at the top of my lungs was: *How can you live like this?*

No, I played it smart. Pretty soon we were sitting at either end of a fallen log, sipping our respective mugs of coffee, just like family.

"Mm, good java," I lied.

"What do you want?" she said.

"Okay, kid, I'll tell you," I said. "The Company is sending me up to San Francisco on a job. I need a field botanist, and I had my pick of anybody in the area, so I decided on you."

I braced myself for an explosion, because sometimes Mendoza's a little touchy about surprises. But she was silent for a moment, with that bewildered expression again, and I just knew she was accessing her chronometer because she'd forgotten what year this was.

"San Francisco, huh?" she said. "But I went through Yerba Buena a century ago, Joseph. I did a complete survey of all the endemics. Specimens, DNA codes, the works. Believe me, there wasn't anything to interest Dr. Zeus."

"Well, there might be now," I said. "And that's all you need to know until we get there."

She sighed. "So it's like that?"

"It's like that. But, hey, we'll have a great time! There's a lot more up there now than fog and sand dunes."

"I'll say there is," she said grimly. "I just accessed the historical record for October 1850. There's a cholera epidemic going on. There's chronic arson. The streets are half quicksand. You really take me to some swell places, don't you?"

"How long has it been since you ate dinner in a restaurant?" I coaxed. She started to say something sarcastic in reply, looked down at whatever was floating in the bottom of her coffee, and shuddered.

"See? It'll be a nice change of scenery," I told her, as she tossed the dregs over her shoulder. I tossed out my coffee, too, in a simpatico gesture. "The Road to Frisco! A fun-filled musical romp! Two wacky cyborgs plus one secret mission equals laughs galore!"

"Oh, shut up," she told me, but rose to strike camp.

It took us longer to get down out of the mountains than I would have liked, because Mendoza insisted on bringing her five potted trees, which were some kind of endangered species, so we had to carry them all the way to the closest Company receiving terminal in Monterey, by which time I was ready to drop the damn things down any convenient cliff. But away they went to some Company botanical garden, and, after requisitioning equipment and a couple of horses, we finally set off for San Francisco.

I guess if we had been any other two people, we'd have chatted about bygone times as we rode along. It's never safe to drag up old memories with Mendoza, though. We didn't talk much, all the way up El Camino Real, through the forests and across the scrubby hills. It wasn't until we'd left San Jose and were picking our way along the shore of the back bay, all black ooze and oyster shells, that Mendoza looked across at me and said: "We're carrying a lot of lab equipment with us. I wonder why?"

I just shrugged.

"Whatever the Company's sending us after, they want it analyzed on the spot," she said thoughtfully. "So possibly they're not sure that it's really what they want. But they need to find out."

"Could be."

"And your only field expert is being kept on a need-to-know basis, which means it's something important," she continued. "And they're sending *you*, even though you're still working undercover in the Church, being Father Rubio or whoever. Aren't you?"

"I am."

"You look even more like Mephistopheles than usual in that robe, did I ever tell you that? Anyway—why would the Company send a friar into a town full of gold miners, gamblers, and prostitutes?" Mendoza speculated. "You'll stick out like a sore thumb. And where does botany fit in?"

"I guess we'll see, huh?"

She glared at me sidelong and grumbled to herself a while, but that was okay. I had her interested in the job, at least. She was losing that thousand-year-stare that worried me so much.

I wasn't worrying about the job at all.

You could smell San Francisco miles before you got there. It wasn't the ordinary mortal aroma of a boom town without adequate sanitation, even one in the grip of cholera. San Francisco smelled like smoke, with a reek that went right up your nose and drilled into your sinuses.

It smelled this way because it had been destroyed by fire four times already, most recently only a month ago, though you wouldn't know it to look at the place. Obscenely expensive real estate where tents and shanties had stood was already filling up with brand-new frame buildings. Hammers pounded day and night along Clay, along Montgomery and Kearney and Washington. All the raw new wood was festooned with red-white-and-blue bunting, and hastily improvised Stars and Stripes flew everywhere. California had only just found out it had been admitted to the Union, and was still celebrating.

The bay was black with ships, but those closest to the shore were never going to sea again—their crews had deserted and they were already enclosed by wharves, filling in on all sides. Windows and doors had been cut in their hulls as they were converted to shops and taverns.

Way back in the sand hills, poor old Mission Dolores—built of adobe blocks by a people whose world hadn't changed in millennia, on a settlement plan first designed by officials of the Roman Empire—looked down on the crazy new world in wonderment. Mendoza and I stared, too, from where we'd reined in our horses near Rincon Hill.

"So this is an American city," said Mendoza.

"Manifest Destiny in action," I agreed, watching her. Mendoza had never liked being around mortals much. How was she going to handle a modern city, after a century and a half of wilderness? But she just set her mouth and urged her horse forward, and I was proud of her.

For all the stink of disaster, the place was *alive*. People were out and running around, doing business. There were hotels and taverns; there were groceries and bakeries and candy stores. Lightermen worked the water between those ships that hadn't yet been absorbed into the city, bringing in prospectors bound for the gold fields or crates of goods for the merchants. I heard six languages spoken before we'd crossed Clay Street. Anything could be bought or sold here, including a meal prepared by a Parisian chef. The air hummed with hunger, and enthusiasm, and a kind of rapacious innocence.

I grinned. America looked like fun.

We found a hotel on the big central wharf, and loaded our baggage into two narrow rooms whose windows looked into the rigging of a landlocked ship. Mendoza stared around at the bare plank walls.

"This is Oregon spruce," she announced. "You can still smell the forest! I'll bet this was alive and growing a month ago."

"Probably," I agreed, rummaging in my trunk. I found what I was looking for and unrolled it to see how it had survived the trip.

"What's that?"

"A subterfuge." I held the drawing up. "A beautiful gift for his Holiness the Pope! The artist's conception, anyway."

"A huge ugly crucifix?" Mendoza looked pained.

"*And* a matching rosary, baby. All to be specially crafted out of gold and—this is the important part—gold-bearing quartz from sunny California, U.S.A., so the Holy Father will know he's got faithful fans out here!"

"That's disgusting. Are you serious?"

"Of course I'm not serious, but we don't want the mortals to know that," I said, rolling up the drawing and sticking it in a carpetbag full of money. "You stay here and set up the lab, okay? I've got to go find some jewelers."

There were a lot of jewelers in San Francisco. Successful guys coming back from the Sacramento sometimes liked to commemorate their luck by having gold nuggets set in watch fobs, or stickpins, or brooches for sweethearts back east. Gold-bearing quartz, cut and polished, was also popular, and much classier looking.

Hiram Gainsborg, on the corner of Ohio and Broadway, had some of what I needed; so did Joseph Schwartz at Harrison and Broadway, although J. C. Russ on the corner of Harrison and Sixth had more. But I also paid a visit to Baldwin & Co. on Clay at the Plaza, and to J. H. Bradford on Kearney, and just to play it safe I went to over to Dupont and Clay to see the firm of Moffat & Co., Assayers and Bankers.

So I was one pooped little friar, carrying one big heavy carpetbag, by the time I trudged back to our hotel as evening shadows descended. I'd been followed for three blocks by a Sydney ex-convict whose intent was robbery and possible murder; but I managed to ditch him by ducking into a saloon, exiting out the back and across the deck of the landlocked *Niantic,* and cutting through another saloon where I paused just long enough to order an oyster loaf and a pail of steam beer.

I'd lost him for good by the time I thumped on Mendoza's door with the carpetbag.

"Hey, honeybunch, I got dinner!"

She opened the door right away, jittery as hell. "Don't shout, for God's sake!"

"Sorry." I went in and set down the carpetbag gratefully. "I don't think the mortals are sleeping yet. It's early."

"There are three of them on this floor, and seventeen downstairs," she said, wringing her hands. "It's been a while since I've been around so many of them. I'd forgotten how loud their hearts are, Joseph. I can hear them beating."

"Aw, you'll get used to it in no time," I said. I held up the takeout. "Look! Oyster loaf and beer!"

She looked impatient, and then her eyes widened as she caught the scent of the fresh-baked sourdough loaf and the butter and the garlic and the little fried oysters . . .

"Oh, gosh," she said weakly.

So we had another nice companionable moment, sitting at the table where she'd set up the testing equipment, drinking from opposite sides of the beer pail. I lit a lamp and pulled the different paper-wrapped parcels from my carpetbag, one by one.

"What're those?" Mendoza inquired with her mouth full.

"Samples of gold-bearing quartz," I explained. "From six different places. I wrote the name of each place on the package in pencil, see? And your job is to test each sample. You're going to look for a blue-green lichen growing in the crevices with the gold."

She swallowed and shook her head, blank-faced.

"You need a microbiologist for this kind of job, Joseph, surely. Plants that primitive aren't my strong suit."

"The closest microbiologist was in Seattle," I explained. "And Agrippanilla's a pain to work with. Besides, you can handle this! Remember the Black Elysium grape? The mutant saccharomyces or whatever it was? You won yourself a field commendation on that one. This'll be easy!"

Mendoza looked pleased, but did her best to conceal it. "I'll bet your mission budget just wouldn't stretch to shipping qualified personnel down here, eh? That's the Company. Okay; I'll get started right after dinner."

"You can wait until morning," I said.

"Naah." She had a gulp of the beer. "Sleep is for sissies."

So after we ate I retired, and far into the hours of the night I could still see lamplight shining from her room, bright stripes through the plank wall every time I turned over. I knew why she was working so late.

It's not hard to sleep in a house full of mortals, if you tune out the sounds they make. Sometimes, though, just on the edge of sleep, you find yourself listening for one heartbeat that ought to be there, and it isn't. Then you wake up with a start, and remember things you don't want to remember.

I opened my eyes and sunlight smacked me in the face, glittering off the bay through my open door. Mendoza was sitting on the edge of my bed, sipping from her canteen. I grunted, grimaced, and sat unsteadily.

"Coffee," I croaked. She looked smug and held up her canteen.

"There's a saloon on the corner. The nice mortal sold me a whole pot of coffee for five dollars. Want some?"

"Sure." I held out my hand. "So . . . you didn't mind going down to the saloon by yourself? There are some nasty mortals in this town, kid."

"The famous Sydney Ducks? Yes, I'm aware of that." She was quietly gleeful about something. "I've lived in the Ventana for years, Joseph, dodging mountain lions! *Individual* nasty mortals don't frighten me anymore. Go ahead, try the coffee."

I sipped it cautiously. It was great. We may have been in America (famous for lousy coffee) now, but San Francisco was already *San Francisco*.

Mendoza cleared her throat and said, "I found your blue-green lichen. It was growing on the sample from Hiram Gainsborg's. The stuff looks like Stilton cheese. What is it, Joseph?"

"Something the Company wants," I said, gulping down half the coffee.

"I'll bet it does," she said, giving me that sidelong look again. "I've been sitting here, watching you drool and snore, amusing myself by accessing scientific journals on bioremediant research. Your lichen's a toxiphage, Joseph. It's perfectly happy feeding on arsenic and antimony compounds found in conjunction with gold. It breaks them down. I suspect that it could make a lot of money for anyone in the business of cleaning up industrial pollution."

"That's a really good guess, Mendoza," I said, handing back the coffee and swinging my legs over the side of the bed. I found my sandals and pulled them on.

"Isn't it?" She watched me grubbing around in my trunk for my shaving kit. "Yes, for God's sake, shave. You look like one of Torquemada's henchmen, with those blue jowls. So Dr. Zeus is doing something altruistic! In its usual corporate-profit way, of course. I don't understand why this has to be classified, but I'm impressed."

"Uh-huh." I swabbed soap on my face.

"You seem to be in an awful hurry."

"Do I?" I scraped whiskers from my cheek.

"I wonder what you're in a hurry to do?" Mendoza said. "Probably hot-foot it back to Hiram Gainsborg's, to see if he has any more of what he sold you."

"Maybe, baby."

"Can I go along?"

"Nope."

"I'm not sitting in my room all day, watching lichen grow in petrie dishes," she said. "Is it okay if I go sightseeing?"

I looked at her in the mirror, disconcerted. "Sweetheart, this is a rough town. Those guys from Australia are devils, and some of the Yankees—"

"I pity the mortal who approaches me with criminal intent," she said, smiling in a chilly kind of way. "I'll just ride out to the Golden Gate. How can I get into trouble? Ghirardelli's won't be there for another two years, right?"

I walked her down to the stable anyway, and saw her safely off before hot-footing it over to Hiram Gainsborg's, as she suspected.

Mr. Gainsborg kept a loaded rifle behind his shop counter. I came in through his door so fast he had it out and trained on me pronto, before he saw it was me.

"Apologies, Father Rubio," he said, lowering the barrel. "Back again, are you? You're in some hurry, sir." He had a white chin beard, wore a waist-coat of red-and-white-striped silk, and overall gave me the disconcerting feeling I was talking to Uncle Sam.

"I was pursued by importuning persons of low moral fiber," I said.

"That a fact?" Mr. Gainsborg pursed his lips. "Well, what about that quartz you bought yesterday? Your brother friars think it'll do?"

"Yes, my son, they found it suitable," I said. "In fact, the color and qual-ity are so magnificent, so superior to any other we have seen, that we all agreed only *you* were worthy of this important commission for the Holy

Father." I laid the drawing of the crucifix down on his counter. He smiled.

"Well, sir, I'm glad to hear that. I reckon I can bring the job in at a thousand dollars pretty well." He fixed me with a hard clear eye, waiting to see if I'd flinch, but I just hauled my purse out and grinned at him.

"Price is no object to the Holy Mother Church," I said. "Shall we say, half the payment in advance?"

I counted out Chilean gold dollars while he watched, sucking his teeth, and I went on: "In fact, we were thinking of having rosaries made up as a gift for the whole College of Cardinals. Assuming, of course, that you have enough of that *particular* beautiful vein of quartz. Do you know where it was mined?"

"Don't know, sir, and that's a fact," he told me. "Miner brought in a sackful a week ago. He reckoned he could get more for it at a jeweler's because of the funny color. There's more'n enough of it in my back room to make your beads, I bet."

"Splendid," I said. "But do you recall the miner's name, in case we do need to obtain more?"

"Ayeh." Mr. Gainsborg picked up a dollar and inspected it. "Isaiah Stuckey, that was the fellow's name. Didn't say where his claim was, though. They don't tell, as a general rule."

"Understandable. Do you know where I might find the man?"

"No, sir, don't know that. He didn't have a red cent until I paid for the quartz, I can tell you; so I reckon the next place he went was a hotel." Mr. Gainsborg looked disdainful. "Unless he went straight for the El Dorado or a whorehouse, begging your pardon. Depends on how long he'd been in the mountains, don't it?"

I sighed and shook my head. "This is a city of temptation, I am afraid. Can you describe him for me?"

Mr. Gainsborg considered. "Well, sir, he had a beard."

Great. I was looking for a man with a beard in a city full of bearded men. At least I had a name.

So I spent the rest of that day trudging from hotel to boardinghouse to tent, asking if anybody there had seen Isaiah Stuckey. Half the people I asked snickered and said, "No, why?" and waited for a punchline. The other half also replied in the negative, and then asked my advice on matters spiritual. I heard confessions for seventeen prostitutes, five drunks, and a transvestite before the sun sank behind Knob Hill, but I didn't find Isaiah Stuckey.

By twilight, I had worked my way out to the landlocked ships along what would one day be Battery and Sansome Streets, though right now they were just so many rickety piers and catwalks over the harbor mud. I teetered up the gangplank of one place that declared itself the MAGNOLIA HOTEL, by means of a sign painted on a bedsheet hung over the bow. A grumpy-looking guy was swabbing the deck.

"We don't rent to no goddam greasers here," he informed me. "Even if you is a priest."

"Well, now, my son, Christ be my witness I've not come about taking rooms," I said in the thickest Dublin accent I could manage. "Allow me to introduce myself! Father Ignatius Costello. I'm after searching for a poor soul whose family's in sore need of him, and him lost in the gold fields this twelvemonth. Do you rent many rooms to miners, lad?"

"Sure we do," muttered the guy, embarrassed. "What's his name?"

"Isaiah Stuckey, or so his dear old mother said," I replied.

"Him!" The guy looked up, righteously indignant now. He pointed with his mop at a vast expanse of puke on the deck. "That's your Ike Stuckey's work, by God!"

I recoiled. "He's never got the cholera?"

"No, sir, just paralytic drunk. You ought to smell his damn *room*, after he lay in there most of a week! Boss had me fetch him out, plastered or not, on account of he ain't paid no rent in three days. I got him this far and he heaved up all over my clean floor! Then, I wish I may be struck down dead if he don't sober up instant and run down them planks like a racehorse! Boss got a shot off at him, but he kept a-running. Last we saw he was halfway to Kearney Street."

"Oh, dear," I said. "I don't suppose you'd have any idea where he was intending to go, my son?"

"No, I don't," said the guy, plunging his mop in its pail and getting back to work. "But if you run, too, you can maybe catch the son of a—" he wavered, glancing up at my ecclesiastical presence "—gun. He ain't been gone but ten minutes."

I took his advice, and hurried off through the twilight. There actually was a certain funk lingering in the air, a trail of unwashed-Stuckey molecules, that any bloodhound could have picked up without much effort—not that it would have enjoyed the experience—and incidentally any cyborg with augmented senses could follow, too.

So I was slapping along in my sandals, hot on Stuckey's trail, when I ran into Mendoza at the corner.

"Hey, Joseph!" She waved at me cheerily. "You'll never guess what I found!"

"Some plant, right?"

"And how! It's a form of *Lupinus* with—"

"That's fascinating, doll, and I mean that sincerely, but right now I could really use a lift." I jumped and swung up into the saddle behind her, only to find myself sitting on something damp. "What the hell—"

"That's my *Lupinus.* I dug up the whole plant and wrapped the root ball in a piece of my petticoat until I can transplant it into a pot. If you've squashed it, I'll wring your neck," she told me.

"No, it's okay," I said. "Look, could we just canter up the street that way? I'm chasing somebody and I don't want to lose him."

She grumbled, but dug her heels into the horse's sides and we took off, though we didn't go very far very fast because the street went straight uphill.

"It wouldn't have taken us ten minutes to go back and drop my *Lupinus* at the hotel, you know," Mendoza said. "It's a really rare subspecies, possibly a mutant form. It appears to produce photoreactive porphyrins."

"Honey, I haven't got ten minutes," I said, wrootching my butt away from the damn thing. "Wait! Turn left here!" Stuckey's trail angled away down Kearney toward Portsmouth Square, so Mendoza yanked the horse's head around and we leaned into the turn. I peered around Mendoza, trying to spot any bearded guy staggering and wheezing along. Unfortunately, the street was full of staggering bearded guys, all of them converging on Portsmouth Square.

We found out why when we got there.

Portsmouth Square was just a sandy vacant lot, but there were wire baskets full of pitch and redwood chips burning atop poles at its four corners, and bright-lit board and batten buildings lined three sides of it. The fourth

side was just shops and one adobe house, like a row of respectable spin-
sters frowning down on their neighbors, but the rest of the place blazed
like happy Gomorrah.

"Holy smoke," said Mendoza, reining up. "I'm not going in there,
Joseph."

"It's just mortals having a good time," I said. Painted up on false fronts,
garish as any Old West fantasy, were names like The Mazourka, Parker
House, The Varsouvienne, La Souciedad, Dennison's Exchange, The Arcade. All of them were torchlit and proudly decked in red, white, and blue,
so the general effect was of Hell on the Fourth of July.

"It's brothels and gambling dens," said Mendoza.

"It's theaters, too," I said defensively, pointing at the upstairs windows
of the Jenny Lind.

"And saloons. What do you want here?"

"A guy named Isaiah Stuckey," I said, leaning forward. His scent was
harder to pick out now, but . . . over *there* . . . "He's the miner who found
our quartz. I need to talk to him. Come on, we're blocking traffic! Let's try
that one. The El Dorado."

Mendoza gritted her teeth but rode forward, and as we neared the El
Dorado the scent trail grew stronger.

"He's in here," I said, sliding down from the saddle. "Come on!"

"I'll wait outside, thank you."

"You want to wait here by yourself, or you want to enter a nice civilized
casino in the company of a priest?" I asked her. She looked around wildly
at the happy throng of mortals.

"Damn you anyway," she said, and dismounted. We went into the El Dorado.

Maybe I shouldn't have used the words *nice civilized casino.* It was a big
square place with bare board walls, and the floor sloped downhill from the
entrance, because it was just propped up on pilings over the ash heaps and
was already sagging. Wind whistled between the planks, and there is no
night air so cold as in San Francisco. It gusted into the stark booths along
one wall, curtained off with thumbtacked muslin, where the whores were
working. It was shantytown squalor no Hollywood set designer would
dream of depicting.

But the El Dorado had all the other trappings of an Old West saloon, with as much rococo finery as could be nailed up or propped against the plank walls. There were gilt-framed paintings of balloony nude women. There was a grand mirrored bar at one end, cut glass glittering under the oil lamps. Upon the dais a full orchestra played, good and loud, and here again the Stars and Stripes were draped, swagged and rosetted in full glory.

At the gambling tables were croupiers and dealers in black suits, every one of them a gaunt Doc Holliday clone presiding over monte, or faro, or diana, or chuck-a-luck, or plain poker. A sideboard featured free food for the high rollers, and a lot of ragged men—momentary millionaires in blue jeans, back from the gold fields for the winter—were helping themselves to pie and cold beef. At the tables, their sacks of gold dust or piles of nuggets sat unattended, as safe as anything else in this town.

I wished I wasn't dressed as a friar. This was the kind of spot in which a cyborg with the ability to count cards could earn himself some money to offset operating expenses. I might have given it a try anyway, but beside me Mendoza was hyperventilating, so I just shook my head and focused on my quarry.

Isaiah Stuckey was in here somewhere. At the buffet table? No . . .

At the bar? No . . . Christ, there must have been thirty guys wearing blue jeans and faded red calico shirts in here, and they all stank like bachelors. Was that him? The beefy guy looking around furtively?

"Okay, Mendoza," I said, "if you were a miner who'd just recovered consciousness after a drinking binge, stone broke—where would you go?"

"I'd go bathe myself," said Mendoza, wrinkling her nose. "But a mortal would probably try to get more money. So he'd come in here, I guess. Of course, you can only *win* money in a game of chance if you already have money to bet—"

"*STOP, THIEF!*" roared somebody, and I saw the furtive guy sprinting through the crowd with a sack of gold dust in his fist. The croupiers had risen as one, and from the recesses of their immaculate clothing produced an awesome amount of weaponry. Isaiah Stuckey—boy, could I smell him *now!*—crashed through a back window, pursued closely by bullets and bowie knives.

I said something you don't often hear a priest say and grabbed Mendoza's arm. "Come on! We have to find him before they do!"

We ran outside, where a crowd had gathered around Mendoza's horse.

"Get away from that!" Mendoza yelled. I pushed around her and gaped at what met my eyes. The sorry-looking bush bound behind Mendoza's saddle was . . . glowing in the dark, like a faded neon rose. It was also shaking back and forth, but that was because a couple of mortals were trying to pull it loose.

They were a miner, so drunk he was swaying, and a hooker only slightly less drunk, who was holding the miner up by his belt with one hand and doing her best to yank the mutant *Lupinus* free with the other.

"I *said* leave it alone!" Mendoza shoved me aside to get at the hooker.

"But I'm gettin' married," explained the hooker, in as much of a voice as whiskey and tobacco had left her. "An' I oughter have me a buncha roses to get married holding on to. 'Cause I ain't never been married before and I oughter have me a buncha roses."

"That is not a bunch of roses, you stupid cow, that's a rare photoreactive porphyrin-producing variant *Lupinus* specimen," Mendoza said, and I backed off at the look in her eyes and so did every sober man there, but the hooker blinked.

"Don't you use that kinda language to me," she screamed, and attempted to claw Mendoza's eyes out. Mendoza ducked and rose with a roundhouse left to the chin that knocked poor Sally Faye, or whoever she was, back on her ass, and her semiconscious fiancé went down with her.

All the menfolk present, with the exception of me, circled eagerly to give the ladies room. I jumped forward and got Mendoza's arm again.

"My very beloved daughters in Christ, is this any way to behave?" I cried, because Mendoza, with murder in her eye, was pulling a gardening trowel out of her saddlebag. Subvocally I transmitted, *Are you nuts? We've got to go after Isaiah Stuckey!* Snarling, Mendoza swung herself back into the saddle. I had to scramble to get up there, too, hitching my robe in a fairly undignified way, which got boffo laughs from the grinning onlookers before we galloped off into the night.

"Go down to Montgomery Street!" I said. "He probably came out there!"

"If one of the bullets didn't get him," said Mendoza, but she urged the horse down Clay and made a fast left onto Montgomery. Halfway along the block we slowed to a canter and I leaned out, trying to pick up the scent trail again.

"Yes!" I punched the air and nearly fell off the horse. Mendoza grabbed my hood, hauling me back up straight behind her.

"Why the hell is it so important you talk to this mortal?" she demanded.

"Head north! His trail goes back toward Washington Street," I said. "Like I said, babe, he sold that quartz to Gainsborg."

"But we already know it tested positive for your lichen," said Mendoza. At the next intersection we paused as I sniffed the air, and then pointed forward.

"He went thataway! Let's go. We want to know where he got the stuff, don't we?"

"Do we?" Mendoza kicked the horse again—I was only grateful the Company hadn't issued her spurs—and we rode on toward Jackson. "Why should we particularly need to know where the quartz was mined, Joseph? I've cultured the lichen successfully. There'll be plenty for the Company labs."

"Of course," I said, concentrating on Isaiah Stuckey's scent. "Keep going, will you? I think he's heading back toward Pacific Street."

"Unless the Company has some other reason for wanting to know where the quartz deposit is," said Mendoza, as we came up on Pacific.

I sat up in the saddle, closing my eyes to concentrate on the scent. There was his earlier track, but . . . yes . . . he was heading uphill again. "Make another left, babe. What were you just saying?"

"What I was *about* to say was, I wonder if the Company wants to be sure nobody else finds this very valuable deposit of quartz?" said Mendoza, as the horse snorted and laid its ears back; it wasn't about to gallop up Pacific. It proceeded at a grudging walk.

"Gee, Mendoza, why would Dr. Zeus worry about something like exclusive patent rights on the most valuable bioremediant substance imaginable?" I said.

She was silent a moment, but I could feel the slow burn building.

"You mean," she said, "that the Company plans to destroy the original source of the lichen?"

"Did I say that, honey?"

"Just so nobody else will discover it before Dr. Zeus puts it on the market, in the twenty-fourth century?"

"Do you see Mr. Stuckey up there anyplace?" I rose in the saddle to study the sheer incline of Pacific Street.

Mendoza said something amazingly profane in sixteenth-century Galician, but at least she didn't push me off the horse. When she had run out of breath, she gulped air and said: "Just *once* in my eternal life I'd like to know I was actually helping to save the world, like we were all promised, instead of making a lot of technocrats up in the future obscenely rich."

"I'd like it too, honest," I said.

"Don't you *honest* me! You're a damned Facilitator, aren't you? You've got no more moral sense than a jackal!"

"I resent that!" I edged back from her sharp shoulder blades, and the glow-in-the-dark mutant *Lupinus* squelched unpleasantly under my behind. "And anyway, what's so great about being a Preserver? You could have been a Facilitator like me, you know that, kid? You had what it took. Instead, you've spent your whole immortal life running around after freaking *bushes*!"

"A Facilitator like you? Better I should have died in that dungeon in Santiago!"

"I saved your *life*, and this is the thanks I get?"

"And as for freaking bushes, Mr. Big Shot Facilitator, it might interest you to know that certain rare porphyrins have serious commercial value in the data storage industry—"

"So, who's making the technocrats rich now, huh?" I demanded. "And have you ever stopped to consider that maybe the damn plants wouldn't *be* so rare if Botanist drones like you weren't digging them up all the time?"

"For your information, that specimen was growing on land that'll be paved over in ten years," Mendoza said coldly. "And if you call me a drone again, you're going to go bouncing all the way down this hill with the print of my boot on your backside."

The horse kept walking, and San Francisco Bay fell ever farther below us. Finally, stupidly, I said:

"Okay, we've covered all the other bases on mutual recrimination. Aren't you going to accuse me of killing the only man you ever loved?"

She jerked as though I'd shot her, and turned around to regard me with blazing eyes.

"You didn't kill him," she said, in a very quiet voice. "You just let him die."

She turned away, and of course then I wanted to put my arms around her and tell her I was sorry. If I did that, though, I'd probably spend the next few months in a regeneration tank, growing back my arms.

So I just looked up at the neighborhood we had entered without noticing, and that was when I really felt my blood run cold.

"Uh—we're in Sydney-Town," I said.

Mendoza looked up. "Oh-oh."

There weren't any flags or bunting here. There weren't any torches. And you would never, *ever* see a place like this in any Hollywood western. Neither John Wayne nor Gabby Hayes ever went anywhere near the likes of Sydney-Town.

It perched on its ledge at the top of Pacific Street and rotted. On the left side was one long row of leaning shacks; on the right side was another. I could glimpse dim lights through windows and doorways, and heard fiddle music scraping away, a half dozen folk tunes from the British Isles, played in an eerie discord. The smell of the place was unbelievable, breathing out foul through dark doorways where darker figures leaned. Above the various dives, names were chalked that would have been quaint and reassuring anywhere else: The Noggin of Ale. The Tam O'Shanter. The Jolly Waterman. The Bird in Hand.

Some of the dark figures leaned out and bid us "G'deevnin'," and without raising their voices too much let us know about the house specialties. At the Boar's Head, a woman was making love to a pig in the back room; did we want to see? At the Goat and Compass, there was a man who'd eat or drink anything, absolutely *anything*, mate, for a few cents, and he hadn't had a bath in ten years. Did we want to give him a go? At the Magpie, a girl was lying in the back on a mattress, so drunk she'd never wake before morning, no matter what anyone did to her. Were we interested? And other dark figures were moving along in the shadows, watching us.

Portsmouth Square satisfied simple appetites like hunger and thirst, greed, the need to get laid or to shoot at total strangers. Sydney-Town, on the other hand, catered to specialized tastes.

It was nothing I hadn't seen before, but I'd worked in Old Rome at her worst, and Byzantium too. Mendoza, though, shrank back against me as we rode.

She had a white, stunned look I'd seen only a couple of times before.

The first was when she was four years old, and the Inquisitors had held her up to the barred window to see what could happen if she didn't confess she was a Jew. More than fear or horror, it was *astonishment* that life was like this.

The other time she'd looked like that was when I let her mortal lover die.

I leaned close and spoke close to her ear. "Baby, I'm going to get down and follow the trail on foot. You ride on, okay? I'll meet you at the hotel."

I slid down from the saddle fast, smacked the horse hard on its rump, and watched as the luminous mutant whatever-it-was bobbed away through the dark, shining feebly. Then I marched forward, looking as dangerous as I could in the damn friar's habit, following Isaiah Stuckey's scent line.

He was sweating heavily, now, easy to track even here. Sooner or later, the mortal was going to have to stop, to set down that sack of gold dust and wipe his face and breathe. He surely wasn't dumb enough to venture into one of these places . . .

His trail took an abrupt turn, straight across the threshold of the very next dive. I sighed, looking up at the sign. This establishment was The Fierce Grizzly. Behind me, the five guys who were lurking paused, too. I shrugged and went in.

Inside the place was small, dark, and smelled like a zoo. I scanned the room. Bingo! There was Isaiah Stuckey, a gin punch in his hand and a smile on his flushed face, just settling down to a friendly crap game with a couple of serial rapists and an axe murderer. I could reach him in five steps. I had taken two when a hand descended on my shoulder.

"Naow, mate, you ain't saving no souls in 'ere," said a big thug. "You clear off, or sit down and watch the exhibition, eh?"

I wondered how hard I'd have to swing to knock him cold, but then a couple of torches flared alight at one end of the room. The stage curtain, nothing more than a dirty blanket swaying and jerking in the torchlight, was flung aside.

I saw a grizzly bear, muzzled and chained. Behind her, a guy I assumed to be her trainer grinned at the audience. The act started.

In twenty thousand years I thought I'd seen everything, but I guess I hadn't.

My jaw dropped, as did the jaws of most of the other patrons who

weren't regulars there. They couldn't take their eyes off what was happen-
ing on the stage, which made things pretty easy for the pickpockets working the room.

But only for a moment.

Maybe that night the bear decided she'd finally had enough, and sum-
moned some self-esteem. Maybe the chains had reached the last stages of
metal fatigue. Anyway, there was a sudden *ping*, like a bell cracking, and
the bear got her front paws free.

About twenty guys, including me, tried to get out through the front door
at the same moment. When I picked myself out of the gutter, I looked up to
see Isaiah Stuckey running like mad again, farther up Pacific Street.

"Hey! Wait!" I shouted; but no Californian slows down when a grizzly is
loose. Cursing, I rose and scrambled after him, yanking up my robe to clear
my legs. I could hear him gasping like a steam engine as I began to close
the gap between us. Suddenly, he went down.

I skidded to a halt beside him and fell to my knees. Stuckey was flat on
his face, not moving. I turned him over and he flopped like a side of meat,
staring sightless up at the clear cold stars.

Massive aortic aneurysm. Dead as a doornail.

"No!" I howled, ripping his shirt open and pounding on his chest,
though I knew nothing was going to bring him back. "Don't you go and die
on me, you mortal son of a bitch! Stupid *jackass*—"

Black shadows had begun to slip from the nearest doorways, eager to begin corpse-robbing; but they halted, taken aback, I guess, by the sight of a
priest screaming abuse at the deceased. I glared at them, remembered who I
was supposed to be, and made a grudging sign of the Cross over the late Isaiah Stuckey.

There was a clatter of hoofbeats. Mendoza's horse came galloping back
downhill.

"Are you okay?" Mendoza leaned from the saddle. "Oh, hell, is that him?"

"The late Isaiah Stuckey," I said bitterly. "He had a heart attack."

"I'm not surprised, with all that running uphill," said Mendoza. "This
place really needs those cable cars, doesn't it?"

"You said it, kiddo." I got to my feet. "Let's get out of here."

Mendoza frowned, gazing at the dead man. "Wait a minute. That's
Catskill Ike!"

"Cute name," I said, clambering up into the saddle behind her. "You knew the guy?"

"No, I just monitored him in case he started any fires. He's been prospecting on Villa Creek for the last six months."

"Well, so what?"

"So I know where he found your quartz deposit," said Mendoza. "It wasn't mined up the Sacramento at all, Joseph."

"It's in Big *Sur*?" I demanded. She just nodded.

At that moment, the grizzly shoved her way out into the street, and it seemed like a good idea to leave fast.

"Don't take it too badly," said Mendoza a little while later, when we were riding back toward our hotel. "You got what the Company sent you after, didn't you? I'll bet there'll be Security Techs blasting away at Villa Creek before I get home."

"I guess so," I said glumly. She snickered.

"And look at the wonderful quality time we got to spend together! And the Pope will get his fancy crucifix. Or was that part just a scam?"

"No, the Company really is bribing the Pope to do something," I said. "But you don't—"

"—Need to know what, of course. That's okay. I got a great meal out of this trip, at least."

"Hey, are you hungry? We can still take in some of the restaurants, kid," I said.

Mendoza thought about that. The night wind came gusting up from the city below us, where somebody at the Poulet d'Or was mincing onions for a *sauce piperade,* and somebody else was grilling steaks. We heard the pop of a wine cork all the way up where we were on Powell Street . . .

"Sounds like a great idea," she said. She briefly accessed her chronometer. "As long as you can swear we'll be out of here by 1906," she added.

"Trust me," I said happily. "No problem!"

"Trust you?" she exclaimed, and spat. I could tell she didn't mean it, though.

We rode on down the hill.

WELCOME TO OLYMPUS,
MR. HEARST

Opening Credits: 1926

"Take ten!" called the director, and lowering his megaphone he settled back in his chair. It sank deeper into the sand under his weight, and irritably settling again he peered out at the stallion galloping across the expanse of dune below him, its burnoosed rider clinging against the scouring blast of air from the wind machines.

"Pretty good so far . . ." chanted the assistant director. Beside him, Rudolph Valentino (in a burnoose that matched the horseman's) nodded grimly. They watched as the steed bore its rider up one wave of sand, down the next, nearer and nearer to that point where they might cut away—

"Uh-oh," said the grip. From the sea behind them a real wind traveled forward across the sand, tearing a palm frond from the seedy-looking prop trees around the Sheik's Camp set and sending it whirling in front of the stallion. The stallion pulled up short and began to dance wildly. After a valiant second or so the rider flew up in the air and came down on his head in the sand, arms and legs windmilling.

"Oh, Christ," the director snarled. *"Cut! Kill the wind!"*

"You O.K., Lewis?" yelled the script boy.

The horseman sat up unsteadily and pulled swathing folds of burnoose up off his face. He held up his right hand, making an OK sign.

"Set up for take eleven!" yelled the assistant director. The horseman clambered to his feet and managed to calm his mount; taking its bridle, he

slogged away with it, back across the sand to their mark. Behind them the steady salt wind erased the evidence of their passage.

"This wind is not going to stop, you know," Valentino pointed out gloomily. He stroked the false beard that gave him all the appearance of middle age he would ever wear.

"Ain't there any local horses that ain't spooked by goddam palm leaves?" the grip wanted to know.

"Yeah. Plowhorses," the director told them. "Look, we paid good money for an Arabian stallion. Do you hear the man complaining? I don't hear him complaining."

"I can't even *see* him," remarked the assistant director, scanning the horizon. "Jeez, you don't guess he fell down dead or anything out there?"

But there, up out of the sand came the horse and his rider, resuming position on the crest of the far dune.

"Nah. See?" the director said. "The little guy's a pro." He lifted the megaphone, watching as Lewis climbed back into the saddle. The script boy chalked in the update and held up the clapboard for the camera. *Crack!*

"Wind machines go—and—take eleven!"

Here they came again, racing the wind and the waning light, over the lion-colored waves as the camera whirred, now over the top of the last dune and down, disappearing—

Disappearing—

The grip and the assistant director groaned. Valentino winced.

"I don't see them, Mr. Fitzmaurice," the script boy said.

"So where are they?" yelled the director. *"Cut! Cut, and kill the goddam wind."*

"Sorry!" cried a faint voice, and a second later Lewis came trudging around the dune, leading the jittering stallion. "I'm afraid we had a slight spill back there."

"Wranglers! Jadaan took a fall," called the assistant director in horrified tones, and from the camp on the beach a half dozen wranglers came running. They crowded around the stallion solicitously. Lewis left him to their care and struggled on toward the director.

The headpiece of his burnoose had come down around his neck, and his limp fair hair fluttered in the wind, making his dark makeup—what was left after repeated face-first impact with dunes—look all the more incongruous. He spat out sand and smiled brightly, tugging off his spirit-gummed beard.

"Of course, I'm ready to do another take if you are, Mr. Fitzmaurice," Lewis said.

"No," said Valentino. "We will kill him or we will kill the horse, or both."

"Oh, screw it," the director decided. "We've got enough good stuff in the can. Anyway, the light's going. Let's see what we can do with that take, as far as it went."

Lewis nodded and waded on through the sand, intent on getting out of his robes; Valentino stepped forward to put a hand on his shoulder. Lewis squinted up at him, blinking sand from his lashes.

"You work very hard, my friend," Valentino said. "But you should not try to ride horses. It is painful to watch."

"Oh—er—thank you. It's fun being Rudolph Valentino for a few hours, all the same," said Lewis, and from out of nowhere he produced a fountain pen. "I don't suppose I might have your autograph, Mr. Valentino?"

"Certainly," said Valentino, looking vainly around for something to autograph. From another nowhere Lewis produced a copy of the shooting script, and Valentino took it. "Your name is spelled?"

"L-e-w-i-s, Mr. Valentino. Right there?" he suggested. "Right under where it says *The Son of the Sheik?*" He watched with a peculiarly stifled glee as Valentino signed: *For my "other self" Lewis. Rudolph Valentino.*

"There," said Valentino, handing him the script. "No more falls on the head, yes?"

"Thank you so much. It's very kind of you to be worried, but it's all right, you know," Lewis replied. "I can take a few tumbles. I'm a professional stunt man, after all."

He tucked the script away in his costume and staggered down to the water's edge, where the extras and crew were piling into an old stakebed truck. The driver was already cranking up the motor, anxious to begin his drive back to Pismo Beach before the tide turned and they got bogged down again.

Valentino watched Lewis go, shaking his head.

"Don't worry about that guy, Rudy," the director told him, knocking sand out of his megaphone. "I know he looks like a pushover, but he never gets hurt, and I mean never."

"But luck runs out, like sand." Valentino smiled wryly and waved at the dunes stretching away behind them, where the late slanting sunlight cast his shadow to the edge of the earth. "Doesn't it? And that one, I think he has the look of a man who will die young."

Which was a pretty ironic thing for Valentino to say, considering that he'd be dead himself within the year and that Lewis happened to be, on that particular day in 1926, just short of his eighteen hundred and twenty-third birthday.

If we immortals had birthdays, anyway.

Flash Forward: 1933

"Oh, look, we're at Pismo Beach," exclaimed Lewis, leaning around me to peer at it. The town was one hotel and a lot of clam stands lining the high-way. "Shall we stop for clams, Joseph?"

"Are you telling me you didn't get enough clams when you worked on *Son of the Sheik*?" I grumbled, groping in my pocket for another mint Life-saver. The last thing I wanted right now was food. Usually I can eat any-thing (and have, believe me) but this job was giving me butterflies like crazy.

"Possibly," Lewis said, standing up in his seat to get a better view as we rattled past, bracing himself with a hand on the Ford's windshield. The wind hit him smack in the face and his hair stood out all around his head. "But it would be nice to toast poor old Rudy's shade, don't you think?"

"You want to toast him? Here." I pulled out my flask and handed it to Lewis. "It would be nice to be on time for Mr. Hearst, too, you know?"

Lewis slid back down into his seat and had a sip of warm gin. He made a face.

"*Ave atque vale*, old man," he told Valentino's ghost. "You're not actually nervous about this, are you, Joseph?"

"Me, nervous?" I bared my teeth. "Hell no. Why would I be nervous meeting one of the most powerful men in the world?"

"Well, precisely." Lewis had another sip of gin, made another face. "Thank God you won't be needing this bootlegger any more. *Vale* Volstead Act, too! You must have known far more powerful men in your time, mustn't you? You worked for a Byzantine emperor once, if I'm not mistaken."

"Three or four of 'em," I corrected him. "And believe me, not one had anything like the pull of William Randolph Hearst. Not when you look at the big picture. Anyway, Lewis, the rules of the whole game are different now. You think a little putz like Napoleon could rule the world today? You think Hitler'd be getting anywhere without the media? Mass communication is where the real power is, kiddo."

"He's only a mortal, after all," Lewis said. "Put it into perspective! We're simply motoring up to someone's country estate to spend a pleasant weekend with entertaining people. There will be fresh air and lovely views. There will be swimming, riding, and tennis. There will be fine food and decent drink, at least one hopes so—"

"Don't count on booze," I said. "Mr. Hearst doesn't like drunks."

"—and all we have to do is accomplish a simple document drop for the Company," Lewis went on imperturbably, patting the briefcase in which he'd brought the autographed Valentino script. "A belated birthday present for the master of the house, so to speak."

"That's all you have to do," I replied. "I have to actually negotiate with the guy."

Lewis shrugged, conceding my point. "Though what was that story you were telling me the other night, about you and that pharaoh, what was his name—? It's not as though there will be jealous courtiers ordering our executions, after all."

I made a noise of grudging agreement. I couldn't explain to Lewis why this job had me so on edge. Probably I wasn't sure. I lie to myself a lot, see. I started doing it about thirteen thousand years ago and it's become a habit, like chain-sucking mints to ward off imaginary nervous indigestion.

Immortals have a lot of little habits like that.

We cruised on up the coast in my Model A, through the cow town of San Luis Obispo. This was where Mr. Hearst's honored guests arrived in his private rail car, to be met at the station by his private limousines. From there they'd be whisked away to that little architectural folly known to later generations as Hearst Castle, but known for now just as The Ranch or, if you were feeling romantic, *La Cuesta Encantada*.

You've never been there? Gee, poor you. Suppose for a moment you owned one of the more beautiful hills in the world, with a breathtaking view of mountains and sea. Now suppose you decided to build a house on top of it, and had all the money in the world to spend on making that house the place of your wildest dreams, no holds barred and no expense spared, with three warehouses full of antiques to furnish the place.

Hell, yes, you'd do it; anybody would. What would you do then? If you were William Randolph Hearst, you'd invite guests up to share your enjoyment of the place you'd made. But not just any guests. You could afford to lure the best minds of a generation up there to chat with you, thinkers and artists, Einsteins and Thalbergs, Huxleys and G. B. Shaws. And if you had a blonde mistress who worked in the movies, you got her to invite her friends, too: Gable and Lombard, Bette Davis, Marie Dressler, Buster Keaton, Harpo Marx, Charlie Chaplin.

And the occasional studio small fry like Lewis and me, after I'd done a favor for Marion Davies and asked for an invitation in return. The likes of us didn't get the private railroad car treatment. We had to drive all the way up from Hollywood on our own steam. I guess if Mr. Hearst had any idea who was paying him a visit, he'd have sent a limo for us too; but the Company likes to play its cards close to the vest.

And we didn't look like a couple of immortal cyborg representatives of an all-powerful twenty-fourth-century Company, anyway. I appear to be an ordinary guy, kind of dark and compact (O.K., *short*) and Lewis . . . well, he's good-looking, but he's on the short side, too. It's always been Company policy for its operatives to blend in with the mortal population, which is why nobody in San Luis Obispo or Morro Bay or Cayucos wasted a second glance on two average cyborg joes in a new Ford zipping along the road.

Anyway we passed through little nowhere towns-by-the-sea and rolling windswept seacoast, lots of California scenery that was breathtaking, if you like scenery. Lewis did, and kept exclaiming over the wildflowers and cypress trees. I just crunched Pep-O-Mints and kept driving. Seventeen miles before we got anywhere near Mr. Hearst's castle, we were already on his property.

What you noticed first was a distant white something on a green hilltop: two pale towers and not much more. I remembered medieval hill towns in Spain and France and Italy, and so did Lewis, because he nudged me and chuckled: "Rather like advancing on Le Monastier, eh? Right about now I'd be practicing compliments for the lord or the archbishop or whoever, and hoping I'd brought enough lute strings. What about you?"

"I'd be praying I'd brought along enough cash to bribe whichever duke it was I had to bribe," I told him, popping another Lifesaver.

"It's not the easiest of jobs, is it, being a Facilitator?" Lewis said sympathetically. I just shook my head.

The sense of displacement in reality wasn't helped any by the fact that we were now seeing the occasional herd of zebra or yak or giraffe, frolicking in the green meadows beside the road. If a roc had swept over the car and carried off a water buffalo in its talons, it wouldn't have seemed strange. Even Lewis fell silent, and took another shot of gin to fortify himself.

He had the flask stashed well out of sight, though, by the time we turned right into an unobtrusive driveway and a small sign that said HEARST RANCH. Here we paused at a barred gate, where a mortal leaned out of a shack to peer at us inquiringly.

"Guests of Mr. Hearst's," I shouted, doing my best to look as though I did this all the time.

"Names, please?"

"Joseph C. Denham and Lewis Kensington," we chorused.

He checked a list to be sure we were on it and then, "Five miles an hour, please, and the animals have right-of-way at all times," he told us, as the gates swung wide.

"We're in!" Lewis gave me a gleeful dig in the ribs. I snarled absently and drove across the magic threshold, with the same jitters I'd felt walking under a portcullis into some baron's fortress.

The suspense kept building, too, because the road wound like five miles of corkscrew, climbing all that time, and there were frequent stops at barred gates as we ascended into different species habitats. Lewis had to get out and open them, nimbly stepping around buffalo pies and other things that didn't reward close examination, and avoiding the hostile attentions of an ostrich at about the third gate up. Eventually we turned up an avenue of orange trees and flowering oleander.

"Oh, this is very like the south of France," said Lewis. "Don't you think?"

"I guess so," I muttered. A pair of high wrought-iron gates loomed in front of us, opening unobtrusively as we rattled through, and we pulled up to the Grand Staircase.

We were met by a posse of ordinary-looking guys in chinos and jackets, who collected our suitcases and made off with them before we'd even gotten out of the car. I managed to avoid yelling anything like "Hey! Come back here with those!" and of course Lewis was already greeting a dignified-looking lady who had materialized from behind a statue. A houseboy took charge of the Model A and drove it off.

". . . Mr. Hearst's housekeeper," the lady was saying. "He's asked me to show you to your rooms. If you'll follow me—? You're in the Casa del Sol."

"Charming," Lewis replied, and I let him take the lead, chatting and being personable with the lady as I followed them up a long sweeping staircase and across a terrace. We paused at the top, and there opening out on my left was the biggest damn Roman swimming pool I've ever seen, and I worked in Rome for a couple of centuries. The statues of nymphs, sea gods, et cetera, were mostly modern or museum copies. Hearst had not yet imported what was left of an honest-to-gods temple and set it up as a backdrop for poolside fun. He would, though.

Looming above us was the first of the "little guest bungalows." We craned back our heads to look up. It would have made a pretty imposing mansion for anybody else.

"Delightful," Lewis said. "Mediterranean Revival, isn't it?"

"Yes, sir," the housekeeper replied, leading us up more stairs. "I believe this is your first visit here, Mr. Kensington? And Mr. Denham?"

"Yeah," I said.

"Mr. Hearst would like you to enjoy your stay, and has asked that I provide you with all information necessary to make that possible," the housekeeper recited carefully, leading us around the corner of the house to its courtyard. The door at last! And waiting beside it was a Filipino guy in a suit, who bowed slightly at the waist when he saw us.

"This is Jerome," the housekeeper informed us. "He's been assigned to your rooms. If you require anything, you can pick up the service telephone and he'll respond immediately." She unlocked the door and stepped aside to usher us in. Jerome followed silently and vanished through a side door.

As we stood staring at all the antiques and Lewis made admiring noises, the housekeeper continued: "You'll notice Mr. Hearst has furnished much of this suite with his private art collection, but he'd like you to know that the bathroom—just through there, gentlemen—is perfectly up-to-date and modern, with all the latest conveniences, including shower baths."

"How thoughtful," Lewis answered, and transmitted to me: *Are you going to take part in this conversation at all?*

"That's really swell of Mr. Hearst," I said. *I'm even more nervous than I was before, O.K.?*

The housekeeper smiled. "Thank you. You'll find your bags are already in your assigned bedrooms. Jerome is unpacking for you."

Whoops. "Great," I said. "Where's my room? Can I see it now?"

"Certainly, Mr. Denham," said the housekeeper, narrowing her eyes slightly. She led us through a doorway that had probably belonged to some sixteenth-century Spanish bishop, and there was Jerome, laying out the contents of my cheap brown suitcase. My black suitcase sat beside it, untouched.

"If you'll unlock this one, sir, I'll unpack it too," Jerome told me.

"That's O.K.," I replied, taking the black suitcase and pushing it under the bed. "I'll get that one myself, later."

In the very brief pause that followed, Jerome and the housekeeper exchanged glances, Lewis sighed, and I felt a real need for another Lifesaver. The housekeeper cleared her throat and said, "I hope this room is satisfactory, Mr. Denham?"

"Oh! Just peachy, thanks," I said.

"I'm sure mine is just as nice," Lewis offered. Jerome exited to unpack for him.

"Very good." The housekeeper cleared her throat again. "Now, Mr. Hearst wished you to know that cocktails will be served at Seven this evening in the assembly hall, which is in the big house just across the courtyard. He expects to join his guests at Eight; dinner will be served at Nine. After dinner Mr. Hearst will retire with his guests to the theater, where a motion picture will be shown. Following the picture, Mr. Hearst generally withdraws to his study, but his guests are invited to return to their rooms or explore the library." She fixed me with a steely eye. "Alcohol will be served only in the main house, although sandwiches or other light meals can be requested by telephone from the kitchen staff at any hour."

She thinks you've got booze in the suitcase, you know, Lewis transmitted.

Shut up. I squared my shoulders and tried to look open and honest. Everybody knew that there were two unbreakable rules for the guests up here: no liquor in the rooms and no sex between unmarried couples. Notice I said "for the guests." Mr. Hearst and Marion weren't bound by any rules except the laws of physics.

The housekeeper gave us a few more helpful tidbits like how to find the zoo, tennis court, and stables, and departed. Lewis and I slunk out into the garden, where we paced along between the statues.

"Overall, I don't think that went very well," Lewis observed.

"No kidding," I said, thrusting my hands in my pockets.

"It'll only be a temporary bad impression, you know," Lewis told me helpfully. "As soon as you've made your presentation—"

"Hey! Yoo-hoo! Joe! You boys made it up here O.K.?" cried a bright voice from somewhere up in the air, and we turned for our first full-on eyeful of La Casa Grande in all its massive glory. It looked sort of like a big Spanish cathedral, but surely one for pagans, because there was Marion Davies hanging out a third-story window waving at us.

"Yes, thanks," I called, while Lewis stared. Marion was wearing a dressing gown. She might have been wearing more, but you couldn't tell from this distance.

"Is that your friend? He's *cute*," she yelled. "Looks like Freddie March!"

Lewis turned bright pink. "I'm his stunt double, actually," he called to her, with a slightly shaky giggle.

"What?"

"I'm his stunt double."

"Oh," she yelled back. "O.K.! Listen, do you want some ginger ale or anything? You know there's no"—she looked naughty and mimed drinking from a bottle—"until tonight."

"Yes, ginger ale would be fine," bawled Lewis.

"I'll have some sent down," Marion said, and vanished into the recesses of La Casa Grande.

We turned left at the next statue and walked up a few steps into the courtyard in front of the house. It was the size of several town squares, big enough to stage the riot scene from *Romeo and Juliet* complete with the Verona Police Department charging in on horseback. All it held at the moment, though, was another fountain and some lawn chairs. In one of them, Greta Garbo sat moodily peeling an orange.

"Hello, Greta," I said, wondering if she'd remember me. She just gave me a look and went on peeling the orange. She remembered me, all right.

Lewis and I sat down a comfortable distance from her, and a houseboy appeared out of nowhere with two tall glasses of White Rock over ice.

"Marion Davies said I was cute," Lewis reminded me, looking pleased. Then his eyebrows swooped together in the middle. "That's not good, though, is it? For the mission? What if Mr. Hearst heard her? Ye gods, she was shouting it at the top of her lungs."

"I don't think it's going to be any big deal," I told him wearily, sipping my ginger ale. Marion thought a lot of people were cute, and didn't care who heard her say so.

We sat there in the sunshine, and the ice in our drinks melted away. Garbo ate her orange. Doves crooned sleepily in the carillon towers of the house and I thought about what I was going to say to William Randolph Hearst.

Pretty soon the other guests started wandering up, and Garbo wouldn't talk to them, either. Clark Gable sat on the edge of the fountain and got involved in a long conversation with a sandy-haired guy from Paramount about their mutual bookie. One of Hearst's five sons arrived with his girlfriend. He tried to introduce her to Garbo, who answered in monosyllables, until at last he gave it up and they went off to swim in the Roman pool. A couple of friends of Marion's from the days before talkies, slightly threadbare guys named Charlie and Laurence who looked as though they hadn't worked lately, got deeply involved in a discussion of Greek mythology.

I sat there and looked up at the big house and wondered where Hearst was, and what he was doing. Closing some million-dollar media deal? Giving some senator or congressman voting instructions? Placing an order with some antiques dealer for the contents of an entire library from some medieval duke's palace?

He did stuff like that, Mr. Hearst, which was one of the reasons the Company was interested in him.

I was distracted from my uneasy reverie when Constance Talmadge arrived, gaining on forty now but still as bright and bouncy as when she'd played the Mountain Girl in *Intolerance,* and with her Brooklyn accent just as strong. She bounced right over to Lewis, who knew her, and they had a lively chat about old times. Shortly afterward the big doors of the house opened and out came, not the procession of priests and altar boys you'd expect, but Marion in light evening dress.

"Hello, everybody," she hollered across the fountain. "Sorry to keep you waiting, but you know how it is—Hearst come, Hearst served!"

There were nervous giggles and you almost expected to see the big house behind her wince, but she didn't care. She came out and greeted everybody warmly—well, almost everybody; Garbo seemed to daunt even Marion—and then welcomed us in through the vast doorway, into the inner sanctum.

"Who's a first-timer up here?" she demanded, as we crossed the threshold. "I know you are, Joe, and your friend—? Get a load of this floor." She pointed to the mosaic tile in the vestibule. "Know where that's from? Pompeii! Can you beat it? People actually died on this floor."

If she was right, I had known some of them. It didn't improve my mood.

The big room beyond was cool and dark after the brilliance of the courtyard. Almost comfortable, too: it had contemporary sofas and overstuffed chairs, little ashtrays on brass stands. If you didn't mind the fact that it was also about a mile long and full of Renaissance masterpieces, with a fireplace big enough to roast an ox and a coffered ceiling a mile up in the air, it was sort of cozy. Here, as in all the other rooms, were paintings and statues representing the Madonna and Child. It seemed to be one of Mr. Hearst's favorite images.

We milled around aimlessly until servants came out bearing trays of drinks, at which time the milling became purposeful as hell. We converged on those trays like piranhas. The Madonna beamed down at us all, smiling her blessing.

The atmosphere livened up a lot after that. Charlie sat down at a piano and began to play popular tunes. Gable and Laurence and the guy from Paramount found a deck of cards and started a poker game. Marion worked the rest of the crowd like the good hostess she was, making sure that everybody had a drink and nobody was bored.

The Hearst kid and his girlfriend came in with wet hair. A couple of Hearst's executives (slimy-looking bastards) came in too, saw Garbo and hurried over to try to get her autograph. A gaunt and imposing grande dame with two shrieking little mutts made an entrance, and Marion greeted her enthusiastically; she was some kind of offbeat novelist who'd had one of her books optioned, and had come out to Hollywood to work on the screenplay.

I roamed around the edges of the vast room, scanning for the secret panel that concealed Hearst's private elevator. Lewis was gallantly dancing the Charleston with Connie Talmadge. Marion made for them, towing the writer along.

"—And this is Dutch Talmadge, you remember her? And this is, uh, what was your name, sweetie?" Marion waved at Lewis.

"Lewis Kensington," he said, as the music tinkled to a stop. The pianist paused to light a cigarette.

"Lewis! That's it. And you're even cuter up close," said Marion, reaching out and pinching his cheek. "Isn't he? Anyway you're Industry too, aren't you, Lewis?"

"Only in a minor sort of way," Lewis demurred. "I'm a stunt man."

"That just means you're worth the money they pay you, honey," Marion told him. "Unlike some of these blonde bimbos with no talent, huh?" She whooped with laughter at her own expense. "Lewis, Dutch, this is Cartimandua Bryce! You know? She writes those wonderful spooky romances."

The imposing-looking lady stepped forward. The two chihuahuas did their best to lunge from her arms and tear out Lewis's throat, but she kept a firm grip on them.

"A-and these are her little dogs," added Marion unnecessarily, stepping back from the yappy armful.

"My familiars," Cartimandua Bryce corrected her with a saturnine smile. "Actually, they are old souls who have re-entered the flesh on a temporary basis for purposes of the spiritual advancement of others."

"Oh," said Connie.

"O.K.," said Marion.

"This is Conqueror Worm," Mrs. Bryce offered the smaller of the two bug-eyed monsters, "and this is Tcho-Tcho."

"How nice," said Lewis gamely, and reached out in an attempt to shake Tcho-Tcho's tiny paw. She bared her teeth at him and screamed frenziedly. Some animals can tell we're not mortals. It can be inconvenient.

Lewis withdrew his hand in some haste. "I'm sorry. Perhaps the nice doggie's not used to strangers?"

"It isn't that—" Mrs. Bryce stared fixedly at Lewis. "Tcho-Tcho is attempting to communicate with me telepathically. She senses something unusual about you, Mr. Kensington."

If she can tell the lady you're a cyborg, she's one hell of a dog, I transmitted.

Oh, shut up, Lewis transmitted back. "Really?" he said to Mrs. Bryce. "Gosh, isn't that interesting?"

But Mrs. Bryce had closed her eyes, I guess the better to hear what Tcho-Tcho had to say, and was frowning deeply. After a moment's uncomfortable silence, Marion turned to Lewis and said, "So, you're Freddie March's stunt double? Gee. What's that like, anyway?"

"I just take falls. Stand in on lighting tests. Swing from chandeliers," Lewis replied. "The usual." Charlie resumed playing: *I'm the Sheik of Araby.*

"He useta do stunts for Valentino, too," Constance added. "I remember."

"You doubled for Rudy?" Marion's smile softened. "Poor old Rudy."

"I always heard Valentino was a faggot," chortled the man from Paramount. Marion rounded on him angrily.

"For your information, Jack, Rudy Valentino was a real man," she told him. "He just had too much class to chase skirts all the time!"

"Soitain people could loin a whole lot from him," agreed Connie, with the scowl of disdain she'd used to face down Old Babylon's marriage market in *Intolerance.*

"I'm just telling you what I heard," protested the man from Paramount.

"Maybe," Gable told him, looking up from his cards. "But did you ever hear that expression, 'Say nothing but good of the dead'? Now might be a good time to dummy up, pal. That or play your hand."

Mrs. Bryce, meanwhile, had opened her eyes and was gazing on Lewis with a disconcerting expression.

"Mr. Kensington," she announced with a throaty quaver, "Tcho-Tcho informs me you are a haunted man."

Lewis looked around nervously. "Am I?"

"Tcho-Tcho can perceive the spirit of a soul struggling in vain to speak to you. You are not sufficiently tuned to the cosmic vibrations to hear him," Mrs. Bryce stated.

Tell him to try another frequency, I quipped.

"Well, that's just like me, I'm afraid." Lewis shrugged, palms turned out. "I'm terribly dense that way, you see. Wouldn't know a cosmic vibration if I tripped over one."

Cosmic vibrations, my ass. I knew what she was doing; carney psychics do it all the time, and it's called a cold reading. You give somebody a close once-over and make a few deductions based on the details you observe. Then you start weaving a story out of your deductions, watching your subject's reactions to see where you're accurate and tailoring your story to fit as you go on. All she had to work with, right now, was the mention that Lewis had known Valentino. Lewis has *Easy Mark* written all over him, but I guessed she was up here after bigger fish.

"Tcho-Tcho sees a man—a slender, dark man—" Mrs. Bryce went on, rolling her eyes back in her head in a sort of alarming way. "He wears Eastern raiment—"

Marion downed her cocktail in one gulp. "Hey, look, Mrs. Bryce, there's Greta Garbo," she said. "I'll just bet she's a big fan of your books."

Mrs. Bryce's eyes snapped back into place and she looked around.

"Garbo?" she cried. She made straight for the Frozen Flame, dropping Lewis like a rock, though Tcho-Tcho snapped and strained over her shoulder at him. Garbo saw them coming and sank further into the depths of her chair. I was right. Mrs. Bryce was after bigger fish.

I didn't notice what happened after that, though, because I heard a clash of brass gates and gears engaging somewhere upstairs. The biggest fish of all was descending in his elevator, making his delayed entrance.

I edged over toward the secret panel. My mouth was dry, my palms were sweaty. I wonder if Mephistopheles ever gets sweaty palms when he's facing a prospective client?

Bump. Here he was. The panel made no sound as it opened. Not a mortal soul noticed as W. R. Hearst stepped into the room, and for that matter Lewis didn't notice either, having resumed the Charleston with Connie Talmadge. So there was only me to stare at the very, very big old man who sat down quietly in the corner.

I swear I felt the hair stand on the back of my neck, and I didn't know why.

William Randolph Hearst had had his seventieth birthday a couple of weeks before. His hair was white, he sagged where an old man sags, but his bones hadn't given in to gravity. His posture was upright and power-fully alert.

He just sat there in the shadows, watching the bright people in his big room. I watched him. This was the guy who'd fathered modern journalism, who with terrifying energy and audacity had built a financial empire that included newspapers, magazines, movies, radio, mining, ranching. He picked and chose presidents as though they were his personal appointees. He'd ruthlessly forced the world to take him on his own terms; morality was what *he* said it was; and yet there wasn't any fire that you could spot in the seated man, no restless genius apparent to the eye.

You know what he reminded me of? The Goon in the *Popeye* comic strips. Big as a mountain and scary, too, but at the same time sad, with those weird deep eyes above the long straight nose.

He reminded me of something else, too, but not anything I wanted to remember right now.

"Oh, you did your trick again," said Marion, pretending to notice him at last. "Here he is, everybody. He likes to pop in like he was Houdini or something. Come on, W.R., say hello to the nice people." She pulled him to his feet and he smiled for her. His smile was even scarier than the rest of him. It was wide, and sharp, and hungry, and young.

"Hello, everybody," he said, in that unearthly voice Ambrose Bierce had described as the fragrance of violets made audible. Flutelike and without resonance. Not a human voice; jeez, *I* sound more human than that. But then, I'm supposed to.

And you should have seen them, all those people, turn and stare and smile and bow—just slightly, and I don't think any of them realized they were bowing to him, but I've been a courtier and I know a grovel when I see one. Marion was the only mortal in that room who wasn't afraid of him. Even Garbo had gotten up out of her chair.

Marion brought them up to him, one by one, the big names and the no-bodies, and introduced the ones he didn't know. He shook hands like a shy kid. Hell, he *was* shy! That was it, I realized: he was uneasy around people, and Marion—in addition to her other duties—was his social interface. O.K., this might be something I could use.

I stood apart from the crowd, waiting unobtrusively until Marion had brought up everybody else. Only when she looked around for me did I step out of the shadows into her line of sight.

"And—oh, Joe, almost forgot you! Pops, this is Joe Denham. He works for Mr. Mayer? He's the nice guy who—"

Pandemonium erupted behind us. One of the damn chihuahuas had gotten loose and was after somebody with intent to kill, Lewis from the sound of it. Marion turned and ran off to deal with the commotion. I leaned forward and shook Hearst's hand as he peered over my shoulder after Marion, frowning.

"Pleased to meet you, Mr. Hearst," I told him quietly. "Mr. Shaw asked me to visit you. I look forward to our conversation later."

Boy, did that get his attention. Those remote eyes snapped into close focus on me, and it was like being hit by a granite block. I swallowed hard but concentrated on the part I was playing, smiling mysteriously as I disengaged my hand from his and stepped back into the shadows.

He wasn't able to say anything right then, because Tcho-Tcho was herding Lewis in our direction and Lewis was dancing away from her with apologetic little yelps, jumping over the furniture, and Marion was laughing hysterically as she tried to catch the rotten dog. Mrs. Bryce just looked on with a rapt and knowing expression.

Hearst pursed his lips at the scene, but he couldn't be distracted long. He turned slowly to stare at me and nodded, just once, to show he understood.

A butler appeared in the doorway to announce that dinner was served. Hearst led us from the room, and we followed obediently.

The dining hall was less homey than the first room we'd been in. Freezing cold in spite of the roaring fire in the French Gothic hearth, its gloom was brightened a little by the silk Renaissance racing banners hanging up high and a lot of massive silver candlesticks. The walls were paneled with fifteenth-century choir stalls from Spain. I might have dozed off in any one of them, back in my days as a friar. Maybe I had; they looked familiar.

We were seated at the long refectory table. Hearst and Marion sat across from each other in the center, and guests were placed by status. The nearer you were to the master and his mistress, the higher in favor or more important you were. Guests Mr. Hearst found boring or rude were moved discreetly farther out down the table.

Well, we've nowhere to go but up, Lewis transmitted, finding our place cards clear down at the end. I could see Hearst staring at me as we took our plates (plain old Blue Willow that his mother had used for camping trips) and headed for the buffet.

I bet we move up soon, too, I replied.

Ah! Have you made contact? Lewis peered around Gable's back at a nice-looking dish of venison steaks.

Just baited the hook. I tried not to glance at Hearst, who had loaded his plate with pressed duck and was pacing slowly back to the table.

Does this have to be terribly complicated? Lewis inquired, sidling in past Garbo to help himself to asparagus soufflé. *All we want is permission to conceal the script in that particular Spanish cabinet.*

Actually we want a little more than that, Lewis. I considered all the rich stuff and decided to keep things bland. Potatoes, right.

I see. This is one of those need-to-know things, isn't it?

You got it, kiddo. I put enough food on my plate to be polite and turned to go back to my seat. Hearst caught my eye. He tracked me like a light-house beam all the way down the table. I nodded back, like the friendly guy I really am, and sat down across from Lewis.

I take it there's more going on here than the Company has seen fit to tell me? Lewis transmitted, unfolding his paper napkin and holding out his wine glass expectantly. The waiter filled it and moved on.

Don't be sore, I transmitted back. *You know the Company. There's probably more going on here than even I know about, O.K.?*

I only said it to make him feel better. If I'd had any idea how right I was . . .

So we ate dinner, at that baronial banqueting table, with the mortals. Gable carried on manful conversation with Mr. Hearst about ranching, Marion and Connie joked and giggled across the table with the male guests, young Hearst and his girl whispered to each other, and a servant had to take Tcho-Tcho and Conqueror Worm outside because they wouldn't stop snarling at a meek little dachshund that appeared under Mr. Hearst's chair. Mrs. Bryce didn't mind; she was busy trying to tell Garbo about a past life, but I couldn't figure out if it was supposed to be hers or Garbo's. Hearst's executives just ate, in silence, down at their end of the table. Lewis and I ate in silence down at our end.

Not that we were ignored. Every so often Marion would yell a pleasantry our way, and Hearst kept swinging that cold blue searchlight on me, with an expression I was damned if I could fathom.

When dinner was over, Mr. Hearst rose and picked up the dachshund. He led us all deeper into his house, to his private movie theater.

Do I have to tell you it was on a scale with everything else? Walls lined in red damask, gorgeous beamed ceiling held up by rows of gilded caryatids slightly larger than lifesize. We filed into our seats, I guess unconsciously preserving the order of the dinner table because Lewis and I wound up off on an edge again. Hearst settled into his big leather chair with its telephone, called the projectionist and gave an order. The lights went out, and after a fairly long moment in darkness, the screen lit up. It was *Going Hollywood,* Marion's latest film with Bing Crosby. She greeted her name on the screen with a long loud raspberry, and everyone tittered.

Except me. I wasn't tittering, no sir; Mr. Hearst wasn't in his big leather chair anymore. He was padding toward me slowly in the darkness, carrying his little dog, and if I hadn't been able to see by infrared I'd probably have screamed and jumped right through that expensive ceiling when his big hand dropped on my shoulder in the darkness.

He leaned down close to my ear.

"Mr. Denham? I'd like to speak with you in private, if I may," he told me.

"Yes, sir, Mr. Hearst," I gasped, and got to my feet. Beside me, Lewis glanced over. His eyes widened.

Break a leg, he transmitted, and turned his attention to the screen again.

I edged out of the row and followed Hearst, who was walking away without the slightest doubt I was obeying him. Once we were outside the theater, all he said was, "Let's go this way. It'll be faster."

"O.K.," I said, as though I had any idea where we were going. We walked back through the house. There wasn't a sound except our footsteps echoing off those high walls. We emerged into the assembly hall, eerily lit up, and Hearst led me to the panel that concealed his elevator. It opened for him. We got in, he and I and the little dog, and ascended through his house.

My mouth was dry, my palms were sweating, my dinner wasn't sitting too well . . . well, that last one's a lie. I'm a cyborg and I can't get indigestion.

But I felt like a mortal with a nervous stomach, know what I mean? And I'd have given half the Renaissance masterpieces in that house for a roll of Pep-O-Mints right then. The dachshund watched me sympathetically.

We got out at the third floor and stepped into Hearst's private study. This was the room from which he ran his empire when he was at La Cuesta Encantada, this was where phones connected him directly to newsrooms all over the country; this was where he glanced at teletype before giving orders to the movers and shakers. Up in a corner, a tiny concealed motion picture camera began to whirr the moment we stepped on the carpet, and I could hear the click as a modified Dictaphone hidden in a cabinet began to record. State-of-the-art surveillance, for 1933.

It was a nicer room than the others I'd been in so far. Huge, of course, with an antique Spanish ceiling and golden hanging lamps, but wood-paneled walls and books and Bakhtiari carpets gave it a certain warmth. My gaze followed the glow of lamplight down the long polished mahogany conference table and skidded smack into Hearst's life-size portrait on the far wall. It was a good portrait, done when he was in his thirties, the young emperor staring out with those somber eyes. He looked innocent. He looked dangerous.

"Nice likeness," I said.

"The painter had a great talent," Hearst replied. "He was a dear friend of mine. Died too soon. Why do you suppose that happens?"

"People dying too soon?" I stammered slightly as I said it, and mentally yelled at myself to calm down: it was just business with a mortal, now, and the guy was even handing me an opening. I gave him my best enigmatic smile and shook my head sadly. "It's the fate of mortals to die, Mr. Hearst. Even those with extraordinary ability and talent. Rather a pity, wouldn't you agree?"

"Oh, yes," Hearst replied, never taking his eyes off me a moment. "And I guess that's what we're going to discuss now, isn't it, Mr. Denham? Let's sit down."

He gestured me to a seat, not at the big table but in one of the comfy armchairs. He settled into another to face me, as though we were old friends having a chat. The little dog curled up in his lap and sighed. God, that was a quiet room.

"So George Bernard Shaw sent you," Hearst stated.

"Not exactly," I said, folding my hands. "He mentioned you might be interested in what my people have to offer."

Hearst just looked at me. I coughed slightly and went on: "He spoke well of you, as much as Mr. Shaw ever speaks well of anybody. And, from what I've seen, you have a lot in common with the founders of our Company. You appreciate the magnificent art humanity is capable of creating. You hate to see it destroyed or wasted by blind chance. You've spent a lot of your life preserving rare and beautiful things from destruction.

"And—just as necessary—you're a man with vision. Modern science, and its potential, doesn't frighten you. You're not superstitious. You're a moral man, but you won't let narrow-minded moralists dictate to you! So you're no coward, either."

He didn't seem pleased or flattered, he was just listening to me. What was he thinking? I pushed on, doing my best to play the scene like Claude Rains.

"You see, we've been watching you carefully for quite a while now, Mr. Hearst," I told him. "We don't make this offer lightly, or to ordinary mortals. But there are certain questions we feel obliged to ask first."

Hearst just nodded. When was he going to say something?

"It's not for everybody," I continued, "what we're offering. You may think you want it very much, but you need to look honestly into your heart and ask yourself: are you ever tired of life? Are there ever times when you'd welcome a chance to sleep forever?"

"No," Hearst replied. "If I were tired of life, I'd give up and die. I'm not after peace and tranquillity, Mr. Denham. I want more time to live. I have things to do! The minute I slow down and decide to watch the clouds roll by, I'll be bored to death."

"Maybe." I nodded. "But here's another thing to consider: how much the world has changed since you were a young man. Look at that portrait. When it was painted, you were in the prime of your life—*and so was your generation.* It was your world. You knew the rules of the game, and everything made sense.

"But you were born before Lincoln delivered the Gettysburg address, Mr. Hearst. You're not living in that world anymore. All the rules have changed. The music is so brassy and strident, the dances so crude. The kings are all dying out, and petty dictators with dirty hands are seizing power. Aren't you, even a little, bewildered by the sheer speed with which everything moves nowadays? You're only seventy, but don't you feel just a bit like a dinosaur sometimes, a survivor of a forgotten age?"

"No," said Hearst firmly. "I like the present. I like the speed and the newness of things. I have a feeling I'd enjoy the future even more. Besides, if you study history, you have to conclude that humanity has steadily improved over the centuries, whatever the cynics say. The future generations are bound to be better than we are, no matter how outlandish their fashions may seem now. And what's fashion, anyway? What do I care what music the young people listen to? They'll be healthier, and smarter, and they'll have the benefit of learning from our mistakes. I'd love to hear what they'll have to say for themselves!"

I nodded again, let a beat pass in silence for effect before I answered.

"There are also," I warned him, "matters of the heart to be considered. When a man has loved ones, certain things are going to cause him grief— if he lives long enough to see them happen. Think about that, Mr. Hearst."

He nodded slowly, and at last he dropped his eyes from mine.

"It would be worse for a man who felt family connections deeply," he said. "And every man ought to. But things aren't always the way they ought to be, Mr. Denham. I don't know why that is. I wish I did."

Did he mean he wished he knew why he'd never felt much paternal connection to his sons? I just looked understanding.

"And as for love," he went on, and paused. "Well, there are certain things to which you have to be resigned. It's inevitable. Nobody loves without pain."

Was he wondering again why Marion wouldn't stop drinking for him?

"And love doesn't always last, and that hurts," I condoled. Hearst lifted his eyes to me again.

"When it does last, that hurts too," he informed me. "I assure you I can bear pain."

Well, those were all the right answers. I found myself reaching up in an attempt to stroke the beard I used to wear.

"A sound, positive attitude, Mr. Hearst," I told him. "Good for you. I think we've come to the bargaining table now."

"How much can you let me have?" he said instantly.

Well, this wasn't going to take long. "Twenty years," I replied. "Give or take a year or two."

Yikes! What an expression of rapacity in his eyes. Had I forgotten I was dealing with William Randolph Hearst?

"Twenty years?" he scoffed. "When I'm only seventy? I had a grandfather who lived to be ninety-seven. I might get that far on my own."

"Not with that heart, and you know it," I countered.

His mouth tightened in acknowledgment. "All right. If your people can't do any better—twenty years might be acceptable. And in return, Mr. Denham?"

"Two things, Mr. Hearst," I held up my hand with two fingers extended. "The Company would like the freedom to store certain things here at La Cuesta Encantada from time to time. Nothing dangerous or contraband, of course! Nothing but certain books, certain paintings, some other little rarities that wouldn't survive the coming centuries if they were kept in a less fortified place. In a way, we'd just be adding items to your collection."

"You must have an idea that this house will 'survive the coming centuries,' then," said Hearst, looking grimly pleased.

"Oh, yes, sir," I told him. "It will. This is one thing you've loved that won't fade away."

He rose from his chair at that, setting the dog down carefully, and paced away from me down the long room. Then he turned and walked back, tucking a grin out of sight. "O.K., Mr. Denham," he said. "Your second request must be pretty hard to swallow. What's the other thing your people want?"

"Certain conditions set up in your will, Mr. Hearst," I said. "A secret trust giving my Company control of certain of your assets. Only a couple, but very specific ones."

He bared his smile at me. It roused all kinds of atavistic terrors; I felt sweat break out on my forehead, get clammy in my armpits.

"My, my. What kind of dumb cluck do your people think I am?" he inquired jovially.

"Well, you'd certainly be one if you jumped at their offer without wanting to know more." I smiled back, resisting the urge to run like hell. "They don't want your money, Mr. Hearst. Leave all you want to your wife and your boys. Leave Marion more than enough to protect her. What my Company wants won't create any hardship for your heirs, in any way. But— you're smart enough to understand this—there are plans being made now that won't bear fruit for another couple of centuries. Something you might not value much, tonight in 1933, might be a winning card in a game being played in the future. You see what I'm saying here?"

"I might," said Hearst, hitching up the knees of his trousers and sitting down again. The little dog jumped back into his lap. Relieved that he was no longer looming over me, I pushed on.

"Obviously we'd submit a draft of the conditions for your approval, though your lawyers couldn't be allowed to examine it—"

"And I can see why." Hearst held up his big hand. "And that's all right. I think I'm still competent to look over a contract. But, Mr. Denham! You've just told me I've got something you're going to need very badly one day. Now, wouldn't you expect me to raise the price? And I'd have to have more information about your people. I'd have to see proof that any of your story, or Mr. Shaw's for that matter, is true."

What had I said to myself, that this wasn't going to take long?

"Sure," I said brightly. "I brought all the proof I'll need."

"That's good," Hearst told me, and picked up the receiver of the phone on the table at his elbow. "Anne? Send us up some coffee, please. Yes, thank you." He leaned away from the receiver a moment to ask: "Do you take cream or sugar, Mr. Denham?"

"Both," I said.

"Cream and sugar, please," he said into the phone. "And please put Jerome on the line." He waited briefly. "Jerome? I want the black suitcase that's under Mr. Denham's bed. Yes. Thank you." He hung up and met my stare of astonishment. "That is where you've got it, isn't it? Whatever proof you've brought me?"

"Yes, as a matter of fact," I replied.

"Good," he said, and leaned back in his chair. The little dog insinuated her head under his hand, begging for attention. He looked down at her in mild amusement and began to scratch between her ears. I leaned back, too, noting that my shirt was plastered to my back with sweat and only grateful it wasn't running down my face.

"Are you a mortal creature, Mr. Denham?" Hearst inquired softly.

Now the sweat was running down my face.

"Uh, no, sir," I said. "Though I started out as one."

"You did, eh?" he remarked. "How old are you?"

"About twenty thousand years," I answered. Wham, he hit me with that deadweight stare again.

"Really?" he said. "A little fellow like you?"

I ask you, is five foot five really so short? "We were smaller back then," I explained. "People were, I mean. Diet, probably."

He just nodded. After a moment he asked: "You've lived through the ages as an eyewitness to history?"

"Yeah. Yes, sir."

"You saw the Pyramids built?"

"Yes, as a matter of fact." I prayed he wouldn't ask me how they did it, because he'd never believe the truth, but he pushed on:

"You saw the Trojan War?"

"Well, yes, I did, but it wasn't exactly like Homer said."

"The stories in the Bible, are they true? Did they really happen? Did you meet Jesus Christ?" His eyes were blazing at me.

"Well—" I waved my hands in a helpless kind of way. "I didn't meet Jesus, no, because I was working in Rome back then. I never worked in Judea until the Crusades, and that was way later. And as for the stuff in the Bible being true . . . Some of it is, and some of it isn't, and anyway it depends on what you mean by true." I gave in and pulled out a handkerchief, mopping my face.

"But the theological questions!" Hearst leaned forward. "Have we got souls that survive us after physical death? What about Heaven and Hell?"

"Sorry." I shook my head. "How should I know? I've never been to either place. I've never died, remember?"

"Don't your masters know?"

"If they do, they haven't told me," I apologized. "But then there's a lot they haven't told me."

Hearst's mouth tightened again, and yet I got the impression he was satisfied in some way. I sagged backward, feeling like a wrung-out sponge. So much for my suave, subtle Mephistopheles act.

On the other hand, Hearst liked being in control of the game. He might be more receptive this way.

Our coffee arrived. Hearst took half a cup and filled it the rest of the way up with cream. I put cream and four lumps of sugar in mine.

"You like sugar," Hearst observed, sipping his coffee. "But then, I don't suppose you had much opportunity to get sweets for the first few thousand years of your life?"

"Nope," I admitted. I tasted my cup and set it aside to cool. "No Neolithic candy stores."

There was a discreet double knock. Jerome entered after a word from Mr. Hearst. He brought in my suitcase and set it down between us. "Thanks," I said.

"You're welcome, sir," he replied, without a trace of sarcasm, and exited as quietly as he'd entered. It was just me, Hearst, and the dog again. They looked at me expectantly.

"All right," I said, drawing a deep breath. I leaned down, punched in the code on the lock, and opened the suitcase. I felt like a traveling salesman. I guess I sort of was one.

"Here we are," I told Hearst, drawing out a silver bottle. "This is your free sample. Drink it, and you'll taste what it feels like to be forty again. The effects will only last a day or so, but that ought to be enough to show you that we can give you those twenty years with no difficulties."

"So your secret's a potion?" Hearst drank more of his coffee.

"Not entirely," I said truthfully. I was going to have to do some cryptosurgery to make temporary repairs on his heart, but we never tell them about that part of it. "Now. Here's something I think you'll find a lot more impressive."

I took out the viewscreen and set it up on the table between us. "If this were, oh, a thousand years ago and you were some emperor I was trying to impress, I'd tell you this was a magic mirror. As it is . . . you know that Television idea they're working on in England right now?"

"Yes," Hearst replied.

"This is where that invention's going to have led in about two hundred years," I said. "Now, I can't pick up any broadcasts because there aren't any yet, but this one also plays recorded programs." I slipped a small gold disc from a black envelope and pushed it into a slot in the front of the device, and hit the PLAY button.

Instantly the screen lit up pale blue. A moment later a montage of images appeared there, with music booming from the tiny speakers: a staccato fanfare announcing the evening news for April 18, 2106.

Hearst peered into the viewscreen in astonishment. He leaned close as the little stories sped by, the attractive people chattering brightly: new mining colonies on Luna, Ulster Revenge League terrorists bombing London again, new international agreement signed to tighten prohibitions on Recombinant DNA research, protesters in Mexico picketing Japanese-owned auto plants—

"Wait," Hearst said, lifting his big hand. "How do you stop this thing? Can you slow it down?"

I made it pause. The image of Mexican union workers torching a sushi bar froze. Hearst remained staring at the screen.

"Is that," he said, "what journalism is like, in the future?"

"Well, yes, sir. No newspapers anymore, you see; it'll all be online by then. Sort of a print-and-movie broadcast," I explained, though I was aware the revelation would probably give the poor old guy future shock. This had been his field of expertise, after all.

"But, I mean—" Hearst tore his gaze away and looked at me probingly. "This is only snippets of stuff. There's no real coverage; maybe three sentences to a story and one picture. It hasn't got half the substance of a newsreel!"

Not a word of surprise about colonies on the Moon.

"No, it'll be pretty lightweight," I admitted. "But, you see, Mr. Hearst, that'll be what the average person wants out of news by the twenty-second century. Something brief and easy to grasp. Most people will be too busy—and too uninterested—to follow stories in depth."

"Play it over again, please," Hearst ordered, and I restarted it for him. He watched intently. I felt a twinge of pity. What could he possibly make of the sound bites, the chaotic juxtaposition of images, the rapid, bouncing, and relentless pace? He watched, with the same frown, to about the same spot; then gestured for me to stop it again. I obeyed.

"Exactly," he said. "Exactly. News for the fellow in the street! Even an illiterate stevedore could get this stuff. It's like a kindergarten primer." He looked at me sidelong. "And it occurs to me, Mr. Denham, that it must be fairly easy to sway public opinion with this kind of pap. A picture's worth a thousand words, isn't it? I always thought so. This is mostly pictures. If you fed the public the right little fragments of story, you could manipulate their impressions of what's going on. Couldn't you?"

I gaped at him.

"Uh—you could, but of course that wouldn't be a very ethical thing to do," I found myself saying.

"No, if you were doing it for unethical reasons," Hearst agreed. "If you were on the side of the angels, though, I can't see how it would be wrong to pull out every trick of rhetoric available to fight for your cause! Let's see the rest of this. You're looking at these control buttons, aren't you? What are these things, these hieroglyphics?"

"Universal icons," I explained. "They're activated by eye movement. To start it again, you look at this one—" Even as I was pointing, he'd started it again himself.

There wasn't much left on the disc. A tiny clutch of factoids about a new fusion power plant, a weather report, a sports piece, and then two bitty scoops of local news. The first was a snap and ten seconds of sound, from a reporter at the scene of a party in San Francisco commemorating the two-hundredth anniversary of the 1906 earthquake. The second one—the story that had influenced the Company's choice of this particular news broad-cast for Mr. Hearst's persuasion—was a piece on protesters blocking the subdivision of Hearst Ranch, which was in danger of being turned into a planned community with tract housing, golf courses, and shopping malls.

Hearst caught his breath at that, and if I thought his face had been scary before I saw now I had had no idea what scary could be. His glare hit the activation buttons with almost physical force: replay, replay, replay. After he'd watched that segment half a dozen times, he shut it off and looked at me.

"They can't do it," he said. "Did you see those plans? They'd ruin this coastline. They'd cut down all the trees! Traffic and noise and soot and—and where would all the animals go? Animals have rights, too."

"I'm afraid most of the wildlife would be extinct in this range by then, Mr. Hearst," I apologized, placing the viewer back into its case. "But maybe now you've got an idea about why my Company needs to control certain of your assets."

He was silent, breathing hard. The little dog was looking up at him with anxious eyes.

"All right, Mr. Denham," he said quietly. "To paraphrase Dickens: Is this the image of what will be, or only of what may be?"

I shrugged. "I only know what's going to happen in the future in a general kind of way, Mr. Hearst. Big stuff, like wars and inventions. I'm not told a lot else. I sincerely hope things don't turn out so badly for your ranch—and if it's any consolation, you notice the program was about protesting the *proposed* development only. The problem is, history can't be changed, not once it's happened."

"History, or recorded history, Mr. Denham?" Hearst countered. "They're not at all necessarily the same thing, I can tell you from personal experience."

"I'll bet you can," I answered, wiping away sweat again. "O.K., you've figured something out: there are all kinds of little zones of error in recorded history. My Company makes use of those errors. If history can't be changed, it can be worked around. See?"

"Perfectly," Hearst replied. He leaned back in his chair and his voice was hard, those violets of sound transmuted to porphyry marble. "I'm convinced your people are on the level, Mr. Denham. Now. You go and tell them that twenty years is pretty much chickenfeed as far as I'm concerned. It won't do, not by a long way. I want nothing less than the same immortality you've got, you see? Permanent life. I always thought I could put it to good use and, now that you've shown me the future, I can see my work's cut out for me. I also want shares in your Company's stock. I want to be a player in this game."

"But—" I sat bolt upright in my chair. "Mr. Hearst! I can manage the shares of stock. But the immortality's impossible! You don't understand how it works. The immortality process can't be done on old men. We have to start with young mortals. I was only a little kid when I was recruited for the Company. Don't you see? Your body's too old and damaged to be kept running indefinitely."

"Who said I wanted immortality in this body?" said Hearst. "Why would I want to drive around forever in a rusted old Model T when I could have one of those shiny new modern cars? Your masters seem to be capable of darned near anything. I'm betting that there's a way to bring me back in a new body, and if there isn't a way now, I'll bet they can come up with one if they try. They're going to have to try, if they want my cooperation. Tell them that."

I opened my mouth to protest, and then I thought—why argue? Promise him anything. "O.K.," I agreed.

"Good," Hearst said, finishing his coffee. "Do you need a telephone to contact them? My switchboard can connect you anywhere in the world in a couple of minutes."

"Thanks, but we use something different," I told him. "It's back in my room and I don't think Jerome could find it. I'll try to have an answer for you by tomorrow morning, though."

He nodded. Reaching out his hand, he took up the silver bottle and considered it. "Is this the drug that made you what you are?" He looked at me. His dog looked up at him.

"Pretty much. Except my body's been altered to manufacture the stuff, so it pumps through me all the time," I explained. "I don't have to take it orally."

"But you'd have no objection to sampling a little, before I drank it?"

"Absolutely none," I said, and held out my empty coffee cup. Hearst lifted his eyebrows at that. He puzzled a moment over the bottlecap before figuring it out, and then poured about three ounces of Pineal Tribrantine Three cocktail into my cup. I drank it down, trying not to make a face.

It wasn't all PT3. There was some kind of fruit base, cranberry juice as far as I could tell, and a bunch of hormones and euphoriacs to make him feel great as well as healthy, and something to stimulate the production of telomerase. Beneficial definitely, but not an immortality potion by a long shot. He'd have to have custom-designed biomechanicals and prosthetic implants, to say nothing of years of training for eternity starting when he was about three. But why tell the guy?

And Hearst was looking young already, just watching me: wonderstruck, scared, and eager. When I didn't curl up and die, he poured the rest of the bottle's contents into his cup and drank it down, glancing furtively at his hidden camera.

"My," he said. "That tasted funny."

I nodded.

And of course he didn't die either, as the time passed in that grand room. He quizzed me about my personal life, wanted to hear about what it was like to live in the ancient world, and how many famous people I'd met. I told him all about Phoenician traders and Egyptian priests and Roman senators I'd known. After a while Hearst noticed he felt swell—I could tell by his expression—and he got up and put down the little dog and began to pace the room as we talked, not with the heavy cautious tread of the old man he was but with a light step, almost dancing.

"So I said to Apuleius, 'But that only leaves three fish, and anyway what do you want to do about the flute player—' " I was saying, when a door in the far corner opened and Marion stormed in.

"W-w-where *were* you?" she shouted. Marion stammered when she was tired or upset, and she was both now. "Thanks a lot for s-sneaking out like that and leaving me to t-t-talk to everybody. They're your guests too, y-you know!"

Hearst turned to stare at her, openmouthed. I really think he'd forgotten about Marion. I jumped up, looking apologetic.

"Whoops! Hey, Marion, it was my fault. I needed to ask his advice about something," I explained. She turned, surprised to see me.

"Joe?" she said.

"I'm sorry to take so long, dear," said Hearst, coming and putting his arms around her. "Your friend's a very interesting fellow." He was looking at her like a wolf looks at a lamb chop. "Did they like the picture?"

"N-n-no!" she said. "Half of 'em left before it was over. You'd think they'd s-stay to watch Bing C-Crosby."

If there's one thing I've learned over the millennia, it's when to exit a room.

"Thanks for the talk, Mr. Hearst," I said, grabbing my black case and heading for the elevator. "I'll see if I can't find that prospectus. Maybe you can look at it for me tomorrow."

"Maybe," Hearst murmured into Marion's neck. I was ready to crawl down the elevator cable like a monkey to get out of there, but fortunately the car was still on that floor, so I jumped in and rattled down through the house like Mephistopheles dropping through a trapdoor instead.

It was dark when I emerged into the assembly hall, but as soon as the panel had closed after me light blazed up from the overhead fixtures. I blinked, looking around. Scanning revealed a camera mount, way up high, that I hadn't noticed before. I saluted it Roman style and hurried out into the night, over the Pompeiian floor. As soon as I had crossed the threshold, the lights blinked out behind me. More surveillance. How many faithful Jeromes did Hearst have, sitting patiently behind peepholes in tiny rooms?

The night air was chilly, fresh with the smell of orange and lemon blossoms. The stars looked close enough to fall on me. I wandered around between the statues for a while, wondering how the hell I was going to fool the master of this house into thinking the Company had agreed to his terms. Gee: for that matter, how was I going to break it to the Company that they'd underestimated William Randolph Hearst?

Well, it wasn't going to be the first time I'd had to be the bearer of bad news to Dr. Zeus. At last I gave it up and found my way back to my wing of the guest house.

There was a light on in the gorgeously gilded sitting room. Lewis was perched uncomfortably on the edge of a sixteenth-century chair. He looked guilty about something. Jumping to his feet as I came in, he said: "Joseph, we have a problem."

"We do, huh?" I looked him over wearily. All in the world I wanted right then was a hot shower and a few hours of shuteye. "What is it?"

"The, ah, Valentino script has been stolen," he said.

My priorities changed. I strode muttering to the phone and picked it up. After a moment a blurred voice answered.

"Jerome? How you doing, pal? Listen, I'd like some room service. Can I get a hot fudge sundae over here at La Casa del Sol? Heavy on the hot fudge?"

"Make that two," Lewis suggested. I looked daggers at him and went on:

"Make that two. No, no nuts. And if you've got any chocolate pudding or chocolate cake or some Hershey bars or anything, send those along, too. O.K.? I'll make it worth your while, chum."

"... so I just thought I'd have a last look at it before I went to bed, but when I opened the case it wasn't there," Lewis explained, licking his spoon.

"You scanned for thermoluminescence? Fingerprints?" I said, putting the sundae dish down with one hand and reaching for cake with the other.

"Of course I did. No fingerprints, and judging from the faintness of the thermoluminescence, whoever went through my things must have been wearing gloves," Lewis told me. "About all I could tell was that a mortal had been in my room, probably an hour to an hour and a half before I got there. Do you think it was one of the servants?"

"No, I don't. I know Mr. Hearst sent Jerome in here to get something out of my room, but I don't think the guy ducked into yours as an afterthought to go through your drawers. Anybody who swiped stuff from Mr. Hearst's guests wouldn't work here very long," I said. "If any guest had ever had something stolen, everybody in the Industry would know about it. Gossip travels fast in this town." I meant Hollywood, of course, not San Simeon.

"There's a first time for everything," Lewis said miserably.

"True. But I think our buddy Jerome has *faithful retainer* written all over him," I said, finishing the cake in about three bites.

"Then who else could have done it?" Lewis wondered, starting on a dish of pudding.

"Well, you're the Literary Specialist. Haven't you ever accessed any Agatha Christie novels?" I tossed the cake plate aside and pounced on a Hershey bar. "You know what we do next. Process of elimination. Who was where and when? I'll tell you this much, it wasn't me and it wasn't Big Daddy Hearst. I was with him from the moment we left the rest of you in the theater until Marion came up and I had to scram." I closed my eyes and sighed in bliss, as the Theobromos high finally kicked in.

"Well—" Lewis looked around distractedly, trying to think. "Then—it has to have been one of us who were in the theater watching *Going Hollywood*."

"Yeah. And Marion said about half the audience walked out before it was over," I said. "Did you walk out, Lewis?"

"No! I stayed until the end. I can't imagine why anybody left. I thought it was delightful," Lewis told me earnestly. "It had Bing Crosby in it, you know."

"You've got pudding on your chin. O.K.; so you stayed through the movie," I said, realizing my wits weren't at their sharpest right now but determined to thrash this through. "And so did Marion. Who else was there when the house lights came up, Lewis?"

Lewis sucked in his lower lip, thinking hard through the Theobromine fog. "I'm replaying my visual transcript," he informed me. "Clark Gable is there. The younger Mr. Hearst and his friend are there. The unpleasant-looking fellows in the business suits are there. Connie's there."

"Garbo?"

"Mm—nope."

"The two silents guys? Charlie and Laurence?"

"No."

"What's his name, Jack from Paramount, is he there?"

"No, he isn't."

"What about the crazy lady with the dogs?"

"She's not there either." Lewis raised horrified eyes to me. "My gosh, it could have been any one of them." He remembered the pudding and dabbed at it with his handkerchief.

"Or the thief might have sneaked out, robbed your room, and sneaked back in before the end of the picture," I told him.

"Oh, why complicate things?" he moaned. "What are we going to do?"

"Damned if I know tonight," I replied, struggling to my feet. "Tomorrow you're going to find out who took the Valentino script and get it back. I have other problems, O.K.?"

"What do you mean?"

"Mr. Hearst is upping the ante on the game. He's given me an ultimatum for Dr. Zeus," I explained.

"Wowie." Lewis looked appalled. "He thinks he can dictate terms to the Company?"

"He's doing it, isn't he?" I said, trudging off to my bedroom. "And guess who gets to deliver the messages both ways? Now you see why I was nervous? I knew this was going to happen."

"Well, cheer up," Lewis called after me. "Things can't go more wrong than this."

I switched on the light in my room, and found out just how much more wrong they could go.

Something exploded up from the bed at my face, a confusion of needle teeth and blaring sound. I was stoned, I was tired, I was confused, and so I just slapped it away as hard as I could, which with me being a cyborg and all was pretty hard. The thing flew across the room and hit the wall with a crunch. Then it dropped to the floor and didn't move, except for its legs kicking, but not much or for long.

Lewis was beside me immediately, staring. He put his handkerchief to his mouth and turned away, ashen-faced.

"Ye gods!" he said. "You've killed Tcho-Tcho!"

"Maybe I just stunned her?" I staggered over to see. Lewis staggered with me. We stood looking down at Tcho-Tcho.

"Nope," Lewis told me sadly, shaking his head.

"The Devil, and the Devil's dam, and the Devil's . . . insurance agent," I swore, groping backward until I found a chair to collapse in. "Now what do we do?" I averted my eyes from the nasty little corpse and my gaze fell on the several shreddy parts that were all that remained of my left tennis shoe. "Hey! Look what the damn thing did to my sneaker!"

"How did she get in here, anyway?" Lewis wrung his hands.

"So much for my playing tennis with anybody tomorrow," I snarled.

"But—but if she was in here long enough to chew up your shoe . . ." Lewis paused, eyes glazing over in difficult thought. "Oh, I wish I hadn't done that Theobromos. Isn't that the way it always is? Just when you think it's safe to relax and unwind a little—"

"Hey! This means Cartimandua Bryce took your Valentino script," I said, leaping to my feet and grabbing hold of the chair to steady myself. "See? The damn dog must have followed her in unbeknownst!"

"You're right." Lewis's eyes widened. "Except—well, no, not necessarily. She didn't have the dogs with her, don't you remember? They wouldn't be-have at table. They had to be taken back to her room."

"So they did." I subsided into the chair once more. "Hell. If somebody was sneaking through the rooms, the dog might have got out and wandered around until it got in here, chewed up my shoe, and went to sleep on my bed."

"And that means—that means—" Lewis shook his head. "I'm too tired to think what that means. What are we going to do about the poor dog? I suppose we'll have to go tell Mrs. Bryce."

"Nothing doing," I snapped. "When I'm in the middle of a deal with Hearst? Hearst, who's fanatic about kindness to animals? Sorry about that, W.R., but I just brutally murdered a dear little chihuahua in La Casa del Sol. Thank God there aren't any surveillance cameras in here!"

"But we have to do something," Lewis protested. "We can't leave it here on the rug! Should we take it out and bury it?"

"No. There's bound to be a search when Mrs. Bryce notices it's gone," I said. "If they find the grave and dig it up, they'll know the mutt didn't die naturally, or why would somebody take the trouble to hide the body?"

"Unless we hid it somewhere it'd never be found?" Lewis suggested. "We could pitch it over the perimeter fence. Then, maybe the wild animals would remove the evidence!"

"I don't think zebras are carrion eaters, Lewis." I rubbed my temples wearily. "And I don't know about you, but in the condition I'm in, I don't think I'd get it over the fence on the first throw. All I'd need then would be for one of Hearst's surveillance cameras to pick me up in a spotlight, trying to stuff a dead chihuahua through a fence. Hey!" I brightened. "Hearst has a zoo up here. What if we shotput Tcho-Tcho into the lion's den?"

Lewis shuddered. "What if we missed?"

"To hell with this." I got up. "Dogs die all the time of natural causes."

So we wound up flitting through the starry night in hyperfunction, leaving no more than a blur on any cameras that might be recording our passage, and a pitiful little corpse materialized in what we hoped was a natural attitude of canine demise on the front steps of La Casa Grande. With any luck it would be stiff as a board by morning, which would make foul play harder to detect.

Showered and somewhat sobered up, I opened the field credenza in my suitcase and crouched before it to tap out my report on its tiny keys.

WRH WILLING, HAD PT3 SAMPLE, BUT HOLDING OUT FOR MORE. TERMS: STOCK SHARES PLUS IMMORTALITY PROCESS. HAVE EXPLAINED IMPOS-SIBILITY. REFUSES TO ACCEPT.

SUGGEST: LIE. DELIVER 18 YEARS PER HISTORICAL RECORD WITH PROMISE OF MORE, THEN RENEGOTIATE TERMS WITH HEIRS.

PLEASE ADVISE.

It didn't seem useful to tell anybody that the Valentino script was missing. Why worry the Company? After all, we must be going to find it and complete at least that part of the mission successfully, because history records that an antiques restorer will, on Christmas 20, 2326, at the height of the Old Hollywood Revival, find the script in a hidden compartment in a Spanish cabinet, once owned by W. R. Hearst but recently purchased by Dr. Zeus Incorporated. Provenance indisputably proven, it will then be auctioned off for an unbelievably huge sum, even allowing for twenty-fourth-century inflation. And history cannot be changed, can it?

Of course it can't.

I yawned pleasurably, preparing to shut the credenza down for the night, but it beeped to let me know a message was coming in. I scowled at it and leaned close to see what it said.

TERMS ACCEPTABLE. INFORM HEARST AND AT FIRST OPPORTUNITY PERFORM REPAIRS AND UPGRADE. QUINTILIUS WILL CONTACT WITH STOCK OPTIONS.

I read it through twice. Oh, O.K.; the Company must mean they intended to follow my suggestion. I'd promise him the moon but give him the eighteen years decreed by history, and he wouldn't even be getting those if I didn't do that repair work on his heart. What did they mean by *upgrade*, though? Eh! Details.

And I had no reason to feel lousy about lying to the old man. How many mortals even get to make it to eighty-eight, anyway? And when my stopgap measures finally failed, he'd close his eyes and die—like a lot of mortals—in happy expectation of eternal life after death. Of course, he'd get it in Heaven (if there is such a place) and not down here like he'd been promised, but he'd be in no position to sue me for breach of contract anyway.

I acknowledged the transmission and shut down at last. Yawning again, I crawled into my fabulous priceless antique Renaissance-era hand-carved gilded bed. The chihuahua hadn't peed on it. That was something, at least.

I slept in the next morning, though I knew Hearst preferred his guests to rise with the sun and do something healthy like ride five miles before breakfast. I figured he'd make an exception in my case. Besides, if the PT3 cocktail had delivered its usual kick he'd probably be staying in bed late himself, and so would Marion. I squinted up at the left-hand tower of La Casa Grande, making my way through the brilliant sunlight.

No dead dog in sight anywhere, as I hauled open the big front doors;

Tcho-Tcho's passing must have been discovered without much commotion. Good. I walked through the cool and the gloom of the big house to the morning room at the other end, where sunlight poured in through French doors. There a buffet was set out with breakfast.

Lewis was there ahead of me, loading up on flapjacks. I heaped hash browns on my plate and, for the benefit of the mortals in various corners of the room, said brightly: "So, Lewis! Some swell room, huh? How'd you sleep?"

"Fine, thanks," he replied. *Other than a slight Theobromos hangover.* "But, you know, the saddest thing happened! One of Mrs. Bryce's little dogs got out in the night and died of exposure. The servants found it this morning."

"Gee, that's too bad." *Anybody suspect anything?*

No. "Yes, Mrs. Bryce is dreadfully upset." *I feel just awful.*

Hey, did you lure the damn mutt into my room? We've got worse things to worry about this morning. I helped myself to coffee and carried my plate out into the dining hall, sitting down at the long table. Lewis followed me.

Right, the Valentino script. Have you had any new ideas about who might have taken it?

No. I dug into my hash browns. *Has anybody else complained about anything missing from their rooms?*

No, nobody's said a word.

The thing is—nobody knew you had it with you, right? You didn't happen to mention that you were carrying around an autographed script for The Son of the Sheik?

No, of course not! Lewis sipped his coffee, looking slightly affronted. *I've only been in this business for nearly two millennia.*

Maybe one of the guests was after Garbo or Gable, and got into your room by mistake? I turned nonchalantly to glance into the morning room at Gable. He was deeply immersed in the sports section of one of Mr. Hearst's papers.

Well, if it was an obsessive Garbo fan he'd have seen pretty quickly that he wasn't in a woman's room. Lewis put both elbows on the table in a manly sort of way. *So if it was one of the ladies after Gable—? Though it still doesn't explain why she'd steal the script.*

I glanced over at Connie, who was sitting in an easy chair balancing a plate of scrambled eggs on her knees as she ate. *Connie wouldn't have done it, and neither would Marion. I doubt it was the Hearst kid's popsy. That leaves Garbo and Mrs. Bryce, who left the movie early.*

But why would Garbo steal the script? Lewis drew his eyebrows together.

Why does Garbo do anything? I shrugged. Lewis looked around uneasily.

I can't see her rifling through my belongings, however. And that leaves Mrs. Bryce.

Yeah. Mrs. Bryce. Whose little dog appeared mysteriously in my bedroom.

I got up and crossed back into the morning room on the pretext of going for a coffee refill. Mrs. Bryce, clad in black pajamas, was sitting alone in a prominent chair, with Conqueror Worm greedily wolfing down Eggs Benedict from a plate on the floor. Mrs. Bryce was not eating. Her eyes were closed and her face turned up to the ceiling. I guess she was meditating, since she was doing the whole lotus position bit.

As I passed, Conqueror Worm left off eating long enough to raise his tiny head and snarl at me.

"I hope you will excuse him, Mr. Denham," said Mrs. Bryce without opening her eyes. "He's very protective of me just now."

"That's O.K., Mrs. Bryce," I said affably, but I kept well away from the dog. "Sorry to hear about your sad loss."

"Oh, Tcho-Tcho remains with us still," she said serenely. "She has merely ascended to the next astral plane. I just received a communication from her, in fact. She discarded her earthly body in order to accomplish her more important work."

"Gee, that's just great," I replied, and Gable looked up from his paper at me and rolled his eyes. I shrugged and poured myself more coffee. I still thought Mrs. Bryce was a phony on the make, but if she wanted to pretend Tcho-Tcho had passed on voluntarily instead of being swatted like a tennis ball, that was all right with me.

You think she might have done it, after all? Lewis wondered as I came back to the table. *She had sort of fixated on me, before Marion turned her on Garbo.*

Could be. I think she's too far off on another planet to be organized enough for cat burglary, though. And why would she steal the script and nothing else?

I can't imagine. What are we going to do? Lewis twisted the end of his paper napkin. *Should we report the theft to Mr. Hearst?*

Hell no. That'd queer my pitch. Some representatives of an all-powerful Company we'd look, wouldn't we, letting mortals steal stuff out of our rooms? No.

Here's what you do: see if you can talk to the people who left the theater early, one by one. Just sort of engage them in casual conversation. Find out where each one of the suspects went, and see if you can cross-check their stories with others.

Lewis looked panicked. *But—I'm only a Literature Preservation Specialist. Isn't this interrogation sort of thing more in your line of work, as a Facilitator?*

Maybe, but right now I've got my hands full, I responded, just as the lord of the manor came striding into the room.

Mr. Hearst was wearing jodhpurs and boots, and was flushed with exertion. He hadn't gotten up late after all, but had been out on horseback surveying his domain, like one of the old Californio dons. He hit me with a triumphant look as he marched past, but didn't stop. Instead he went straight up to Mrs. Bryce's chair and took off his hat to address her. Conqueror Worm looked up and him and cowered, then ran to hide behind the chair.

"Ma'am, I was so sorry to hear about your little dog! I hope you'll do me the honor of picking out another from my kennels? I don't think we have any chihuahuas at present, but in my experience a puppy consoles you a good deal when you lose an old canine friend," he told her, with a lot more power and breath in his voice than he'd had last night. The PT3 was working, that much was certain.

Mrs. Bryce looked up from her meditation, startled. Smiling radiantly she rose to her feet.

"Why, Mr. Hearst, you are too kind," she replied. No malarkey about ascendance to astral planes with him, I noticed. He offered her his arm and they swept out through the French doors, with Conqueror Worm running after them desperately.

What happens when we've narrowed down the list of suspects? Lewis tugged at my attention.

Then we steal the script back, I told him.

But how? Lewis tore his paper napkin clean in half. *Even if we move fast enough to confuse the surveillance cameras in the halls—*

We'll figure something out, I replied, and then shushed him, because Marion came floating in.

Floating isn't much of an exaggeration, and there was no booze doing the levitation for her this morning. Marion Davies was one happy mortal. She spotted Connie and made straight for her. Connie looked up and offered a glass.

"I saved ya some arranch use, Marion," she said meaningfully. The orange juice was probably laced with gin. She and Marion were drinking buddies.

"Never mind that! C'mere," Marion told her, and they went over to whisper and giggle in a corner. Connie was looking incredulous.

And are you sure we can rule the servants out? Lewis persisted.

Maybe, I replied, and shushed him again, because Marion had noticed me and broken off her chat with Connie, her smile fading. She got up and approached me hesitantly.

"J-Joe? I need to ask you about something."

"Please, take my seat, Miss Davies." Lewis rose and pulled the chair out for her. "I was just going for a stroll."

"Gee, he's a gentleman, too," Marion said, giggling, but there was a little edge under her laughter. She sank down across from me, and waited until Lewis had taken his empty plate and departed before she said: "Did you—um—come up here to ask Pops for m-money?"

"Aw, hell, no," I said in my best regular-guy voice. "I wouldn't do something like that, Marion."

"Well, I didn't really think so," she admitted, looking at the table and pushing a few grains of spilled salt around with her fingertip. "He doesn't pay blackmailers, you know. But—y-you've got a reputation as a man who knows a lot of secrets, and I just thought—if you'd used me to get up here to talk to him—" She looked at me with narrowed eyes. "That wouldn't be very nice."

"No, it wouldn't," I agreed. "And I swear I didn't come up here to do anything like that. Honest."

Marion just nodded. "The other thing I thought it might be," she went on, "was that you might be selling some kind of patent medicine. A lot of people know he's interested in longevity, and it looked like he'd been drinking something red out of his coffee cup, you see." Her mouth was hard. "He may be a millionaire and he's terribly smart, but people take advantage of him all the time."

"Not me," I said, and looked around as though I wanted to see who might be listening. I leaned across the table to speak close to her ear. "Listen, honey, the truth is—I really did need his advice about something. And he was kind enough to listen. But it's a private matter and believe me, *he's* not the one being blackmailed. See?"

"Oh!" She thought she saw. "Is it Mr. Mayer?"

"Why, no, not at all," I answered hurriedly, in a tone that implied exactly the opposite. Her face cleared.

"Gee, poor Mr. Mayer," she said. She knitted her brows. "So you didn't give W.R. any kind of . . . spring tonic or something?"

"Where would I get something like that?" I looked confused, as I would be if I were some low-level studio dick who handled crises for executives and had never heard of PT3.

"Yeah." Marion reached over and patted my hand. "I'm sorry. I just wanted to be sure."

"I don't blame you," I said, getting to my feet. "But please don't worry, O.K.?"

She had nothing to worry about, after all. Unlike me. I still had to talk to Mr. Hearst.

I strolled out through the grounds to look for him. He found me first, though, looming abruptly into my path.

"Mr. Denham." Hearst grinned at me. "I must commend you on that stuff. It works. Have you communicated with your people?"

"Yes, sir, I have," I assured him, keeping my voice firm and hearty.

"Good. Walk with me, will you? I'd like to hear what they had to say." He started off, and I had to run to fall into step beside him.

"Well—they've agreed to your terms. I must say I'm a little surprised." I laughed in an embarrassed kind of way. "I never thought it was possible to grant a mortal what you're asking for, but you know how it is—the rank and file aren't told everything, I guess."

"I suspected that was how it was," Hearst told me placidly. His little dachshund came racing to greet him. He scooped her up and she licked his face in excitement. "So. How is this to be arranged?"

"As far as the shares of stock go, there'll be another gentleman getting in touch with you pretty soon," I said. "I'm not sure what name he'll be using, but you'll know him. He'll mention my name, just as I mentioned Mr. Shaw's."

"Very good. And the other matter?"

Boy, the other matter. "I can give you a recipe for a tonic you'll drink on a daily basis," I said, improvising. "Your own staff can make it up."

"As simple as that?" He looked down at me sidelong, and so did the dog. "Is it the recipe for what I drank last night?"

"Oh, no, sir," I told him truthfully. "No, this will be something to prolong your life until the date history decrees that you *appear* to die. See? But it'll all be faked. One of our doctors will be there to pronounce you dead, and instead of being taken away to a mortuary, you'll go to one of our hospitals and be made immortal in a new body."

That part was a whopping big bald-faced lie, of course. I felt sweat beading on my forehead again, as we walked along through the garden and Hearst took his time about replying.

"It all sounds plausible," he said at last. "Though of course I've no way of knowing whether your people will keep their word. Have I?"

"You'd just have to trust us," I agreed. "But look at the way you feel right now! Isn't that proof enough?"

"It's persuasive," he replied, but left the sentence unfinished. We walked on. O.K., I needed to impress him again.

"See that pink rose?" I pointed to a bush about a hundred yards away, where one big bloom was just opening.

"I see it, Mr. Denham."

"Count to three, O.K.?"

"One," Hearst said, and I was holding the rose in front of his eyes. He went pale. Then he smiled again, wide and genuine. The little dog *whuffed* at me uncertainly.

"Pretty good," he said. "And can you 'put a girdle round about the earth in forty minutes'?"

"I might, if I could fly," I said. "No wings, though. You don't want wings, too, do you, Mr. Hearst?"

He just laughed. "Not yet. I believe I'll go wash up now, and then head off to the tennis court. Do you play, Mr. Denham?"

"Gee, I just love tennis," I replied, "but, you know, I got all the way up here and discovered I'd only packed one tennis shoe."

"Oh, I'll have a pair brought out for you." Hearst looked down at my feet. "You're, what, about a size six?"

"Yes, sir," I said with a sinking feeling.

"They'll be waiting for you at the court," Hearst informed me. "Try to play down to my speed, will you?" He winked hugely and ambled away.

I was on my way back to the breakfast room with the vague hope of drinking a bottle of pancake syrup or something when I came upon Lewis.

He was creeping along a garden path, keenly watching a flaxen-haired figure slumped on a marble bench amid the roses.

"What are you doing, Lewis?" I said.

"What does it look like I'm doing?" he replied *sotto voce.* "I'm stalking Garbo."

"All right . . ." I must have looked dubious, because he drew himself up indignantly.

"Can you think of any other way to start a casual conversation with her?" he demanded. "And I've worked out a way—" He looked around and transmitted the rest, *I've worked out quite a clever way of detecting the guilty party.*

Oh yeah?

You see, I just engage Garbo in conversation and then sort of artlessly mention that I didn't catch the end of Going Hollywood *because I had a dreadful migraine headache, so I went back to my room early, and would she tell me how it came out? And if she's not the thief, she'll just explain that she left early too and has no idea how it turned out. But! If she's the one who took the script, she'll know I'm lying, because she'll have been in my room and seen I wasn't there. And she'll be so disconcerted that her blood pressure will rise, her pulse will race, her pupils will dilate, and she'll display all the other physical manifestations that would show up on a polygraph if I happened to be using one! And then I'll know.*

Ingenious, I admitted. *Worked all the time for me, when I was an Inquisitor.*

Thank you. Lewis beamed.

Of course, first you have to get Garbo to talk to you.

Lewis nodded, looking determined. He resumed his ever-so-cautious advance on the Burning Icicle. I shrugged and went back to La Casa del Sol to change into tennis togs.

Playing tennis with W. R. Hearst called for every ounce of the guile and finesse that had made me a champion in the Black Legend All-Stars, believe me. I had to demonstrate all kinds of hyperfunction stunts a mortal wouldn't be able to do, like appearing on both sides of the net at once, just to impress him with my immortalness; and yet I had to avoid killing the old man with the ball, and—oh yeah—let him win somehow, too. I'd like to see Bill Tilden try it some time.

It was hell. Hearst seemed to think it was funny, at least; he was in a great mood watching me run around frantically while he kept his position in center court, solid as a tower. He returned my sissy serves with all the force of cannon fire. His dog watched from beyond the fence, standing up on her hind legs to bark suspiciously. She was *sure* there was something funny about me now. Thank God Gable put in an appearance after about an hour of this, and I was able to retire to the sidelines and wheeze, and swear a tougher hour was never wasted there. Hearst paused before his game long enough to make a brief call from a courtside phone. Two minutes later, there was a smiling servant offering me a glass of ice-cold ginger ale.

Gable didn't beat Hearst, either, and I think he actually tried. Clark wasn't much of a toady.

I begged off to go shower—dark hairy guys who play tennis in hyper-function tend to stink—and slipped out afterward to do some reconnoitering.

Tonight I planned to slip in some minor heart surgery on Hearst as he slept, to guarantee those eighteen years the Company was giving him. The trick was going to be getting in undetected. There had to be another way to reach Hearst's rooms besides his private elevator, but there were no stairs visible in any of the rooms I'd been in. How did the servants get up there?

Prowling slowly around the house and bouncing sonar waves off the outside, I found a couple of ways to ascend. The best, for my purposes, was a tiny spiral staircase that was entered from the east terrace. I could sneak through the garden, go straight up, find my way to Hearst's bedroom, and depart the same way once I'd fixed his heart. I could even wear the tennis shoes he'd so thoughtfully loaned me.

I was wandering in the direction of the Neptune pool when there was a hell of a racket from the shrubbery ahead of me. Conqueror Worm came darting out, yapping savagely. I was composed enough not to kick him as he raced up to my ankles. He growled and backed away when I bared my teeth at him in my friendliest fashion.

"Hi, doggie," I said. "Poor little guy, where's your mistress?"

A dark-veiled figure that had been standing perfectly still on the other side of the hedge decided to move, and Cartimandua Bryce walked forward calling out: "Conqueror! Oh! Conqueror, you mustn't challenge Mr. Denham." She came around the corner and saw me.

There was a pause. I think she was waiting for me to demand in astonishment how she'd known it was me, but instead I inquired: "Where's your new dog?"

"Still in Mr. Hearst's kennels," she replied, with a proud lift of her head. "Dear Mr. Hearst is having a traveling basket made for her. Such a kind man!"

"He's a swell guy, all right," I agreed.

"And just as generous in this life as in his others," she went on. "But, you know, being a Caesar taught him that. Ruling the Empire either ennobled a man or brought out his worst vices. Clearly, our host was one of those on whom the laurel crown conferred refinement. Of course, he is a very old soul."

"No kidding?"

"Oh, yes. He has come back many, many times. Many are the names he has borne: Pharaoh, and Caesar, and High King," Mrs. Bryce told me, in as matter-of-fact a voice as though she was listing football trophies. "He has much work to do on this plane of existence, you see. Of course, you may well wonder how I know these things."

"Gee, Mrs. Bryce, how do you know these things?" I asked, just to be nice.

"It is my gift," she said, with a little sad smile, and she sighed. "My gift and my curse, you see. The spirits whisper to me constantly. I described this terrible and wonderful affliction in my novel *Black Covenant*, which of course was based on one of my own past lives."

"I don't think I've read that one," I admitted.

"A sad tale, as so many of them are," she said, sighing again. "In the romantic Scottish Highlands of the thirteenth century, a beautiful young girl discovers she has an uncanny ability to sense both past and future lives of everyone she meets. Her gift brings inevitable doom upon her, of course. She finds her long-lost love, who was a soldier under Mark Antony when she was one of Cleopatra's handmaidens, and is now a gallant highwayman—I mean her lover, of course—and, sensing his inevitable death on the gallows, she dares to die with him."

"That's sad, all right," I agreed. "How'd it sell?"

"It was received by the discerning public with their customary sympathy," Mrs. Bryce replied.

"Is that the one they're doing a screenplay on?" I inquired.

"No," she said, looking me up and down. "That's *Passionate Girl*, the story of Mary, Queen of Scots, told from the unique perspective of her faithful terrier. I may yet persuade Miss Garbo to accept the lead role But, Mr. Denham—I am sensing something about you. Wait. You work in the film industry—"

"Yeah, for Louis B. Mayer," I said.

"And yet—and yet—" She took a step back and shaded her eyes as she looked at me. "I sense more. You cast a long shadow, Mr. Denham. Why—you, too, are an old soul!"

"Oh yeah?" I said, scanning her critically for Crome's radiation. Was she one of those mortals with a fluky electromagnetic field? They tend to receive data other mortals don't get, the way some people pick up radio broadcasts with tooth fillings, because their personal field bleeds into the temporal wave. I couldn't sense anything out of the ordinary in Mrs. Bryce, though. Was she buttering me up because she thought I could talk Garbo into starring in *Passionate Girl* at MGM? Well, she didn't know much about my relationship with Greta.

"Yes—yes—I see you in the Mediterranean area—I see you dueling with a band of street youths—is it in Venice, in the time of the Doges? Yes. And before that . . . I see you in Egypt, Mr. Denham, during the captivity of the Israelites. You loved a girl . . . yet there was another man, an overseer . . ." Conqueror Worm might be able to tell there was something different about me, but his mistress was scoring a big metaphysical zero.

"Really?"

"Yes," she said, lowering her eyes from the oak tree above us, where she had apparently been reading all this stuff. "Do you experience disturbing visions, Mr. Denham? Dreams, perhaps of other places, other times?"

"Yeah, actually," I couldn't resist saying.

"Ah. If you desire to seek further—I may be able to help you." She came close and put her hand on my arm. Conqueror Worm prowled around her ankles, whining like a gnat. "I have some experience in, shall we say, arcane matters? It wouldn't be the first time I have assisted a questing soul in unraveling the mystery of his past lives. Indeed, you might almost call me a detective . . . for I sense you enjoy the works of Mr. Dashiell Hammett," she finished, with a smile as enigmatic as the Mona Lisa.

I smiled right back at her. Conqueror Worm put his tail between his legs and howled.

"Gosh, Mrs. Bryce, that's really amazing," I said, reaching for her hand

and shaking it. "I do like detective fiction." And there was no way she could have known it unless she'd been in my room going through my drawers, where she'd have seen my well-worn copy of *The Maltese Falcon.* "Did your spirits tell you that?"

"Yes," she said modestly, and she was lying through her teeth, if her skin conductivity and pulse were any indication. Lewis was right, you see: we can tell as much as a polygraph about whether or not a mortal is truthful.

"You don't say?" I let go her hand. "Well, well. This has been really interesting, Mrs. Bryce. I've got to go see how my friend is doing now, but, you know, I'd really like to get together to talk with you about this again. Soon."

"Ah! Your friend with the fair hair," she said, and looked wise. Then she stepped in close and lowered her voice. "The haunted one. Tell me, Mr. Denham . . . is he . . . inclined to the worship of Apollo?"

For a moment I was struck speechless, because Lewis does go on sometimes about his Roman cultural identity, but then I realized that wasn't what Mrs. Bryce was implying.

"You mean, is he a homo?"

"Given to sins of the purple and crimson nature," she rephrased, nodding.

Now I knew she had the Valentino script, had seen Rudy's cute note and leaped to her own conclusion. "Uh . . . gee. I don't know. I guess he might be. Why?"

"There is a male spirit who will not rest until he communicates with your friend," Mrs. Bryce told me, breathing heavily. "A fiery soul with a great attachment to Mr. Kensington. One who has but recently passed over. A beautiful shade, upright as a smokeless flame."

The only question now was, why? One thing was certain: whether or not Lewis had ever danced the tango with Rudolph Valentino, Mrs. Bryce sure wished she had. Was she planning some stunt to impress the hell out of all these movie people, using her magic powers to reveal the script's whereabouts if Lewis reported it missing?

"I wonder who it is?" I said. "I'll tell him about it. Of course, you know, he might be kind of embarrassed—"

"But of course." She waved gracefully, as though dismissing all philistine considerations of closets. "If he will speak to me privately, I can do him a great service."

"O.K., Mrs. Bryce," I said, winking, and we went our separate ways through the garden.

I caught up with Lewis in the long pergola, tottering along between the kumquat trees. His tie was askew, his hair was standing on end, and his eyes shone like a couple of blue klieg lights.

"The most incredible thing just happened to me," he said.

"How'd you make out with Garbo?" I inquired, and then my jaw dropped, because he drew himself up and said, with an effort at dignity:

"I'll thank you not to speculate on a lady's private affairs."

"Oh, for crying out loud!" I hoped he'd had the sense to stay out of the range of the surveillance cameras.

"But I can tell you this much," he said, as his silly grin burst through again, "she absolutely did not steal my Valentino script."

"Yeah, I know," I replied. "Cartimandua Bryce took it after all."

"She— Really?" Lewis focused with difficulty. "However did you find out?"

"We were talking just now and she gave the game away." I explained. "Oldest trick in the book, for fake psychics: snoop through people's belongings in secret so you know little details about them you couldn't have known otherwise, then pull 'em out in conversation and wow everybody with your mystical abilities.

"What do you want to bet that's what she was doing when she sneaked out of the theater? She must have used the time to case people's rooms. That's how the damn dog got in our suite. It must have followed her somehow and gotten left behind."

"How sordid," Lewis said. "How are we going to get it back, then?"

"We'll think of a way," I said. "I have a feeling she'll approach you herself, anyhow. She's dying to corner you and give you a big wet kiss from the ghost of Rudolph Valentino, who she thinks is your passionate dead boyfriend. You just play along."

Lewis winced. "That's revolting."

I shrugged. "So long as you get the script back, who cares what she thinks?"

"I care," Lewis protested. "I have a reputation to think about!"

"Like the opinions of a bunch of mortals are going to matter in a hundred years!" I said. "Anyway, I'll bet you've had to do more embarrassing things in the Company's service. I know I have."

"Such as?" Lewis demanded sullenly.

"Such as I don't care to discuss just at the present time," I told him, flouncing away with a grin. He grabbed a pomegranate and hurled it at me, but I winked out and reappeared a few yards off, laughing. The lunch bell rang.

I don't know what Lewis did with the rest of his afternoon, but I suspect he spent it hiding. Myself, I took things easy; napped in the sunlight, went swimming in the Roman pool, and relaxed in the guest library with a good book. By the time we gathered in the assembly hall for cocktail hour again, I was refreshed and ready for a long night's work.

The gathering was a lot more fun now that I wasn't so nervous about Mr. Hearst. Connie got out a Parcheesi game and we sat down to play with Charlie and Laurence. The Hearst kid and his girlfriend took over one of the pianos and played amateurish duets. Mrs. Bryce made a sweeping entrance and backed Gable into a corner, trying out her finder-of-past-lives routine on him. Marion circulated for a while, before getting into a serious discussion of real estate investments with Jack from Paramount. Mr. Hearst came down in the elevator and was promptly surrounded by his executives, who wanted to discuss business. Garbo appeared late, smiling to herself as she wandered over to the other piano and picked out tunes with one finger.

Lewis skulked in at the last moment, just as we were all getting up to go to dinner, and tried to look as though he'd been there all along. The ladies went in first. As she passed him, Garbo reached out and tousled his hair, though she didn't say a word.

The rest of us—Mr. Hearst included—gaped at Lewis. He just straightened up, threw his shoulders back, and swaggered into the dining hall after the ladies.

My place card was immediately at Mr. Hearst's right, and Lewis was seated on the other side of me. It didn't get better than this. I looked nearly as smug as Lewis as I sat down with my loaded plate. Cartimandua Bryce had been given the other place of honor, though, at Marion's right, I guess as a further consolation prize for the loss of Tcho-Tcho. Conqueror Worm was allowed to stay in her lap through the meal this time. He took one look at me and cringed down meek as a lamb, only lifting his muzzle for the tidbits Mrs. Bryce fed him.

She held forth on the subject of reincarnation as we dined, with Marion drawing her out and throwing the rest of us an occasional broad wink, though not when Hearst was looking. He had very strict ideas about courtesy toward guests, even if he clearly thought she was a crackpot.

"So what you're saying is, we just go on and on through history, the same people coming back time after time?" Marion inquired.

"Not all of us," Mrs. Bryce admitted. "Some, I think, are weaker souls and fade after the first thundering torrent of life has finished with them. They are like those who retire from the ball after but one dance, too weary to respond any longer to the fierce call of life's music."

"They just soita go ova to da punchbowl and stay there, huh?" said Connie.

"In a sense," Mrs. Bryce told her, graciously ignoring her teasing tone. "The punchbowl of Lethe, if you will; and there they imbibe forgetfulness and remain. Ah, but the stronger souls plunge back headlong into the maelstrom of mortal passions!"

"Well, but what about going to Heaven and all that stuff?" Marion wanted to know. "Don't we ever get to do that?"

"Oh, undoubtedly," Mrs. Bryce replied, "for there are higher astral planes beyond this mere terrestrial one we inhabit. The truly great souls ascend there in time, as that is their true home; but even they yield to the impulse to assume flesh and descend to the mundane realms again, especially if they have important work to do here." She inclined across the table to Hearst. "As I feel *you* have often done, dear Mr. Hearst."

"Well, I plan on coming back after this life, anyhow," he replied with a smile, and nudged me under the table. I nearly dropped my fork.

"I don't know that I'd want to," said Marion a little crossly. "My g-goodness, I think I'd rather have a nice rest afterwards, and not come back and have to go fighting through the whole darned business all over again."

Hearst lifted his head and regarded her for a long moment.

"Wouldn't you, dear?" he said.

"N-no," Marion insisted, and laughed. "It'd be great to have some peace and quiet for a change."

Mrs. Bryce just nodded, as though to show that proved her point. Hearst looked down at his plate and didn't say anything else for the moment.

"But anyway, Mrs. Bryce," Marion went on in a brighter voice, "who else do you think's an old soul? What about the world leaders right now?"

"Chancellor Hitler, certainly," Mrs. Bryce informed us. "One has only to look at the immense dynamism of the man! This, surely, was a Teutonic Knight, or perhaps one of the barbarian chieftains who defied Caesar."

"Unsuccessfully," said Hearst in a dry little voice.

"Yes, but to comprehend reincarnation is to see history in its true light," Mrs. Bryce explained. "Over the centuries his star has risen inexorably, and will continue to rise. He is a man with true purpose."

"You don't feel that way about Franklin Delano Roosevelt, do you?" Hearst inquired.

"Roosevelt strives," said Mrs. Bryce noncommittally. "But I think his is yet a young soul, blundering perhaps as it finds its way."

"I think he's an insincere bozo, personally," Hearst said.

"Unlike Mussolini! Now there is another man who understands historical destiny, to such an extent one knows he has retained the experience of his past lives."

"I'm afraid I don't think much of dictators," said Hearst, in that castle where his word was law. Mrs. Bryce's eyes widened with the consciousness of her misstep.

"No, for your centuries—perhaps even eons—have given you the wisdom to see that dictatorship is a crude substitute for enlightened rule," she said.

"By which you mean good old American democracy?" he inquired. Wow, Mrs. Bryce was sweating. I have to admit it felt good to sit back and watch it happen to somebody else for a change.

"Well, of course she does," Marion said. "Now, I've had enough of all this history talk, Pops."

"I wanna know more about who *we* all were in our past lives, anyway," said Connie. Mrs. Bryce joined in the general laughter then, shrill with relief.

"Well, as I was saying earlier to Mr. Gable—I feel certain he was Mark Antony."

All eyes were on Clark at this pronouncement. He turned beet red but smiled wryly.

"I never argue with a lady," he said. "Maybe I was, at that."

"Oh, beyond question you were, Mr. Gable," said Mrs. Bryce. "For I myself was one of Cleopatra's maidens-in-waiting, and I recognized you the moment I saw you."

Must be a script for *Black Covenant* in development, too.

There were chuckles up and down the table. "Whaddaya do to find out about odda people?" Connie persisted. "Do ya use one of dose Ouija boards or something?"

"A crude parlor game," Mrs. Bryce said. "In my opinion. No, the best way to delve into the secrets of the past is to speak directly to those who are themselves beyond the flow of time."

"Ya mean, have a seance?" Connie looked intrigued. Marion's eyes lit up.

"That'd be fun, wouldn't it? Jeepers, we've got the perfect setting, too, with all this old stuff around!"

"Now—I don't know—" said Hearst, but Marion had the bit in her teeth.

"Oh, come on, it can't hurt anybody. Are you all done eating? What do you say, kids?"

"Aren't you supposed to have a round table?" asked Jack doubtfully.

"Not necessarily," Mrs. Bryce told him. "This very table will do, if we clear away dinner and turn out the lights."

There was a scramble to do as she suggested. Hearst turned to look at me sheepishly, and then I guess the humor of it got to him: an immortal being sitting in on a seance. He pressed his lips together to keep from grinning. I shrugged, looking wise and ironic.

Marion came running back from the kitchen and took her place at table. "O.K.," she yelled to the butler, and he flicked an unseen switch. The dining hall was plunged into darkness.

"Whadda we do now?" Connie asked breathlessly.

"Consider the utter darkness and the awful chill for a moment," replied Mrs. Bryce in somber tones. "Think of the grave, if you are tempted to mock our proceedings. And now, if you are all willing to show a proper respect for the spirits—link hands, please."

There was a creaking and rustling as we obeyed her. I felt Hearst's big right hand enclose my left one. Lewis took my other hand. *Good Lord, it's dark in here*, he transmitted.

So watch by infrared, I told him. I switched it on myself; the place looked really lurid then, but I had a suspicion about what was going to happen and I wanted to be prepared.

"Spirits of the unseen world," intoned Mrs. Bryce. "Ascended ones! Pause in your eternal meditations and heed our petition. We seek enlightenment! Ah, yes, I begin to feel the vibrations—there is one who approaches us. Can it be? But yes, it is our dear friend Tcho-Tcho! Freed from her disguise of earthly flesh, she once again parts the veil between the worlds. Tcho-Tcho, I sense your urgency. What have you to tell us, dear friend? Speak!"

I think most of the people in the room anticipated some prankster barking at that point, but oddly enough nobody did, and in the strained moment of silence that followed Mrs. Bryce let her head sag forward. Then, slowly, she raised it again, and tilted it way back. She gasped a couple of times and then began to moan in a tiny falsetto voice, incoherent sounds as though she were trying to form words.

"Woooooo," she wailed softly. *"Woooo woo woo woo! Woo woooo!"*

There were vibrations then, all right, from fourteen people trying to hold in their giggles. Mrs. Bryce tossed her head from side to side.

"Wooooo," she went on, and Conqueror Worm sat up in her lap and pointed his snout at the ceiling and began to talk along with her in that way that dogs will, sort of *wou-wou, wou-wou wou,* and beside me Hearst was shaking with silent laughter. Mrs. Bryce must have sensed she was losing her audience, because the woo-woos abruptly began to form into distinct words:

"I have come back," she said. *"I have returned from the vale of felicity because I have unfinished business here. Creatures of the lower plane, there are spirits waiting with me who would communicate with you. Cast aside all ignorant fear. Listen for them!"*

After another moment of silence Marion said, in a strangling kind of voice: "Um—we were just wondering—can you tell us who any of us were in our past lives?"

"Yes . . . " Mrs. Bryce appeared to be listening hard. *"There is one . . . she was born on the nineteenth day of April."*

Connie sat up straight and peered through the darkness in Mrs. Bryce's direction. "Why, dat's my boithday!" she said in a stage whisper.

"Yes . . . I see her in Babylon, Babylon that is fallen . . . yea, truly she lived in Babylon, queen of cities all, and carried roses to lay before Ishtar's altar."

"Jeez, can ya beat it?" Connie exclaimed. "I musta been a priestess or something."

"Pass on now . . . I see a man, hard and brutal . . . he labors with his hands. He stands before towers that point at heaven . . . black gold pours forth. He has been too harsh. He repents . . . he begs forgiveness . . ."

I could see Gable gritting his teeth so hard the muscles in his jaws stood out. His eyes were furious. I wondered if she'd seen a photograph of his father in his luggage. Or had Mrs. Bryce scooped this particular bit of biographical detail out of a movie magazine?

Anyway he stubbornly refused to take the bait, and after a prolonged silence the quavery voice continued:

"Pass on, pass on . . . There is one here who has sailed the mighty oceans. I see him in a white cap . . ."

There was an indrawn breath from one of Hearst's executives. Somebody who enjoyed yachting?

"Yet he has sailed the seven seas in another life . . . I see him kneeling before a great queen, presenting her with all the splendor of the Spanish fleet . . . this entity bore the name of Francis Drake."

Rapacious little pirate turned cutthroat executive? Hey, it could happen.

"Pass on now . . ." I could see Mrs. Bryce turn her head slightly and peer in Lewis's direction through half-closed eyes. *"Oh, there is an urgent message . . . there is one here who pleads to speak . . . this spirit with his dark and smoldering gaze . . . he begs to be acknowledged without shame, for no true passion is shameful . . . he seeks his other self."*

Yikes! transmitted Lewis, horrified.

O.K. She wanted to convince us Rudolph Valentino was trying to say something? He was going to say something, all right. I didn't care whether Lewis *or* Rudy were straight or gay or swung both ways, but this was just too mean-spirited.

I pulled my right hand free from Lewis's and wriggled the left one loose from Hearst's. He turned his head in my direction and I felt a certain speculative amusement from him, but he said nothing to stop me.

So here's what Hearst's surveillance cameras and Dictaphones recorded next: a blur moving through the darkness and a loud crash, as of cymbals. Tcho-Tcho's voice broke off with a little scream.

Next there was a man's voice speaking out of the darkness, but from way high up in the air where no mortal could possibly be—like on the tiny ledge above the wall of choir stalls. If you'd ever heard Valentino speak (like I had, for instance) you'd swear it was him yelling in a rage: *"I am weary of lies! There is a thief here, and if what has been stolen is not returned tonight, the djinni of the desert will avenge. The punishing spirits of the afterlife will pursue! Do you DARE to cross me?"*

Then there was a hiss and a faint smell of sulfur, and gasps and little shrieks from the assembled company as an apparition appeared briefly in the air: Valentino's features, and who could mistake them? His mouth was grim, his eyes hooded with stern determination, just the same expression as Sheik Ahmed had worn advancing on Vilma Banky. Worse still, they were eerily pallid against a scarlet shadow. Somebody screamed, really screamed in terror.

The image vanished, there was another crash, and then a confused moment in which the servants ran in shouting and the lights were turned on.

Everybody was sitting where they had been when the lights had gone out, including me. Down at the end of the table, though, where nobody was sitting, one of Mr. Hearst's collection of eighteenth-century silver platters was spinning around like a phonograph record.

Everyone stared at it, terrified, and the only noise in that cavernous place was the slight rattling as the thing spun slowly to a stop.

"Wow," said the Hearst kid in awe. His father turned slowly to look at me. I met his eyes and pulled out a handkerchief. I was sweating again, but you would be, too, you know? And I used the gesture to drop the burnt-out match I had palmed.

"What the hell's going on?" said Gable, getting to his feet. He stalked down the table to the platter and halted, staring at it.

"What is it?" said Jack.

Gable reached out cautiously and lifted the platter in his hands. He tilted it up so everybody could see. There was a likeness of Valentino smeared on the silver, in some red substance.

"Jeez!" screamed Connie.

"What *is* that stuff?" said Laurence. "Is it blood?"

"Is it ectoplasm?" demanded one of the executives.

Gable peered at it closely.

"It's ketchup," he announced. "Aw, for Christ's sake."

Everyone's gaze was promptly riveted on the ketchup bottle just to Mr. Hearst's right. Hard as they stared at it, I don't think anybody noticed that it was five inches farther to his right than it had been when the lights went out.

Or maybe Mr. Hearst noticed. He pressed his napkin to his mouth and began to shiver like a volcano about to explode, squeezing his eyes shut as tears ran down.

"P-P-Pops!" Marion practically climbed over the table to him, thinking he was having a heart attack.

"I'm O.K.—" He put out a hand to her, gulping for breath, and she realized he was laughing. That broke the tension. There were nervous guffaws and titters from everyone in the room except Cartimandua Bryce, who was pale and silent at her place. Conqueror Worm was still crouched down in her lap, trembling, trying to be The Little Dog Who Wasn't There.

"Gee, that was some neat trick somebody pulled off!" said young Hearst.

Mrs. Bryce drew a deep breath and rose to her feet, clutching Conqueror Worm.

"Or—was it?" she said composedly. She swept the room with a glance. "If anyone here has angered the spirit of Rudolph Valentino, I leave it to his or her discretion to make amends as swiftly as possible. Mr. Hearst? This experience has taken much of the life force from me. I must rest. I trust you'll excuse me?"

"Sure," wheezed Hearst, waving her away.

She made a proudly dignified exit. I glanced over at Lewis, who stared back at me with wide eyes.

Nice work, he transmitted. I grinned at him.

I wouldn't go off to your room too early, I advised. *Give her time to put the script back.*

O.K.

"Well, I don't know about the rest of you," Hearst said at last, sighing, "but I'm ready for some ice cream after that."

So we had ice cream and then went in to watch the movie, which was *Dinner at Eight*. Everybody stayed through to the end. I thought it was a swell story.

Lewis and I walked back to La Casa del Sol afterward, scanning carefully, but nobody was lurking along the paths. No horrible little dog leaped out at me when I turned on the light in my room, either.

"It's here," I heard Lewis crowing.

"The script? Safe and sound?"

"Every page!" Lewis appeared in my doorway, clutching it to his chest. "Thank God. I think I'll sleep with it under my pillow tonight."

"And dream of Rudy?" I said, leering.

"Oh, shut up." He pursed his lips and went off to his room.

I relaxed on my bed while I listened to him changing into his pajamas, brushing his teeth, gargling and all the stuff even immortals have to do before bedtime. He climbed into bed and turned out the light, and maybe he dreamed about Rudy, or even Garbo. I monitored his brainwaves until I was sure he slept deeply enough. Time for the stuff he didn't need to know about.

I changed into dark clothes and laced up the tennis shoes Hearst had loaned me. Opening my black case, I slid out its false bottom and withdrew the sealed prepackaged medical kit I'd been issued from the Company HQ in Hollywood before coming up here. With it was a matchbox-sized Hush Field Unit.

I stuck the Hush Unit in my pocket and slid the medical kit into my shirt. Then I slipped outside, and raced through the gardens of La Cuesta Encantada faster than Robin Goodfellow, or even Evar Swanson, could have done it.

The only time I had to pause was at the doorway on the east terrace, when it took me a few seconds to disable the alarm and pick the lock; then I was racing round and round up the staircase, and so into Hearst's private rooms.

I had the Hush Field Unit activated before I came anywhere near him, and it was a good thing. There was still a light on in his bedroom. I tiptoed in warily all the same, hoping Marion wasn't there.

She wasn't. She slept soundly in her own room on the other end of the suite. I still froze when I entered Hearst's room, though, because Marion gazed serenely down at me from her life-sized nude portrait on the wall. I looked around. She kept pretty strange company: portraits of Hearst's mother and father hung there too, as well as several priceless paintings of the Madonna and Child. I wondered briefly what the pictures might have to say to one another, if they could talk.

Hearst was slumped unconscious in the big armchair next to his telephone. Thank God he hadn't been using it when the Hush Field had gone on, or there'd be a phone off the hook and a hysterical night operator sending out an alarm now. He'd only been working late, composing an editorial by the look of it, in a strong confident scrawl on a lined pad. His dachshund was curled up at his feet, snoring. I set it aside gently and, like an ant picking up a dead beetle, lifted Hearst onto his canopied bed. Then I turned on both lamps, stripped off Hearst's shirt, and took out the medical kit.

The seal hissed as I broke it, and I peeled back the film to reveal . . .

The wrong medical kit.

I stared into it, horrified. What was all this stuff? This wasn't what I needed to do routine heart repair on a mortal! This was one of our own kits, the kind the Base HQ repair facilities stocked. I staggered backward and collapsed into Hearst's comfy chair. Boy, oh boy, did I want some Pep-O-Mints right then.

I sat there a minute, hearing my own heart pounding in that big quiet house.

All right, I told myself, talented improvisation is your forte, isn't it? You've done emergency surgery with less, haven't you? Sure you have. Hell, you've used flint knives and bronze mirrors and leeches and . . . there's bound to be something in that kit you can use.

I got on my feet and poked through it. O.K., here were some sterile Scrubbie Towelettes. I cleansed the area where I'd be making my incision. And here were some sterile gloves, great; I pulled those on. A scalpel. So far, so good. And a hemostim, and a skin plasterer, yeah, I could do this! And here was a bone laser. This was going to work out after all.

I gave Hearst a shot of metabolic depressant, opened him up, and set to work, telling myself that somebody was going to be in big trouble when I made my report to Dr. Zeus . . .

Hearst's ribs looked funny.

There was a thickening of bone where I was having to use the laser, in just the places I needed to make my cuts. Old trauma? Damned old. Funny-looking.

His heart looked funny, too. Of course, I expected that. Hearst had a heart defect, after all. Still, I didn't expect the microscopic wired chip attached to one chamber's wall.

I could actually taste those Pep-O-Mints now. My body was simulating the sensation to comfort me, a defense against the really amazing stress I was experiencing.

I glanced over casually at the medical kit and observed that there was an almost exact duplicate of the chip, but bigger, waiting for me in a shaped compartment. So were a bunch of other little implants.

Repairs and upgrade. This was the right kit after all.

I set down my scalpel, peeled off my gloves, took out my chronophase, and opened its back. I removed a small component. Turning to Hearst's phone, I clamped the component to its wire and picked up the receiver. I heard weird noises and then a smooth voice informing me I had reached Hollywood HQ.

"This is Facilitator Joseph and *what the hell is going on here?*" I demanded.

"Downloading file," the voice replied sweetly.

I went rigid as the encoded signal came tootling through the line to me. Behind my eyes flashed the bright images: I was getting a mission report, filed in 1862, by a Facilitator Jabesh . . . assigned to monitor a young lady who was a passenger on a steamer bound from New York to the Isthmus of Panama, and from there to San Francisco. She was a recent bride, traveling with her much older husband. She was two months pregnant. I saw the pretty girl in pink, I saw the rolling seas, I saw the ladies in their bustles and the top-hatted guys with muttonchop whiskers.

The girl was very ill. Ordinary morning sickness made worse by *mal de mer*? Jabesh—there, man in black, tipping his stovepipe hat to her—posing as a kindly doctor, attended her daily. One morning she fainted in her cabin and her husband pulled Jabesh in off the deck to examine her. Jabesh sent him for a walk around the ship and prepared to perform a standard obstetric examination on the unconscious girl.

Jabesh's horrified face: almost into his hands she miscarried a severely damaged embryo. It was not viable. His frantic communication, next, on the credenza concealed in his doctor's bag. The response: PRIORITY GOLD, with an authorization backed up by Executive Facilitator General Aegeus. The child was to live, at all costs. He was to make it viable. Why? Was the Company making certain that history happened *as written* again? But how could he save this child? With what? Where did he even start?

He downloaded family records. Here was an account of the husband having had a brother "rendered helpless" by an unspecified disease and dying young. Some lethal recessive? Nobody could make this poor little lump of flesh live! But the Company had issued a Priority Gold.

I saw the primitive stateroom, the basin of bloody water, Jabesh's shirt-sleeves rolled up, his desperation. The Priority Gold blinking away at him from his credenza screen.

We're not bound by the laws of mortals, but we do have our own laws. Rules that are never broken under any circumstances, regulations that carry terrible penalties if they're not adhered to. We can be punished with memory effacement, or worse.

Unless we're obeying a Priority Gold. Or so rumor has it.

Jabesh repaired the thing, got its heart-bud beating again. It wasn't enough. Panicked, he pulled out a few special items from his bag (I had just seen one of them) and did something flagrantly illegal: he did a limited augmentation on the embryo. Still not enough.

So that was when he rolled the dice, took the chance. He did something even more flagrantly illegal.

He mended what was broken on that twisted helix of genetic material. He did it with an old standard issue chromosome patcher, the kind found in any operative's field repair kit. They were never intended to be used on mortals, let alone two-month-old embryos, but Jabesh didn't know what else to do. He set it on automatic and by the time he realized what it was doing, he was too late to stop the process.

It redesigned the baby's genotype. It surveyed the damage, analyzed what was lacking, and filled in the gaps with material from its own pre-loaded DNA arsenal. It plugged healthy chromosome sequences into the mess like deluxe Tinkertoy units until it had an organism with optimal chances for survival. That was what it was programmed to do, after all. But it had never had to replace so much in a subject, never had to dig so deeply into its arsenal for material, and some of the DNA in there was very old and very strange indeed. Those kits were first designed a hundred thousand years ago, after all, when *Homo sapiens* hadn't quite homogenized.

By the time the patcher had finished its work, the embryo had been transformed into a healthy hybrid of a kind that hadn't been born in fifty millennia, with utterly unknown potential.

I could see Jabesh managing to reimplant the thing and get the girl all tidy by the time her gruff husband came back. He was telling the husband she needed to stay off her feet and rest, he was telling him that nothing in life is certain, and tipping his tall hat, good day, sir, and staggering off to sit shaking in his cabin, drinking bourbon whiskey straight out of a case bottle without the least effect.

He knew what he'd done. But Jabesh had obeyed the Priority Gold.

I saw him waiting, afraid of what might happen. Nothing did, except that the weeks passed, and the girl lost her pallor and became well. I could see her crossing at Panama—there was the green jungle, there was the now visibly pregnant mother sidesaddle on a mule—and here she was disembarking at San Francisco.

It was months before Jabesh could summon the courage to pay a call on her. Here he was being shown into the parlor, hat in hand. Nothing to see but a young mother dandling her adored boy. Madonna and child, to the life. One laughing baby looks just like another, right? So who'd ever know what Jabesh had done? And here was Jabesh taking his leave, smiling, and turning to slink away into some dark corner of history.

The funny thing was, what Jabesh had done wasn't even against the mortals' law. Yet. It wouldn't become illegal until the year 2093, because mortals wouldn't understand the consequences of genetic engineering until then.

But I understood. And now I knew why I'd wanted to turn tail and run the moment I'd laid eyes on William Randolph Hearst, just as certain dogs cowered at the sight of me.

The last images flitted before my eyes, the baby growing into the tall youth with something now subtly different about him, that unearthly voice, that indefinable quality of endlessly prolonged childhood that would worry his parents. Then! Downloaded directly into my skull before I could even flinch, the flashing letters: PRIORITY GOLD. *REPAIR AND UPGRADE.* Authorized by Executive Facilitator General Aegeus, that same big shot who'd set up Jabesh.

I was trapped. I had been given the order.

So what could I do? I hung up the phone, took back my adapter component, pulled on a fresh pair of gloves, and took up my scalpel again.

How bad could it be, after all? I was coming in at the end of the story, anyway. Eighteen more years weren't so much, even if Hearst never should have existed in the first place. Any weird genetic stuff he might have passed on to his sons seemed to have switched off in them. And, looking at the big picture, had he really done any harm? He was even a decent guy, in his way. Too much money, enthusiasm, appetite for life, an iron will, and unshakable self-assurance . . . and a mind able to think in more dimensions than a human mind should. O.K., so it was a formula for disaster.

I knew, because I remembered certain men with just that kind of zeal and ability. They had been useful to the Company, back in the old days before history began, until they had begun to argue with Company policy. Then the Company had had a problem on its hands, because the big guys were immortals. Then the Company had had to fight dirty, and take steps to see there would never be dissension in its ranks again.

But that had been a long time ago, and right now I had a Priority Gold to deal with, so I told myself Hearst was human enough. He was born of woman, wasn't he? There was her picture on the wall, right across from Marion's. And he had but a little time to live.

I replaced the old tired implants with the fresh new ones and did a repair job on his heart that ought to last the required time. Then I closed him up and did the cosmetic work, and got his shirt back on his old body.

I set him back in his chair, returned the editorial he had been writing to his lap, set the dog at his feet again, gathered up my stuff, turned off the opposite lamp, and looked around to see if I'd forgotten anything. Nope. In an hour or so his heart would begin beating again and he'd be just fine, at least for a few more years.

"Live forever, oh king," I told him sardonically, and then I fled, switching off the hush field as I went.

But my words echoed a little too loudly as I ran through his palace gardens, under the horrified stars.

———

Hearst watched, intrigued, as Lewis slid the Valentino script behind the panel in the antique cabinet. With expert fingers Lewis worked the panel back into its grooves, rocking and sliding it gently, until there was a click and it settled into the place it would occupy for the next four centuries.

"And to think, the next man to see that thing won't even be born for years and years," Hearst said in awe. He closed the front of the cabinet and locked it. As he dropped the key in his waistcoat pocket, he looked at Lewis speculatively.

"I suppose you're an immortal, too, Mr. Kensington?" he inquired.

"Well—yes, sir, I am," Lewis admitted.

"Holy Moses. And how old are you?"

"Not quite eighteen hundred and thirty, sir."

"Not quite! Why, you're no more than a baby, compared to Mr. Denham here, are you?" Hearst chuckled in an avuncular sort of way. "And have *you* known many famous people?"

"Er—I knew Saint Patrick," Lewis offered. "And a lot of obscure English novelists."

"Well, isn't that nice?" Mr. Hearst smiled down at him and patted him on the shoulder. "And now you can tell people you've known Greta Garbo, too."

"Yes, sir," said Lewis, and then his mouth fell open, but Hearst had already turned to me, rustling the slip of paper I had given him.

"And you say my kitchen staff can mix this stuff up, Mr. Denham?"

"Yeah. If you have any trouble finding all the ingredients, I've included the name of a guy in Chinatown who can send you seeds and plants mail-order," I told him.

"Very good," he said, nodding. "Well, I'm sorry you boys can't stay longer, but I know what those studio schedules are like. I imagine we'll run into one another again, though, don't you?"

He smiled, and Lewis and I sort of backed out of his presence salaaming.

Neither one of us said much on the way down the mountain, through all those hairpin turns and herds of wild animals. I think Lewis was scared Hearst might still somehow be able to hear us, and actually I wouldn't have put it past him to have managed to bug the Model A.

Myself, I was silent because I had begun to wonder about something, and I had no way to get an answer on it.

I hadn't taken a DNA sample from Hearst. It wouldn't have been of any use to anybody. You can't make an immortal from an old man, because his DNA, no matter how unusual it is, has long since begun the inevitable process of deterioration, the errors in replication that make it unusable for a template.

This is one of the reasons immortals can only be made from children, see? The younger you are, the more bright and new-minted your DNA pattern is. I was maybe four or five when the Company rescued me, not absolute optimum for DNA but within specs. Lewis was a newborn, which is supposed to work much better. Might fetal DNA work better still?

That being the case . . . had Jabesh kept a sample of the furtive work he'd done, in that cramped steamer cabin? Because if he had, if Dr. Zeus had it on file somewhere . . . it would take a lot of work, but the Company *might* meet the terms of William Randolph Hearst.

But they wouldn't actually ever really do such a thing, would they?

We parked in front of the general store in San Simeon and I bought five rolls of Pep-O-Mints. By the time we got to Pismo Beach I had to stop for more.

End Credits: 2333

The young man leaned forward at his console, fingers flying as he edited images, superimposed them, and rearranged them into startling visuals. When he had a result that satisfied him, he put on a headset and edited in the sound, brief flares of music and dialogue. He played it all back and nodded in satisfaction. His efforts had produced thirty seconds of story that would hold the viewers spellbound, and leave them with the impression that Japanese Imperial troops had brutally crushed a pro-Republic riot in Mazatlan, and Californians from all five provinces were rallying to lend aid to their oppressed brothers and sisters to the south.

Nothing of the kind had occurred, of course, but if enough people thought it had, it just might become the truth. Such things were known to happen.

And it was for everyone's good, after all, because it would set certain necessary forces in motion. He believed that democracy was the best possible system, but had long since quietly acknowledged to himself that government by the people seldom worked because people were such fools. That was all right, though. If a beautiful old automobile wouldn't run, you could always hook it up to something more efficient and tow it, and pretend it was moving of its own accord. As long as it got where you wanted it to go in the end, who cared?

He sent the story for global distribution and began another one, facts inert of themselves but presented in such a way as to paint a damning picture of the Canadian Commonwealth's treatment of its Native American neighbors on the ice mining issue. When he had completed about ten seconds of the visual impasto, however, an immortal in a gray suit entered the room, carrying a disc case.

"Chief? These are the messages from Ceylon Central. Do you want to review them before or after your ride?"

"Gosh, it's that time already, isn't it?" the young man said, glancing at the temporal chart in the lower left hand corner of the monitor. "Leave them here, Quint. I'll go through them this evening."

"Yes, sir." The immortal bowed, set down the case, and left. The young man rose, stretched, and crossed the room to his living suite. A little dog rose from where it had been curled under his chair and followed him sleepily.

Beyond his windows the view was much the same as it had been for the last four centuries: the unspoiled wilderness of the Santa Lucia mountains as far as the eye could see in every direction, save only the west where the sea lay blue and calm. The developers had been stopped. He had seen to it.

He changed into riding clothes and paused before a mirror, combing his hair. Such animal exploitation as horseback riding was illegal, as he well knew, having pushed through the legislation that made it so himself. It was good that vicious people weren't allowed to gallop around on poor sweating beasts anymore, striking and shouting at them. He never treated his horses that way, however. He loved them and was a gentle and careful rider, which was why the public laws didn't apply to him.

He turned from the mirror and found himself facing the portrait of Marion, the laughing girl of his dreams, forever young and happy and sober. He made a little courtly bow and blew her a kiss. All his loved ones were safe and past change now.

Except for his dog; it was getting old. They always did, of course. There were some things even the Company couldn't prevent, useful though it was.

Voices came floating up to him from the courtyard.

". . . because when the government collapsed, of course Park Services didn't have any money anymore," a tour docent was explaining. "For a while it looked as though the people of California were going to lose La Cuesta Encantada to foreign investors. The art treasures were actually being auctioned off, one by one. How many of you remember that antique movie script that was found in that old furniture? A few years back, during the Old Hollywood Revival?"

The young man was distracted from his reverie. Grinning, he went to the mullioned window and peered down at the tour group assembled below. His dog followed him and he picked it up, scratching between its ears as he listened. The docent continued: "Well, that old cabinet came from here! We know that Rudolph Valentino was a friend of Marion Davies, and we think he must have left it up here on a visit, and somehow it got locked in the cabinet and forgotten until it was auctioned off, and the new owners opened the secret drawer."

One of the tourists put up a hand.

"But if everything was sold off—"

"No, you see, at the very last minute a miracle happened." The docent smiled. "William Randolph Hearst had five sons, as you know, but most of their descendants moved away from California. It turned out one of them was living in Europe. He's really wealthy, and when he heard about the Castle being sold, he flew to California to offer the Republic a deal. He bought the Castle himself, but said he'd let the people of California go on visiting Hearst Castle and enjoying its beauty."

"How wealthy is he?" one of the visitors wanted to know.

"Nobody knows just how much money he has," said the docent after a moment, sounding embarrassed. "But we're all very grateful to the present Mr. Hearst. He's actually added to the art collection you're going to see and—though some people don't like it—he's making plans to continue building here."

"Will we get to meet him?" somebody else asked.

"Oh, no. He's a very private man," said the docent. "And very busy, too. But you will get to enjoy his hospitality, as we go into the refectory now for a buffet lunch. Do you all have your complimentary vouchers? Then please follow me inside. Remember to stay within the velvet ropes . . ."

The visitors filed in, pleased and excited. The young man looked down on them from his high window.

He set his dog in its little bed, told it to stay, and then left by a private stair that took him down to the garden. He liked having guests. He liked watching from a distance as their faces lit up, as they stared in awe, as they shared in the beauty of his grand house and all its delights. He liked making mortals happy.

He liked directing their lives, too. He had no doubt at all of his ability to guide them, or the wisdom of his long-term goals for humanity. Besides, it was fun.

In fact, he reflected, it was one of the pleasures that made eternal life worth living. He paused for a moment in the shade of one of the ancient oak trees and looked around, smiling his terrible smile at the world he was making.

HELLFIRE AT TWILIGHT

On a certain autumn day in the year 1774, a certain peddler walked the streets of a certain residential district in London.

His pack was full, because he wasn't really making much of an effort to sell any of his wares. His garments were shabby, and rather large for him, but clean, and cut with a style making it not outside the powers of imagination that he might in fact be a dashing hero of some kind. One temporarily down on his luck, perhaps. Conceivably the object of romantic affection.

He whistled as he trudged along; doffed his hat and made a leg when the coaches of the great rumbled by, spattering him with mud. When occasionally hailed by customers, he stopped and rifled through his pack with alacrity, producing sealing wax, bobbins of thread, blotting paper, cheap stockings, penny candles, tinderboxes, soap, pins and buttons. His prices were reasonable, his manner deferential without being fawning, but he was nonetheless unable to make very many sales.

Indeed, so little notice was taken of him that he might as well have been invisible when he slipped down an alley and came out into one of the back lanes that ran behind the houses. This suited his purposes, however.

He proceeded along the backs of sheds and garden fences with an ease born of familiarity, and went straight to a certain stretch of brick wall. He balanced briefly on tiptoe to peer over; then knocked at the gate in a certain pattern, *rap-a-rap rap.*

The gate was opened by a maid, with such abruptness it was pretty evident she'd been lurking there, waiting for his knock.

"You ain't half behind your time," she said.

"I was assailed by profitable custom," he replied, sweeping off his hat and bowing. "Good morning, my dear! What have you for me today?"

"Gooseberry," she said. "Only it's gone cold, you know."

"I shan't mind that one whit," the peddler replied, swinging his pack round. "And I have brought you something particularly nice in return."

The maid looked at his pack with eager eyes. "Oooo! You never found one!"

"Wait and see," said the peddler, with a roguish wink. He reached into the very bottom of his pack and brought out an object wrapped in brown paper. Presenting it to the maid with a flourish, he watched as she unwrapped it.

"You *never!*" she cried. She whipped a glass lens out of her apron pocket and held the object up, examining it closely.

"Masanao of Kyoto, that is," she announced. "Here's the cartouche. Boxwood. *Very* nice. Some sort of funny little dog, is it?"

"It's a fox, I believe," said the peddler.

"So it is. Well! What a stroke of luck." The maid tucked both lens and netsuke into her apron pocket. "You might go by Limehouse on your rounds, you know; they do say there's all sorts of curious things to be had there."

"What a good idea," said the peddler. He hefted his pack again and looked at her expectantly.

"Oh! Your pie, to be sure. La! I was that excited, I did forget." The maid ran indoors, and returned a moment later with a small pie wrapped in a napkin. "Extra well lined, just as you asked."

"Not a word to your good master about this, however," said the peddler, laying his finger beside his nose. "Eh, my dear?"

"Right you are," said the maid, repeating the gesture with a knowing wink. "He don't miss all that old parchment, busy as he is, and now there's ever so much more room in that spare cupboard."

The peddler took his leave and walked on. Finding a shady spot with a view of the Thames, he sat down and ever so carefully lifted the pie out of its parchment shell, though he was obliged to peel the last sheet free, it having been well gummed with gooseberry leakage. He spread the sheets out across his lap, studying them thoughtfully as he bit into the pie. They were closely written in much-blotted ink, ancient jottings in a quick hand.

"'Whatte to fleshe out thys foolyshe farye play? Too insubstancyal. Noble courte of Oberon nott unlike Theseus his courte. The contrast invydious. Yet too much wit in that lyne and the M of Revylls lyketh it not. Lovers not sufficienclye pleasing of themseylves. Thinke. Thinke, Will. Thinke,'" he read aloud, through a full mouth.

"'How yf a rustick brought in? None can fynde fawlt there by Jesu. Saye a weaver, bellowes-mender or some suche in the woodes by chance. Excellent good meate for Kempe. JESU how yf a companye of rusticks??? As who should bee apying we players? Memo, speake wyth Burbage on thys . . .'"

At that moment he blinked, frowned, and shook his head. Red letters were dancing in front of his eyes: TOXIC RESPONSE ALERT.

"I *beg* your pardon?" he murmured aloud. Vaguely he waved a hand through the air in front of his face, as though swatting away flies, while he ran a self-diagnostic. The red letters were not shooed away; yet neither did his organic body appear to be having any adverse reactions to anything he was tasting, touching, or breathing.

But the red letters did fade slightly after a moment. He shrugged, had another mouthful of pie and kept reading.

"'Cost of properteyes: not so muche an it might be, were we to use agayne the dresses fro thatt Merlyne playe—'"

TOXIC RESPONSE ALERT, cried the letters again, flashing bright. The peddler scowled in real annoyance and ran another self-diagnostic. He received back the same result as before. He looked closely at the pie in his hand. It appeared wholesome, with gooseberry filling oozing out between buttery crusts, and he was rather hungry.

With a sigh, he wrapped it in a pocket handkerchief and set it aside. Carefully he packed the Shakespeare notes in a flat folder, and slid it into his pack; took up the pie again and walked away quickly in the direction of St. Paul's.

There was a stately commercial edifice of brick built on a slope, presenting its respectable upper stories level with the busy street above. The side facing downhill to the river, however, looked out on one of the grubbier waste grounds in London, thickly grown with weeds. Little winding dog paths crossed the area, and the peddler followed one to an unobtrusive-looking door set in the cellar wall of the aforementioned edifice. He did not knock, but stood patiently, waiting as various unseen devices scanned him. Then the door swung inward and he stepped inside.

He walked down an aisle between rows of desks, at which sat assorted gentlemen or ladies working away at curious blue-glowing devices. One or two people nodded to him as he passed, or waved a languid pen. He smiled pleasantly, but proceeded past them to a low flight of stairs and climbed to a half-landing, which opened out on private offices. One door bore a sign in gold lettering that read REPAIRS.

The peddler opened the door, looked in, and called hesitantly:

"Yoo-hoo, Cullender, are you receiving?"

"What the hell is it *now*?" said someone from behind a painted screen. A face rose above the screen, glaring through what appeared to be a pair of exceedingly thick spectacles. "Oh, it's you, Lewis. Sorry—been trying to catch the last episode of *Les Vampires*, and there's an Anthropologist over in Cheapside who keeps transmitting on my channel, all in a panic because he thinks—well, never mind. What can I do for you?"

Lewis set the half-eaten pie down on Cullender's desk blotter. "Would you mind very much scanning this for toxins?"

Cullender blinked in surprise at it. He switched off the ring holo, removed it, and came around the screen to unwrap the handkerchief.

"Gooseberry," he observed. "Looks all right to me."

"Well, but when I take a bite of it, I get this Red Alert telling me it's toxic," said Lewis, holding his fingers up at eye level and making jerky little stabs at the air to signify flashing lights. Cullender frowned, perplexed. He took off his wig, draped it over a corner of the screen, and scratched his scalp.

"You ran a self-diagnostic, I suppose?"

"I certainly did. I appear to be fit as a fiddle."

"Where'd you get it?"

"From the cook of a certain collector of rare documents," said Lewis, lowering his voice.

"Oh! Oh! The, er, Shakespeare correspondence?" Cullender looked at the pie with new respect. He turned it over carefully, as though expecting to find the front page of *Loves Labours Wonne* stuck there.

"I've already peeled the parchment off," said Lewis. "But I did wonder, you know, whether some sort of chemical interaction with old parchment, or the ink perhaps . . . ?"

"To be sure." Cullender took hold of the pie with both hands and held it up. He stared at it intently. His eyes seemed to go out of focus, and in a flat voice he began rattling off a chemical analysis of ingredients.

"No; nothing unusual," he said in a perfectly normal voice, when he had done. He took a bite of the pie and chewed thoughtfully. "Delicious."

"Any flashing red letters?"

"Nary a one. Half a minute—I've thought of something." Cullender went to a shelf and took down what appeared to be a small Majolica ware saucer. He held it out to Lewis. "Spit, there's a good fellow."

"I beg your pardon?"

"Just hoick up a good one. Don't be shy. It's the latest thing in noninvasive personnel chemistry diagnostics."

"But I've already run a diagnostic," said Lewis in tones of mild exasperation, and spat anyway.

"Well, but, you see, this gives us a different profile," said Cullender, studying the saucer as he swirled its contents to and fro. "Yes . . . yes, I thought as much. Ah ha! Perfectly clear now."

"Would you care to enlighten me?"

"It's nothing over which you need be concerned. Merely a crypto-allergy," said Cullender, as he stepped into a back cubicle and rinsed off the dish.

"I'm sorry?"

"Had you lived your life as a mortal man, you'd have been allergic to gooseberries," said Cullender, returning to his desk. "*But*, when we underwent the process that made us cyborgs, our organic systems were given the ability to neutralize allergens. Nonetheless, sometimes a little glitch in the software reads the allergen as an active toxin—sends you a warning, when in fact you have nothing to fear from the allergen at all—a mere false alarm. Don't let it trouble you, my friend!"

"But I've eaten gooseberries plenty of times," said Lewis.

"You may have become sensitized," said Cullender. "Had a mortal acquaintance once became allergic to asparagus at the age of forty. One day he's happily wolfing it down with mayonnaise—next day he's covered in hives the size of half crowns at the mere smell of the stuff."

"Yes, but I'm a cyborg," said Lewis, with a certain amount of irritation.

"Well—a minor error in programming, perhaps," said Cullender. "Who knows why these things happen, eh? Could be sunspots."

"There haven't been any," said Lewis.

"Ah. True. Well, been in for an upgrade recently?"

"No."

"Perhaps you ought, then," said Cullender. "And in the meanwhile, just avoid gooseberries! You'll be fine."

"Very well," said Lewis stiffly, tucking his handkerchief back in his pocket. "Good day."

He turned and left the Repairs office. Behind him, Cullender surreptitiously picked up the rest of the pie and crammed it into his mouth.

Lewis proceeded down the hall to the cloakroom, where he claimed a change of clothes and continued to the showers. He bathed, attired himself in a natty ensemble and neat powdered wig that made him indistinguishable from any respectable young clerk in the better offices in London, and went back to the cloakroom to turn in his peddler's outfit. The pack went with it, save for the folder containing the Shakespeare notes.

"Literature Preservation Specialist Grade Three Lewis," said the cloak warden meditatively. "Your case officer's expecting you, you know. Upstairs."

"Ah! I could just do with a cup of coffee," said Lewis. He tucked the folder under his arm, set his tricorn on his head at a rakish angle, and went off down the hall to climb another flight of stairs.

Having reached the top, and having passed through no less than three hidden panels, he stepped out into the Thames Street coffee room that sat above the London HQ of Dr. Zeus Incorporated.

The coffee room, in its décor, reflected the Enlightenment: rather than being dark-paneled, low-beamed, and full of jostling sheep farmers clutching leathern jacks of ale, it was high-ceilinged and spacious, with wainscoting painted white, great windows admitting the (admittedly somewhat compromised) light and air of a London afternoon, and full of clerks, politicians, and poets chatting over coffee served in porcelain cups imported from China.

Lewis threaded his way between the tables, smiling and nodding. He heard chatter of Gainsborough's latest painting, and the disquiet in the American colonies. Three periwigged gentlemen in tailored silk of pastel Easter egg colors discussed Goethe's latest. Two red-faced, jolly-looking elders pondered the fall of the Jesuits. A tableful of grim men in snuff-colored broadcloth debated the fortunes of the British East India Company. Someone else, in a bottle-green waistcoat, was declaring that Mesmer was a fraud. And, over in a secluded nook, a gentleman of saturnine countenance was watching the room, his features set in an expression compounded of equal parts disdain and boredom.

Ave, Nennius! Lewis transmitted. The gentleman turned his head, spotted Lewis, and stifled a yawn.

Ave, Lewis. He took out his watch and looked at it in a rather pointed fashion, as Lewis came to his table and removed his hat.

"Your servant, sir!" said Lewis, aloud. "Dr. Nennys? I believe I had the pleasure of your acquaintance at Mr. Dispater's party, some weeks ago."

"I believe you are correct, sir," said Nennius. "Pray have a seat, won't you? The boy's just bringing a fresh pot."

"Too kind of you," said Lewis, as he settled into a chair. He held up the folder containing the parchments, waggled his eyebrows in a triumphant manner, and set it down at Nennius's elbow. "I believe you collect antiquities, sir, do you not? If you will do me the kindness of examining these papers, I believe you will find much to engage your interest!"

Don't lay it on with a trowel, for gods' sake, transmitted Nennius, but aloud said merely: "Indeed? Let us see."

He opened the folder and studied its contents, while a waiter brought another pot of coffee and a fresh cup and saucer for Lewis.

"Would you be dining, sir? Cake or something?"

Lewis felt the pangs of appetite. "Have you any apple pie?"

"Yes, sir," said the waiter, "Bring you a nice one," and he withdrew.

"We—ell," said Nennius, "Very interesting . . . some prime examples here. Private correspondence, notes, what appears to be a script page or two . . ." He lifted out one parchment, and pursed his lips in annoyance as it brought two other pages with it, glued together by fruit filling. "Rather a lot of work for the conservators, however."

Lewis spread out his hands in a gesture of apology. "At least we have them. Before I made the contact, she was using them to light the boiler. Poor old fellow! I expect he'll have apoplexy when he finds out. Still, 'History—' "

" '—Cannot Be Changed,' " said Nennius, finishing the statement for him. "So somebody ought to profit from it. Eh? Not a bad job overall, Lewis." He closed the folder and studied his nails as the waiter brought a sturdy-looking little apple tart and set it before Lewis. The waiter left, and, as Lewis was happily breaking into the crust with a fork, Nennius said: "Still, they're pulling you out. Sending you down to the Chilterns."

"Mm! Lovely country thereabouts," said Lewis, noting in satisfaction that no red letters flashed in his field of vision. He had another mouthful of pie. "What's the quarry, pray?"

"*If* it really exists, it's a Greek scroll or codex that would be anywhere from three thousand to seventeen hundred years old," said Nennius. "On the other hand, it may be a fraud. The sort of thing that would be cobbled together and sold to an impressionable young Briton on a grand tour. Your job's to find it—which may in itself be a bit tricky—and obtain it for the Company, which may be more difficult still."

"And determine whether it's authentic or otherwise, I assume," said Lewis.

"Of course, of course." Nennius took out a calfskin folder nearly identical to the one Lewis had given him and deftly switched them. "Your directions and letter of introduction are in there. Scholar wanting employment, highly recommended, encyclopedic knowledge of all things Greek and Latin, expert curator of papyrus, parchment, and et cetera. The gentleman in question has an extensive library." Nennius smiled as he said the last word.

"Sounds easy!" said Lewis, not looking up from his pie. "Hours of browsing through a splendid classical library? Now, that's my idea of a posting!"

"How nice that you bring your customary enthusiasm to the job," Nennius drawled. "Though we don't believe your specific quarry will be in the library, in fact. More likely hidden in a box of some kind, somewhere in one of the tunnels. Perhaps in an altar."

"Tunnels?" Lewis knitted his brows in perplexity. "Wherever am I being sent?"

"West Wycombe," said Nennius, with just a trace of malicious amusement. "To the estate of Baron leDespencer."

"Ah," said Lewis politely, lifting another forkful of flaky pastry crust.

"That would be Baron leDespencer, Sir Francis Dashwood," said Nennius. The bit of pie fell off Lewis's fork.

"I *beg* your pardon?" he stammered. Looking around hastily, he leaned forward and lowered his voice. "Surely you don't mean that fellow with the, the, er—"

"Notorious hellfire club? I'm afraid I do, yes," said Nennius in a leisurely fashion, taking a sip of his coffee.

"But I'm a *Literature Preservation Specialist*," said Lewis.

"So I understand. And Dashwood has one of the most extensive libraries of pornography, both ancient and modern, in the world. I know of some operatives who'd positively leap at the chance to have a peek at it," said Nennius. "You ought to have ample time, whilst you're searching for the scroll. Which is something entirely different, by the way. It may, or may not, contain an account of the rituals performed during the Eleusinian Mysteries."

"But *we* know all about the Eleusinian Mysteries!" said Lewis. "I attended them myself! And managed to record them, I might add."

"Yes, but your old holiday holoshots aren't the sort of thing the Company can sell to wealthy collectors," Nennius pointed out. "He's expecting you on the fifteenth. You'll do famously, I'm quite sure. Good day, sir. You'll excuse me, I trust; I have an engagement at the Cocoa Tree."

He rose, took up a silver-headed walking stick and strolled out, leaving Lewis with the check.

In the dim gray hours of the fifteenth of the month, Lewis stepped down from the coach, caught his valise as the coachman threw it down to him, and looked blearily around at High Wycombe.

Its appearance lived up to its reputation as the capital of the British chair manufacturing industry.

There was a tavern that looked as though its interior was dark-paneled, low-beamed, and full of jostling upholsterers clutching leathern jacks of ale. It did not look as though it might be open and serving breakfast, however. Lewis sighed, and started the trudge to West Wycombe.

In spite of his worries, his spirits rose as he went along. The road was good, free of mudholes; the country rolling and wooded, beautiful in the brightening air. The dawn chorus of birds began. When the sun rose at last, it struck an answering gleam from a curious feature high on a hill: what appeared to be the steeple of a church, surmounted not with a cross but with a golden ball, like an echo of the sun itself.

"How charmingly neoclassical," Lewis thought to himself, and was surprised, on accessing his database of local information, to discover that it was in fact St. Lawrence's church, and had been "restored and improved" by Sir Francis Dashwood himself.

The birds sang on. The autumn meadows were full of gamboling hares, and fleecy sheep, and the occasional prosperous and happy-looking shepherd. Rose brambles were bright with scarlet fruit. When the great house came into view at last, that too was all sunlight and peace: a great Palladian mansion of golden stone, trimmed with white.

Lewis scanned the countryside for suspicious-looking altars, standing stones, or at least a wicker man or two. There weren't any. No black hounds watched him from behind trees, either. Only, as he entered the park and started down the wide, pleasant drive, an elderly pug limping along on its solitary business stopped to regard him. It coughed at him in a querulous sort of way, and then lost interest in him and wandered on through drifts of fallen leaves.

At the end of the drive Lewis came to the tremendous entrance portico, Greek Revival looking strangely comfortable in its setting. Within, like an immense lawn jockey, a statue of Bacchus towered beside the door. Bacchus too looked comfortable. Lewis smiled nervously up at him as he knocked.

He gazed about as he waited for someone to open the door; there were panels painted with representations of scenes from classical literature, including one of Bacchus crowning Ariadne. Lewis was studying it with his head craned back, mouth agape, when the door was abruptly opened. He looked down and found himself being regarded by an elderly gentleman, far too well dressed to be a butler.

"You're not the postman," he said.

"No, sir. Your servant, sir!" Lewis removed his hat and bowed. "Lewis Owens. Is Lord leDespencer within?"

"He is," said the gentleman. "Owens? You'd be the librarian?"

"I hope to be, sir," said Lewis, drawing forth and offering his letter of introduction. The gentleman took it and waved him within in an absent-minded way, as he broke the seal and perused the letter's contents. Lewis slid past him and set down his valise in the Great Hall.

He scanned, but was unable to pick up any currents of mortal agitation; only a droning like a well-run beehive, and fragments of mortal thought: . . . *Just get them geraniums potted . . . it doesn't hurt quite so much now, I shall be better presently . . . he asked for jugged hare special, and here you've gone and used up all the . . . damn, however shall I get that grease spot out? . . . I could quite fancy a cup of chocolate just now . . . see, he put all his money in barley futures, but . . .*

Lewis tended to become enthralled by mortal dramas, however ordinary, so he was startled from his reverie when the gentleman said, without warning: " '*Vilia miretur vulgus; mihi flavus Apollo—*' "

" '*—Pocula Castalia plena ministret aqua,*' " responded Lewis automatically. The old gentleman smiled at him.

"I see your patron is not mistaken in you. My apologies, young man; the last candidate Sir Francis considered for the post was something of an impostor. Paul Whitehead, sir, at your service."

"Whitehead, the author of *Manners* and other celebrated satires!" Lewis cried, bowing low. "Oh, sir, what an honor—"

They were interrupted at this moment by the butler hurrying in, hastily rearranging his cravat.

"I beg your pardon, Mr. Whitehead—so sorry—is the gentleman a friend?"

"I think it likely," said Mr. Whitehead, looking dazed. "You have, in fact, *read* something of mine? Good God, sir! And here I thought myself quite forgotten."

He drew breath to laugh and coughed instead, a hard racking cough. John hurried forward to take his arm, but he held up his hand.

"I'm quite all right. Never mind, John. Come along, Mr. Owens; Sir Francis will be delighted to see you."

He led Lewis through splendid rooms, all done in a rather old-fashioned Italian Renaissance style and perhaps with too many statues to be in the best of taste.

"My understanding was that the library was in some disarray," said Lewis delicately.

"Well, it ought to be properly catalogued," said Mr. Whitehead. "We never got around to it; and now that so many of the books from Medmenham have been conveyed over here—why, it is in a sad condition."

Lewis cleared his throat. "That would be the, er, famous abbey?"

"Of the monks of St. Francis of Wycombe." The old man rolled his eyes. "*Famous*, is it? I daresay. For a secret society, we had an extraordinary number of tattlers. Not that any of them are up to much lechery nowadays. But there it is: 'In the days of me youth I could bill like a dove . . . tra la la la.' "

They emerged from the house into wide garden acreage, in which the neoclassical theme continued; temples, arches, and yet more statues, crowded around a lake. In the near foreground, however, a small and somewhat wobbly-looking pavilion of pink silk had been pitched on the lawn.

As they approached it, Lewis heard a man's voice saying: "I shouldn't do it, Francis. You will almost certainly have your left hand cut off by the Grand Turk."

"Bad Francis," said a child's voice.

"I believe you've found your librarian, Francis," said Mr. Whitehead, leading Lewis around to the front of the pavilion. Inside, seated on a Turkish carpet, were two tiny children, a dish of quartered oranges and sweetmeats, and a man in late middle age. He wore a dressing gown and a turban.

"What?" he said. "Oh. Pray excuse me; we're being Arabs."

"Quite all right," said Lewis.

"May I present Mr. Lewis Owens, Sir Francis?" said Mr. Whitehead, not without a certain irony. "Mr. Owens—Lord leDespencer, Sir Francis Dashwood."

Further introduction was delayed at this point, because the little boy lunged for the sweetmeats and crammed a fistful of them in his mouth quick as lightning, occasioning the little girl to scream shrilly: "Papa, he went and done it after all!"

"And may I present my children? Francis and Frances Dashwood." Sir Francis clapped twice, and a nurse came from the portico. "I name them all after me; so like the Roman custom, don't you think? Take them back to the harem, Mrs. Willis. Fanny, remember your manners. What must we do when we meet infidel gentlemen?"

The little girl drew a curtain over her head, then rose to her feet and made an unsteady curtsey. The nurse scooped up the baby, levered the gooball of sweets out of his mouth with a practiced hand, and bore him away despite his screams of rage. The little girl followed her, tripping only once on the trailing curtain.

"Won't you sit down, Mr. Owens?" said Sir Francis, indicating the carpet beside him. Mr. Whitehead had already gone to the portico and fetched himself a garden chair.

"With gratitude, sir," said Lewis, crawling awkwardly into the tent. Sir Francis offered him the dish, and he helped himself to an orange quarter. Seen close to, Sir Francis looked nothing like a notorious rake and blasphemer; he had a good-natured face, with shrewd eyes and none of the bloated fogginess of the habitual drinker.

"Here's his letter," said Mr. Whitehead, handing it to Sir Francis, who held it out at arm's length and peered at it.

"Why, sir, you come to us highly recommended," he said after a moment. "It would appear you are quite the scholar."

"Dr. Franklin is too kind," said Lewis, doing his best to look abashed.

"And you've some experience restoring old papers! That's an excellent thing; for, you know, some of my library is exceeding rare and, like mortal flesh, prone to crumble with age." Sir Francis tucked the letter into his pocket and gave Lewis a sidelong look. "I suppose you were, er, advised as to its nature?"

"Oh." Lewis blushed. "Yes. Yes, my lord, I was."

"I don't imagine you're a prudish young fellow; Franklin would scarce have sent you if you were inclined that way. Mr. Williams was a sad disappointment, yes indeed; let us hope his successor fares better." Sir Francis took up a piece of orange and bit into it.

"I expect you have heard stories, of course," he added.

"Er—yes," said Lewis. Sir Francis chortled.

"Most of them are wildest exaggeration. Yet we had some rare times in our day, Paul, had we not? Good food, good drink, good company. Taste the sweets of life, my boy, whilst you're able; for all too soon we fade like summer flowers."

"Too soon indeed," said Mr. Whitehead with a sigh. "Albeit a firm belief in eternal life in the hereafter is a great comfort."

"Quite so," Sir Francis agreed, looking solemn. "Still, we're not entirely withered yet, hey? I was thinking only the other evening, we really ought to have another 'chapter meeting' with some of our brother monks." He winked broadly at Lewis. "Quite a bit of fun, and really nothing of which to be ashamed. Paul knows of a respectable house with the most agreeable, good-natured girls—charmers all, discreet, free of the pox, but with a certain amount of *intellectual* furniture, you know."

"Ah! Like the hetaerae of ancient Greece?" Lewis inquired.

"Exactly!" said Sir Francis, and seized his hand and shook it enthusiastically. "Just so. And, after all, in men of our years, good conversation hath its virtue too. Not that I expect a young man to believe me."

He popped a sweetmeat in his mouth and crawled out of the tent on hands and knees. "Come along," he said briskly. "We'll show you the library."

Lewis found himself employed. It couldn't have been easier; he had a pleasant room, was free to keep his own hours, and had a place at Sir Francis's table. On his second evening in residence he had a difficult encounter with a dish of syllabub that proved to contain gooseberries, but managed to ignore the flashing lights and keep smiling at his host's witticisms.

And the library was a treasure trove.

It was true that a great deal of it consisted of erotica, inclining to the eclectic rather than the perverse. Lewis found a splendid copy of the earliest translation into English of the *Kama Sutra.* And the library certainly needed putting into order: *Gulliver's Travels* jostled for shelf space with books on the Kabbalah, or on architecture, or *Foxe's Book of Martyrs,* or Ovid's *Amores.* There were indeed a couple of fairly ancient scrolls and codices: a second-century copy of Euripides' *The Bacchae,* and a copy of Aristophanes' *The Frogs* that was nearly as old.

There were a few fakes, too, most notably a work on alchemy purporting to have been written by Aristotle; these were well done, clearly by a someone who had had access to a cache of very old papyrus and knew a few tricks for compounding period-formula inks. Lewis recognized the hand of a certain forger active in the last century, who had worked from the Eugenikos manuscripts. This unknown Russian was quite a celebrity in the faked document trade; Lewis, noting that Sir Francis had traveled to Russia in his youth, suspected that he may have been sold a number of phonies from the same artist.

At the end of a week, he sat down at his artfully concealed field credenza and sent the message:

> *DASHWOOD MISSION SUCCESS SO FAR. HAVE GAINED ACCESS TO LIBRARY. MUCH TO INTEREST COMPANY INVESTORS! WILL REQUIRE TWO DRUMS PAPYRO-FIX AND ONE OF PARCH-FIX. KINDLY SHIP BY EARLIEST POST.*
>
> *HOWEVER, NO SIGN OF QUOTE ELEUSINIAN MYSTERY SCROLL UNQUOTE. NO SIGN OF PAGAN ORGIES YET. NO ORGIES OF ANY KIND, IN FACT. SUGGEST INFORMANT MISTAKEN?*

After an hour the reply came back, in glaring yellow letters:

> PAPYRO-FIX AND PARCH-FIX HAVE SHIPPED.
> LOOK HARDER, LEWIS.

"This is excellent bacon, my lord," said Lewis, at the breakfast table.

"Eh?" Sir Francis looked up from watching the nurse attempting to feed his offspring porridge. "Ah. Good pigs hereabouts."

Lewis wondered how to gracefully transition from pigs to the subject at hand, and couldn't think of a way.

"I wondered, my lord, whether (since it is the Sabbath) I might not have the day to walk in the gardens," he said.

"What? Oh, by all means!" said Sir Francis. "Yes, you'll enjoy that. A man of classical education will find much to engage his attention," he added, winking so broadly that his little daughter was fascinated, and sat there at table practicing outrageous winks, until her nurse quelled her with a deadly look.

Lewis slipped forth after breakfast and had hoped to spend a profitable day spying out likely places where a scroll might be hidden, but he had got no farther than the Temple of Venus when Sir Francis popped out of a folly.

"There you are! It occurred to me that you'd benefit from a guide; there's rather a lot to see," he cried heartily.

"You're too kind, my lord," said Lewis, concealing his irritation.

"Oh, not at all." Sir Francis cleared his throat a little self-consciously and went on: "Well! The temple of Venus. Note, sir, the statue."

"Which one?" Lewis inquired politely, for there were before him nearly thirty figures decorating the slope up to the temple, among the bright fallen leaves: boys bearing shields, various smaller figures of fauns, nymphs, cherubs, and what looked suspiciously like a contingent of garden gnomes.

"Venus herself," said Sir Francis, leading the way up the hill. "The one actually in the temple, you see? Regard the rather better execution than in all the little figures; I got those at a bargain price, though, by God. Someone's plaster yard in Genoa had gone bankrupt and was closing out its stock. This, sir, is a copy of the Venus de Medici; rather fine, don't you think?"

"Profoundly so," said Lewis, wondering whether Sir Francis was guiding him away from something. Sir Francis stepped back and swung his hand up to point at the dome of the temple.

"And, see there? Look closely. It's a little hard to make out, at this angle, but that's Leda and Jove in the guise of a swan."

Lewis stepped back and looked.

"Oh," he said. "Oh! Well. She, er, certainly looks happy."

"I think the sculptor caught perfectly the combination of ecstatic convulsion and divine-regarding reverie," said Sir Francis. "Pity we can't have it down here where it might be better viewed, but . . . well, perhaps better not. Awkward to explain to the children."

"I expect it would be, yes."

"And down *here* we put Venus's Parlor," Sir Francis went on. "That one represents Mercury, you see? Rather an ironic reminder to incautious youth. Observe the many elegant references to sweet Venus's portal of bliss, or, as some have called it, the Gate of Life itself, whence we all are come."

"How evocative, my lord," said Lewis, stammering rather.

"And that yonder is a temple to the nymph Daphne," said Sir Francis, pointing. "Must have the laurels trimmed back somewhat, so as to disclose it with more art. I put that in during my druidical days."

"I beg your pardon?"

"Was going to worship trees, once," said Sir Francis. "Applied to Stukeley—the Head Druid, you know—for initiation and all that. Got a charter to start up a grove, as it happened; but they grew vexed with me and withdrew it. No sense of humor, those fellows."

"Not the eighteenth-century ones, at any rate," Lewis murmured.

"And I don't know that I see much to worship in mere *trees*, in any case," said Sir Francis. "They're not good company, eh?" He nudged Lewis. "Same thing with the Freemasons; I always did my best to behave with them, but 'pon my soul I couldn't keep a straight face. Though I trust I give no offense, sir?"

"Oh, none, I assure you."

"I suppose I ought to have inquired whether you were a Christian," said Sir Francis.

"I frankly own myself a pagan," confided Lewis. "Though I have Christian friends."

"Oh, I too! I'd never mock Christ himself, you know; it's the institution I can't abide. Loathsome, cruel, sanctimonious greedy hypocrites! But regard my little church up there, on the hill; what d'you think of that, sir, hey?"

"I did wonder what the golden ball was for," said Lewis.

"It represents the Sun," said Sir Francis. "To my mind, much the more appropriate symbol for the 'Light of the World,' wouldn't you say? But certain folk took umbrage, of course. Though I expect I only made things worse by having drinking parties up there, for I had it built hollow, you know, with seats inside. Then I slipped and nearly broke my neck climbing down out of it . . . dear, dear." He began to snicker shamefacedly. "Still, you ought to have seen the vicar's expression!"

They walked on a little, and Sir Francis pointed out the lake, with its swans and authentic fleet of small ships, useful for mock sea battles at parties ("Though last time a fire broke out—burning wadding flew everywhere—so we haven't fired the cannons in years"). On an island in the center of the lake was another folly, with yet more statues.

"Looks rather like the temple of Vesta in Rome," Lewis observed.

Hastily he added, "At least, as it might have looked before it became a ruin."

"Ah! You saw that, did you?" said Sir Francis. "Very good! That was my intent, you know. You *are* a scholar, sir. I sketched the ruins myself, once. Dearly loved classical Rome when I was a young man. Still think its religion was quite the most sensible men have ever made for themselves."

"You know, I've thought that too," said Lewis.

"Have you?" Sir Francis turned to him, positively beaming. "Their gods are so like *us*, you know; ordinary people, with faults and family quarrels. Some of them quite dreadful, but others rather endearing. Much more likely to have made this dirty, silly world than some remote Perfection in th' ether. Or wouldn't you say?"

"It has always seemed that way to me," said Lewis, thinking wistfully of his human ancestry. He considered Sir Francis, and decided to cast out a hook. "Of course, there wasn't much prospect of an afterlife for mere mortals in antiquity."

"Not so!" said Sir Francis. "Or what would you make of the Eleusinian Mysteries, then?"

Lewis drew a deep breath and thanked Mercury, god of schemers.

"Well, what can one make, my lord? The Eleusinian rites are unknown, because their initiates were sworn to secrecy," he said.

"Ha! I can tell you how much an oath of secrecy's worth," said Sir Francis, shaking his head. "Depend upon it, my young friend, people blabbed. Life everlasting was offered to mortals long before St. Paul and his cronies claimed the idea."

True enough, thought Lewis, reflecting on the Company's immortality process. "So it's rumored, my lord; but, alas, we've not a shred of proof for that, have we?"

"That's as may be," said Sir Francis blandly. "If I were to tell you that there are certain sacred groves in Italy where satyrs yet dance, you'd think me mad; yet I have seen something pretty near to them. Ay, and nymphs, too!"

Lewis did his best to look like a man of the world. "Well, I could name you a nymph or two here in England, if it comes to that," he said, attempting a nudge and wink. Sir Francis clapped him on the back.

"I dare say you could! Yes, we really must have another chapter meeting. I'll sponsor you, if you like."

"Oh, sir, what kindness!"

"Not at all," said Sir Francis, looking immensely pleased. "We've needed some young blood in our ranks. I'll send to Twickenham for Whitehead; he'll arrange it."

Lewis looked at the box of fragments and shook his head sadly. The pornographic papyrus was in shocking condition, nearly as bad as some of the Dead Sea scrolls would be; though this damage seemed due to recent abuse of some kind. Worse still, some of the little bits were gummed together with something, and it wasn't gooseberry jam. Lewis had begun to have a queasy notion as to the circumstances of his immediate predecessor's departure.

"Well, let's see if we can't put things to rights," he muttered to himself, and set out the larger pieces. Three nymphs, five satyrs, and . . . possibly a horse? And a flute player? And a lot of bunches of grapes. Three sets of unattached, er, bits. Part of a . . . duck?

Frowning, the tip of his tongue between his teeth in intense concentration, Lewis sorted through all the fragments of wildly posturing limbs. With a cyborg's speed in analysis, he began to assemble the bits of the puzzle.

"There . . . and *he* goes there and *she* goes there and . . . no, that doesn't look anatomically possible, does it? Ah. But if this leg goes up *this* way . . . no, that's an elbow . . . oh, it's a *centaur!* Well, that makes much more sense. Silly me."

The door to the library opened, admitting a draft and Sir Francis. Lewis spread out his hands to prevent the reassembled orgy scene from sailing across the tabletop.

"There you are, Owens," Sir Francis said. He sounded a trifle hesitant. Lewis looked up at him sharply, but he did not meet Lewis's gaze; instead he kept his eyes on the papyrus as he approached.

"Well! H'em. What a splendid job you're doing! Deplorable state that one was in; should have had this seen to ages ago, I suppose. But, then, I've been busy these last years bringing myrtles to Venus myself, rather than reading about other people doing it. Eh?"

"Very wise, my lord."

He pulled out a chair and sat at the table, looking on in silence a moment as Lewis went back to fitting fragments together.

"I remember acquiring that one as though it were yesterday," Sir Francis said. "I was seeing Naxos. My guide was a shrewd man; you could trust him to find you absolutely anything. Girls fair or dark, plump or slender, whatever your mood; and the very best houses for drinking, you know, whether you wanted wine or stronger spirits. If you wanted to see temples, he could find those too; and I had but to mention that I was interested in antiquities, and, by God, sir, he showed me . . ."

"A certain shop?" said Lewis, carefully applying Papyro-Fix from a plain jar, with a tiny brush. He fitted two fragments together. They reunited so perfectly it would have been impossible to say where they had been sundered. "A dark little place down a winding street?"

"Look at that! I declare, sir, you are a very physician of books! . . . But no, it wasn't such a shop. I've seen those places; they're all too eager to snare a young fool on his first Grand Tour, and sell him Homer's very lyre and Caesar's own laurels to boot. All impostures, you may be certain. No . . . this was another sort of place entirely."

Lewis was silent, waiting for him to continue. He looked up and saw Sir Francis gazing out the window, where the autumn forest showed now black branches through the drifting red and gold.

"The man led me up a mountainside," said Sir Francis. "A mountain of golden stone, only thinly greened over with little gnarled holm oaks, and with some sort of herb that gave off an aromatic perfume in the sunlight. And, what sunlight! White as diamond, clear and hot. The sunlight of the very morning of the world. Transparent air, and the dome of blue overhead so deep a man could drown in it.

"Well, the path was less than a goatpath, and we climbed for the best part of an hour, through thorns half the time, and how I cursed the fellow! He kept pointing out a little white house, far up the mountainside, lonely and abandoned-looking. But I followed him, very surly indeed as you may imagine by the time we'd gained the house at last.

"Up there it was a little better; there was a great old fig tree that cast pleasant shade. I threw myself down in the coolness and panted, as an eagle sailed past—at eye level, sir—and the sea so far below was nothing but a blue mist, with little atomies of ships plying to and fro.

"I could hear murmuring coming from the house, but no other noises at all, not so much as the cry of a bird, and the drone of the insects had ceased. It was all very like a dream, you know; and it became more so when I got to my feet and went inside.

"There in the cool and the dark, a row of antique faces regarded me. They were only the heads of statues that had been ranged along a shelf, but upon my life I took them for persons at first, perhaps interrupted in conversation.

"My guide introduced the old man and his daughter. He'd been a scholar, evidently—dug amongst the ruins and through forgotten places to amass his collection—penniless now, and selling off the better pieces when he could find buyers. She was a beauty. Very Greek, gray-eyed and proud. Brought me a cup of cold water with all the grace of Hebe.

"Well, we commenced to do business. I'd a well-lined purse—stupid thing to carry in such country, of course, but some god or other protects young idiots from harm. He sold me the scrolls at once. His daughter brought out a few painted urns, very fine some of them, and I bought one or two. I had my man ask if there were any more. They talked that over be-tween them, the father and his girl, and at last she signed for us to follow her.

"We went out through the back of the house. There was a spring, trick-ling from the rock, and a sort of pergola joining the back of the house to a grotto there. It was all deep in vine-shade, with the little green grapes hanging down. Blessedly refreshing. That Achaean charmer led me back into the shadows, and I was upon point of seeing whether I might coax a kiss from her when—there—on my life and honor, sir, I tell you I looked on the face of God."

"What did you see?" said Lewis, enthralled.

"I think it must have been a little temple, once," said Sir Francis. "It cer-tainly felt sacred to me. There were figures carved at the back of the grotto, into the living rock; Bacchus with all his train of satyrs and nymphs, coming to the rescue of Ariadne. Primitive, but I tell you, sir, the artist *could do faces*. The revelers were so jolly, you wanted to laugh with them—and, oh, the young Divinity, immortal and human all at once, smiling so kindly on that poor girl, seduced and deserted on her island! Holding out his hand to save her, and, in his compassion, granting her the golden crown of eternal life.

"It was a revelation, sir. That's what a God ought to be, I said to myself: wild joy in flesh and blood! And, being flesh and blood, generous enough to preserve we wretched mortals from death's affliction.

"I was desperate to buy the panel, but it wasn't to be had; no indeed. The girl had brought me in there simply to show some few small bronzes, stacked on the floor for want of room in the cottage. I sought by gestures to convey I wished to break the figures free of the wall; she understood well enough, and favored me with a look that nearly froze my blood. You'll think me a booby, sir, but I wept.

"I never close my eyes at night but I see that grotto still. I have had the god's likeness made many times, by some tolerably good painters, and bought me several images of him; yet none can compare with his countenance as I saw it on that bright morning in my youth.

"And I cannot but believe that, for a brief moment on that morning, I escaped this world's confines and walked in the realm of the ineffable."

"An enchanting story, my lord," said Lewis. He looked down at the bits of paper before him, fragments of some long-dead mortal's imagination.

How different their perception is, from ours. How I wish . . .

"Not the story I came in here to tell, alas," said Sir Francis, looking sheepish. "The past rules the present when you reach my age; you'll understand in your time, my boy. I, er, haven't quite been able to arrange the party. Not the initiation party into the Order, in any case. Paul's been ill, and our friend Dr. Franklin sends his regrets, but he's otherwise engaged— still trying to salvage something from this calamity with the Americans, I've no doubt."

"I quite understand," said Lewis.

"And Bute's quite taken up with his gardening now . . . Montagu sent word he'd certainly come, but for the entertainment he owes his guest— you've heard of Omai, the wild South Seas fellow? Captain Cook brought him back for show, and he's been feted in all the best homes. *I* said, bring him with you; we'll initiate a noble savage! But it seems his time's all bespoke with garden parties . . . well. You see how it is."

"Quite," said Lewis. "Perhaps another time, then."

"Oh, indeed! In point of fact, sir . . ." Sir Francis turned his head to peer at the doorway, then turned back and spoke with lowered voice. "I had contemplated something else, a rather more exclusive affair entirely. We haven't had one in a while; but now and again the need presents itself, and you being such an agreeable pagan, I thought . . ."

Lewis, scarcely believing his luck, put down the brush and leaned forward.

"This wouldn't have anything to do with a certain mystery we spoke of in the garden, would it?"

"Yes! Yes! You understand?" Sir Francis looked desperately hopeful.

"I believe I do, my lord. Trust me, you may count on my discretion," said Lewis, setting a finger beside his nose.

"Oh, good. Although, you know . . ." Sir Francis leaned in and spoke so low that if he hadn't been a cyborg, Lewis couldn't have made out what he was saying. "It won't be quite as, er, jolly as the services at the abbey. Perhaps we'll have a little dinner party first, just to warm us up, but then things will be rather solemn. I hope you won't be disappointed."

"I'm sure I shan't be," said Lewis.

When Sir Francis had left, after several winks, nudges, and hoarse declarations of the need for *utter secrecy*, Lewis jumped up and did a buck-and-wing down the length of the library.

There were certain comings and goings over the next week, nothing to indicate anything out of the ordinary to the unsuspecting observer, but significant. Sir Francis packed his present mistress, the children and their nurses off to Bath, with a great many sloppy kisses and endearments. Guests arrived at odd hours: Sir Francis's half-brother John, and another elderly gentleman who turned out to be a Regius Professor of Civil Law.

Lewis, placidly piecing together ancient carnal acrobatics, scanned the household as he worked, and picked up more snippets of information. He learned that the seamstress had been given a great deal of last-minute work to do, because someone's costume hadn't been tried on in three years and didn't fit anymore. A young pig was driven over from an outlying farm and made a nasty mess in the kitchen garden, about which the cook complained; then Sir Francis himself went down and slaughtered it, somewhat inexpertly, judging from the noise and the complaints of the laundress who had to get the blood out of his garments.

The gardener was sent off with a shovel and wheelbarrow, and was gone all day, and grumbled when he returned; the footman and butler loaded a table and several chairs into a wagon, and drove them away somewhere.

Lewis was applying Parch-Fix to a codex purporting to tell the secrets of the Vestal Virgins when he heard the trumpets announcing a coach's arrival. He scanned; yes, a coach was coming up the drive, containing five . . . no, six mortals.

He set the brush down and closed his eyes, the better to focus.

Jingling ring of metal-shod wheels on gravel, with dreadful tooth-grinding clarity. The hollow thunder of the horse's hooves slowing to distinct *clop-clop-clop*, like the final drops in a rain shower, counterpointed by slippered feet crossing the marble floor of the entry hall in the house below.

Boom! Sir Francis seemed incapable of using a door without flinging it wide.

"Ladies! Ladies, my charmers, my beauties, welcome, welcome one and all! Dear Mrs. Digby, it has been an age! How d'ye do? By Venus and her son, my dear, you're looking well!"

"La, bless you, my lord, and ain't you the 'oney-tongued flatterer!"

"Never in the world, sweetheart. Sukey! Pretty Bess! My arm, ladies, pray step down, mind your gown there—welcome once again—ah, Joan, you did come after all! We'd have missed you sorely. A kiss for thee, my love—and who's this? A new rose in the bouquet?"

"That's our young miss. Ain't been with us long. We reckoned she'd do for— " And here the voice dropped to a whisper, but Lewis made it out: *"For our you-know-who."*

"Ah!" Sir Francis likewise resorted to an undertone. *"Then a chaste kiss for you, fair child. Welcome! Where's Mr. Whitehead?"*

"I'm just getting my hat—"

"A word in your ear, my lord—'e ain't well. 'Ad a fainting fit and frighted us something awful. Sukey brought 'im round with a little gin, but 'e's that pale—"

"I know—I know, my dear, but—Ah, here you are, Paul! What a rascal you are, swiving yourself into collapse with a carriageful of beauties! Eh? I declare, you're like a spawning salmon. Couldn't wait until tonight, could you?"

" 'Ere then, dearie, you just take my arm—"

"What nonsense—I'm perfectly well—"

"Bess, you take 'is other arm—come now, lovey, we'll just go inside for a bit of a lie-down afore dinner, won't we?"

"Perhaps that would be best—"

"Yes, let's give this rampant stallion a rest before the next jump. John! Have Mrs. Fitton send up a restorative."

"At once, my lord."

The voices louder now, because everyone had come indoors, but more muffled and indistinct. Lewis pushed back from the table and tilted his head this way and that, until he could pick up sounds clearly once more. There was Sir Francis, whispering again: *"—looks dreadful, poor creature. We ought to have done this sooner."*

" 'E looked well enough this fortnight past, when 'e was down to London. My sister's 'usband, 'e done just the same—sound as a bell at Christmas, and we buried 'im at Twelfth Night. Well, we must just 'ope for the best, that's what my mother used to say, my lord. What think you of the girl?"

"A little obscured by the veil, but she seems a pretty creature. She's observed all the . . . er . . . ?"

"Yes, my lord, you may be sure of that. And you 'ave a boy?"

"A capital boy! You shall meet him presently."

"Oh, good, 'cos I didn't care for t' other young gentleman at all . . ."

Lewis sneezed, breaking his focus and sending a bit of Vestal Virgin flying. "Drat," he muttered. He got down on hands and knees to retrieve her from under the table and wondered once again, as he did so, just what exactly had happened to his predecessor.

Any unease he might have felt, however, was being rapidly overpowered by a certain sense of hopeful anticipation. A dinner party composed almost entirely of old men and nubile and willing ladies! Was it possible his perpetual bad luck was about to change, if only for an evening's bliss?

He had repaired the Vestal Virgins and was busily pasting the spine back on a copy of *A New Description of Merryland* when Sir Francis's butler entered the library, bearing a cloak draped over his arm.

"I beg your pardon, sir, but my lord requests your presence in the garden. You are to wear this." He held up the cloak, which had a capacious hood.

"Ah! A fancy dress party, is it?" Lewis took the cloak and slung it around his shoulders. The hood fell forward, blinding him. John, unsmiling, adjusted it.

"If you say so, sir. You want to go out by the east door."

"Right-ho! I'm on my way," said Lewis, and trooped off with an eager heart.

In the garden he encountered a huddle of other cloaked figures, and was greeted by the foremost of them, who in speaking revealed himself as Sir Francis: "That you, young Owens? We're just waiting for the ladies, bless 'em. Ah, they approach!"

Indeed, a procession was winding its way around the side of the house. Lewis saw five cloaked figures, and the foremost carried a torch held high. The gentlemen bowed deeply. Lewis followed suit.

"Goddess," said Sir Francis, "We mortals greet you with reverence and longing. Pray grant us your favor!"

"My favor thou shalt 'ave, mortal," said she of the blazing torch. "Come with me to yon 'allowed shrine, and I shall teach thee my 'oly mystery."

"Huzzay!" said the old Regius Professor, under his breath. He gave Lewis a gleeful dig in the ribs. His elbow was rather sharp and Lewis found it quite painful. All discomfort fled, however, when a little cloaked figure came and took his hand.

They paired up, a lady to each gentleman. Sir Francis took the arm of the torch-bearer, and led them away through the night in solemn procession, like a troupe of elderly Guy Fawkes pranksters. The line broke only once, when one of the gentlemen stumbled and began to cough; they stopped and waited until he recovered himself, and then moved on.

Lewis, checking briefly by infrared, saw that the procession was moving in the general direction of the high hill crowned by the Church of the Golden Ball. Most of his attention was turned on the girl who walked beside him. Her hand was warm; she was young, and shapely, and walked with a light step. He wondered what she looked like.

The procession did not climb the hill, but wound around its base. Presently Lewis was able to drag his attention away from the girl long enough to observe another church that lay straight ahead of them, seemingly dug into the hill. As they drew closer, he saw that it was only a façade of flint, built to conceal the entrance to a tunnel.

The famous Hellfire Caves! thought Lewis, and his heartbeat quickened.

They entered through gates, to a long tunnel cut through chalk, and here they must go single file. To his amazement, Lewis felt his racing heart speed into a full-blown panic attack; it was all he could do not to break from the line and run. He scanned the strata above his head: wet chalk, fractured and unstable. Plenty of rational reasons to fear this place; no need to summon demons from the unconscious . . .

The little girl reached forward and gave his hand a squeeze. It made him feel better.

They followed the tunnel gradually downhill, past niches opening off to the left, and then around in a loop that seemed to have taken them in a complete circle. It was black as pitch but for the torch flaring ahead of them, and silent, and damp, and cold as the grave. Another long straight descent; then a tight maze of turns and multiple openings where anyone but a cyborg might have had difficulty keeping a sense of direction. But now light showed ahead, down a straight passage, and Lewis picked up the scent of food.

They emerged into a great open chamber, well lit by flaring torches. Four figures stood perfectly motionless against the far wall. Each was draped in a black veil that dropped from the crown of the head nearly to the floor, in long straight lines. Each wore a mask. Two were black and featureless; two were painted in black and gold, resembling insect faces.

In the center of the room, looking incongruous, was a dining table set for ten.

Sir Francis's voice boomed into the silence, shattering the tension with echoes: "And now, a pause in our solemnities! Supper in Hell, my friends! Though I promise you, you shall not be long *tantalized*. Tantalus, hey? In Hades? D'y'get the joke?"

"What a witty fellow you are, my lord, to be sure," said the lady with the torch dryly. She threw back her hood to reveal a svelte woman in early middle age. Her hair was a flaming and unnatural red. Painted, plastered, and upholstered as she was, she had nonetheless maintained a certain charm.

All the party now threw off their cloaks, and Lewis blinked in surprise. The gentlemen, himself excepted, wore white jackets and pantaloons, as well as extraordinary floppy blue and red hats embroidered on the front with the words *Love and Friendship*. The ladies wore white robes, cut in what must have been intended as a Greek fashion; all save the youngest, who, like Lewis, wore ordinary street dress. Her features remained hidden by her veil, however.

"It's cold in here," complained a buxom wench somewhat past her prime. "Why couldn't we done this at the Abbey? It's ever so nice there. Remember the times we used to have?"

"I know, my dear, a thousand apologies—" said Sir Francis. "But the Abbey's not so convenient as it was, I fear—"

"And we ain't a-doing of our sacred rites in no profane place, Sukey Foster, so just you shut your cake'ole," reproved her mistress. She cast a somewhat anxious eye upon Sir Francis. "All the same, dearie, I 'ope I'll get a cushion to put under my bum this time? That altar ain't 'arf cold and 'ard."

"Everything has been seen to, dear Demeter," Sir Francis assured her.

"Very kind of you, I'm sure, Lord 'Ermes," she replied. Gazing around at the assembled party, she spotted Lewis. " 'Ere now! Is 'e the . . . ?"

"Yes," Sir Frances replied.

"Well, ain't you the pretty fellow!" Demeter pinched Lewis's cheek.

"Might we perhaps sit?" said the old professor. "My leg is positively throbbing, after that march."

"Yes, please," said Whitehead faintly. He looked sweating and sick, a ghastly contrast with his clownish attire. Lewis scanned him, and winced; the mortal was terminally ill.

They shuffled to their places. To his disappointment, Lewis found himself seated far down the table from the little girl in the veil. The masked figures, who had been still as statues until now, came to life and served in eerie silence. A whole roast pig was brought from a side passage, as well as a dish of fruit sauce, loaves of barley bread, and oysters. Chocolate was poured from silver urns. ("No wine?" said the professor in disappointment. Sir Francis and Madam Demeter gave him identical looks of disapproval, and he blushed and muttered "Oh! So sorry—forgot.")

Lewis, cold, hungry, and depressed, took a reckless gulp of chocolate and at once felt the rush of Theobromine elevating his spirits.

They feasted. Perhaps to make up for the lack of alcoholic cheer, the mortal party became terrifically loud, in riotous laughter and bawdy witticisms that made Lewis blush for the veiled girl. She sat in silence at her end of the table, except for once when she began to lift her veil and: " 'Ere! Just you keep your face covered, girl!" said Madam Demeter.

" 'Ow the bloody 'ell am I supposed to eat anything?" the girl demanded.

"You pushes the cloth forward, and slips little bites under, like you was a proper lady," explained Sukey. "That's how I done it, when it was me."

The girl said nothing more, but folded her arms in a monumental sulk. Lewis, well into his second cup of chocolate and with his cyborg nervous system now definitely under the influence of Theobromine, regarded her wistfully. He thought she looked enchanting. He wondered if he could rescue her from her degrading life.

How to do it? . . . Not enough money in the departmental budget. They'd all laugh at me anyway. But what if I went to one of the gambling houses? I could count cards. Prohibited of course but the Facilitator class operatives do it all the time, for extra pocket money. Nennius himself, in fact. Win enough to set her up with, with a shop or something. Poor child . . .

"Have another slice of this excellent pork, my boy!" roared Sir Frances, reaching across to slap meat on his plate. "And you haven't tried the fruit sauce! It's sublime!"

"Thanks," Lewis shouted back, leaning out of the way as a servant buried the pork in dollops of fruit compote. He leaned back in, took up a spoon, and began shoveling compote into his mouth, aware he needed to take in solid food.

No sooner had he set the spoon down, however, than the red letters began to flash before his eyes with all the vividness of migraine distortion: TOXIC RESPONSE ALERT!

"God Apollo," he groaned. Peering down at his plate, he made out one or two gooseberry seeds in the syrupy mess, when the flashing letters allowed him to see anything. "What have I done to myself?"

He sat very still and waited for the flashing to stop, but it didn't seem to; too late, he wondered if the Theobromine might have combined badly with whatever it was in the gooseberries to which his organic body objected.

Judge, then, with what sense of dread he heard the *ping-ping-ping* of spoon against water glass, and the creaking chair as Sir Francis rose to his feet to say: "Now, my dears! Now, my esteemed brothers in revelry! Let us put aside our jollity! Our sacred business begins!"

"Huzzay!" shrieked the old professor.

"A little more decorum, sir, if you please," said Madam Demeter. "This is a solemn h'occasion, ain't it?"

"I'm sorry, my dear, it's my sense of enthusiasm—"

"Quite understandable, sir," said Sir Francis. "But we ought to remember that we have a new celebrant amongst us, who, though but a youth, has shown a true spirit of—er—Mr. Owens, are you quite all right?"

Lewis opened his eyes to behold a revolving wheel of faces staring at him, peeping in and out between the flashing red letters.

"Quite," he said, and gave what he hoped was a confident smile. The smile went on longer than he had intended it to; he had the distinct impression it was turning into a leer and dripping down one side of his face.

"Ah; very well then; I think we'll commence. Brothers and sisters! Let us drink together from the cup that will bind us in immortality," said Sir Francis, and Lewis was aware that a servant was stepping up behind him and leaning down to offer something. Blinking at it, he beheld a figured wine krater, a modern copy, showing Bacchus rescuing Ariadne. He took it and drank.

Water, barley, pennyroyal . . . a memory buried for fifteen hundred years floated up into his consciousness. Lewis tasted it again.

"The *kykeon!*" he exclaimed, rather more loudly than he had meant to. "And you've even got the formula right! Well done!"

In the absolute silence that followed, he became aware that everyone was staring at him. *You idiot, Lewis!* he thought, and meekly passed the krater to Sir Francis. All the others at table drank without speaking. When the empty krater had been placed in the center of the table at last, Sir Francis cleared his throat.

"The time has come. Behold my caduceus."

This provoked a shrill giggle from the professor, quickly shushed by the ladies on either side of him.

"If you ain't going to take this seriously, you didn't ought to be here," said Bess severely.

Lewis peered and made out that Sir Francis had produced a staff from somewhere and was holding it up. It was in fact a caduceus, very nicely carved, and the twining serpents' scales had been gilded, and their eyes set with faceted stones that glittered in the torchlight.

"I speak now as Hermes, servant of Jove," said Sir Francis. "I but do his immortal will."

"And I am Demeter, goddess of all that grows," intoned the lady, with a theatrical flourish. " 'Ow weary I am, after the bountiful 'arvest! I will sleep. I trust in Jove; no 'arm shall come to my dear daughter Persephone, 'oo wanders on Nysa's flowery plain."

Sir Francis indicated to Lewis that he ought to rise. Lewis got up so hastily his chair fell backward with a crash, and he was only prevented from going with it by the masked servant, who steadied him. The veiled girl rose, too, and dragged from beside her chair a basket.

"I am Persephone, goddess of the spring," she announced. "Blimey, what a lovely great flower do I see! I shall pick it straightaway!"

Sir Francis took Lewis by the arm and led him to the dark mouth of another tunnel, opposite the one by which they had entered. Persephone followed on tiptoe, grabbing a torch from one of the wall sockets as she came. They went down the tunnel a few yards, and stopped. Persephone drew a deep breath and screamed at the top of her lungs: "Owwwwww! What dark god is this 'oo ravishes me away from the light of the world? Ow, 'elp, 'elp, will nobody 'ear my distress? Father Jove, where art thou?"

"Quickly now," Sir Francis whispered, and they hurried on through the darkness, around a corner, around another and another, deeper into the labyrinth, and Lewis heard water rushing somewhere ahead. They passed through another, smaller chamber, where there was a low stone altar; Lewis nearly fell over it, but Sir Francis caught him again and the girl took his other arm. Somehow they made it into the next passage and shortly came out into another chamber.

"The river Styx," announced Sir Francis, with a wave of his caduceus. "Here Hermes of the winged heels can conduct no farther. Away! He flits! He flies, back to lofty Olympus!" Throwing out his arms and springing into air with quite a remarkable balletic grace for a man his age, even crossing his ankles before he came down, and landing so lightly that his wig scarcely moved on his head, he turned and ran back up the passageway.

Lewis stood staring after him. The girl tugged on his sleeve.

"We're supposed to get in the boat," she said.

Lewis turned around to look. They stood on the edge of a dark stream that rushed through the cavern. On the farther shore was the entrance to yet another black passage. Before them was moored a quaint little boat, beautifully if morbidly carved with skulls and crossed bones, painted in black and gold.

"Oh," said Lewis. "Yes, of course! But where's Charon?"

" 'Oo?" said Persephone.

"The ferryman," said Lewis, making punting motions.

"Oh. Nobody told me nothing about no ferrymen; I reckon you're supposed to get us across," said the girl.

"Right! Yes! In we go, then," said Lewis, who was finding the red flashes subsiding somewhat, but in their place was an increasing urge to giggle. "My hand, madam! Yo-heave-ho and hoist the anchor!"

" 'Ere, are you all right?" The girl squinted at him through her veil.

"Never better, fair Persephone!" Lewis cast off and seized up the pole. He propelled them across with such a mighty surge that—

"Bleeding Jesus, mister, look out! You'll—"

The boat ran aground and Lewis toppled backward, falling with a tremendous splash into the dark water. He came up laughing hysterically as he dogpaddled toward the boat, with his wig bobbing eerily in his wake.

"Oh, God Apollo, I've drowned in the river Styx—well, this *is* a first for me—but I wouldn't be *mister*, you know, the technical term is *mystes*—"

Persephone stuck her torch in a rock crevice, grabbed his collar, and hauled him ashore. "You been drinking, ain't you?" she said in exasperation.

"No, actually—it's the drinking chocolate, it has an odd effect on our nervous systems—we cyb—I mean, we . . . Owenses," said Lewis through chattering teeth, for the water had been like ice.

"Ow, your shoes'll be ruined and—give me the bleeding pole, we got to fish your wig out. Damn it, I ain't wearing this veil another minute," said Persephone, and tore it off.

Lewis caught his breath.

She was a very young girl, pale by torchlight, but with roses in her cheeks. Her hair was red. Her eyes, rather than the blue or green one might expect, were black as the stream from which she'd pulled him. His heart—not the cyborg mechanism that pumped his blood—contracted painfully.

"*Mendoza?*" he whispered.

" 'Oo's that? 'Ere, what's wrong?" she demanded. "You ain't going be sick, are you? You look like you seen a ghost."

"I—you—you look like someone I knew," said Lewis. "I must apologize—"

A throaty scream came echoing down the passage from the banqueting chamber.

"*My child!*" cried Madam Demeter, in tones she had clearly picked up from watching Mr. Garrick at Drury Lane. "*Ooooh, my chiiiiild! She is quite rrrravished away! Ow, somebody 'elp me quick! Wherever could she be?*"

"Bugger," said Persephone. "We got to go on. Come on, get up! You need a 'and?"

"Please—" Lewis let her haul him to his feet. He stood swaying, wondering if she was a hallucination, as she stuck the torch in his nerveless hand, retrieved his sopping wig, and grabbed up the basket. She did not wait, but started ahead of him through the dark doorway. Coming to himself, he ran squelching after her.

Only a few yards on they emerged into the last chamber; there was no way to exit but back the way they had come. It was a small room, very cold and damp indeed, and empty but for a squarish stone object in the middle of the floor. There were some carvings on the side; Lewis recognized it for a Roman sarcophagus. Persephone sat down on it and began to rummage through the basket.

"You want to get out of them wet clothes," she advised. She held up one end of a length of white cloth. "This ain't much, but at least it's dry."

He stared at it in incomprehension, trying to clear his wits. She sighed, set the basket down, and began to unbutton his waistcoat.

"Don't tell *me* you ain't drunk. Come on, old dear, we ain't got all night," she said. " 'Ark at 'em going on!"

"*I am Hecate, her what rules the night! I know where your daughter got to, Mistress Demeter!*"

"*Pray, speak thou!*"

"*Well, I hears this scream, see? And I says to all-seeing Helios, lord of the sun, I says, Whatever was that noise? Sounded like a virgin pure being carried off! And Helios says, he says, Oh that was fairest Persephone being ravished. It was that Lord Hades done it!*"

" *'E never!*"

"*S'welp me God! She's gone to the Otherworld to be Queen of the Dead!*"

"*My CHIIIIILD! Almighty Jove, is there no rrrrremedy!*"

Lewis stood nervelessly, letting the little girl peel off his soaked garments, until she unfastened his trousers.

"I—perhaps I'd better do that," he said, clutching at himself and backing away.

"Please yourself," she said, and matter-of-factly began to strip down.

"*Madam, be content!*" A male voice came echoing down the passageway. "*It is the will of All-Seeing Jove!*"

"*Whaaaaaat? What perfidy is this? It shall not be!*"

"'Ow they do go on," said Persephone. Lewis, hopping on one foot as he tried to get his breeches off, turned to answer her and nearly fell over; for she had skinned out of her garments with the speed of frequent practice, and stood unconcernedly brushing out her hair. He stared. She didn't seem to notice.

"*. . . why then, sir, 'Eaven shall learn a goddess may be wrathful, too! I shall with'old my gracious bounty from the woooorld! See if I don't! The green corn shall wither in the field, and mortal men shall staaaarve!*"

"They're getting louder!" said Lewis. "Oh, dear, they're not coming in here, are they?"

"Naow, just as far as the room with the h'altar," said Persephone. "This is the sacred grotto. Nothing in 'ere but the sacred scroll."

Lewis managed to get his breeches off. Clutching them to his lap, he shuffled crabwise to the basket, rummaging for something with which to clothe himself. He pulled out a voluminous length of gauze embroidered with flowers.

"That's mine, ducky," said Persephone, sliding past him to take it. Her bare breast grazed his arm. He started so violently he dropped the sodden bundle he'd been holding. Persephone looked down. Her eyes widened.

"*. . . wander through the barren world, mourning the 'ole time for my dearest daughter! Oooooh, the perfidy of Jove!*"

"I'm sorry," said Persephone. "This ain't 'arf awkward. Look, if we was anyplace else, I'd do you proper, a nice-looking boy like you; only I can't 'ere, on account of it'd be sacrilege."

"It would?" said Lewis piteously.

"'Ere will I rest awhile amid this sheltering grove, and in the shape of somebody's old wet nurse I will appear. But, soft! 'Oo approaches wretched Demeter? I perceive they are the daughters of some king or other.'"

"Why, who is this poor old thing as sits beside our washing well? Cheer up, good lady. You shall come home with us and nurse our young brother."

"Didn't 'is Lordship h'explain?" Persephone rolled her eyes. "I thought you'd done this afore." She pulled the embroidered shift over her head, and yanked it down smartly to cover herself.

"Well—yes—but—it was a long time ago, and . . ." His distress seemed to aggravate the TOXIC RESPONSE ALERT. He squeezed his eyes tight shut, and made an effort to sober up.

"Nooooow I am alone with the mortal babe, I will reward the kindness done to me! So! So! 'Ey presto! Another pass through the flaaaaames, and he shall become immortal—"

"Ow my gawd, lady, you'll burn up my baby!"

"Now look what you went and done, foolish mortal! The spell's broke—"

"I can't do you because I'm being the Queen of h'Avernus," Persephone explained. "Which it would be h'adultery, see, on account of me being married to the Lord of the Dead and all. Do your breechclout up like a nice bloke, won't you? I know it don't seem fair, what with 'is lordship and that lot getting to fornicate like mad. But it's in aid of Mr. Whitehead, you know."

"Oh," said Lewis, blinking back tears as she fastened his loincloth in place for him and then draped a white scarf over her hair.

"Poor old thing's dying," said Persephone. "Ever such a nice gentleman, 'e is. I wonder why the nice ones always dies on you? But this way 'e won't be scared, see—"

"—build a temple to meee, and so my divine wrath shall be appeeeeeeased! Nay, more! I shall grant eternal life to 'im as performs my sacred rites!"

"We thank thee, merciful goddess!" Now it became an exchange between the woman's voice and the chorus of male voices:

"What 'ave you done?"

"We have feasted; we drank the kykeon!"

"Fasted," Lewis corrected absently.

"What'll you do next?"

"We're taking something out!"

"What'll you do with it?"

"We're going to put it in something else!"

"Then come forward, mortals, and be'old the Sacred Flame! Die in the fire of my h'embrace, to live eternally!"

"Whu-huh-HEY!"

"I'm just as glad I ain't got to watch this part," remarked Persephone, settling down on the tomb lid. "Between you and me, Mrs. Digby ain't so young as she was, and the thought of 'er on that h'altar with 'er knees up—it's enough to curl your 'air, ain't it?"

"I suppose so," said Lewis, sitting down beside her.

Sounds of violent carnal merriment echoed down the passageway. Persephone twiddled her thumbs.

"So, er, 'ow'd you learn about the old gods and all that?" she asked.

Lewis stared into the darkness, through a hazy roil of red letters and memories.

"I was a foundling baby, left in a blanket by a statue of Apollo," he said. "In Aquae Sulis."

"Where's that?"

"I mean, Bath. It's in Bath. I was raised by a . . ." Lewis pondered how to explain a twenty-fourth-century corporation with the ability to time-travel and collect abandoned human children for the purpose of processing them into cyborg operatives. "By a wealthy scholar with no particular religious views. But I always rather liked the idea of the gods of old Rome."

"Fancy that," said Persephone. "Mrs. Digby, she learned it off his lordship. Ever such a comfort, for poor working girls, she says."

"You shouldn't be doing this," said Lewis, taking her hand in his. "You should have a better life. If I helped you—if I set you up in business, or something—"

"That's the liquor talking, dearie," said Persephone, not unkindly. "Lord love us, you ain't nothing but a clerk; you ain't got any money. And it ain't such a bad life; things is 'igh-class at Mrs. Digby's, you know. *Much* rather do that than be somebody's scullery maid."

"I'm so sorry," Lewis whispered.

"It's all right; it's what we're born to, ain't it?" she said. She inclined her head to listen to the tumult coming from the altar chamber. "I reckon it's time for the seed, then."

From her basket she produced a pomegranate, and, digging into the rind with her thumbs, prized it open. She picked out a seed and crunched it.

Lewis watched her hopelessly. She offered him the fruit.

" 'Ave some?"

"Yes," said Lewis. "Yes, for you. I will." He took a handful of ruby seeds and ate, and the bittersweet juice ran down his chin. She reached up a corner of her veil and wiped it clean. They huddled together for warmth, there on the lid of the tomb.

"Go to it, Paul!"

"Bravo, Whitehead! That's the spirit!"

"Huzzay!"

"That's it, lovey, that's the way, ooh! Lord, plenty of life in this one yet! That's it. You just rest in my arms, my dear. There ain't nothing to be afraid of. Think about them Elysium Fields . . . that's my darling, that's my sweet gentleman . . ."

"Hup! Ho! Ha! Whitehead's soul is to Heaven fled!"

"I 'ope they don't take all night," said Persephone, a little crossly. "Blimey, I'm cold." She rummaged in her basket again and pulled out a flask. Unstoppering it, she had a gulp of its contents and sighed, wiping her mouth with the back of her hand.

"Nothing like a bit of this to take the chill off," she said, and passed the flask to Lewis. He drank without thinking, and handed it back.

"Oh," he said. "That was gin, wasn't it?"

Chants of rejoicing echoed down the tunnel.

"Eh? 'Course it was. I think our cue's coming up now—"

"I'm afraid gin combines rather badly with Theobromine," said Lewis unsteadily.

"With what?" Persephone turned her face to him. He watched in fascination as she became an equation of light and shadow, and then an image of stained glass shining with light. She was telling him something—she was rising and taking his hand, leaving trails of colored light where she moved—

He felt a gentle impact at the back of his head and a tremendous happiness. He was flying down the tunnel, bearing her along with him—the sundering water, rippling with subtle colors, was easily bounded across. He roared the ancient hymn as he came, and heard the eternal masses echoing it back from Paradise.

"Evohe! Evohe! Iacchus! Evohe!" He was in the cave with the altar but it was full of light, it was glowing like summer, and no longer cold but warm.

"I have taken in the seed, and see what I bring into the light!" Persephone

declared. The mortals knelt around him, crowding close, weeping and laughing and catching at his hands.

"Blessed Iacchus, give us hope!"

"Iacchus! The boy Iacchus is come!"

"Iacchus, take away our fear!"

"Make us immortal, Iacchus!"

Demeter and Persephone were greeting each other, with elaborate palms-out rapture, and Persephone was saying: *"Behold my son, which is Life come out of Death!"*

"Please, Iacchus!" He looked down into old Whitehead's pleading face, sweating and exhausted. *"Let me not be lost in the dark!"*

He wept for the mortal man, he touched his face and promised him the moon, he promised them all the moon, he babbled any comforting nonsense he could think of. He tried to stretch out his hand to Persephone but she had receded somehow, on the golden sea of faces. Everything was golden. Everything was melting into golden music.

Lewis opened his eyes. He looked up; he looked down; he looked from side to side. Doing anything more ambitious than this seemed a bad idea.

He was in bed in the room allotted to him by Sir Francis. Someone had laid him out as carefully as a carving of a saint on a tomb, with the counterpane drawn up to his chest. They had put one of his nightshirts on him, too. It seemed to be morning.

He closed his eyes again and ran a self-diagnostic. His body told him, quite pointedly, that he'd been extremely stupid. It implied that if he ever subjected it to that kind of abuse again, he was going to find himself in a regeneration tank for at least six months. It stated further that it required complex carbohydrates *right now*, as well as at least two liters of fluid containing high concentrations of calcium, magnesium, and potassium. He opened his eyes again and looked around to see if anything answering that description was within reach.

No; the nearest fluid of any kind was water on a table beside his bed, in a crystal vase containing a few sprays of late hedgeroses. It looked exquisitely wet. He wondered whether he could get the roses out and drink from the vase without making too much of a mess. His body told him it didn't care whether he made a mess. Groaning, he prepared to sit up.

At that moment he heard the approach of footsteps, two pair. They were accompanied by a slight rattle of china.

The door opened and Sir Francis stuck his head into the room. Seeing Lewis awake, his face brightened extraordinarily.

"Mr. Owens! Thank all the gods you're with us again at last! You . . . er, that is . . . that *is* you, Mr. Owens?"

"I think so," said Lewis. Little lightning flashes of headache assailed him.

Sir Francis bustled into the room, waving the butler in after him. Lewis found his gaze riveted on the covered tray the butler carried. Sir Francis sat down on the edge of the bed, staring at Lewis no less fixedly.

"D'you recall much, eh?"

"Not a great deal, my lord," said Lewis. "That wouldn't happen to be breakfast, would it?"

The butler lifted the napkin to disclose a pitcher, a small pot of honey, and a dish of little cakes. Sir Francis twisted his fingers together self-consciously.

"That's, er, milk and honey and, ah, the closest my cook could approximate to ambrosia. The honey comes from Delos," he said, with a peculiar tone of entreaty in his voice.

Lewis dragged himself into a sitting position, though his brain quailed against the red-hot lining of his skull. The butler set the tray on his lap; he grabbed up the pitcher, ignoring the crystal tumbler provided with it, and drank two quarts of milk straight down without pausing to breathe. Sir Francis watched with round eyes as he gulped the ambrosia cakes one after another, and, seizing up a spoon, started on the honey.

"Wonderful stuff," said Lewis, remembering his manners. "Might I have a little more?"

"Anything you like," said Sir Francis, beckoning distractedly at John. Lewis held the pitcher up.

"Another round of this, please, and three or four loaves of bread?"

"With jam, sir?"

"No! No jam. Thank you."

John took the pitcher and hurried out of the room.

"I don't wonder you've an appetite," said Sir Francis. "That was an astonishing evening, my boy. We're all greatly indebted to you. Never saw anything quite like that in my life."

"But—I received the impression you'd—er, enacted certain rites before," said Lewis, scraping the bottom of the honey jar with the spoon.

"Why, so we had. But never with such remarkable results!" said Sir Francis. "What an improvement on your predecessor. *He* was no fit vessel for Divinity at all! Treated the ladies most disrespectfully. I sent him packing; then we discovered he'd helped himself to the spoons. Apprehended him in the very act of boarding the coach with my best silver coffee urn in his trunk too, would you credit it?

"Not at all like you. Such Olympian presence! Such efficacy! Whitehead looked positively well. 'How d'ye feel now, Paul?' I said, and bless me if he didn't reply, 'Why, sir, I declare I could pile Mount Pelion upon Mount Ossa, and straightwise mount to Heaven!' "

"I'm gratified, my lord," said Lewis cautiously. "Though I confess the evening is somewhat indistinct in my memory."

"I expect it would be, sir. I suspect *you* were scarcely there at all! Eh?" Sir Francis winked at him. "But I'll leave you in peace; John will lay out your clothes. All fresh-laundered; though the wig's at the barber's for a fresh setting and powdering. It was in a sad state, I fear. And I've taken the liberty of having a new pair of shoes made; one of yours seems to have gone missing in the Styx. You'll find them in the bottom of your wardrobe."

"New shoes?" Lewis said. "Made overnight?"

"Overnight? Bless you, no! You've slept for three days! A very Endymion," Sir Francis told him. He lingered shyly by the door a moment, his eyes downcast. "You have rendered me a greater service than I can ever repay. Your servant, sir."

Lewis enjoyed an unaccustomed luxury of idleness over the next few days; the servants tiptoed in his presence, looked on him with awe, and leaped to bring him anything he requested. He used the time to access and review his memory, and found, to put it mildly, some difference between what his conscious mind had perceived and what his augmented perception had recorded.

He was chagrined by this, but his embarrassment was ameliorated somewhat by the relaxation of pressure as regarded his mission for the Company.

DASHWOOD OBJECTIVE OBTAINED, he transmitted on his credenza, long past midnight when he was unlikely to be disturbed by a servant. *ATTENDED "ELEUSINIAN RITE" AND CAN REPORT THAT IT IS NOT, REPEAT NOT AUTHENTIC. DETAILS WELL-KNOWN IN ANTIQUITY WORKED INTO A PLAUSIBLE FAKE. SOURCE SCROLL NOT LOCATED BUT SUSPECT THE EUGENIKOS FORGER. AWAITING FURTHER ORDERS.*

He sent the message and relaxed, but almost at once a reply shot out of the ether:

OBTAIN SOURCE SCROLL. CLIENT MADE SUBSTANTIAL OFFER.

Lewis gnawed his lower lip. He sent:

BUT IT'S A FAKE.
IRRELEVANT.
BUT IT WOULDN'T FOOL ANYONE WHO'D ATTENDED THE MYSTERIES.
CLIENT IS MORTAL. WON'T KNOW DIFFERENCE.

With a certain sense of moral outrage, Lewis transmitted:

ACKNOWLEDGED. UNDER PROTEST. VALE.

He knew well enough, now, where the object of his quest was.

With a heavy heart, in the small hours following an evening during which Sir Francis had been particularly pleasant company, Lewis packed his valise. He drew on his cloak and slipped down through the dark house, and out a side door into the garden. He switched to night vision; the surrounding countryside leaped into focus, lurid green, unearthly. Pausing only to hide his bag in a clump of rhododendron, he set out.

He went quickly, though it was a long cold walk just the same. Once, a bat shrieked overhead; he looked up in time to see its smear of red light vanishing into the trees. Once a fox crossed his path, and stopped to regard him with eyes like fire. He missed the little girl walking at his side, and wondered whether he'd be too great a fool if he sought her out once he returned to London. He wondered whether he could bear watching her grow old and die.

This question so preoccupied him that he almost failed to notice that he was being followed. After a while, however, the laboring mortal heartbeat and steam-bellows breath distracted him, and he looked back. There, a great way off, a scarlet blur made its way along the track. Its dark lantern pulsed with heat. A poacher? Lewis shrugged and picked up his pace, until he reached the entrance to the Hellfire Caves.

The gates had been locked; a moment's work with his cloak pin and Lewis had them open. Fighting panic once more, he hurried into true Stygian blackness, rendered more ghostly by his vision. Emerging from the maze into the banqueting chamber, he nearly shouted at what he took at first to be a lurking figure; but it was only a pair of serving tables stacked up on end, draped with oilcloth.

Muttering to himself, Lewis went on. In the chamber with its altar, he was almost surprised to see no spot of residual heat glowing still from Mrs. Digby's bum. At the River Styx he proceeded soberly, poling himself across in the little boat with all the dignity of Charon, and stepped out dryshod on the other shore. There, trampled and forgotten in the chalk, Lewis spotted Persephone's veil.

He bent and picked it up. He regarded it a long moment before folding it carefully and tucking it away inside his shirt, next to his heart.

In the Inner Temple, he lifted the lid from the sarcophagus. Within was a box of alabaster, something Egyptian from the look of it. He lifted the lid on that and found a box of cypress wood, a modern piece painted with figures of maenads dancing. Within, he found the scroll.

Lewis unrolled it, examined it briefly, and sighed. Yes: the work of the clever Russian. *Let him not speak, he who has witnessed the rites sacred to holy Demeter and her slender-ankled daughter! But bear witness, oh furies, that this scribe breaks no oath in relating the true nature of what he has seen with his silent pen* . . . He returned the scroll to its box, tucked it under his arm, and walked back toward the starlight.

He was on his way to the maze when he heard the crunch of footsteps coming. In a panic, he turned back and dodged into one of the alcoves opening off the banqueting chamber. There he stood, absolutely still as the mortal shuffled into the chamber.

It was Sir Francis, peering about by the single ray of light his lamp gave forth.

Lewis held his breath. *Do not see me, mortal man . . . you will not see me, mortal . . .*

A bat swooped through. Sir Francis gasped and dropped his lantern, which unfortunately did not go out; rather, its shutter was knocked open by the impact. The chamber was flooded with light.

Oh, crumbs.

Sir Francis bent to pick up the lantern, straightened with it, and looked full into Lewis's face. His gaze fell to the box under Lewis's arm.

"Oh, dear," he said. "I was afraid of something like this."

Lewis, ready to babble out an apology, was quite unprepared for what happened next. Scuffing sharp-edged gravel out of the way, Sir Francis knelt down laboriously.

"Please," he said. "Which one are you? Apollo? Hermes? I was sure I recognized you, t'other night. Forgive my old eyes, I pray; I might have seen you more clearly, once."

"I am only a messenger," said Lewis, praying to both gods for help.

"Just as you wish, my lord," said Sir Francis, and he nearly winked. He regarded the scroll box sadly. "Must you take it away? We were idle merry boys once, and we did blaspheme; but only as boys do. I had rather hoped you had come to dwell among us at last. We need you, we poor mortals."

"But you no longer need this." Lewis held up the scroll box, wondering if he could wink out without dropping it.

"I suppose not," said Sir Francis, slumping. He clasped his hands. "Please, tell me, Bright One—will my friend die?"

"You know he must," said Lewis, as gently as he could.

"Oh, Paul," said Sir Francis. He said nothing more for a moment, as a tear rolled down his cheek. He looked up at Lewis hopefully. "But if *you* are here—why then, it's a sign! The gods are not unkind. They must care for us. It's all true, isn't it? We *will* go to Paradise, and revel in the Elysian Fields, just as She promised us."

"Believe, it, mortal man," said Lewis. *For all I know, it may be true.*

He reached down his hand as though in blessing, setting it on Sir Francis's head. Concentrating, he generated a pulse designed to have an effect on the temporal lobe of the mortal brain.

Sir Francis gasped in pleasure. He heard celestial choirs, had visions of glory, and *knew* a sublime truth impossible to put into words. The ecstasy was enough to send him into a dead faint.

Lewis picked him up and staggered out with him, far away through the night fields to the great house, where he laid Sir Francis down before the statue of Bacchus. He paused only a moment, leaning forward with his hand on the wall, gasping for breath; then he knocked, loud enough to rouse the servants.

Long before the fearful mortals had come to the door, he had retrieved his valise from the shrubbery and fled in the direction of London.

No more than a month later, a certain peddler wandered the streets of a certain district of London. The streets were crowded and filthy, even in this somewhat better-class part of the district. The mad king squatted on his throne, the American crisis was going from bad to worse, nay, the whole globe was reeling in chaos that would soon spit forth another age, and the first snow of winter had begun to drift out of a sullen and steely sky.

The peddler's garments were shabby, not really adequate for the weather, and yet he carried himself with a style making it not outside the powers of imagination that he might in fact be a dashing hero of some kind. One temporarily down on his luck, perhaps. Conceivably the object of romantic affection.

He doffed his hat to all he met, and, when meeting any who looked as though he or she might know, discreetly inquired whether they knew the way to Mrs. Digby's establishment.

Hoping, even as foolish mortals do, for some sign of a compassionate universe.